Moo

Ann Victoria Roberts made her successful fiction debut with *Louisa Elliott*, which became a bestseller and was translated into several languages. This was followed by its sequel, *Liam's Story*, a novel of the Great War, inspired by the discovery of a family diary, and by a third novel, *Dagger Lane*. She is married to a Master Mariner and knows the sea and the north-east coast of England well. She divides her time between her home in York and a cottage in Whitby.

Beryl.

By the same author

Louisa Elliott
Liam's Story
Dagger Lane

MOON RISING

A novel set in Whitby

Ann Victoria Roberts

ARROW

Published by Arrow Books in 2000

3 5 7 9 10 8 6 4 2

First published in the United Kingdom in 2000 by
Chatto & Windus
Arrow Books Limited
20 Vauxhall Bridge Road, London SW1V 2SA

Random House Australia (Pty) Limited
20 Alfred Street, Milsons Point, Sydney,
New South Wales 2061, Australia

Random House New Zealand Limited
18 Poland Road, Glenfield,
Auckland 10, New Zealand

Random House (Pty) Limited
Endulini, 5a Jubilee Road, Parktown 2193, South Africa

Random House Group Limited Reg. No. 954009
www.randomhouse.co.uk

A CIP catalogue record for this book
is available from the British Library

Papers used by Random House are natural,
recyclable products made from wood grown in sustainable forests.
The manufacturing processes conform to the environmental
regulations of the country of origin

ISBN 0 09 928148 1

Typeset by Deltatype Ltd, Birkenhead, Merseyside
Printed and bound in Great Britain by
Cox & Wyman Ltd, Reading, Berks

In memory of my father, George,
1908–1982
He never judged and always kept an open mind.

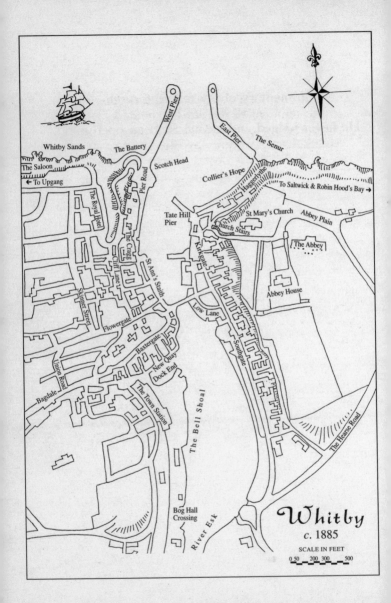

Whitby

c. 1885

SCALE IN FEET

0 50   200 300   500

The wind suddenly shifted to the north-east, and the remnant of the sea-fog melted in the blast; and then, *mirabile dictu*, between the piers, leaping from wave to wave as it rushed at headlong speed, swept the strange schooner with all sail set...

Bram Stoker, *Dracula*

One

After years of promising to return, in the end I was called back to Whitby by the coincidence of two deaths. It seemed strange that my second cousin, Bella Firth, and my great-uncle, Thaddeus Sterne, with more than fifty years separating them in age, should quit the world within days of each other, the former unnoticed by the world at large, the latter, as befitting a well-known local personage, with considerable public grief.

Although I'd known at heart there was no choice, I'd debated briefly about sending my condolences from London, telling myself that the Firths would understand, and that no one was likely to notice one mourner less amongst the crowd at Old Uncle Thaddeus's funeral. Or even to recognise me after so many years. Besides, the journey was not one I would normally have chosen to make in the first week of January.

With the short afternoon closing in, I closed my eyes, dozed, then woke with a sudden jolt to find that the train had stopped. It took me a moment to identify the sounds, but somewhere in the darkness ahead the engine was releasing regular gouts of steam; enough to suggest to my sleeping mind the rush of waves across a sandy beach and a buffeting wind along the piers. Even so, I shivered. Rubbing at the window with my glove, I saw that in the last half-hour a few dancing flakes of snow had become a misty blur of white.

Alice, my maid, compressed her lips in what was more of a grimace than a smile. 'We'll be lucky to reach York at this rate, ma'am, never mind Whitby.'

Acknowledging the truth of that, I opened my gold pendant to see the tiny clock-face inside. It was one of the first presents ever given to me by my late husband, Henry, and could still arouse a smile whenever I paused to think of it. A man whose hobby was collecting timepieces was bound to be concerned by punctuality and, as I had been brought up amongst people who navigated their lives as well as their ships by the sun, misunderstandings were to be expected. There had been plenty, although I think most of them were eventually smoothed out. I worked hard to make up for my shortcomings, but if he did not always appreciate my eccentricities, at least Henry Lindsey was good to me. I was fond of him always, but it was not until I was widowed that I realised how much I'd loved him too.

After his death, the business had become my sole responsibility, and I was thankful that Henry and I had worked together, since without that experience everything would have ground to a halt. I'd have been lost, an innocent in the marketplace, at the mercy of grief and loneliness and the packs of wily, marauding males. Now, almost two years later, with a pair of reliable partners installed, I was able to think about taking time off before time took care of me. I was still a year under forty, but I felt older by a decade.

Recently, as my grief for Henry found its proper place, I'd begun to feel that I should take stock of my life before I moved on, assess the value of things I had too long accepted as natural or immutable laws.

2

I thought those two deaths in Whitby might show me where to start.

But the weather seemed intent on holding everything up. It was past six already and impossible in the darkness to say where we were. As I peered through the murky glass there came a sudden groan, the train lurched forward with a muffled clanking of chains and buffers and, startled, I felt my heart lurch with it. Once more under way, we could hear and feel the difficulties ahead, locomotive wheels biting and failing on snow-covered tracks, with corresponding gasps from the engine. If tedium had already given way to irritation, here was the point where it turned to anxiety. In normal circumstances it would not have mattered to me what time we arrived, since there were several connections to Whitby throughout the evening; but if heavy snow was already falling north and east of York, it was doubtful whether the line across the moors would be open.

I had to be in Whitby by noon the next day. The knowledge pressed me, while the snow threatened to make a nonsense of this journey and everything connected with it. Half an hour later, when the train finally crawled into the station at York, I made an effort to be one of the first on to the platform. Leaving Alice to deal with the luggage, I hailed a porter, then strode off to the enquiry office. All trains were at a standstill because of the blizzard, although the main lines north and south would be cleared as soon as possible; with luck, the clerk said, it should take no more than a few hours. But when I mentioned Whitby and the North York Moors, he grimaced and shook his head. Not even twentieth-century wonders could overcome the weather and Whitby's geographic isolation.

As I hastened away, I was vaguely aware of a tall,

heavily built man standing to one side of me in the crowd. I moved round him and hurried off to find Alice. A few minutes later, with the porter in tow, we made our way to the hotel, only to find the place unbearably crowded. People jostled and elbowed their way to the front desk, where it seemed the prize of a room might be had for those who pushed hardest. The atmosphere was that of a race-track or auction-sale, but the reception staff were impassive, refusing to be intimidated, or indeed to catch anyone's eye until each traveller was properly attended to. Eventually, having drawn myself up to my full height, I managed to secure some attention, and the use of a room at the back of the hotel. It was barely larger than a broom cupboard, and Alice was unimpressed, but there was an easy chair as well as a wash-stand and a military-style bed, and it was better than nothing.

Since there was no room for two people to move about at once, I glanced in the glass, secured a few recalcitrant curls and adjusted my raven's-wing hat, and left Alice to arrange our overnight things. I headed back through the foyer to the station con-course. Cold though it was, I felt in need of fresh air and exercise after all those hours cooped up on the train. Head down against the swirl of snowflakes coming in from the left, I almost cannoned into a large man, well muffled against the weather, who was approaching from the right. With an apology and a quick side-step I managed to avoid his steadying arms, and only as I continued on my way did I question a sudden sense of familiarity. From his height and build I thought he might be one of my innumerable cousins, a distant member of the Sterne clan returning home, as I was, for Old Uncle Thaddeus's funeral, and thus better avoided. But when I turned to look again, he was no longer to be seen.

The air was acrid with soot and sulphur, alive with the chuntering of engines and sudden, echoing bursts of steam; perhaps not the ideal place to go walking, but infinitely preferable to the fug of overcrowded public rooms. Evidently I was not alone in my opinion, since the platforms were by no means deserted, despite the icy wind funnelling through that great arcade. It was dark between the iron pillars, with dazzling pools of light here and there, shadows moving and flickering with the wind, and, at the far end of the platform, an extraordinary display which had drawn quite a crowd. Illuminated by electric lights just within the arch, snow was whirling and falling in an endless cascade, like goose-down at Christmas, to lie as invitingly as a freshly made bed across the tracks.

At least it seemed that way to me, but then I was thinking longingly of featherbeds and soft white linen. The fall of flakes was mesmeric. The crowd grew and we stood gazing up at the station's proscenium arch like an audience at a first night. Strangers were talking to one another, and I was aware but not listening, when a man behind me said with gruff amusement: 'If one could only reproduce that effect on stage, the show would be a sell-out for the season!'

I knew the voice, its quality and intonation, even though the pitch was deeper than I remembered. At first I thought he was speaking to someone else, and was terrified to turn, but when I did, I saw only the man I'd run into outside the hotel, whose eyes I'd felt gazing at me earlier in the queue at the information desk. My mouth twitched into a polite half-smile as my eyes skimmed over him and away, and then flashed back with shock.

5

The broad-brimmed hat shadowed his face; removing it, he bowed briefly and gave a wry smile, quite at variance with the intensity of his gaze. 'Well,' he said. 'It is Damaris Sterne – just as I thought.'

Under the bright lights his eyes were unchanged, and in the shock of recognition my smile froze. It was a long time since anyone had called me by my given name, but I did not correct him. For several seconds I stood in rigid disbelief; then, hard on the heels of shock came a surge of guilt so hot it seemed to scorch my face and throat. The pain made nonsense of the years between: our last meeting might have been a matter of days ago instead of half a lifetime.

I was totally unprepared. I took a step backwards and almost fell; would have done so had it not been for the steadying hand at my elbow. Even so, a stranger's help would have been more welcome. Angrily, I shook him off, not wanting to be reminded of the first time, all those years ago, when he'd pulled me back from the edge of a cliff.

Struggling to regain my composure, I looked round for Alice, then remembered where she was. I longed for safety and somewhere to hide, and regretted this bitter cold place.

'So,' he said quietly, 'you do remember, after all.' It was a statement, uttered with more regret than satisfaction.

Of course I remembered – how could I forget? – but he had changed so much, and for several seconds my mind refused to accept the truth. I peered up at him more closely, trying to reconcile the man before me with the younger image in my mind. I noticed a puffiness around the eyes, a thickening of the neck, and the fact that his coat, with a suggestion of his old theatrical flamboyance about the astrakhan collar,

6

was good but by no means new. Beneath the broad-brimmed hat his grey hair was neat, and his beard, less pepper than salt, was styled like the King's. He was much heavier than I remembered, and it seemed to me his girth spoke of too many years of soft living, in which a powerful physique had been allowed to turn to fat. I found the change disconcerting, but it was the greyness which upset me most. In his prime he had been strikingly attractive, with strong, regular features and thick brown hair. By contrast, his beard in those days was a bright, coppery red, almost the same colour as my own wild curls. When we met, his beard had been the first thing I noticed.

But if the change in him was unsettling, his presence was a shock. And most unwelcome. So I turned away to hide my emotions. 'I'm sorry,' I said, trying to sound dismissive and in control of the situation, 'I don't know you at all – and if you persist in bothering me, sir, I shall be forced to summon the police.'

He had the nerve to chuckle. 'Come now, you don't mean that.'

'Oh, but I do.' The words were ground out as I fought hard to control my trembling. I wanted to march away but was afraid my legs would not carry me far enough. 'Please leave me alone.'

'But I mean you no harm,' he protested mildly, and with a typically expansive gesture indicated the walking stick and his apparent infirmity. 'Unless you were to measure your step to mine, I couldn't even keep up with you.'

He made my urge to run seem ridiculous. Nevertheless, I forced my reluctant limbs into motion – one or two people around us were beginning to find our conversation more interesting than that cascade of snow. 'What do you want?'

'Should I want anything?' he asked reproachfully

as we turned together and walked slowly down the platform. 'Isn't it enough that I should see you and recognise you, and be overjoyed that you've changed so little in the years between?'

'You think I haven't *changed*?' I demanded, more affronted than otherwise, but unable to restrain a mocking burst of laughter.

'Oh, Damaris,' he said, annoying me further by his use of that old name, 'we've both changed – how could we not? – and even more, no doubt, than appears to the eye. I was young and fit in those days, and you – you were just a girl, scrambling up and down cliffs and striking a pose for every photographer in sight. Even so,' he added slyly, with a nod at my headgear, 'I thought I recognised you on the train, in spite of your fine feathers. I wasn't sure at first, until I saw you striding forth along the platform, your whole body bent against the wind . . .'

I was uncertain just how much of a compliment that was, the implication being that fine ladies strolled, never *strode forth*. I saw an edge, too, in the mention of photographers, which made my jaw tighten. Struggling for a suitably sarcastic response, I said: 'You flatter me,' while wondering what to do. It struck me that I was being teased out of further denials, and that he was determined to keep my company for the duration. I suppose I could have denied him that by walking away or making a fuss, or as a last resort by reporting him as a nuisance to the stationmaster, but that was never a serious consideration. The logical side of my mind – which was rapidly recovering from its shock – was aware that this journey of mine was in part an attempt to settle old scores, and my present companion was certainly worthy of adding to the list. Unlooked for and unexpected, but if I had ever longed for a chance to make him suffer – and I had – then this was my opportunity to do so.

With that thought, I felt better. Stronger, more able to handle the situation. I set the shock aside and donned the mildly flirtatious, woman-of-the-world mask that had served me so well in business. As we reached the barrier I gave him a sidelong glance and, as I caught his eye, a conspiratorial smile to go with it. 'Well, now, since you've penetrated my disguise, won't you join me for dinner? Be my guest and allow me – for old times' sake – to repay your hospitality?' As he appeared to hesitate, I said: 'But just let's be clear about something. My name's no longer Damaris, it's Marie – Marie Lindsey. *Mrs* Lindsey, as a matter of fact.'

He smiled and gave a mocking little bow. 'Thank you, Mrs Lindsey – although there's no need, I –'

'But my dear man, there's *every* need,' I assured him, bestowing my most winning smile. 'In fact, I insist.'

Quiet corners were difficult to find in a hotel which was full to overflowing, but the management had opened up all public rooms in an attempt to accommodate everyone in some degree of comfort. Waiters were doing brisk service to and from the bar, and some judicious tipping secured us a table for dinner an hour hence. In the meantime, leaving my companion with his whisky, I went to find Alice.

I told her to be sure to have a good meal belowstairs, and, since I would no doubt be late, to make use of the bed in my absence. She said she would lie down with the quilt over her, and I agreed to wake her when I came up. What she thought of my chance encounter I do not know – possibly not very much, since the world of shipping and finance had ensured me many male acquaintances – but it would have

9

surprised her to know the details of my former relationship with the man I was going downstairs to meet.

Not that I had any intention of revealing those details – indeed, keeping them secret had cost me a great deal over the years. For my own benefit while married, of course; but I had often wondered how my companion, always a friend to the rich and famous, would have fared had the matter become public knowledge.

He was probably less concerned now than he would have been, but there was still his wife to think of, the precious and inimitable Florence. She'd had her own lovers – though in the courtly, romantic sense, of course, since she was worshipped for her delicate beauty and worked hard at preserving the illusion of purity. Not for her the sweaty conflict of human congress, nor even, as far as I was aware, the passionless contact of the marital bed. We never met but I always thought of her as being perfectly untouchable, rather like a Burne-Jones portrait in the flesh: regular, faultless, and *dull*.

She was twenty when they married, but he had known her for almost two years. I was eighteen when he and I first met. Except in the vital matter of colouring, some might say that Florence and I were not unalike; both tall, both reed-thin, and although she had the exquisite profile – which I certainly could not boast – I had the kind of curly red hair that Burne-Jones might have died for. The kind that always attracted attention, the kind her husband admired so much.

When I thought of the intensity I had shared with him, I wondered how on earth he could have married her. But although dear Florence had no money, she did have beauty, and – they tell me – the kind of fey charm that seemed to captivate romantic

10

young men. Amongst her suitors at home in Dublin she'd even had young Oscar Wilde begging for her hand.

Anyway, she turned Oscar down. Perhaps his wit threatened to eclipse her beauty, I don't know, but she chose instead an older, more robust-looking man with some intriguing social and professional prospects. He was captivated by her looks, and because he was over thirty and it was about time he married, and because he could suddenly afford to, he asked her to be his wife. At least, that's what he told me. Some years later, when the mistakes were destroying him and the fabric of his life was falling into shreds, he packed a bag, stepped on a train and travelled to Whitby.

More than two decades had passed since then. That morning I would have said my perceptions were normal, yet in the last hour time had become distorted, making the distant past suddenly more real than the present. Until I rejoined my companion, that is, and found myself disconcerted afresh by his appearance.

As I took a seat beside him, he raised his glass and made some heavy-handed comment about the weather, to the effect that it had managed, extraordinarily, to bring us together once again. I felt that twice in twenty-one years hardly constituted a coincidence, and said so. He tried another tack. 'I heard you mention Whitby – do you still live there?'

That enquiry prompted a taut smile. 'Heavens, no – my husband and I lived mostly in London.' At his quick glance I shook my head. 'No, we're not neighbours – that is, if you're still in Chelsea? My home's in Hampstead, overlooking the Heath.'

He chuckled then with surprise. At first I imagined it was at the distance I'd travelled in life – after all, I'd come a long way since last we met – but then he recovered himself and said ruefully: 'Obviously, you know much more of me . . .'

'Difficult not to – or rather it was, once upon a time. There was always something in the London papers.' That was perhaps an exaggeration, but there had been enough in theatre notices and society columns over the years to keep me abreast of his activities. In hopes of discovering more, I managed to force out the words convention demanded, even though they almost choked me. 'I was sorry,' I said, 'to read about Irving, last year.'

His face was still; there was a pause. 'Yes, he hadn't been well for some time. Even so, it was a great shock. Ironically, it was his farewell tour – we were in Bradford, at the Theatre Royal – he was playing in *Becket*.' Looking into his glass, he said quietly: 'I still miss him. We were friends, you know, for over thirty years.'

Exasperated by his loyalty, I had to turn my glance away. With a sigh that just might have passed for one of regret, I said: 'Yes, great friends, I remember. But goodness, how he used you!'

He bridled a little at that. 'Irving was a great man – the greatest actor of his generation. I was privileged to be close to him.'

'He was certainly a great actor – one of the best of any generation. And you served him well,' I agreed sardonically, 'far beyond the call of duty. But what did he ever give you, for heaven's sake, other than the chance to watch him nightly from the wings?'

'We were friends,' he declared, half turning his shoulder. Obviously, the subject was still a painful one. For a moment, I wondered whether Irving's flamboyant style had landed them both in trouble, but when he turned to face me again, he was wearing a determined smile. 'Let's talk of other things. You, for instance. You seem to know all about

12

my life, while I know nothing of yours. What is it that takes you back to Whitby after all these years?'

There was such irony present – in the fact of our meeting and its circumstance, even in his sudden curiosity – that I wanted, quite desperately, to laugh. Mad, hysterical laughter was bubbling away inside me, and I was almost afraid of what might happen next. I considered making some excuse and returning to my room. There, at least, I could pretend that nothing mattered. It was over, done with, all in the past; I was a middle-aged woman, a wealthy widow; no longer the impulsive and impressionable girl I'd been when we met. And my adversary was no longer young, but approaching sixty. So why did I tremble when I looked at him? Why did those grey eyes continue to remind me of things that were best forgotten?

It was perhaps as well that our table became available, and that over dinner we were obliged to discuss – I was about to say, less contentious subjects, but for me, in his company, most things were contentious. I don't recall what we ate, only that there were several courses, and by the end of it my stomach was too heavy to suffer from any kind of nervous rebellion. I drank more than usual too, which for once was more steadying than otherwise, so that I was able to talk about my life with equanimity, relating the story of how I'd met my husband, the decade of challenge and excitement I'd enjoyed while working with him in the City. When I met him, Henry Lindsey had been a childless widower, and, much to his regret, we had not been blessed with children. But that, as I explained to my companion, didn't grieve me overmuch; I preferred the challenge of charter parties to children's parties, and lucrative cargoes to lace-trimmed cradles.

It was a practised little speech, but, thinking it

13

frank and original, he was both impressed and amused. There was a certain amount of truth in what I said so glibly, and although the unvarnished facts were much less palatable, this was not the place to divulge them. For the time being it was enough for him to know that I was childless. But that was another reason for envying the inestimable Florence. She might have hated sex and disliked her husband – as he'd once claimed – but at least she had his son.

The shortage of tables for dining meant that we were encouraged to take our coffee elsewhere. At last we found a pair of wing-back chairs in a corner of the reading room, and a young waiter keen to earn his tips. He kept up the fire and made sure we were well supplied with coffee and spirits, especially after midnight, when many people had retired to their rooms. I could have done the same, but the coincidence of our meeting gripped me as much as it did my companion. Having once broached Pandora's box, we found it impossible to shut the lid. To my surprise as much as my dismay I realised that the details of our affair had not been forgotten by him, and that he could recall incidents and events just as well as I.

The intimacy of those hours after midnight brought everything back. Shadows and secrecy, whispered confessions, fears and passions so powerful they seemed still alive. The memories were unsettling, and the pain of them made me angry, but in some respects I think my anger was an advantage, since it took the edge off caution and common politeness, and brought out levels of honesty that might have shocked anyone else. Perhaps they shocked him too, but I'd kept a seal on my tongue for long enough, and on this occasion it did me good to say what I thought, to allow myself free rein with never a care for the consequences.

I may have railed against fate, sitting there in my chair by the fire, but my companion had the grace not to remind me that others would have given much to be in my shoes. Mostly I was aware of that, and in bad moments had only to think of my cousin Bella to be profoundly thankful; but just then that was no consolation. Bella was dead, which was another reason to be angry. If the Fates had to have their sacrifice, I demanded of the man by my side, why did it have to be Bella – why couldn't it have been her twin, Isa, lying there in her shroud?

Isa, dead, would have been a matter for rejoicing, and, difficult or not, I knew I would have returned to Whitby under far worse circumstances than this, just for the pleasure of dancing on her grave.

Those sentiments, expressed so vehemently, did surprise him. He'd never forgotten the consequences of my friendship with Bella; what he did not know was how Isa came to be involved. To anyone else those details might not have been important, but he was part of that time, and suddenly I was as eager to tell him as he was to listen. I'd shouldered the burden alone for more years than I cared to recall, and wanted rid of it. Let him feel the weight, I thought; let him wince and stagger while he studied the options. And let him try to decide what should be done to redress the balance.

Two

There was no need to remind him of the day we met. He'd always had a passion for the sea and storms, and I know he remembered that one in Whitby, because he wrote about it so vividly in that strange book of his. Under all the embroidery of a novel, events were much the same – the storm, the Russian ship, the wrecks – the great black hound, of course, was the legendary Whitby barghest, the one we'd talked about amongst all the other legends and folk-tales that abound along that coast.

As I recall, it was about the time of low water, which would have been around two o'clock that afternoon, when the excitement began. What shipping we'd seen that week had mostly passed on the horizon, beating well out to sea to avoid being driven inshore by those northeasterly gales, but the coastguard had spotted a brigantine in trouble just off the Nab. It was far too close and coming closer, and I felt anxiety grip like a claw. I knew it couldn't be the *Lillian*, a ship in which I had a special interest: it was too early in the season for her return from the Mediterranean. Even so, I strained to see her lines more clearly, and was thankful to discover from a harassed coastguard that she was in fact the *Mary and Agnes* of Scarborough.

Thankful – but only in one sense. There were still

men and boys aboard, precious to someone, in danger of their lives. I was glad to see the lifeboat being wheeled out to stand on its carriage by the slipway, but at that, like flies to a carcass, people were suddenly gathering to watch. Experiencing a moment's contempt, I turned back to the task in hand. I was working with Jack Louvain that day, and, because of the exceptionally high tide, we'd been transporting vital photographic equipment away from the quayside shop to his private rooms. By the time he'd decided to stop and take photographs, the piers and cliffs – which in truth were places to be avoided in weather like that – were thronged with sightseers.

Battered by the gale, fighting against it, loaded with camera and tripod and precious glass plates, we struggled to a suitable vantage point on the west cliff. The wind that seemed determined to push us back inland was equally determined to drive the ship ashore, and it soon became evident that the Master of the brigantine had given up the battle and was making for the harbour. Whether or not this was a wise move remained to be seen, since huge waves were battering the pier ends and breaking over the lighthouses on either side. On the clifftop we could barely stand, but Mr Louvain had me hanging on to the tripod while he attempted to set up the camera for a view of the ship coming in – perhaps successfully between the piers, or more dramatically against the rocks. Either way, he was determined to capture a photograph, if only I could hold the camera still.

On the beach below the slipway, the lifeboat was standing by, while people kept saying it should be out there already, offshore, when disaster was just a hairbreadth away. I could have told them there were rules to be obeyed, that a ship had to have struck before the boat could be launched, but I'd neither the breath nor the inclination to argue. For a moment it seemed all would be well, but then the brigantine was swamped by a massive wave and came up wide of the harbour mouth, beam on, helpless in the face of that howling gale. Jack Louvain was yelling at me to keep steady, but I was already on my knees under the tripod, trying so hard to hold it down that everything was clenched, including my teeth.

'Take it, take it!' I muttered desperately, knowing the ship had two chances – either she would roll again and not right herself, or she'd be forced to strike the shore. Praying for the latter, I opened my eyes long enough to see her being lifted bodily by the next wave, and another, as she was swept towards us; but I was not prepared for the unearthly sound as she was driven sideways on to the beach. There came a terrible, deep-throated grinding, topped by almost human groans of protest as every timber jarred, as planking splintered and canvas cracked, and seas gushed over the decks.

Whether Jack Louvain got his picture or not, in that moment I neither knew nor cared. My hands were still clamped around the tripod legs but I was too shocked to hold things steady. In common with everyone else I simply watched in horror as masts and spars collapsed and the ship sank into the pounding seas. Along the beach, the lifeboat was launched from its cradle into the foam. Not very well, either. In fact it was dangerously poor, a case of haste and frustration almost causing another disaster. Those first minutes were agonising. Most of the crew were known to me; two were close neighbours. I crawled forward to watch them fighting the waves, and, relying on the force of the wind, I suppose I was leaning out too far; the grass was slippery beneath me and spray was whipping up from the beach.

I peeled damp strands of hair from my eyes and

face, and I remember my irritation as Jack Louvain shouted at me. I looked round and saw in the crowd behind me a man with a red beard, glaring so ferociously I thought I must know him. In my momentary confusion I almost slipped, but in the next instant he had my arm and was dragging me back from the edge.

He was tall and well-built; well dressed too, but that didn't curb my annoyance. I was furious at the interference, even more so at being manhandled by a complete stranger, but Jack couldn't have cared less. His concerns were to capture a record of wild skies, wilder seas, and that broken ship with her crew struggling to survive.

It seemed we were all fighting just then, the lifeboatmen having a time of it too, with their boat being pushed back by both wind and tide. They'd barely rounded the second nab, and were still a hundred yards from the brigantine when the boat grounded in the shallows, and oars were smashed with a crack like guns going off. In that moment of astonishment I freed myself, and was so angry I delivered a punch to my captor's midriff that made him grunt, probably more with surprise than pain. Even so, it jarred my wrist and I winced. We glared at each other in furious antipathy; then, with arms that were like iron bands, he simply lifted me out of the way and addressed himself to the problem at hand.

Speechless with rage, I watched as this man in his fine tweeds crouched down on the muddy grass. While Jack Louvain changed plates he held everything steady with apparent ease. I wanted to beat them both over the head – preferably with the tripod in question – but my attention was distracted by cries from the beach. People had descended by the cliff path and were wading into the foam, making every effort to re-launch the lifeboat. It was an impossible task, and the boat had to be abandoned, but at least the lifeboatmen were safe, which was more than could be said for the crew of the brigantine.

While a breeches-buoy was being rigged, we moved closer to the wreck for better pictures. It seemed to take for ever, and the light was not good, but finally the apparatus was secured and Jack got busy as the first man was pulled ashore. He was just a boy really, and looked more like a drowned rabbit by the time he'd been dunked a few times in those ferocious seas. Of those that followed him, some were so exhausted they had to be carried up the cliff path, and one looked so inert I thought he was dead. As they brought him past on a makeshift stretcher his hands and face looked waxen, his hair was in tangled strands, and there was even a skein of seaweed around his neck like some travesty of a rope. The sight struck me with horror. When I looked again at the brigantine, I saw my mind's own ghost-ship, the *Merlin* of Whitby, wrecked off Tallinn with the loss of all hands when I was just seven years old. All drowned, including my father and grandfather, in the icy Baltic seas of early spring.

It was like the rekindling of an old nightmare. I shivered convulsively, and for a moment could have been sick. I doubt whether Jack Louvain would have noticed, but his new assistant did, and, mistaking the cause, was suddenly bent on ushering me up to the warmth and shelter of the Saloon. Although a mug of hot tea would have been welcome, I had no desire to be escorted out again by those who were busily ministering to the needs of shipwrecked mariners. In the scheme of things a local girl, muddied and bedraggled, was of no concern at all. That this man regarded me differently made me pause; in fact his

20

chivalry was so unexpected it went straight to my heart, melting my antipathy like ice in the sun. So I shook my head and said I was all right, which in truth I was. But I was also flattered by his attention. It didn't occur to me at the time that he might be stirred by my physical activity and that uncontrollable display of emotion.

I had been ready to resent him for his station in life and the attitude that went with it, but he seemed a practical man, confident and energetic, and I found I admired that almost as much as his fine grey eyes and flourishing red beard. As we started to pack up, I stole surreptitious glances and wondered who he was, what he was doing in Whitby so late in the year. The odds favoured a connection with the new coastal railway, since we'd seen engineers of many and various persuasions in recent years, and most of them were easygoing, adaptable men. Strangely, I thought him not grave enough for a lawyer or a banker, yet I discovered later that he was a barrister who managed the complicated financial affairs of a most extraordinary business. In fact when I found out all that he did, I was amazed; even more to find that he was famous in his own world, on hobnobbing terms with the cream of London society, and a personal friend of the actress Ellen Terry. To begin with, of course, I had no idea of that, which was perhaps as well, since I would not have dared to speak to him otherwise, much less flirt so outrageously.

Even so, when he turned to me and said: 'Fine fellows – such bravery warms the heart,' I could not resist pointing out that the lads manning the lifeboat were fishermen by profession, every one a volunteer and fiercely proud of the fact. He was impressed by that, I could tell, and, equally, I knew I'd made a more personal impression. I could see that Jack had

21

warmed to him too, and against the battering of wind and rain was attempting to convey his thanks. He had run out of photographic plates and was intending to take everything back to his rooms rather than the studio, and I knew he expected me to lend a hand. Although there was chaos on the beach, it seemed all the crew were now accounted for, and in spite of the interest of the crowd I could hardly bear to stand and watch the brigantine breaking up in the surf. But just as I was regretting this untimely separation from the red-bearded gentleman, he relieved me of the heavy tripod and began to walk along with us.

We communicated mainly by gesture as the wind whipped words away. I gathered he'd introduced himself, but I missed his name, and then, when it was a little easier to talk in the shelter of town, Jack monopolised things by offering to forward copies of the photographs taken that afternoon. I could see he regretted not capturing our escort too, and would have liked him to pose for the camera. It was late, however, and the light was going, and thanks to our work that morning the studio was upside down.

Jack and I exchanged a look of frustration, and in between talk of tides and flooding tried to persuade the gentleman to call by for a sitting the following day. Unfortunately he had an early start next morning, but in the course of that conversation it became clear that he thought me Jack Louvain's paid assistant. Catching Jack's cautionary smile I said nothing to put him right, just found myself thankful for the storm. I suppose an old plain serge gown looks not so much different from a good one when both are damp and mud-spattered; and for those who must go out, it was the kind of day when thick plaid shawls were infinitely preferable to fancy hats.

Once we reached Jack's lodgings and the photographic equipment was safely installed, he used the excuse of the hour and the weather to usher me home. I was not displeased by the suggestion, just annoyed when, in the very next breath, he offered our companion a tot of whisky as a restorative. If anyone deserved warmth and restoration, I thought, it was me; but then unattached young women were not encouraged to drink whisky with bachelor gentlemen in the privacy of their rooms.

With as much grace as I could muster I wished them both good-night and turned to leave; a moment later I was struggling to restrain a broad grin as our new acquaintance refused Jack's invitation and offered to walk along with me as far as his hotel. I had great difficulty in affecting a casual mien as we left Jack standing in the doorway and made our way together down the street.

I half expected him to be staying at the Royal Hotel with its panoramic views, and was a little disappointed to find him at a more modest establishment nearby. Shouting against the wind, he told me he was on business, visiting a number of theatres in northern parts, with the prospect of a tour in mind. What kind of a tour escaped me, so I commiserated about the weather instead. At that he simply laughed and said it was a bonus – he loved the excitement and exhilaration of a storm.

Since we were almost blown away, I laughed and nodded while trying to restrain my skirts from flying above my knees. He watched me and grinned like a schoolboy. 'I always think there's nothing quite like a good blow to banish megrims and rouse the blood. What say you, Miss Sterne? Dangerous but thrilling, don't you agree?'

I did indeed and laughed again. Many a time had I thrilled to pounding waves, skipped over salt-sprayed rocks, and run along the cliffs in a mad March gale, drunk with freedom and a sense of danger. But whether my heart raced in response to the idea or the look in his eye I was not entirely sure. I would have liked to detain him in order to find out, but the evening was closing in, black clouds were scudding over the abbey, and a distant awareness told me I was cold and hungry and should go home. As I began a reluctant farewell, there came an explosion from the coastguard station, followed by the screeching and clattering of gulls. A moment later we saw the fierce red glitter of stars hundreds of feet above, and the slow fall of warning lights to call the lifeboatmen back to duty.

'What is it?' he demanded. 'What's happening?'

'Another ship,' I said, starting to run, and he was with me at once. Dashing to a vantage point above the Battery, we looked across the harbour and out to sea, but it was hard to see anything clearly beyond the black mass of the east cliff and a line of shifting white turbulence below. Then the clouds broke on a clear patch of sky, long enough to show something dark amidst the rising fog of spume and spray. Just beyond the foot of the east cliff, a small vessel was struggling against the mountainous waves, masts jerking and falling in a seemingly hopeless fight for survival. It was like watching a puny child pushing against the knees of a towering Goliath. That small weight was being forced steadily towards the Scaur, the hidden shelf of rock which juts out beneath the east cliff into the sea. The currents ran from west to east across the harbour mouth, and innumerable ships had come to grief there. If the schooner were to be saved, it seemed her only chance was a shallow draught and plenty of water under the keel. That, and a master with iron nerve. But first she had to

24

reach a point beyond the pier ends in order to make the turn.

Through driving mist and spray we saw the second lifeboat make ready for action. All the while the little ship struggled to gain distance from the rocks. Her master had both skill and daring, and with all sail set he brought his vessel round in an extraordinary manoeuvre. A moment later the schooner was racing before the storm, leaping the seething white waters of the Scaur, diving through waves and spray to gain the safety of the piers.

It was a mad moment as she came through. After such prolonged and desperate suspense, the muttered urgings of the crowd exploded in a frenzy of yells and cheers that almost drowned the voice of the storm. I jumped up and down; my companion waved his hat, both of us yelling like lunatics before he swept me off my feet and swung me round in an excess of delight. Laughing and giddy, I clung to him as he set me down, and there was a moment in which almost anything might have happened – laughter, a breathless kiss, or even a gentlemanly apology. But that momentary tension was broken by a groan from the crowd. The ship's master had thought his danger past as he gained the protection of the piers; he lowered sail too soon, lost steerage, and was rapidly driven forward on to the sands of Collier's Hope.

We all stood helpless, like statues, picturing the inevitable before it happened. Anchors were dropped to no avail. As she struck, the groans from the crowd seemed to echo the noise below. All around us were despairing cries and anguished faces, a muttering of belated wisdoms, shaking heads and dragging feet as people started to move away.

'I expect the poor devils will be all right?'

'Yes, I expect so,' I said miserably, watching

scurrying figures and a gathering of lights amidst the gloom on the far side. 'Nothing much worse than a dunking.'

His hand, warm at my waist, slid away, and I was suddenly conscious of a coldness there, giving the coming night a keener edge. I turned with a regretful smile; the spectacle was over, there was no further reason for him to stay. Instead of the expected goodnight, however, he said urgently: 'In that case, let's go across there and see those brave fellows – make sure they're all right.'

So that was what we did, hurrying down to the harbour and across the bridge to the east side. When we reached Tate Hill the crew were only then being brought ashore, staggering on terra firma after several days and nights of storm-tossed seas. One turned aside to be violently sick against the pier wall. Someone said it was the captain, but in the darkness it was hard to tell one from another.

They were foreign – Russians, I think – and it's hard to say how much of English they understood; nevertheless, there were plenty of bystanders from nearby hostelries, all eager to offer congratulations and commiserations in equal measure.

My companion was bright-eyed as we moved amongst the crowd, wanting to see the ship, to know what she was carrying, by what route and from which ports. I had the feeling that if he could have gone aboard the *Dmitry* he would have, and, in spite of their trials and the shipwreck, he even seemed envious of the Russian crew. He certainly admired them. After all the drama, most of Whitby was in a celebratory mood, and I felt it too; but somehow I had not expected the same from a well-travelled and sophisticated stranger. That he was so taken up by these local events impressed me, and seemed to forge a bond between us.

26

As the bedraggled sailors were ushered through an open doorway into the warm and smoky taproom of the Duke of York, we stood in a sheltered corner across the way, for a while just watching and listening. Then, from the gathering darkness beyond, audible once the babble of voices ceased, came the hiss and boom of the tide as it worked against the stranded ship. The sound made me shiver.

'We should move,' he said then, tightening his arm around me; but having noticed the Church Stairs curving up to the right, he wanted to know where they led.

'To the graveyard,' I said, 'and the abbey.'

In those conditions it was mad, but there was a wildness about that evening. I knew what it would be like on top, and tried to dissuade him; nevertheless, when he headed for the steps I had to follow. I couldn't let an inexperienced visitor out on the east cliff alone.

Between Tate Hill and the parish church were 199 broad stone steps sweeping up the cliff, with an iron rail to either side and the even steeper climb of the Donkey Road running parallel below. We would have been more sheltered there, but he had already set off, the first few yards easy until the wind took hold, until each grip on the iron rail became a hand-over-hand haul to the top.

The moon appeared as we crested the cliff, round and full, dazzling between racing banks of cloud. The gale whipped and tore at my heavy serge gown; it was like being punched and beaten, almost impossible to breathe up there, but my companion would not accept defeat until he'd seen the abbey's ruined Gothic silhouette, with the squat outline of the church before it, clinging to the cliff like a gull with wings outstretched. In scudding moonlight the surrounding graves seemed to be moving across the cliff, like ranks of militia marching out to battle with the sea.

It was unnerving, as though the whole cliff was on the move. I clung for safety to one of the memorials, while he advanced without me, leaning forward into the wind. 'We should go back!' I yelled, summoning all the puny force at my disposal. A moment later, a particularly ferocious gust made him grab at an upright stone; after that he turned and made his way back to me. But he was laughing in spite of the danger, enjoying the buffeting like a child's game, where I was fearful, dizzy with the racing moonlight and eager to get back to safer ground.

'Another time,' he conceded, taking pity at last and clamping me to his side as we headed for the steps. Going down was worse than coming up, although he kept me safe enough. I don't know who was more breathless, he or I, but at the foot, by the Duke of York, we paused to recover ourselves. I released my plaid shawl from its secure knot, and draped its heavy folds more becomingly over my head and shoulders, while my companion smoothed his hair and rescued his soft-brimmed hat from inside his coat. With a grin he knocked it back into shape, wedged it firmly on his head, and took my arm again.

'I think we should eat,' he said then, as though the matter had been decided, 'but not here – the landlord will be too taken up with his unexpected guests. Do you know of a good place nearby?'

Briefly, cautions instilled by my late grandmother sprang to mind, and were overcome almost at once by thoughts of a hot meal. With her upright stoicism, no doubt she would have been appalled by such weakness, but I was much too hungry to refuse. Besides, I reminded myself, I was supposed to be a free spirit and could now please myself. Justified, I led the way down Kirkgate.

The White Horse advertised good stabling and a good table, and was one of those old-fashioned hotels still retaining an air of the last century in its bare boards and well-scrubbed orderliness. As I slipped off my shawl and made an attempt to pin back damp, unruly hanks of curls, my companion grinned as he smoothed his own hair, then reached out to mine. 'Allow me,' he said, and gently released the pins I'd been trying to secure. 'It will dry more easily this way.'

With ease, and all in a moment, he arranged my hair loosely around my shoulders, took my shawl and my arm as though I were a society lady, and led me into the saloon bar. His demeanour was so controlled, almost formal as he ordered drinks and enquired about food, that I could scarcely credit his impulsiveness earlier, and wondered whether I'd imagined that madness on the cliff. I had a moment's panic, feeling completely out of my depth, but fortunately the dining room was so lacking in frills it reminded me of my grandmother's house, and in spite of my workaday clothes I managed to relax. In my companion's eyes it might have seemed a rather bare and comfortless place, but his eyes lit up when I told him the novelist Charles Dickens had stayed there, and had probably eaten in the same room. From then on our conversation continued with remarkable ease, as though we were not strangers at all, but old acquaintances delighted to meet again after too long apart.

The fire was drawing well, the place was warm, and the food when it came was heartening and plentiful. Being a stranger to the area, he ordered fried fish which I'm sure was very good, but I was too familiar with fish soup, fish pie, fish baked, smoked and boiled, to want so much as a smell of it on my plate. I asked for the cold roast meats, served with piping-hot fried potatoes and lots of mustard, and barely spoke above a yes or a no until it was finished.

Three

Looking back from a distance of more than two decades, I see myself at that time as a rather wilful but inexperienced girl, lapping up the admiration of a sophisticated older man. He was not trying to seduce me, not then; he was simply enjoying my company, my wide-eyed attention, and his own ability to impress. And I was impressed, not so much by his traveller's tales of America and the Continent – living in Whitby, cheek by jowl with seafarers, I was used to those – but by his life in London, and his work with the Lyceum Theatre Company.

At first, when he mentioned the Lyceum, I thought he meant some kind of college or institute; I thought he was a schoolmaster. But then, seeing my confusion, he explained, and when I blushed at my own ignorance he wanted to know why, whereupon we both laughed at my mistake, the more so every time we met each other's eyes. He said he would tell Irving, and even though I didn't realise then who Irving was, I begged him not to; but he said he felt very much like a schoolmaster at times, trying to control an unruly class of children. He only wished he could threaten them all with the cane; Irving especially.

Although I still didn't know his name, and was too embarrassed to ask, I discovered quickly that he was

31

the Lyceum's business manager, dealing with finance, arranging theatrical tours and publicity, deciphering contracts as well as drawing them up. Even then, when my experience of the world was so limited, I grasped enough to wonder how one man could fulfil such duties, especially when they seemed to include writing speeches and reshaping plays for production. But he enjoyed that, he said; writing had always been something of a hobby, and involvement in the creative side compensated for the drier, more disciplined world of finance.

I'd been to amateur concerts and watched pierrots on the beach, but in those days the theatre meant little to me. I recognised a few actors and actresses, whose faces appeared regularly in printed advertisements, but they were like beings from another world; and to find myself in company with a man who inhabited that world seemed strangely unreal. Nevertheless, it explained to me why Jack Louvain had looked so excited earlier; especially when I discovered that the Lyceum in London was renowned not only for its drama, but most of all for its unique and innovative sets. I paid special attention in order to relate everything to Jack, but found myself longing to see one day what was so vividly described.

I would probably have forgotten the name of the Lyceum's new production, *Faust*, except that I had cause to remember it afterwards, just as I had cause to remember Mr Irving. Impressed at the time by tales of his extravagance, I recall particularly that he'd insisted on going all the way to Bavaria – which I gathered was somewhere in Germany, but not on the Baltic as far as I knew – to study the style of architecture, just to be sure of having the most authentic backdrops. While he was there, he'd even called their chief scene-painter over from London to make sketches of the local doorways and windows.

The scenery had been designed and was now under construction, while the play was currently in rehearsal and promising well. At that my new friend paused for a moment, as though afraid of being indiscreet, but then with a sigh of exasperation went on to complain about the expense of staging one play while another was in rehearsal. What Irving refused to worry about – refused even to *think* about, he muttered grimly – was money. The responsibility for that was put on *his* shoulders, and, as Irving kept saying, if he was worried about the wages bill, then he must either juggle the accounts or go out and find additional funding.

It was as if he could say these things to me because I didn't know these people, nor even fully understand what he was talking about. But his tone and the sudden glitter in his eyes made me nervous; even his beard bristled fiercely in the lamplight. He was a big man, two or three inches over six feet tall and powerfully built, and I was unfamiliar with his temperament. I sensed anger and a barely suppressed frustration, a crackle of tension with regard to this man Irving, that changed his demeanour completely.

'Of course,' he added tersely, 'to him these are just vulgar details, and he mustn't be distracted by them, not while his creative genius is at work. And he is a genius, don't mistake me there – but raising money isn't easy at the best of times, and just now . . .' he shrugged and leaned back. 'The public pocket isn't bottomless, and what if the play should flop? We'll be in hock up to our eyebrows – either that,' he finished with a snort of exasperation, 'or bankrupt!'

My face must have reflected my feelings, for he gazed at me in bemusement before realising the

33

cause of my anxiety. He laughed then and relaxed, patted my hand apologetically, and said he was just being foolish. As usual, Irving would pull the rabbit out of the hat and they'd have another classic to go on drawing the crowds.

But by now my bewilderment was so apparent that he insisted on changing the subject. He wanted to know about Jack Louvain and how I'd come to be the photographer's assistant, since it was not an occupation generally associated with young women.

That was awkward. I hated to prevaricate, and would have preferred not to go into it, but found myself telling the truth as it stood at the time: that I wasn't *employed* by Mr Louvain, except as an occasional model, and had been helping him that day purely as a friend. With the exceptionally high tide came the risk of flooding, and we'd been moving props and equipment out of the way. But he wanted to know more about the modelling, what it involved, and whether any of my pictures were for sale. I felt the answers were somewhat embarrassing, but his interest and enthusiasm led me on until, almost without knowing it, I was embarked upon the story of my life.

He was a sympathetic listener, drawing me out with encouraging smiles and questions. Such attention is seductive in itself, and besides, those expressive grey eyes studied my face with interest, seeming to like what they saw. Life stories inevitably encompass troubles, and I was young enough then to be indignant about mine. I found myself telling him heatedly of the sequence of events which had led to my present situation, about the trials of my previous employment and the argument with Old Uncle Thaddeus. I even told him something of how I felt about Jonathan Markway, one of the sons of the

34

house where I'd worked, and he seemed to under-stand those mixed feelings too. The events of the day had brought Jonathan vividly to mind, and my chief concerns revolved around the fact that at present he was away at sea, facing the kind of dangers we'd witnessed that afternoon. And besides that, he didn't know what had happened to make me lose my job. I hated to think what he would be told about that when he came home.

The last of those worries might well have seemed unimportant or immature to anyone else, but, to his credit, my companion did not dismiss it. Offering me the benefit of his wisdom, he did his best to be reassuring. After that, afraid that I was being a mite serious, I managed to amuse him with a description of Thaddeus Sterne's apoplexy when he discovered I was posing for photographs on the quayside, dressed as a local fisherlass. But, bad end or not, I declared boldly, now that I was lodging with a fisherman's family on the Cragg, I was a free spirit and could please myself.

With a raised eyebrow, my companion wondered aloud what Old Uncle Thaddeus would have said had I decided to embrace a career on the stage. We both laughed then, and with the clearing of our plates he wanted to know whether I would have something other than the tea I'd asked for with my meal. He was having whisky, so after some hesita-tion I ordered port wine, it being almost the only alcoholic drink I could taste in those days without gagging. It went to my head almost at once, making the rest of our conversation – about local dialects – even more amusing than it might have been. He was keen to have me translate various words and phrases picked up during the day, while I volunteered a few more for his entertainment.

We were still in high spirits as we left, and I felt as

though I'd never had such a wonderful time. Outside, the wind seemed less angry, although the tide was well up and licking at the bridge as we crossed the harbour. It was a daunting prospect and on the far side, by Jack Louvain's studio, waves were already running along the road. With linked hands, we raced across to the safety of Golden Lion Bank, and, at the top, turned along narrow Cliff Lane towards his hotel and my lodgings on the Cragg.

It was a familiar route for me, although within moments I realised that the main thoroughfare beyond would have been safer and more sensible. Here were few shops and fewer passers-by, and to bring a strange man this way, with dark alleys to left and right, was like issuing a direct invitation. As a warm hand slid around my waist I was suddenly alarmed. This is where you pay for your meal and the evening's entertainment, I thought; with your back against the wall and a hand across your mouth to silence any protests.

I'd seen enough furtive struggles in the shadows to be under no illusion about men and their desires, or their means of taking what they wanted. While delicate young ladies might be protected from the realities of life, the rest of us were not, and it was my experience that gentlemen found that idea titillating. So I tensed against his arm, urging a few more steps, bringing us closer to our destination. Nearby on the right was the entrance to Pier Lane, no more than a narrow footpath and easy to miss if you were unaware of its existence, which led down to the harbour below. Between these two points lay the maze of steps and stairs, yards and alleys that comprised the Cragg. If I had to run, once I was in Pier Lane he would never find me, not if he searched for a week. With safety in reach I could afford to relax a little, slow my steps, give in to the excitement of the moment. And I must confess I wanted to, despite my fears.

A little breathless, I told him my lodgings were no more than a few yards away, and that his hotel was just around the corner. We stopped by the school wall and my blood was racing as he raised his fingers to my cheek. His touch was gentle, even hesitant, I thought with surprise, remembering our closeness earlier. He made some reference to the blow I'd delivered that afternoon, which made me laugh, and then he thanked me for a pleasant evening. It was so formal, I felt let down. The kiss I'd been wanting and half dreading was not to be. So I tried to put an inch or two more between us, to seem as though I didn't want it anyway. I thanked him for the meal we'd shared, and just as I was thinking how polite we'd become, he bent his head and kissed my lips. A sweet kiss, a soft kiss, an almost unimpeachable kiss from an older man to a young girl.

Except I was eighteen years old, full of vanity and port wine, and he was an attractive stranger from another world. I wanted to know that he found *me* attractive. I didn't want to have to pay over the odds for the privilege, but nor did I want to be treated like a piece of Dresden china. So I kissed him back with warmth and enthusiasm, and hugged him while he recovered from his surprise. I'm sure I was babbling some nonsense or other as he buried his fingers in my hair and turned his mouth again to mine, but a moment later my words were lost in the depths of a passionate response. I could hardly breathe he held me so close, and it seemed he released me only to enfold me closer still. I don't think I was ever more aware of a man's strength, yet until that moment I had been used to thinking of myself as lithe and strong. He could have taken me then and there, if he'd been of a mind to do so, and I would have been powerless to stop him. The fact that he set me down, hugged me more gently, and on a deep breath kissed my brow and cheeks and lips in a kind of benediction, was due to his restraint, not mine.

Feeling soft and slightly dazed, I made my way back to the Cragg. For several months I had been lodging with my cousin Bella's family, the Firths, and although always aware of shortcomings in the household, I'd grown used to them. Dusty boards and grubby walls, tattered furnishings, and what seemed a perpetual stack of unwashed pots in the scullery, were everyday matters, but the difference between their way of life and what I would have chosen for myself was never more marked than it was that night when I returned home.

The fire was out and the kitchen was cold; the wind was whistling in the chimney and a sudden draught made me shiver. The house seemed deserted, and I wondered where Bella and her mother could be. I imagined the younger children were in bed, although it was still too early for the menfolk to be back. It was a Saturday night, when most fishermen seemed driven to congregate in the nearest taverns, and even more so when the weather was bad. An unfortunate habit, when funds were lowest and families most in need; but what made it worse in this case was that Bella's father had an inclination to violence when he'd been drinking, which meant the rest of us had to keep out of his way.

It was not a failing confined to Whitby, I knew that; nor indeed to any particular community. Magnus Firth wasn't even a local man, he was from Orkney, with a tendency to mutter and growl which made him even more difficult to understand. Old Uncle Thaddeus said the man was a bully and his wife Martha a slattern; what's more, the family were several rungs below me on the social ladder, and I had no business living there. In essence he was right, but I found his opinions both harsh and offensive.

Anyway, Martha Sterne had been my father's cousin, and in the early days I thought her much misjudged. She'd been a fine-looking woman once, with something of an education, and I often wondered how she'd come to marry an ignorant man like Magnus Firth. She didn't talk about that, but she did like to talk about my parents, especially my mother. I hungered for information about her, who she was and what she was like when she first came to Whitby, a wild Scottish fisherlass of nineteen with an incomprehensible tongue and a captivating manner. The story went that she'd charmed my father within days, and they were married less than two weeks later; but in Robin Hood's Bay my father's family were neither captivated nor amused by that impulsiveness.

So, instead of living in Bay, which would have been more usual, the young couple had settled in Whitby, where my father had introduced his wife to his cousin Martha, who had also married outside the accepted circle. In speaking of those days, Martha managed to imply that they had all been very close; certainly, she'd befriended my mother when she was alone and my father at sea. Six months ago, when I'd been in need, her daughter Bella had befriended me, and now I felt driven by a fierce sense of loyalty to defend them both.

I'd always seen my father's family as critical and unbending, stern by nature as well as by name, in little need of affection and undeserving of sympathy. Yet that night, for the first time, I began to discern that they'd had certain standards, long ago abandoned by Cousin Martha, which commanded respect. Standards of conduct that may have been exacting but, in a strange way, made for a sense of rightness and safety. After my evening at the White Horse I found myself longing suddenly for the company of people with discipline and good manners, for a clean house with whitewashed walls and scrubbed tables, for an array of polished utensils, and a cheerful fire of driftwood crackling in the grate. In that moment, I experienced such a powerful wave of nostalgia for my grandmother's house, I felt quite sorry for myself.

Trying to ignore the grimness before me, I lit a stub of candle and headed for the stairs. The house was old, built two or three centuries before in typical old Whitby style, at a time when seafarers' homes were stacked against the cliff like boxes, mostly one room deep but four and five storeys high. They were like ships inside, with spiral staircases linking each floor, oak-panelled walls in almost every room, and large square-paned windows overlooking the harbour. My room at the top had the smallest windows but the most panoramic view, and was the thing I liked best about living there.

I climbed the stairs, creeping past the bedrooms on the first two landings, up to my eyrie beneath the eaves. The tiles lifted and clattered with every passing gust, doors and windows rattled, and, in spite of its position against the cliff, with every good blow the house seemed to shake. It had been a week of storms, and with exceptionally high tides and heavy rain inland it was no surprise that the harbour was flooded. From my window I could see most of it below the bridge, turbulent waters silvered by moonlight, the bridge itself a narrow line repeatedly dashed by spray. Closer, between Tate Hill and the East Pier, the black hull of the Russian ship, the *Dmitry*, was being pounded by breakers; even against the storm, I could hear it shifting and grinding in protest.

It was a disturbing sound, but with it I remembered a warm hand at my waist, the strength with which my gentleman friend had held me, and the concern he'd shown earlier, pulling me back from the cliff edge when I could so easily have slipped. I hoped I might see him again, even though it seemed unlikely; more than that, I stared hard at the moon and earnestly wished for it. Yet I couldn't even give him a name, and my sensitivity in that respect – not daring to ask, even though he'd picked up mine from Jack Louvain – now seemed foolish.

I was still moongazing when I heard steps on the stair. As I turned, Bella burst in, breathless and dishevelled, her cheeks flushed from the day's excitements. '*Damsy* – where did you get to all day? I was starting to think you'd been swept off the pier! I've been looking all over – where've you been?'

Despite the questions, she gave me no chance to reply, but flung herself down on my bed and at once began to tell me that a German barque had broken free of its moorings on the Bell Shoal, threatening to take half a dozen others with it; two ships had been wrecked on the beaches, and now there was a force of floodwater sweeping downriver which everyone said would carry the bridge away for certain.

'And it looks more than likely, I must say. There are whole trees and a dead sheep jammed underneath, and they say two little bairns and an old woman from Ruswarp have been drowned already –'

'I met up with Jack Louvain,' I said, not wanting to hear about drownings. 'I was helping to move things out of the studio, when we heard about the *Mary and Agnes*. Jack wanted to take pictures, so –'

I told her of the brigantine and our struggles on

41

the cliff, but when I mentioned the lifeboat she interrupted again, big-eyed and earnest, telling me the town was abuzz with argument, not just the launching rules but whether the coxswain had done right in that aborted rescue attempt; some said rules were rules, and a good cox wouldn't let impatience colour his judgement, but others – Bella's father amongst them – thought the lifeboat committee had a cursed cheek to question the ability and bravery of a man like the coxswain, whose courage was legendary.

But courage was not in question, I knew that. 'Were you there?' I asked Bella.

'No, I was helping up at Spital Bridge.'

'Well, I was there, and all I can say is, he frightened me near to death, coming in like that. He should have gone further out. I was so worried, trying to see the lifeboat lads were all right, I nearly went over the cliff – would have done too, if it hadn't been for – well, the gentleman who was helping us out.'

'What gentleman?' she asked suspiciously.

So then I had to explain – and it was gratifying, I must admit – all about the day's adventures, including my picnic at the studio with Jack Louvain, followed by supper at the White Horse with the gentleman from London. And then there had been those passionate kisses on Cliff Lane . . .

'Oh, he kissed you, did he?' Bella said with sudden reproof. 'Did you like it?'

I thought about that, smiling, remembering the prickliness of rough tweeds, the feel of his beard against my cheek, and the wonderfully privileged smell of cigars and whisky and freshly laundered linen. Touching chilly fingers to my own lips I knew that he'd stirred me, and if the events of today were never to be repeated, they would certainly not be forgotten.

I knew also that Bella would not understand, so I stretched out on the bed beside her, and said with satisfaction, 'Yes, it was nice. And so was he. And what's more,' I added with a sly smile, 'it wasn't a bit like kissing a dead cod!'

It was a joke between us, one of Bella's most disparaging phrases, generally accompanied by a shudder of distaste. In spite of that, she was never without admirers. I thought my comment would make her laugh, but it didn't. She simply pulled a face and asked: 'Did he offer you anything?'

I was shocked by the implication. 'No, of course he didn't! Why should he?'

'Why?' she repeated, as though addressing a simpleton. 'Because most of them think we're fair game, or haven't you noticed? He bought you a meal – maybe he thought you were part of the bargain.'

The fact that such thoughts had gone through my own head a short while previously did not make me any the less angry. 'Well, he didn't,' I declared, 'he wasn't like that. Anyway, why are you being so hateful, Bella? It was only a bit of fun – I thought you'd enjoy it too.'

'What, second-hand?' she scoffed, sliding off the bed and feeling for her shoes on the floor. 'It's bad enough *first*-hand!'

With that she went, banging the door behind her, leaving me stinging at those unexpected barbs. I was astonished by her reaction and I could do nothing but stare after her, going over the conversation in my mind, looking for the point where it had gone awry. It must have been my fault, I decided at last; perhaps I'd been too full of myself and the evening's success, although I couldn't think why she should be so provoked. We'd shared experiences before, laughed at male vanities, bemoaned men's heedless cruelties; I was generally Bella's confidante and sympathiser, and would have done nothing willingly to hurt her.

Mystified, hurt, I snuffed the candle and lay stretched out in bed. After a while I began to ask myself other questions, such as why Bella should be so contemptuous. Was she jealous? There was no need – she was a striking girl, with glossy brown hair and rosy cheeks, attractive in anyone's book. For some reason, though, she thought little of it, while I was just the opposite, looking for my ideal in most of the men I met. In those days I longed to be admired, but I was tall and angular, with a mass of red hair which generally seemed to attract more jests than compliments. I blamed the Sternes, of course, for my height and build, as I did for most of the ills in my life. They were all long-limbed and square-shouldered, the majority with sun-bleached hair and eyes that seemed drawn to the horizon, as if perpetually in search of a sail.

Perhaps a large single sail, I used to think in my more impatient moments, atop a dragon-headed longship, bringing their long-lost relatives from across the North Sea. Ten centuries might have passed since the last of the Viking raids, but anyone meeting Old Uncle Thaddeus out on the cliffs could have been forgiven for thinking the raids were more recent events. He was an imposing figure for all his years, and to me, with his thick white hair and flowing beard, he resembled nothing more closely than a Viking chieftain; all he needed was chain mail and a horned helmet to complete the image.

The family origins were generally regarded as having been in Denmark or Norway, and according to the earliest local records, Sternes were certainly in Robin Hood's Bay at the time of the Dissolution, when Whitby Abbey had been stripped of its lands

44

and possessions. They were fishermen and boat-owners, then as now, and for some reason, genera-tions of intermarriage had not blunted either mental or physical fitness to any noticeable degree. The majority of the men were as able as they were clever, and I never knew one who was not a good seaman, although not all chose the sea for a living. Of the women, most were staunchly independent, known for a certain stoic endurance as much as for their good teeth and regular features. By and large they were handsome but serious, women who under-stood about living in a largely female community, helping each other whenever they could, and bring-ing up children without a man in the house.

The rhythm of their lives was in tune with the seasons and the demands of men who were away from home for eight or nine months of the year. It seemed to me that this had always been so, and it chafed at me like some kind of manacle. Perhaps, if I'd lived with my own mother I would have seen things differently; but my background wasn't alto-gether of the established pattern, so I didn't feel part of it, despite being raised by a woman who was a Sterne through and through. As a girl I couldn't bear the idea of being stuck on the same bit of beach as aunts and grandmothers and great-grandmothers before me. My need was to strike out, make my own footprints in the sand; and yet, ironically, I came in the end to a destiny that was very much part of what the Sternes were about. It was just that I travelled by a different route.

Grandmother, being a Sterne by birth as well as by marriage, was not short of relatives or moral support after my father and grandfather were lost at sea. If nothing else, the women of the family understood tragedies like that. They could be kind and helpful in

their somewhat humourless fashion, but philan-
thropists they were not. Most would have starved
rather than borrow money from a friend. That was
lauded as a virtue, of course, but there were two
sides to it, and it was hard being on the wrong one,
especially in winter, when food and fuel were low.

With the loss of the *Merlin* our small branch of the
family was suddenly orphaned and penniless. It was
hardly a novel situation, which is probably why it
excited less concern at the time than perhaps the
victims felt it warranted; after all, investing in
shipping can be a risky business, especially when the
venture is inadequately backed. I'm sure there have
been many heroic gambles which have paid off
handsomely, and a few foolhardy ones too; but there
have been many more foolhardy failures, and the
tale of the *Merlin* is probably one of the latter. My
father and grandfather, sailing as mate and master,
were joint owners of the trim little schooner and a
sizeable part of her cargo, which was tantamount to
putting every egg in the same basket – something I
would never do today. But times were different then,
and who knows what levels of need or desperation
drove them to it. There's no denying that success
would have made them a fortune at that time of
year, but an unexpected and particularly ferocious
storm put an end to their lives as well as their hopes,
and had long-lasting and far-reaching consequences
for everyone.

My mother, who was living in Whitby and
expecting her third child, went into labour within
hours of receiving the news. The poor little baby
lived for a day and a night, while Mother took a
week to die of childbed fever.

My brother Jamie and I were too stunned to know
what was going on. We knew our mother was ill,
and I knew that dead meant gone, but Jamie always

thought she was coming back. He was four and I was seven, and the only home we had known was in Whitby. After the tragedy, however, everything had to be sold in an attempt to meet the demands of creditors, and we were taken back to Robin Hood's Bay. It was a place we had visited, but we did not know it well, and all those people who said they were related were much less familiar to us than our old friends and neighbours on the Cragg. They were Father's family, of course, and he was usually away most of the year, so his absence was not unusual, but Mother's going left a huge hole in our lives that no one attempted to repair.

In those early days Grandmother seemed a remote and somewhat grim figure, but she must have been numb with shock for a long time. Somehow – and I was too young to grasp this at the time – somehow she coped with the loss of her husband and only son, a daughter-in-law who may not have been all she would have wished but was still family, huge debts, and the sudden responsibility of two young children. It was hard for us to accept an unsmiling stranger in place of the pretty, laughing, loving young woman who had been our mother, and unfortunately, by the time Grandmother was ready to take comfort from our presence instead of regarding us as a burden, we had become set in our reserve and our view of her had become fixed. She was my grandmother and I was her namesake, but I cannot say I ever discovered what she was like as a woman. It was a shame then and it grieves me still.

She always said we could not expect charity from our relatives. Old Uncle Thaddeus, who had buried two wives and had no living offspring to support, would have given her his last penny had she been willing to accept it, but she always refused. I didn't understand at the time, and it was never put into words, but they were first cousins and she'd married his brother. Whether he'd always hankered after her I don't know, but I imagine she was concerned to keep a respectable distance between them. She did not want anyone – relative, friend or enemy – suggesting that Damaris Sterne was taking advantage of such a wealthy and influential man. Or worse, that he was paying her for something that would not stand scrutiny.

Instead, she gave up her home and rented a tiny house just off the Square, taking on a variety of domestic jobs which were fitted into the requirements of the day. She was generally respected for that, and we were certainly well looked after, better clothed and fed than many children in the surrounding area. But what I remember most is the bare, scrubbed poverty of those years, and a longing for human warmth. Even while I sat on the broad stone wall and stared out to sea, I longed for the familiar smells of the kitchen at home, the big easy chair, like a nest before the fire, where Jamie and I would sit on Mother's knee listening to stories. There were no easy chairs in Grandmother's house; easy chairs, she said, were for invalids and old men. The only chair with any padding at all was an upright one, and that was Grandmother's. Woe betide Jamie and me if we sat in it.

After a while, probably when Grandmother was beginning to recover, she started to tell us stories, not so much of mermaids and water-sprites, but of her family, the Sternes, their travels and adventures, connections with Cook and Nelson, and even one who was part of the escort that took Napoleon to Elba. If her intention was to give us a sense of identity she certainly succeeded, but in the course of it she fired Jamie with such a desire for exploration that nothing less than Her Majesty's Navy would do.

He was off fishing as a boy, stowing away more than once to escape going to school, and eventually, thanks to Old Uncle Thaddeus, he was allowed to go into the Navy with something approaching good grace. If not, he would have run off anyway.

Given her ideas on gentility and our general lack of funds, the most she could do for me was to teach me things that she trusted would be of use one day. Housewifery, of course; simple accounts, elocution and good manners. In her youth she'd travelled extensively with my grandfather, and learned enough of French and German to carry her through. The phrases she taught Jamie and me went with the kind of history and geography not always taught in schools, but they were relevant to a seagoing community which earned its bread trading with northern Europe and the Baltic States.

She expected me to marry and obviously hoped I would marry well – although she must have wondered sometimes at my chances. I know she made every effort to introduce me to all our relatives within striking distance, in the hope that one day such connections would pay off. As they did, eventually, although perhaps not in the way she envisaged. At the time I found it humiliating, since neither of us had the clothes to impress, and I was one of those girls who just kept on growing. In spite of my awkwardness – or perhaps because of it – she had me trained as a lady's maid by the Misses Sterne who lived a couple of miles inland. In return for their training, girls received board and lodging for six months and tuppence a week pin money. If they were any good – and most were by the time they'd finished – they received decent references and were introduced to a respectable employment agency in Whitby.

I had two posts through the agency, my first as

under-housemaid in a large house north of Malton, then after that as lady's maid to a doctor's wife in Middlesbrough. It was not a good place, and when Old Uncle Thaddeus wrote to say that he was concerned about my grandmother's health, I was glad to come home at once. There I discovered to my chagrin that Grandmother had been unwell for some time, typically keeping this fact to herself. She was virtually confined to the house and could no longer get up and down stairs. When I would have remonstrated, she said with an echo of her old sharpness: 'It's no good – I'm an old woman now and this body's about worn out.'

In spite of things I found myself smiling. It sounded as though she was about to discard the old, worn-out shell for something bright and new; and then I thought about it and hoped she was right.

I arrived home in the middle of December '84, and over Christmas the nights were so bitterly cold I stacked the fire regardless of cost, to keep the cottage warm. One night, I remember going upstairs and falling asleep at once, only to wake in the early hours, shivering and wondering what was wrong. The air was like ice, and when I went down I found the fire out and the kitchen door standing open. Snow was drifting in across the stone floor, while out in the yard it was perhaps an inch deep. At first I didn't see her. Against white walls in her white cambric nightdress, and covered in snow, she might not have been there. I thought she must still be in the house, and searched again. It was when I came back, with the intention of looking over the broad, protecting wall, that I saw her, huddled at the foot.

She was frozen and barely breathing, and, if she was conscious of me at all, gave no sign. Somehow I managed to get her inside and into bed. The fire was barely smouldering but the fire-bricks were warm, so

I took one out and wrapped it in a blanket to place at her feet. Some time later I was able to boil a kettle and make tea, and by that time she'd wakened. Trying not to sound anxious or even bemused by what had happened, I asked if she remembered going outside. I thought it might have been a need for the privy, but she shook her head at that.

To my astonishment, for it was unlike her to be fey, she said she'd gone in answer to my grandfather's voice, calling to her from the cliffs. But when she went outside she realised that he was aboard his ship in the bay. Unable to reach him, in her disappointment she sank down against the wall. 'I suppose I was dreaming,' she murmured wistfully, 'of when we were young...'

I felt a *frisson* of alarm, which might have been superstitious fear or the intimation of approaching death. I thrust such ideas away, but was suddenly aware of my own helplessness. I sent for Old Uncle Thaddeus, and he came at once to spend a little time with my grandmother. Briefly, before he left, I saw by his contorted features how much he'd always cared for her. To my shame, I can still recall my embarrassment and, because my feelings for him were at best equivocal, I allowed myself to be resentful. He had always admired her, respected her, and by comparison I felt I was judged, and found wanting. But still, whether he was aware of my childishness or not, he sent for Grandmother's closest relatives and, as she deteriorated, I was grateful for the help the women gave me. It was agony to hear those rasping breaths, impossible to persuade her to drink more than an occasional mouthful of water. In the evening of the following day she gave up the fight, and for her sake I was thankful.

It was a frosty, starlit evening, very still over the

water as I went outside. There were a few fishing cobles coming in, but I found myself – foolishly, no doubt – scanning the bay for the sails of a schooner, white sails against a dark sea, my grandfather's ship, perhaps, waiting to ferry the departing soul of Damaris Sterne to a longed-for reunion...

Foolish or not, remembering that night brought back a wave of grief so strong it caught me unawares. I was young then, and ten months seemed a long time, long enough, surely, to get over such a bereavement. But the silly spat with Bella had touched a well-spring somewhere, and I found myself crying for what seemed no reason at all.

Four

Expecting to wake early, I had hoped to get to the station to check train times, so that I could plan a chance meeting with my new friend before he left. It was not to be, however. During the night the storm finally blew itself out, and we were all so exhausted after a week of hardly any sleep at all that the entire household slept on like logs, well into Sunday morning. When I finally poked my head out of the jumble of shawls and blankets, the sun was up and shining from a clear blue sky, the gulls were crying, and someone in the house was frying bacon over a wood fire.

My stomach, which had no right to grumble, complained as though I'd not eaten for a week. Although there was little chance of bacon for me, I hurried through my ablutions with cold water and a sliver of carbolic soap, and hastily dragged a brush through my hair before donning my best winter skirt and bodice. Fortunately they had not been worn for some time and were dry, whereas everything else was still damp and smelling of wet wool and seaweed.

Magnus Firth rarely spoke to me directly, but just as I was hoping to skip through the kitchen with a light word in passing, he blocked my way with his foot and demanded to know where I had been the

53

day before. I glanced at Bella, bent over the fire, but she only shrugged. Her father was at the table, hunched over a breakfast that made my mouth water.

'So where were ye?'

'With Mr Louvain,' I said quickly, 'the photographer. Helping him get pictures of the wrecks.'

'That's not what I heard,' he said. Dipping chunks of bread into the fat on his plate, he handed them to the waiting children. 'I heard you were seen with a fancy stranger.'

I could not imagine why it should be any concern of his, but was afraid to say so. Unwashed and unshaven, with his shaggy black hair and thick, powerful arms, he was the kind of man to make any woman nervous, and he certainly had that effect on me.

'A visitor,' I said. 'Mr Louvain wanted me to show him round.'

For a long moment, Magnus Firth eyed me narrowly. 'Aye, well, just ye remember – we'll have no bastard bairns in this house.'

I felt myself flush from breast to scalp, more with fury than embarrassment. 'You've no right –'

'I've every right,' he stated aggressively. 'I might not be one of your *grand* Sterne relations, but I'm your cousin by marriage, and you're residing under *my* roof, missy, dinna forget that.'

Anger almost overrode caution, but not quite. I would have loved to tell him that *his* roof was really Cousin Martha's, her inheritance from those relations he despised so roundly; but I had to content myself with a tart word of agreement in order to get out in one piece. *Why*, I was thinking as I ran down the steps, *why did I ever come to this house?* But then Bella caught up with me, pushed a rough-hewn chunk of bread and bacon into my hand, and begged me not to be angry.

'Last night, Damsy – I'm sorry. I was just mad at you having a good time without me. I'd been shifting boats and canvas all day, and then I came back to find I'd missed most of the fun. I didn't mean it.'

I couldn't stay angry with Bella for long, and I was grateful for the sandwich, so I grinned and bit into it at once. I'd almost forgotten how good bacon tasted – I had certainly forgotten what day it was until the bells of the parish church started ringing, and Bella asked jokingly whether I was hurrying to morning service.

'Not this week,' I retorted, which was another joke of sorts, since I had been saying much the same thing all summer. But I didn't want to confess that I meant to go to the station, so I told Bella I was intending to call at the studio, to see whether all was well after last night's flooding.

'Pity – now the tide's down, we could've gone to see the wreck.'

'Which one?' I countered, but as I said that we dropped down some steps and rounded a corner and the lower harbour was laid out before us, the Russian ship looming large on the sands of Collier's Hope. During the hours of darkness, the lashing tail of the storm had beaten the *Dmitry* of Narva almost to matchwood, denuding her of masts and spars, stripping her decks and holing her below the water-line so that her cargo of silver sand spilled out, shining, in the morning sun.

Children were playing around the wreck, and a group of fishermen were casting knowledgeable eyes over it; amongst a group of onlookers on the nearby pier was a man setting up a camera and tripod. I could not see his face and it took me a moment to identify the tall, spare outline of Frank Sutcliffe, one of Jack Louvain's friends and rivals. He was an excellent photographer, better than all the others put together, Jack said; even better than himself. I wasn't qualified to judge, but he certainly seemed to work harder and longer hours. But there again, he was married with a family, and unlike others could not afford to play the artist.

All along the harbourside was evidence of last night's flooding. Mud and silt clogged the gutters, and bits of flotsam littered every corner and recess. When we reached the studio we found Jack gazing morosely at a wet and muddy floor. He was relieved to see us, and handed over mop and broom as though they were painful to him. I was less enthralled by the idea of cleaning up in my best clothes, but what really annoyed me was the failure of my secret plan to go to the station. It was with very ill grace that I tucked up my skirts and started work.

Only when we were finished, when the floor was clean again and most of the furniture and props had been returned to their proper places, did Jack mention the early caller. It seemed that our friend of the day before had stopped by on his way to the station, to leave a note in the box. He asked for photographs of both wrecks (if possible) to be sent to him at the Lyceum Theatre, whereupon he would forward his cheque; and on the back of the envelope he had scribbled in pencil: 'Wonderful portraits displayed on the wall opposite the door. The cartes-de-visite of fisherfolk look very fine – would you send me a set?'

Reading the note for myself, I had difficulty not laughing aloud, since I knew very well where my portraits were displayed. But Jack read my face and, with a rueful chuckle, said: 'I see, it's not my work he admires – it's you!'

I protested, blushing, while trying to decipher the signature. I'd just made out the surname, Stoker, when Jack said significantly: 'You know who he is, don't you? Business manager to our most eminent Shakespearian actor –' and while my mouth was still open, framing a reply, he handed over a small carte-de-visite portrait of a distinguished-looking couple, the man older and somewhat hawk-faced, the woman recognisable even to me as reputedly one of the most beautiful and talented in England. The picture-card was not Jack's, but seemed to be one of those bought in for collectors, part of a series featuring actors and actresses in popular roles. On the reverse it claimed to be the only authorised photograph of the Lyceum Theatre's great actor-manager, Henry Irving, with his leading lady, Ellen Terry.

'Of course,' I muttered, wincing at my own stupidity, '*Irving* and *Ellen* – that's who they are, and I didn't realise. He must have thought me so ignorant!'

'He enclosed the picture with his note,' Jack said importantly, taking it from me and showing it to Bella. 'There's no mistake – Mr Bram Stoker really is who he says he is. And to think he was helping me out there on the cliffs, and I missed getting a picture of him!'

Bella wrinkled her nose at me. 'Well, Damsy got a good meal out of it, anyway!'

'I told you he was a gentleman,' I said quickly, hoping to forestall any more disclosures. 'He was just being kind, that's all.'

I caught a speculative glance from Jack, but he said nothing more. He was tactful and I appreciated it. In fact I liked him a lot, and I often wished he'd been

57

taller or more distinguished-looking, or perhaps a little less devoted to his work, since he was eligible in other ways. But although he liked to tease, and even paid me compliments from time to time, I didn't think he was very much interested in me, except as an occasional model.

Several days later, as I was passing the studio, he called me in to show me a letter he'd had in response to the photographs. It was short, but very appreciative, praising the quality of the pictures as well as their artistic merit. Jack was almost glowing with pride and I was just as thrilled, feeling part of the merit was mine. Not just for my face on two or three cards, but for the fact that I'd spent several hours in his company.

Even so, a little while later, I stood for a moment gazing up at the group of framed enlargements on the wall. The one that claimed my attention showed me seated amongst the rocks, holding a withy basket and wearing the typical working dress of a Whitby fishergirl. Caught by the breeze and in sepia tones, even my hair showed to advantage, while the short, striped flannel petticoat and turned-up overskirt made an attractive pattern against the rocks. I thought it a very pleasing and romantic portrait of myself gazing wistfully out to sea; nevertheless, I imagine one of the main attractions to the male collector would have been the several inches of calf and ankle so carelessly displayed. Even though local men thought nothing of it when we turned up our skirts for working on the beach, Whitby's summer visitors were often shocked, and the fishergirls were not above some deliberate teasing.

I'd never been concerned about it previously, much to Old Uncle Thaddeus's horror. But suddenly I realised that what bothered him was not that I was dressing up like a fishergirl, nor even doing the work

– though he regarded it as a big step down from domestic service – but the fact that I was posing for photographs for strange men to gaze at. The idea obviously appalled him. And it was Mr Stoker who made me think of it. If I'd been ignorant before, all at once I pictured him gazing upon my naked feet and ankles, and found myself growing warm from head to toe.

Jack startled me, his words so appropriate I feared he could read my mind. 'Quite a compliment, really,' he said, 'because when you think about it, he must spend most of his time in London, in company with beautiful women – all those actresses and so forth. Not to mention society ladies,' he added with a sidelong smile. 'But still, thinking about it, in London I suppose good photographers must be ten a penny, too.'

'Oh no,' I said earnestly, confident in my powers of discernment, 'not *good* photographers. Even in London, I'm sure they're not common.'

With a grin Jack patted my shoulder. 'Well, maybe we've proved something of a novelty, eh, Damsy?'

'Yes, probably,' I agreed, feeling unexpectedly flat. I wanted to bask in the compliments, enjoy the idea of being admired and in Mr Stoker's possession, but all I could think about was that he was in London, and that he would soon forget Whitby's photographers and fishergirls. Together with his pictures of wrecks and storms, after a few days of curiosity we would be mislaid, pushed to the back of a drawer and forgotten.

After the ferocity of those October gales, November was a cold but quiet month; then, as the winds and storms of winter began to settle into their usual habits, and ice started forming on ropes and halyards, the sailing ships began to come home. Regular

Whitby vessels took up their winter moorings in the upper harbour, and itinerant visitors made arrangements for caulkings and bottom-scrapings at various shipyards along the River Esk.

Almost against my will I started to look out for the *Lillian*, the ship which had borne Jonathan Markway southwards in the spring, and would no doubt soon be bringing him home again. But before I could grow too sentimental, I told myself that his mother would be looking out for him too; and when he asked what had happened to Damsy Sterne, she would have great pleasure in telling him her version of the truth. I could see her, inflated with self-righteous indignation as she told him what a red-handed thief I was; and it wouldn't matter that he could put her right at once, because the damage had been planned and implemented more than half a year ago, while he knew nothing about it. She'd had her victory, and it was far too late now to change anything.

I still minded a great deal. My pride was hurt, and I could never bear that kind of injustice. I would have liked to speak to Jonathan, but wasn't sure I'd be given the opportunity. So, I looked out for him, while trying to pretend a more impersonal concern for the ship.

It was a busy time in Whitby, quite different from the summer. In summer, there was always a kind of tea-party gaiety about the harbour, as though we were children showing off for the benefit of rich relations. But with winter came a different kind of visitor, and the town was suddenly full of men, fathers, brothers and husbands, bringing with them a hearty, no-nonsense virility, a demand for plain speaking and straight dealing. These were men who knew the warts and the wrinkles, for whom the frills and furbelows were unnecessary decorations. Even so, in my experience there was still a level of deception, since they only ever spent the winters at home, while their women worked hard to eliminate conflicts and make everything right. Homes and children were polished to an almost unnatural brightness, and both the table and the hearth must always shine a welcome.

As the forest of masts thickened in the upper harbour, I was reminded of early childhood, watching every day for my father's ship, and, with the time of year, confusing his imminent arrival with the coming of Christmas. 'I Saw Three Ships Come Sailing In . . .' might have been written especially for me. To me in those days, my father seemed like God and Father Christmas and the Three Wise Men all rolled into one, and with his passing the season was never the same again. Nevertheless, we did have some fun that year on the Cragg, and Bella and I enjoyed making simple presents for the children.

In less busy moments, however, I caught myself wondering what I'd done in exchanging the indoor life of a domestic servant for the misery of selling fish in winter. It was bitterly cold standing at a stall on the open quayside, and not much better scouring local beaches for mussels and limpets for bait. Bella and I and the other girls walked miles, taking our lives in our hands as we went up and down the cliffs at low tide. They were high and steep and unstable, sections of clay and shale liable to give way at unexpected moments. We risked our necks most days, and woe betide us if we were not successful. Without bait for the long-lines, Magnus couldn't fish, and although he sometimes had other irons in the fire – not always legal – it was mostly true to say that if he couldn't fish, the family didn't eat.

Even so, after successful trips the catch had to be sold, and not only on the quayside. Sometimes, while Martha bundled herself in shawls and petticoats to mind the stall, Bella and I would walk miles inland with heavy baskets of fish, and, if there was a glut, we would take the train a few stops up the line towards Middlesbrough and walk the moorland farms from there.

As we blew on our chilblains and eased our cracked and blistered feet in heavy boots, Bella and I often agreed that death had to be preferable to a life of flither-picking, skaning mussels, and hawking fish. Sometimes one of us – usually me – would draw comparisons with the phrase 'a fate worse than death', and we'd giggle and make jokes about the idea of ruination. But Bella always said it was a matter of public opinion; you were only ruined if you got caught, or fell for a baby, or had a reputation worth spoiling. Faced by her mother's example, she swore she'd rather have the idle existence of a rich man's mistress than that of a poor man's wife, no matter what folks said; and if only a rich man would make her an offer, she'd be away on the next train. Or she would if she could, if it wasn't for her father . . .

It was meant to be a joke, so we laughed together. Some might have thought she meant it, but I didn't. I never believed she would do that. There had been too many snide references to 'my' Mr Stoker for me to be convinced that Bella would walk the path she warned me against. Even so, her remarks were disparaging enough to put dents in my dreams; after a while I simply stopped talking about him – or even hazarding guesses as to when Jonathan Markway's ship might be back. Anyway, like my employment with the Markways, Jonathan was now part of the past – had to be. It was just that I was anxious about him.

To keep our spirits up as we walked the frozen lanes together, I would air various wild schemes for aiding our escape from the Cragg. One of them involved Jack Louvain and his sets of picture-cards. He always said that photographs of Whitby fisher-folk sold like cod on Fridays, especially to city dwellers, since they were the next-best thing to taking a day trip to the seaside to view us in person. In the wider world we were not as popular as Highlanders in full dress, or even foreigners in the quaint costumes of their native lands, but we were quaint enough in the clothes we wore to work. As Jack said, apart from his commissioned portrait sittings, we were his chief source of income. From time to time, however, he liked to produce slightly different sets of pictures, for what he called a more limited but lucrative market. Hoydenish girls, shawls and starched bonnets cast aside, in rather less of the local costume than might be seen on Whitby's quays. Striped petticoats, tight-laced bodices with a bit of bosom and a lot of bare throat, and legs often bared to the thigh. The poses were wistful or merry, depending on the scene. Perhaps seated on an oak barrel or pile of nets, the girls were sometimes dressed as boys or masked like smugglers, or several would be posed together in a tableau. And all in front of the main backdrop in Jack Louvain's studio, the one he'd painted himself, with the view from the West Pier, looking up towards Sandsend.

He'd used the word *artistic* when putting the idea to me, but I'd known he wanted something saucy, and not even my rebelliousness stretched that far. After I'd mentioned Old Uncle Thaddeus, Jack hadn't asked again, but I knew he'd mentioned it to Bella once or twice. And she claimed she'd have done it. It wasn't so very different from the photo-graphs he'd taken before, and for the right price she might even have risked it; but Jack, she said, wanted too much for too little.

She called him mean, but I disagreed. Jack had his costs to meet. I thought that if she could contemplate the risk of her father finding out, then she should do it, since with the money gained we could almost double my dwindling nest-egg and make what I called *a proper investment*. But those words always produced a groan from Bella. She thought my idea of investing in shipping was as miraculous as ice on a hot summer day. Attractive while it lasted, until the ship went down or the broker cheated you, or there was a sudden glut on the market. She'd heard all about investments in shipping from her mother; and where had it got Martha Sterne, or that famous legacy of hers? The only thing left was the house, and even that rattled and shook in the wind. No, she said, she'd rather wait for the boats to come home, and sell what cargo was landed.

Her point was valid enough, but even then I was aware of its limitations. Like Cousin Martha, I had shipping in my blood and, no matter how hard I tried at times to ignore it, I kept coming back to the same thing. It was hardly a new idea: it had been shared in Whitby for generations, by spinsters, widows, adventurous youths and elderly gentlemen alike. It wasn't wildly foolish to invest in part-shares of the cargoes carried in and out of Whitby, but it was risky. What was needed was a calm head and good advice. And money. Money that the investor had to be willing to lose. My excitement always calmed itself at that, especially when I thought of Cousin Martha and her solace in the gin bottle. Despite that, the quayside was the very place to set me going again, since from there it was possible to see almost every ship in the harbour. When I'd identified them all and wondered yet again, worryingly, where the *Lillian* might be, I would pass the time counting cargoes and trying to assess their values.

During our quiet times, Bella's favourite topic was my life in service. To me it was like telling stories at bedtime to the young ones, since Bella knew every jest, every moment of sadness and every cause of indignation, yet still wanted me to repeat them. She loved the idea of life indoors, of becoming a cook in a grand kitchen, with unlimited food and warmth, huge menus to interpret and minions to do her bidding. It was a fantasy for her, just as I dreamed of owning shares and outdoing Old Uncle Thaddeus. When I paused to think, however, I realised that Bella's fantasy was not – or should not have been – unattainable.

I remember asking whether she'd always wanted to go into service. She just shrugged and looked away, so I gathered it had been important. Eventually, she said: 'Well, it was talked about when we left school, but Isa got to go, so I had to stay.'

It was the old story, but I felt angry anyway. Bella's sister Isa generally got most of what she wanted, while Bella seemed destined to pick up what was left. It seemed such a shame. Isabella and Arabella were twins, beautiful girls with beautiful names, even though they were rarely used in full. As children they'd fascinated me, since when they were very young they'd been almost impossible to tell apart. I'd soon learned the difference, however; I had good reason to know which was Isa.

In retrospect, I suppose she resented me. When visiting the Firths with my mother, I took her sister's attention; also, as a small child I had pretty clothes and hair-ribbons, and the temptation of brilliant red hair that curled of its own accord. She was for ever pulling at it, yanking it out by the handful. I had dolls to play with, too, dolls that Bella and I were happy to share. Isa never wanted to share anything, and once expressed her resentment by deliberately smashing the china head of my favourite against a stone wall. I was so angry, I banged her head against the wall in much the same way. Thankfully, it didn't break like china, but raised a lump the size of an egg. It seemed she never forgave me for that.

Isa was the elder by a few minutes, and had revealed herself as a much tougher and more forceful individual. It was almost as though she'd taken a hold on the lion's share of energy and self-interest at birth, and had spent the years between honing them. More often than not it seemed to me she treated her sister with contempt, as though Bella was fit for only menial tasks. I felt she was envious of Bella's looks, since small physical differences had certainly become more marked over the years. Smaller boned than Bella, Isa was thinner and harder in every sense, wearing a perpetually narrowed expression that marred her features and stopped her from being attractive.

On leaving home she'd started out in Scarborough, then moved on to Middlesbrough, which was a convenient distance away. She was dutiful, sending money often enough to ensure a good name at home, but she didn't visit very often, whereas Bella had been required first of all to mind the house and children, and then to become the family's mainstay as Cousin Martha gradually gave up.

'If you wanted to go into service,' I said once, with all the ignorance at my disposal, 'you should have fought harder. Honestly, Bella, you give in too easily, sometimes.'

'Oh, I do, do I?' she remarked crossly. 'I fought hard enough for you, if you remember! Anyway,' she added a moment later, 'you know what my father's like, he wouldn't let me go. Isa always talked back to him, always got the beltings – he was glad to see the back of her. I could always calm him down, though, so it was better for me to stay.'

That was difficult to deny, but even so it seemed wrong to me that Bella should be the sacrificial lamb for the entire family. I felt for her, and was constantly looking for ways out that we could both embrace. But we were hemmed in on so many sides. What we were doing for a living was no more than scraping enough to survive, making our contribution to the Firth family coffers so we could all eat and I could continue to reside under their roof. I told myself that I was biding my time until something better came along, but after six months I was very much aware that what had been enjoyable in the summer was fun no longer. I was beginning to feel trapped.

Five

It was a long time before I realised what was going on. A combination of fear and ignorance, I suspect, kept me from realising the truth. Obviously, Bella did not want me to know; she was horribly ashamed, not just of her father but of her own role in that tangle of family relationships.

They all worked hard at keeping things dark, at finding excuses for this or that strange comment or action, and because I was aware of those efforts – although not the reasons behind them – I told myself that it was not my place to question too closely. I was not used to large families; I had no experience of the lies and subterfuge needed to keep the balance between thoughtless children and unpredictable adults. At times, I must confess, it felt as though we were all trundling along in a shaky old cart which was threatening to collapse at any moment. The pothole that finally tipped me out on to the hard road of reality was young Lizzie.

I'd often wondered why Bella was so hard on her. God forgive me, but there was a time when I thought Bella was jealous of her twelve-year-old sister. I even remonstrated with her, and had the extraordinary experience of witnessing Bella – tough, worldly-wise Bella – in tears. The next day she wouldn't speak to me; when she did, she flatly refused to explain beyond insisting that she loved Lizzie and would never do anything to hurt her.

'But why do you snap at her all the time, and tell her to clear off whenever your father tries to be nice to her?'

She wouldn't say, but the question was answered for me just after the New Year. The weather was so bad in the first week of January that fishing came to a halt. Magnus Firth had been hanging around the house for days, morose and ill-tempered by turns, watching and waiting for the weather to improve sufficiently for the brave to get out of the harbour. Fish were so scarce that whoever could do that – and get back in again with the next tide, of course – stood to make a tidy profit on his catch. In order to fish, however, the long-lines had to be baited, and so while there was a chance of getting out with the boats, bait had to be either bought or collected. Bella and I took three of the younger children with us to the beach, leaving Lizzie at home with her mother because she had a cough.

We'd not been out long when Davey fell into one of the rockpools and soaked himself through. It was a bitterly cold day and although we hadn't done much we were glad of an excuse to take him home. When we entered the kitchen he was still shivering and moaning for his mother, but she was nowhere to be seen. Instead, for one shocked instant that seemed to go on for ever, we were faced by Magnus Firth with Lizzie across his knee and his hand beneath her skirts. I suppose there might have been an innocent explanation but for the flurry of movement that followed. The girl dived away and ran upstairs, while Magnus shuffled awkwardly in his chair and looked shamefaced.

Somehow, while I stood there wondering just what it was I'd witnessed, Bella managed to behave as usual. She pushed the children towards the stairs, telling Davey to take off his wet things, she'd be up shortly; but once they were gone she rounded on her father with a face like fury. She caught him by the shoulder as he was about to go out, spun him round and, to my horror, punched him in the face. 'You old bastard!' she hissed at him, 'you promised to leave her alone! You've got me and Mam – aren't two of us *enough*?'

For a split second I think he was as amazed as I was. Then, with a howl of rage, he smacked her in return, hard with the flat of his hand, a blow that sent her reeling across the kitchen towards the fire. I moved to intercept but he was there before me, yanking his eldest daughter upright and smacking her again for good measure. 'Don't you dare strike me,' he growled into her face. 'And just remember this, you little bitch – I don't make bargains with anybody, least of all you!'

He flung Bella away from him, like a rag doll, into the chair he had so recently vacated, and wiped the blood from his nose. The baby, who had been sleeping in the corner, suddenly started screaming, but I felt weak, incapable, paralysed; then Magnus seemed to realise I'd been witness to everything. On his way to the door he turned and pinned me against the wall. He held his hand open in front of my face. It was a large hand, badly scarred and calloused, crisscrossed with the ingrained lines of tar and oil and lamp-black; I gazed at it in revulsion. Then he made a fist. 'This is what you'll get,' he promised me under his breath, 'if you utter one single word of what goes on in this house . . .'

When he'd gone I sank limply to my knees, gazing at Bella who was more distressed but far less shocked than I was. While the baby howled, she sobbed into her apron, then cursed her father roundly as she noticed blood pouring from her split lip. As she went to the sink to rinse her mouth, I pulled myself together and picked up the baby, rocking him to still the noise.

Clearing my throat, I said tentatively: 'What's going on, Bella? What was he doing?'

'Nothing,' she said gruffly. 'Forget it. You didn't see anything.'

I knew I'd seen something, it was just that I didn't understand. But Bella's defensive tone made it impossible for me to ask again.

Minutes later, Cousin Martha came in, carrying a basket with a few items of shopping. I thought I spied a gin bottle beneath the groceries, which may have had something to do with her reasons for going out. Before Bella could ask or accuse, however, her mother said brightly: 'Just had to pop out for a bit of bacon for your dad's tea,' and when neither of us replied she carried on talking in similar vein, about the weather, the man in the grocer's shop, the people she'd passed, the conversation she'd had with an old neighbour. She never mentioned Bella's swollen mouth or the cloth she was holding, stained with blood. I wanted to shriek at her.

Bella didn't shriek, and nothing of any import was said. Nothing about what Magnus Firth might or might not have been doing to Lizzie, nor about the exchange of blows, the threats, and nothing at all about the implications. I was very confused. I felt sure I'd drawn the correct conclusions, appalling though they were, but as the atmosphere settled, it almost seemed as though I'd imagined the whole thing. Except for Bella's colourful bruises, of course, and Lizzie, who refused to come downstairs for the rest of the day and wouldn't speak to anyone.

But I looked at them all in a different light after that. I'd never been particularly fond of Douglas, who at seventeen was a younger, more shadowy version of his father. He was deep and dark somehow, and, although he never did anything to me, I used to catch occasional looks from him which made me uneasy. In spite of his silence and cowed way of walking, I always had the feeling that he was biding his time, waiting to pounce; but then, after the incident in the kitchen, it struck me that Douglas was far more likely to turn on his father than offer any sort of violence to me. As for Ronnie, well, he was a kind lad, eager to please and easy to terrify. He probably had no more idea of what was going on than the younger ones had; just a feeling of perpetual unease, a knowing that no matter what happened, their father would always be right while they were wrong. And if they dared to speak out, he would seal their mouths with violence.

Although Bella was no stranger to blows, her father rarely marked her face. This time the bruises caused plenty of comment, most of it jesting, particularly from the men; but everyone knew who had caused them, and when we went out that night there were drinks bought and sympathetic glances behind her back. The fishermen were tough characters – they had to be to survive; some of their fights and enmities amounted almost to feuds – but amongst that hard community of men, I had come to realise that Magnus Firth was neither liked nor respected. He called the locals clannish, and kept himself and his boys close, but he could complain of nothing more than a scrupulous fairness, the kind of courtesy afforded to all outsiders. He fished the local waters like the rest of them, but he had never been accepted – and it was not because he was a foreigner. Bella, being female and undeniably attractive, was different.

Buoyed up by a few drinks and friendly banter,

she managed to enjoy herself while we were out, and I was glad I'd insisted on the idea. It was not until we were approaching the house that she suddenly broke down.

'God, I hate this place – *I hate it!*'

She cried on my shoulder, tears of such anguish and distress I hardly knew what to do. For both our sakes I longed to get away and take her with me, but at my suggestion she became even more distraught, saying she could not leave poor Lizzie to cope with Magnus on her own. She would have to stay at home until the little ones grew up – unless the sea took her father first. 'And if there's any justice in this world at all,' she muttered vehemently, 'it'll take him soon.'

Justice of a kind, I thought; except that with no man to provide for them, the family would be practically destitute. I said nothing, but took advantage of the break in Bella's grief to get her inside. The house was quiet, the kitchen fire no more than a few glowing embers. Cousin Martha was asleep in the chair, with bottle and glass beside her, while baby Magnus was snoring, flushed of cheek and nose, in the nearby linen basket. It struck me that he might have been dosed with gin to keep him quiet – it seemed to be Cousin Martha's answer to everything.

Neither of us was sober, but somehow we negotiated the spiral staircase up to my room. Bella flopped on the bed while I staggered about, stripping off my clothes, wincing with cold until I found my flannel nightdress and slipped it over my head. With the addition of a thick woollen shawl across my shoulders, I was ready to climb into bed. I coaxed Bella out of her skirt and bodice, replaced the shawl around her shoulders, and invited her in with me. We hugged each other, rubbing backs and arms to get warm. Tears could not survive against that, and she was soon smiling. I kissed and hugged her close, trying to convey sisterly care and affection, together with the kind of sympathy words could not express. I was afraid that if I tried, she would simply clam up and turn away from me, so I continued to hold her, tucking her head beneath my chin and letting her rest against my somewhat bony breast.

It was a comfort to me too. The physical warmth reminded me of my mother, and I had been thinking of her a lot since coming to this house. From my window I could see a certain group of rooftops marking the courtyard where we'd lived years ago. It made me aware of sadness and longing, a desire to turn back the clock and somehow make everything right, then and now.

After a while the candle guttered and, not wanting to disturb Bella who seemed to be asleep, I reached over carefully to snuff it out. Still awake, she clutched at my hand, drawing it back against the warmth of her cheek. 'Do you hate me, Damsy?'

'No, of course not,' I said, stroking her hair. 'Why should I hate you?'

'Because of *him*,' she murmured. 'You know – because of what he's done.'

I paused and searched for the right words. 'I don't know what he's done,' I said honestly, 'but if this afternoon is anything to judge by, then whatever it is, I don't think it's your fault. How can it be? Whatever was done, he did it, not you. I hate him, your father – but I don't hate you.'

I was saying only what I believed, what seemed so obvious to me, but Bella hugged me tight with gratitude. She was trembling too, with cold or anxiety, I could not be sure which. I pulled up the blankets around her shoulders and held her close.

'But,' she whispered hesitantly, 'I let him do things to me, don't you see? I shouldn't, should I? And it started just like this afternoon. Him being nice as ninepence, sitting me on his knee, giving me a cuddle, telling me I was his favourite. And I believed him, I thought he must love me best if he wanted to do things like that. But the trouble is,' Bella added, her voice deepening with pain, 'I could only be best so long as I did what he wanted. And when I wanted it to stop, he wanted to punish me. So I kept on, all these years – and now –' she broke off, swallowing hard, 'now he's started on Lizzie. Little Lizzie. That's why I saw red. I'm sorry.'

The images in my mind were an assault in themselves. I shuddered and hugged her closer. 'There's no need to be sorry. How could you help it?'

'I didn't want you to know,' she whispered brokenly, 'that's why I'm sorry. It's disgusting – he's disgusting.'

'Yes, he is,' I said warmly, 'but it's not your fault. You were just a child, like Lizzie – what could you do?'

It was a rhetorical question but Bella shook her head violently. 'I don't know – *I don't know* – and that's God's truth. But I should have done something – I knew it was wrong, I've always known, but I went along with it, I let him do those things. And now – oh, God!' She turned and clung to me, sobbing brokenly. 'I wanted to kill him, Damsy – this afternoon, when I saw him with Lizzie, I wanted to *kill* him . . .'

'You were angry,' I said soothingly, hoping I was saying the right thing. 'In your place I'd have felt the same way.' Picturing his brutality, I shivered. I'd always been wary of him, but this new knowledge was frightening, it opened up areas of wickedness and depravity I'd never suspected, and made me suddenly suspicious of all men.

Bella and I generally spent a lot of time together

during the day, but after that incident in the kitchen she began to spend nights in my room as well. It was awkward, because my bed was very narrow, not big enough for two, and – rather against my better judgement – we swapped my bed for her wider one. She said she felt safer with me, that we were cosy together in that little room under the eaves, and it's true we were; but I'd become used to being on my own, and Bella invaded my privacy. I liked some time to read, straining my eyes with a candle sputtering away on a chair by the bed: it was my pleasure at the end of a long, cold day.

As with many other things, the essence of this pleasure was not discovered until it had become a rarity. I was very fond of Bella, and had long admired her spirit and toughness, but after a while – after the kitchen incident, that is – I began to wonder whether it was no more than a surface disguise. She was still tough enough on the outside, in everyday life, but with me she became another Bella, more dependent somehow, needing my reassurance and advice on everything. She would hold my hand or link arms whenever we went out, and the nights spent in my bed became more usual than otherwise. To begin with it was flattering. I felt I was helping her, I was her backbone, her support; we stood together against the icy winds of fate. If I was uneasy about recent developments then I told myself not to be selfish, Bella needed me.

The hugs and squeezes of friendship became warmer, in a literal as well as metaphorical sense. One night, when she had been telling me how much she disliked men and their kisses – which, apart from my experience with Mr Stoker, I could understand – we became quite silly in demonstrating to each other how we would like to be kissed. It was fun at first, and we could hardly pucker our lips for giggling;

then it became warmer, a little more serious, a little more *just so*, with a teasing of lips and teeth and tongue that roused the blood more, I think, than either of us intended. We pressed against each other and, with closed eyes and burning lips, travelled the sensual journey from tenderness to passion. As the experiment went on, it was like being in an exquisitely drugged state, where all rational thought has ceased to be. In the midst of some inner fantasy, I was being kissed and caressed to oblivion by a delightful but faceless other being, so completely transported that none of the usual barriers came into play. I let myself go, floating on outstretched wings until I reached some extraordinary peak of sensation, and with a delightful shudder came plummeting down to earth.

If it was intensely pleasurable, it was also strangely shocking. There was a sense of aloneness afterwards which had me clinging to Bella as though to a lifeline, while she clung and quivered in return. But it was not until later that it started to bother me, when it happened again, and was no longer such a spontaneous expression of comfort or joy. Next day and in the days that followed I became seized with severe unease, not to say guilt, at the realisation of what we had done. I was fond of Bella, she was my dearest friend, but I did not look on her with desire in my heart; and although she was beautiful and I could acknowledge that with no more than a touch of envy, the thought of her did not really excite me.

Unfortunately, neither did the sight of any man in Whitby, and for a while I worried about what was happening. Then, as fate would have it, something occurred to take my mind off Bella. Towards the end of January I met Jonathan Markway crossing the bridge.

Six

I had been avoiding Southgate for months. Ever since my dismissal from the Markways', that stretch opposite the boatyards, where they had their ship-chandlery, had been forbidden territory for me.

A year ago, ironically, I'd been congratulating myself on being accepted for the position of general maid in a household where they also employed a cook and a daily woman. It was, after all, only a short time after my grandmother's funeral in Bay, when everything had been sold and the house given up, and I was urgently in need of employment. I was looking for a live-in position, but most of the local vacancies were daily, and the agency ones were all too far away for my liking. Old Uncle Thaddeus was still being kind to me then, and, knowing I was reluctant to leave the area, he recommended me to the Markways.

He'd known the family as business acquaintances for decades, but told me little about Mrs Markway, beyond the fact that the chandlery had belonged to her father and that she was the real business head, the one to be reckoned with. She spent much of her time in the shop, while her husband and elder son dealt mostly with the warehouse. The younger son, Jonathan, was serving an apprenticeship at sea.

He would have been about nineteen then, I

imagine, and he was at home that day I went to be interviewed. We came face to face suddenly, on the top landing, as his mother was showing me the house. He was shy, I could tell by the way he looked at me and then as quickly glanced away. Yet in that first sweep of his dark eyes he seemed to absorb every detail of my appearance, from my red hair to the good black dress I was wearing that day. Awareness brought warmth to my cheeks and I was glad Mrs Markway had her back to us, that her attention was on the layout of the upper rooms and the work I would have to do.

In the light of what happened later, I dare say I should have paid more attention to that momentary sense of alarm, but I was young then and thought myself invulnerable. And I should have listened to Cook, who tried her best to warn me about Mrs Markway, a woman who doted on her sons. She was determined to have the best for them, and the best, in her opinion, was to be found by her side, running the family business and making money. Jonathan might have rebelled and gone off to sea, but then, for Mrs Markway, nothing less than his own command would do, and for that he would have to apply himself to book-work as well as the more practical aspects of seamanship. Young women were not part of the plan – especially not servant girls, not even those with good family connections.

I was too much aware of my position to want to dispute that. Of the two sons, Dick was pleasant enough, a slow-moving and determined young man, dependable where the chandlery was concerned, but not my sort at all. As for Jonathan, he was already apprenticed to the sea, and, as I said pertly to Cook when she warned me, I'd already sworn on my mother's grave that I wouldn't marry a seafarer. She said I'd soon change my mind when I discovered they were the only ones available in Whitby, but I paid no attention.

Generally, I tried to keep clear of the top floor when the boys were at home, but for all my fine words, and in spite of my prejudices, I couldn't help but find Jonathan attractive. He was dark and graceful, with his father's Cornish-Breton looks, and a similar taciturnity of manner. Because of that, for a long time our exchanges were mostly restricted to civilities, but one day I was bold enough ask about the books on his shelf, classic novels beside a treatise on navigation, a set of mathematical tables and volumes on rigging and ship stability.

He knew I came from a seafaring family, and, as I explained, at home in Bay books had been important. My father had left a complete set of the Waverley Novels – all of which I'd struggled to read since I was old enough to understand – and Grandmother had possessed some ancient histories which had been in the family for generations. Not even Old Uncle Thaddeus could persuade her to part with those. While she lived, if he wanted to borrow the histories, he had to pay a fee for the privilege, and they had to be returned within the month. He grumbled, but he paid up and respected her for it. I'm not sure that he admired me so much for selling them to him.

That conversation broke the ice, and afterwards Jonathan and I often talked. He lent me his books and I lent him those favourites of mine that I'd managed to keep. And when I evinced an interest in his studies, he was happy to show off a little, explaining the finer points of sail against the coarser advantages of the new steamships, and his desire to understand and master both. For the time being, he said, pointing out his ship at her winter moorings on the Bell Shoal, he was pleased to be aboard a lively brigantine, as fast and seaworthy as any man might desire. I smiled at his description, and, whenever he was aboard during the day, would steal a minute or two by the upstairs window, seeking out the *Lillian* amongst a score of others, trying to pinpoint Jonathan amongst the shipwrights and carpenters working aloft or on deck. Just a glimpse of him could cheer the day's humdrum tasks for me, which should have told me much about my feelings. I found it was harder to ignore the tension between us whenever we happened to be alone.

That last evening, he was lingering in the yard as I came out of the kitchen for a breath of air. It was my habit before going up to the cramped quarters I shared with Cook at the back of the first landing, a moment of peace and quiet before bed. Instinctively, as he approached, I moved into deeper shadow. Lamps were still lit, and with windows on every side there was little chance of the meeting being entirely unobserved.

He said he would be leaving early the next morning, and wanted to say goodbye while we had this chance to be alone. A rush of innocent delight brought a blush to my cheeks, and I was glad of the darkness. But then the full import of his words reached me and suddenly I was tongue-tied; my smile became an anxious frown as I struggled for a reply.

'I'll miss you,' he said earnestly; and: 'I'll miss you, too,' I whispered at last, aware that the words were true. Suddenly, I had to remind myself of all my firm intentions in order not to give way to foolishness.

Unaware of my conflict, he went on: 'I just wanted to say – if you want to borrow any of my books while I'm gone – the novels, I mean – then it's all right. I know you like to read. I'll mention it to my mother . . .'

'Thank you,' I managed, while my throat felt close to choking.

'Take whichever ones you want ...'

I promised I would, all the time wanting to hold him, not his books. But then, leaning closer, he whispered: 'I hope you're still here when I come back ...' He was only a little taller than I, and, for one panic-stricken moment, as his eyes caught the lamplight, I thought he was about to kiss me. Instead he reached for my hand, and the lightness of his touch travelled through me like a shock.

'I expect it'll be near Christmas,' he added gently, but at the time we were barely into March and that reminder was all I needed to bring me to my senses. 'Well, then,' I responded breathlessly, jerking my hand free, 'I'll pray for good weather and a safe return. Now, we'd better go indoors, before your mother wonders what we're up to out here –'

I ran upstairs after that, to stand rigidly by the window until I heard Cook coming up, when I slipped into bed and turned my face to the wall. Early next morning, watching Jonathan leave, I was acutely aware that I'd have given anything to be going with him, to be climbing into the boat, crossing that open stretch of water and boarding the brigantine waiting for the tide ...

If Mrs Markway seemed remarkably cool after that, I tried not to feel that her ill-temper was directed solely at me. It lasted for several weeks, until the day she surprised me leaving Jonathan's room with one of his books in my hand. I'd returned *Gulliver's Travels* and was borrowing *Tristram Shandy*, but beside my bed was another volume, an anthology of verse that I'd been reading for some time. Mrs Markway took one look and accused me of stealing the books. My protests only made things worse. According to her I was wicked, a liar and a thief; nothing I could say would deflect her. Indeed, at every mention of Jonathan's name she became more incensed and, when Cook spoke up for me, Mrs Markway flew into a rage and threatened to sack her too. With her jowls quivering, she told me to pack my things at once and leave – she would not have me in the house a moment longer. She even examined every single one of my own books, to be sure, she said, that none of them had been stolen from her son and secreted away.

The injustice left me open-mouthed with shock. Like someone blind, when she'd gone, I felt for my other possessions and placed them in my box, while Dick hovered in embarrassment on the landing, ready to help me carry it down.

Fortunately the month was April and the weather was good, and although I might have lacked many things I was not without relatives. By the time I arrived in Robin Hood's Bay, however, it was early evening, and Old Uncle was on his way to a public meeting, long white hair and beard gleaming in the dusk. He was not pleased to see me, and had no time to talk, so I had to go on to the house and wait until he returned. His housekeeper took me through to the kitchen, where she gave me something to eat, but I felt very much like the condemned man abandoned to the contemplation of his sins. During that time, the anger that had waxed and waned during my walk built up again, fuelled by anguish, frustration, and the absolute conviction that Old Uncle was not going to believe me.

It was not the best way to begin an important discussion.

From his expression as he looked down at me, I knew immediately that he'd assumed I was in the wrong. That set light to my temper and I flung accusations like Roman candles, all kinds of things that had little to do with the problem in hand, but everything to do with my sense of injury. His influence had secured me the job, I said, so surely he could use that same influence to set Mrs Markway straight – to make her retract those accusations and clear my name.

His response to that was a curt demand as to why he should do such a thing when the whole affair was my own fault. The issue of the books was a matter for regret, but if I was so unwise as to set my cap at young Markway, then I must be prepared to take the consequences. How the boy's mother went about dismissing her servants did not concern him. Furthermore, he was not used to being spoken to in such a manner, especially by a mere chit of a girl. Eliza Markway was a difficult woman, he'd grant me that, but I should have thought twice before making a play for her favourite son. Good sense should have shown me better than that! He would try to help me for the sake of my grandmother, but what, he demanded coldly, did I think I was going to do next? Having chastised me, he went on to say I could stay as a guest, but only for a few days, until I had somewhere else to go. He would do his best to find me another position, but without references it wouldn't be easy.

By that time I didn't want his help. Shaking with fury, on the verge of tears, I told him I would find my own jobs and never bother him again.

I wish now that I could recall sweeping out with pride, but I was trembling so badly I fumbled at the door and almost tripped over the threshold. Old Uncle tried to prevent me from leaving, even called after me from the front gate, but I couldn't wait to be gone. I ran off down the precipitous main street, slipping and sliding on cobbles all the way down to the Wayfoot, where house walls suddenly became defence walls and the sturdy little town met the sea.

I could go no further, unless I wanted to drown myself, and for a fleeting moment I was even foolish enough to consider that as a dramatic form of revenge. But I stopped, and, like the child I was, sank down, sobbing furiously, on a smooth rock-seat, where fishermen sat while mending their nets. The night was calm and cool and after a while it soothed me. I tried to think what to do, while the tide lapped at a row of cobles drawn up on the beach, and gulls muttered on their rooftop nests.

To my mind, there's freedom and there's being cast adrift, and in that moment I was adrift like a boat at the slack of the tide. I could have been turned either way. That I turned back to Whitby, and ultimately took refuge with my cousin Bella and her family, might have seemed arbitrary, but Bella was also a friend, and, in retrospect, I can see that I headed back to Whitby mainly because I was too proud to apologise to Old Uncle Thaddeus. I felt also that no matter what I'd done, the Firths were unlikely to judge me harshly. Anyway, a long and lonely walk seemed easier than having to explain myself to my other relatives in Bay. In my mind's eye they assumed ranks of blank incomprehension, row upon row of kind, sensible, practical women, who would no more have understood my predicament than ever have found themselves in it.

But if the issue of the books might have been hard for them to grasp, they must have found it more difficult still to understand my present situation. And they were mostly kind women. I had no doubt that Mrs Markway, who wished me no good at all, was continuing to enjoy her self-righteousness at my expense.

Thoughts and emotions flashed through my mind

that January day as I watched her son Jonathan coming towards me. How I wished he'd come home a few weeks ago – things might have been different then! – but seeing him now, so clean and slender and handsome, I felt branded. Not just by his mother's accusations, nor even by the smell of fish and the basket on my arm, but by my association with the Firths. I wondered whether everyone in Whitby knew about Magnus and his daughters and, if they did, what they were saying about me, living under his roof. As Jonathan came closer, I wished I could turn back the clock. Or at least look as though I was profiting from something, if only the wages of sin.

He had never been mine, nor I his; even so, seeing the light in his eyes I felt I had betrayed something. The low winter sun, dazzling and revealing, almost blinded me as he stopped to speak. I was squinting so badly it was necessary to edge round in order to see his face, and when I did I wished I hadn't. He might have been pleased to see me at first glance, but now that he could see me properly – looking so much less than my best with that heavy basket of fish – his dark eyes revealed his embarrassment. It could have been shyness and a genuine dismay at my fall in fortune, but I felt besmirched by recent events and was prepared for condemnation. At his greeting, which would surely have thrilled me before Christmas, I was suddenly angry.

'By the way, how's your mother getting on?' I demanded waspishly before he could think what to say. 'I haven't seen her since she sacked me for stealing your books.'

A flush of colour stained his tanned skin and he looked away, upriver, to where ships moored on the Bell Shoal made a dark forest of masts against the bright sky. Watching his reaction, I told myself he was trying to identify the lines of his own ship, his means of escape from all this. It seemed an age before he drew breath, before he turned back to me with lowered brows and a glance that glittered suddenly.

'Yes,' he said at last, stiffly, 'I heard about that, and I'm truly sorry. I thought I'd explained, but there was obviously a misunderstanding somewhere. I wish it could be set straight, but – well, since it's too late for that, I can only apologise, especially about – well, about you losing your job.'

While I looked stonily downriver, wondering whether it was an apology I could accept, he paused and shook his head. 'My mother isn't well, you know – it's difficult.'

I was so astonished, and he was so obviously embarrassed by the conversation, I didn't try to keep him. Gone were the more civil questions that had been on my mind before, such as where had he been, why were they late coming home, and had it been a good trip? For one painful moment our eyes met, and then I heard myself expressing regret, and on that note we parted, he to his work aboard a ship being repaired and refitted, and I to mine, hawking fish. I cursed myself for a fool, but afterwards, when my tortured pride had settled again, it struck me that I might have misunderstood that statement about his mother. He may have meant that she was physically unwell, therefore it would have been unkind to challenge her decisions; on the other hand he could have been suggesting that his mother was going a little mad, even losing her reason. On reflection I thought the latter was most likely, and tried to feel sorry. I didn't succeed. I felt sorrier for myself.

Sorrier, but more or less cured of my infatuation with Jonathan Markway. At least I told myself that. With his dark curly hair and whipcord slenderness he'd become more good-looking than ever during the months he'd been away; except I kept thinking of Grandmother's old saying, *handsome is as handsome does*, and felt he'd let me down just by not being there when he was needed. Another reason for never marrying a seaman, I decided, while trying not to compare that kind of life with the one I was living at present.

I rarely caught so much as a glimpse of the other Markways, although Bella kept her ears open for gossip. She heard the old man had a mistress over towards Bay, and Mrs M. was making everybody pay for it, including the customers. So maybe she was a little mad, after all. I found myself feeling sorry for Jonathan, cooped up in the same house, but had no opportunity to express it. When I saw him, it was rarely to speak to and never to exchange more than the briefest of greetings. For several weeks, during the worst time of the year, he remained before me like a reminder of what might have been. Bella told me to forget him, he wasn't worth sighing over, but that was easier said than done.

When I had time to dream I thought instead of Mr Stoker and wished he would come back, like a knight in shining armour, to rescue me. He was a man, not a boy, and wielded more power than anyone I knew, save Old Uncle Thaddeus. But his concerns were not in Whitby, they were in London, where that new play he'd told me about was doing very well indeed. The spectacle of Henry Irving's *Faust*, with its storms and apparitions, its sulphurous infernos and angelic visions, had apparently made headlines in the daily newspapers. Jack Louvain told me that there were even electric sword-fights, which neither he nor I could envisage, but we spent many an entertaining hour talking about the possibilities. For different reasons, perhaps, each of us had a passionate interest in the production and would have loved to see it, but not even Jack could afford the costs involved.

Nevertheless, as spring approached he started paying me for the jobs I did around the studio, cleaning and tidying, and mounting and filing the endless sets of cartes-de-visite ready for the influx of visitors in the summer. To have the value of my work recognised, and put on a professional basis, did more to cheer me than anything else that winter. For the first time I felt I was doing something worthwhile, something respectable, something of which Uncle Thaddeus might not entirely disapprove.

Seven

In the dark days of February, however, even spring seemed a long way off. February was always a bad month, the lowest point of the year on the east coast, when snow and freezing cold gave way to easterly winds and downpours that continued for days on end. While the wind-driven rain searched out chinks and gaps in leaking roofs and ill-fitting windows, everything was perpetually damp, and the touch of unwarmed clothes on any naked patch of skin was like the cold, clammy kiss of a shroud. We shivered with emptiness too. In all my life I have never been so hungry, or so dependent on the state of the weather, on the boats going out and coming in, returning with their precious and perishable cargoes.

There were times, depending on the tides, when we were up at two and three in the morning, skaning half-frozen mussels from their shells, fingers stiff and swollen with chilblains, often cut and bleeding from the day before. Even so, if the weather was suitable for fishing, the work had to be done; and those who wanted to eat – as Magnus Firth delighted in reminding me – had to be prepared to bait the lines. Mussels were the best for cod, but they were pricey, having been brought across country by train from Ireland and the west coast. We'd fetch them in bags from the station, skane them, soak them in water for a few hours to plump them up, then start baiting the lines, each line with more than two hundred lethal hooks. At least four lines were prepared for every trip, and I swear I remember the pain of every one. But the worst thing was if the boats did not go out: then the lines had to be stripped and cleaned again, for the bait soon went off.

I hated Magnus Firth and despised him too, but I was virtually as dependent upon him as his wife and children. More often than not I wished him dead, yet at the same time when he went out fishing I prayed for his safe return because I could not bear to think what would happen if he didn't come back. And there was the matter of Bella's brothers, who deserved better than the fate I wished on their father.

We always made sure they ate before they went out in the boat, even if it was no more than oatcakes and fried potatoes, since it was not unknown for men to die from the cold out there on the open sea. Bella and I kept the children fed, and we were helped by contributions from Isa, who generally brought cooked meat and pies when she came home. Just occasionally Magnus would be out for a short time and come back flushed with some secret success. Then it was off to the nearest pub to booze all night. Mysteriously, when he came back, he still had money in his pockets. I learned not to ask questions about that.

Although much of the time that winter we were cold and hungry, the situation did have its advantages. When Magnus was fishing, he was busy for twelve and fourteen hours a day, too exhausted for anything other than sleep when he came home; and money was so short all round that Cousin Martha's credit was limited, her gin strictly rationed by Bella. To keep occupied, she knitted endlessly, unravelling the best parts of old ganseys to make sea-boot socks and mufflers for the boys. She looked melancholy and haggard, but I liked her better for it.

For several weeks the intensity of common need kept the whole family pulling together, and for a while I was lulled into thinking that things were not so bad, my being there was making a difference, and that I was welcomed for my contributions.

We saw little of Isa during the bad weather, but when she did come home, her first words on spying me were invariably spiteful. Why was I still living with the Firths, she would demand, when I'd been trained for better things than skaning mussels and baiting long-lines? Watching me work, she would point out any one of a dozen inadequacies, making me feel clumsy and stupid for even trying. But she never offered to help and, with prudish disapproval, even managed to puncture the gallows humour shared by Bella and myself.

What almost brought us to blows, however, was my new, paid employment at the studio. Only a few hours a week, but I was proud of it, and she was jealous. I know now that she'd carried a torch for Jack Louvain for years, ever since he had persuaded her to sit for a portrait while she was still at school. The portrait was so flattering it was almost sinful, and people who knew the Firth twins were astonished to be told it was Isa. Jack Louvain seemed to prefer her to Bella, and I swear she came closer to simpering in his company than she ever did elsewhere. It obviously galled her that I was often alone with him in the studio – something she no doubt dreamed about during her time off in Middlesbrough – and she managed to intimate that I was providing sexual favours in return for money.

Furious, I pushed my hands up close to her face. 'Look – see what a mess they are! You think I'd put myself through this kind of agony if I was getting paid for selling my body? Or don't you think my body's worth more than a few shillings a week?'

Somehow we survived. We knew the worst quarter of the year was behind us when activity in the harbour intensified and ships began to leave. Every day a few more moved out under tow, and I began to watch for Jonathan Markway's ship, the *Lillian*, wondering where they would be bound. I suppose I should have been glad that he was going away again; after all, he was still a reminder, and an uncomfortable one at that, of different and arguably better times. Instead, I scanned the harbour each morning with an increasing sense of anxiety, wondering whether I'd see him again before he left. And then, when I did see him, when he stopped by the stall to speak to me, I found I could barely answer for the pulse beating hard at my throat.

It was one of those crisp, bright mornings, bitterly cold but dry, that make you glad to be alive. The sun was just above the cliff, making a picture of ships in the upper harbour and dazzling off the water; then a train pulled in at the station, so Dock End and New Quay were suddenly alive with carts and carriages. The bustle prompted people to stop and buy, and Bella and I were busily serving one customer after another, barely noticing individuals until the moment of speech. Then, in a sudden lull, Jonathan was there before me in his peaked cap and reefer jacket, looking uncertain and apprehensive, and indefinably different. Taller perhaps, and a little thinner in the face; certainly paler than the last time we'd spoken, when he was so recently returned from sea.

After an exchange of civilities we were both tongue-tied. Bella asked whether he'd had a good leave, and he said not as good as he'd hoped; he was

93

glad to be going back. At that I found my voice, and asked when and where he was going next.

'We'll be away in the next few days – Baltic most like, then the Mediterranean.'

'Very nice,' I managed inanely. 'Is that where you went last time?'

He nodded. 'There and the Black Sea. We had bad weather coming back, across the Bay of Biscay, that's why we were so late coming home. Had to put into St Nazaire for repairs. We were lucky, though,' he said with a deprecating grin, 'there were times when I thought we weren't going to make it at all!'

If he thought to impress me, it was the worst thing he could have said. I gritted my teeth and looked down, trying not to show the alarm I felt at the thought of wrecks and drownings. 'Oh, I see, that was it. I did wonder. Well, if you will go to sea for a living,' I remarked tersely, 'what else can you expect?'

With that the conversation stopped dead, and we were both at a loss. I bent to my basket and added some more fish to the stall, busily rearranging everything while Bella served another customer.

'It's my life,' he said at last, enigmatically, and whatever interpretation he wanted me to put on that, I had to respect it. If he'd challenged me, I might have said the same. But I managed to apologise, and at that he unbent a little, volunteering something else: that he was hoping to sit for his Mate's ticket next time home.

'So it won't be long before I'm free.'

'From what? The sea?'

'From my apprenticeship,' he said slowly, shaking his head as though he couldn't believe such animosity from one who, once upon a time, had seemed to understand. And to tell the truth, nor could I. 'I'll have my own wages,' he went on, 'I'll be my own

man. Free to choose what I do next, and where I go.'
And who I see, was implied but not said.

For a moment longer I held his gaze. 'Well, best of luck,' I said challengingly. 'Who knows where I'll be by then?'

He looked up and down the quay, at all the women wrapped like bundles in layers of skirts and shawls against the cold. I thought I knew what he was thinking, but when he turned back to me, all he said was: 'Somewhere a bit warmer, I hope.'

'Oh, I'm sure,' I said, forcing a laugh and waving a mittened hand. 'This is only temporary, you know – next year it could be the Bay of Naples!'

We all laughed at that, even Bella, but there was something burning and serious in Jonathan's dark eyes. 'In that case, I shall have to keep looking for you, won't I?'

Something in me was burning too, but before I could answer Bella nudged me and a customer intervened, and while I was serving her Jonathan backed away. 'Look – I've got to go – work to do. I'll see you later, perhaps?'

I said yes, no doubt; but he didn't come back that day, though I hung around for a while and made a point of being at the stall early the next morning. All day there was much activity aboard the remaining ships: an intensity of hammering and banging, a raising and lowering of new sails, of berths and moorings being changed while stores were loaded for the coming voyages. At flood of the tide the steam tugs were as active as water rats, and it was difficult to see through the smoke exactly which ships were moving where. I was afraid of losing sight of the *Lillian*, and every time the bridge opened I was on tenterhooks in case Jonathan was leaving without saying goodbye.

Between times I hovered near the bridge, hoping I

might identify him aboard the brigantine, or he might notice me and remember. Bella could mock all she liked, but now that we'd spoken again I felt a need to explain and apologise. I wanted him to think well of me, to carry with him a memory of friendship rather than disappointment and misunderstanding.

Just before sunset, as the last stalls were packing up and I was about to go home, he called out to me from the bridge. 'At last,' he said breathlessly as he hurried to my side, 'I'm glad you're still here! There's been no chance to get away, and I haven't got long now, worst luck. The owners finally made a decision, and we're sailing tonight with the tide.'

He stopped for breath, relief and anxiety in his smile, while I was conscious of pleasure at seeing him, coupled with disappointment at his news. 'Oh, I see. Well, it was good of you to come, but never mind. If you've got to get back ... ?'

'Not just yet – in a little while, half an hour or so –'

It was half an hour more than we might have had, and since it didn't seem to matter where we went, we walked along the railway as far as the old ford at Bog Hall, keeping the brigantine in sight as the tide came up. There was so much to say, yet it seemed we were both too aware of each other to speak; and then when we did, it was only to blurt out simultaneous apologies. But in the end we got his mother and my Uncle Thaddeus out of the way, and managed to put aside any lingering sense of injury.

With the old Esk Inn behind us we stood on the stone quay and looked up and down the river, glassy now in the evening light, saying nothing of any moment, except for both of us wishing he might stay. I wanted to catch hold of time, stop the ship from sailing, keep Jonathan by my side, but the river was rising with the tide, masts above the muddy expanse of the Bell Shoal were coming upright again, and it was time for him to go.

He turned to me then in mute appeal, and I felt the breath catch in my throat as he removed his cap and leaned towards me. Cold lips touched mine, melting to warmth as one kiss became another and we clung together in dizzying, tremulous joy. As my shawl fell back he laid his smooth cool cheek against mine, wrapping his arms around me as though he would never let me go.

'It's been almost a year,' he whispered, 'and I've thought about you so much. I really hoped –'

Overwhelmed by a conflict of emotions, I stopped his lips with my fingers. 'No, Jonathan, you mustn't. I don't want you to think about me at all. It's not worth it.'

He protested at once, crushing my hand in his as he held it to his chest. 'My mother was wrong in what she said and did – it wasn't your fault, none of it was –'

'No, but the rest of it is,' I insisted, stepping back. 'Where I'm living, what I'm doing – it's all been a mistake, you don't understand.'

'Then put it right – move out. You don't have to stay there.'

'It's not so easy as that. I want to leave, but I can't, not yet.' Even as I longed to seize the moment I feared the very things Jonathan represented: risk, loneliness, pain. I didn't want anyone to have that kind of hold over me – or to expect devotion until death in return.

I felt these things, yet without the words to express them I could only gaze at him intensely while he struggled to read my meaning. Voices hailed us then, jocular and teasing, as a couple of railwaymen crossed the inn yard. The moment was broken. Aware of time pressing as dusk fell, we turned to retrace our steps with a sense of chilled urgency that had not been present before.

When we reached the bridge I felt a tug of emotion quite unlike any that had preceded it. Jonathan didn't kiss me in that public place, but took my hand before we parted, gazing at me with such undisguised longing, I had to look away. 'It's going to be a long time. Will you write to me, Damsy?'

But that was too close to commitment, and besides, I couldn't bear the idea of waiting for words from him, words that might never come. 'No,' I said awkwardly, aware that I was hurting him. 'Don't ask me that.'

He took a deep breath. 'Will I see you then, when I get back?'

'If I'm still here,' I said, struggling for lightness, 'I'm sure you will.'

He looked downcast, and I hated myself for it. 'Well,' he sighed, squeezing my fingers hard. 'Whatever you do – wherever you go – leave word for me with someone. Bella or that photographer fellow you work for. Promise?'

So I promised, and he left me then. I watched him disappear into the dusk, hurrying home to collect his things before going aboard the *Lillian*. They would be heading north to the Tyne first of all, for a cargo of coal, and from there, most like, across to Sweden for timber. He'd assured me of the ship's good qualities, of the fact that she was a fine seaboat even in a storm, and her master an excellent seaman. I was glad of that. I needed to believe he would be safe.

Two hours later, without a word to anyone else, I slipped out of the house and went back to St Ann's Staith to await the opening of the bridge. Several ships were due to leave, and the brigantine was already under tow. She came through first, her figurehead gleaming, eager to be over the bar with sails unfurled, catching the offshore wind and away.

There were men on deck and in the rigging, but in the darkness it was hard to identify them. The mast light and red, port-side lantern cast little more than a glow as the ship swept silently past in the wake of her noisy, thrashing tug. I kept moving too, around and between the groups of people, trying to keep my eyes on individuals just a few yards away. I'd reached the pier before I spotted Jonathan coiling mooring-ropes on the stern. He looked up to scan the onlookers and for a moment his face was sharply illumined, deep-shadowed, intense, so close I could see the line between his brows and the grim set of his mouth. I stopped to call out to him, but he was unaware and the ship sailed on.

I had to run to catch up. I ran the length of the pier and was almost at the lighthouse before he saw me and his face lifted suddenly in a delighted grin. He raised his hand and I waved frantically, wishing him God speed, safe voyage, good trip, all the things women have been saying down the centuries to their departing menfolk. I watched and waved until the tug dropped her tow and the night wind filled the unfurling sails, and then, when she'd slipped away like a ghost into the night, I turned back towards town, wondering what was the matter with me, why on earth I was breaking my heart over a man going off to sea.

Eight

Whenever I talked of leaving Whitby, of finding employment that would provide a more secure existence, Bella carried on alarmingly, accusing me of everything from snobbery to ingratitude. She even brought Jonathan into it, claiming I'd changed since seeing him again. I denied it, but felt unsettled anyway, and being with him that afternoon had stirred up more than one kind of longing.

I was restless and dissatisfied, and whether it was Jonathan or just spring fever, his words about moving on had struck a resounding note. It was echoed shortly afterwards, and more directly, by Jack Louvain.

As I posed for him one fine evening after Easter, he remarked quietly: 'It must be nearly a year, Damaris, since I took those first photographs of you . . .' Lightly, he adjusted my shoulder to the position he wanted, and turned my chin towards him, scrutinising me with those bright eyes of his. Frowning, he ran his fingers over the skin at my temple, then felt behind my ears and under my jaw.

'You've lost a lot of weight,' he said reproachfully. When I apologised, he simply shook his head, ducking once more under the black cloth. 'No, it's just that you look haunted – all eyes and cheekbones – like tragedy personified.' He paused to gaze through the big, fish-eye lens of the camera, then announced with muffled triumph, 'But in fact it's rather wonderful, we should have some excellent pictures . . .'

I was not quite sure what to make of that, but knew better than to speak while he was busy. In flattering evening light, and framed by an open cottage doorway, I had hoped for something rather more appealing than tragedy; as perhaps had Jack, to begin with. After much thought and several changes of position, he exposed a couple more plates and then called a halt. 'Tomorrow,' he said, 'at daybreak on the west side, we'll try again. The light will be more searching, and with any luck we'll catch the boats going out. I've a fancy,' he added with a dry smile, 'to portray you as the beautiful girl recently bereaved of her fisherman lover.'

With a hoot of derision I turned to face him. 'Fisherman lover? For heaven's sake, don't tell anybody who knows me, will you? They might take it seriously!'

I thought he would laugh, but instead he pursed his lips and remarked disapprovingly that I was starting to sound like Bella. Then, as we made our way back to the studio, he said: 'You know, when you first sat for me, last year, you said staying with the Firths was only temporary – and again, when you started working for me, you said it was just for a while, until you found a proper job. Why haven't you done anything? Why are you still here?'

He was not being cruel, but I chose to pretend he was and reacted huffily, which provoked him to anger. 'Damaris, shut up and listen to me. You weren't born to this life you've adopted, nor have you married into it. You don't need me to tell you how hard it is – bad enough for men, never mind the women, and they work even harder. But you don't

101

have to do it. You could get out and leave it behind if you really wanted to. So why don't you, before it's too late?'

He caught me on the raw and I had to swallow hard before I could answer. 'It's not as easy as that.'

'Why not? Just pack up your things and leave. You've no obligation to the Firths. Surely, after all you've done for them this winter, they must be obliged to you!'

I tried to protest that they'd given me a roof over my head, but Jack was unimpressed. I'd paid for it, he said, just as I'd paid for everything else, friendship as well as food. 'I haven't said anything before,' he went on, 'because it's not my business to interfere, but I am concerned about you. If it's money you need, I could perhaps lend you some – but only on condition you leave that house and get out of Whitby.'

'Oh, thank you,' I said, feeling hurt, 'that's *most* kind.'

'For heaven's sake, I didn't mean that the way it sounded. I'd miss you, of course I would. We've been friends, I think, apart from anything else. But the Firths aren't good for you, Damaris – they're taking all your heart and energy and good sense. You work so hard for them – you'd put in less hours as a scullery-maid at the Royal! – and for what?' In an eloquent gesture his arms embraced the empty air, and then, with quiet emphasis, he said: 'They're not your responsibility, you know – they survived before you came, and I swear to you they'll survive after you've gone!'

It sounded callous, but there was truth in what he was saying and it struck home painfully. 'You don't like Bella, that's your trouble,' I said harshly, needing something to hit him with, but it was no instrument at all.

'You're right, I don't,' he admitted with a shrug. Then, with somewhat shocking frankness, he said, 'I don't like the way she uses her body in men's company – like an open invitation. It wouldn't be so bad if she meant it, but –'

'She does not!'

Jack turned his head to look at me. 'Damaris, my job involves studying people, watching them, interpreting their actions, the way they stand. I try to put these things into my work. I know what Bella's doing.'

'Oh, you do, do you? And you're a man,' I said contemptuously, 'so I suppose you've chanced your arm and had it bitten off. And *that's* why you don't like Bella.'

He had the temerity to laugh at that. 'Who, me?' he said, 'make a play for Bella Firth? No, not true. It's just that I don't care for whores, and she's one in the making.'

'Well, if she is,' I cried furiously, before dashing away, 'then it's a man who's made her so!'

I was so upset by that exchange I deliberately ignored our appointment at daybreak, which made me reluctant to face the telling-off I knew he would give me when next we met. Two days passed in which I worked on the quayside, flirted with passing visitors, and even had my photograph taken with a few of them by an opportunist rival of Jack's. It was a silly gesture of defiance that I should have known he would hear about, and it made the situation worse.

On the third day I caught sight of him twice but he ignored me, and by that evening I'd started to worry about my job at the studio. He always said he let me help him because I was neat and capable and he trusted me with the equipment, but I was not the only capable one in Whitby; and as for acting as his

103

model occasionally, well, there were plenty of other girls around. So, when work was finished for the day, I went back home with Bella to wash and change before going to see Jack Louvain. That I would have to apologise was obvious; what worried me, however, was that he might question me about Bella, want to know what I meant by that parting shot.

But he was too angry to recall such a minor detail in the face of behaviour he classified as appallingly rude, totally bad-mannered, and infuriatingly ungrateful. He had given me work, he said, because he thought I had something more than the average pretty girl's vanity. He'd imagined I had character and intelligence, enough to grasp the right opportunities and make something of myself. He'd looked forward to seeing what I might do with the hand fate dealt me. Of late, though, I'd proved something of a disappointment, and in the last few days he'd come to agree with Thaddeus Sterne, that I was indeed blind and foolish and unutterably vain.

'I don't know,' he exclaimed, just when I thought he'd finished, 'you seem determined to make an enemy of every friend you've ever had!' He paced the studio floor, eyes dark with fury, while I burned with shame in the doorway. 'You didn't turn up on Wednesday morning, and didn't even bother to send word. Why? The light was perfect, but because I waited for you, I lost the chance of working elsewhere. I can't afford that kind of whim, Damaris. Then, when I heard you'd posed for Henderson, I just couldn't believe it – you must have known how he'd crow about that!'

I did know, and felt ashamed. Rivalry between the different photographers was intense. There were at least half a dozen of them plying their trade in Whitby in the summer, each one eager to produce the best pictures with the best models. If commissioned portrait studies were bread and butter to the professionals, collectors' sets of local characters were the jam, and picturesque studies of the town and harbour were like a blob of cream on top. More than mere survival was at stake. Reputations were involved, together with style and identity, especially in a market awash with ideas copied from professionals and amateurs alike. For the lucky few there might even be medals, awards and a touch of fame. There was much at stake, and I had played the fool with someone who trusted me. Jack Louvain had every right to be angry.

'I'm sorry,' I murmured, feeling tearful and upset. I hated to seem stupid and ill-mannered, hated him to think that I was driven by something as small and petty as vanity. But perhaps he understood something of my dilemma, or my eyes pleaded more eloquently than I realised.

His glare softened under my gaze, and with an exasperated sigh he sank down on to the chair used by his sitters. 'All right,' he said tersely, 'we'll forget it this time. But don't let me down like this again. In future, tell me if you have to break an appointment. It may not be convenient, but at least I'll have been warned.'

I gave him my promise, thankfully and with considerable relief. After that, on the surface at least, our relationship returned to its old level. As the weeks passed and the number of visitors increased I found myself working at the studio most days. There was plenty to do, and I was pleased to note that Jack was trusting me with more and more of the mundane jobs; he even gave me a key to go in whether he was there or not. He became busy with sittings and commissions during the day, and most evenings and early mornings he was out with his camera, trying to capture the kind of photographs people wanted to buy as souvenirs.

He rarely mentioned Bella and neither did I. It was as though she had become a taboo subject. I tried to forget the things he had said because I did not want to believe them, but found myself taking more note of the work I did for the Firths, the hours spent on the market during the day, or hawking crab and lobster around the grand kitchens of the west cliff. If I compared the hourly rate Jack Louvain paid me with the number of hours I worked for the Firths, then Magnus should have been paying me a handsome wage, not just my meals and a couple of shillings' pin money. It seemed I was working for nothing while paying the Firths for my room. It was iniquitous, but I'd locked myself into this position and was not sure how to get out of it.

Had it been winter, when the entire community struggled for survival, I could not have said anything, but the weather was good now, fish were plentiful and lobsters fetching an excellent price. Magnus Firth was so busy we hardly saw him, which meant he had to be doing well. I steeled myself to speak to Bella, and my opportunity came a few days later. She was wearing a blouse I'd not seen before, the children had been given new clothes for Whitsuntide, and even Cousin Martha was talking about summer dresses. It seemed I was the only one who was having to do without, and that hurt, not just because it was the custom to have something new, but because my appearance was important to me.

I used my sense of injustice to raise the matter of work and wages. Bella was surprised at the complaint. 'But you live with us as family – we don't get paid either.'

'But neither you nor the boys pay rent – I do. If I'm

to stay here,' I said heavily, knowing it was useless to talk about leaving, 'I have to get something else besides working at the studio. I've slipped into the habit of helping out, and it's no good. If your father would pay me a proper wage it might be all right, but he won't, will he?'

'He can't afford it,' she said defensively.

With his fishing and smuggling activities I thought he probably could, but I was not prepared to argue the point. Determined to waste no more time, I decided to begin my search for other employment the very next day, and with that in mind, set water to heat so that I could bathe that evening and wash my hair. Generally Bella and I performed our ablutions together, rinsing each other's hair, brushing and drying it before the warm embers of the kitchen fire. On this occasion, however, because my request was out of step, and because it heralded change and possibly an ill wind, I was made to feel unreasonable.

But I persisted, seeing to the necessary jobs myself while Bella carried on with preparations for the evening meal. I thought she was going to be difficult, but afterwards, when her mother had gone out and the men were away to the pub, she decided to take advantage of the fire and hot water too.

I busied myself arranging the screen of towels and clothes-horses, while she went upstairs to settle one of the children. When she came down, I'd been soaking in the tub for several minutes, my mind preoccupied with plans for the next day. I'd hoped Bella would be useful as a sounding board but she seemed more interested in scrubbing my back.

Within moments, my senses were alert to the fact that her friendly assistance had become more persuasive, that Bella was caressing me rather than helping me wash. But I wanted no more of that. I dunked myself deliberately, coming up in a splash of water that made her sit back in protest. I lathered my hair, and then grabbed the soap to scrub myself quickly all over.

She was offended by the rejection and left me to rinse my own hair, but a little later, when she had bathed and dried herself, Bella stood with what seemed deliberate provocation before the fire's dying embers. Her stance reminded me of what Jack had said, and I realised she knew instinctively how to show herself to advantage. With her lovely face and figure, she appeared to be what every man desired, yet the irony was that she disliked men. I found it doubly ironic that she should wish to bestow all her warmth and sensuality on me, who would have been happier without it.

I didn't want her softness, I wanted to feel a man's arms around me, be aware of a man's strength and protection, no matter how illusory. Almost sick with longing, I thought of Jonathan, remembering the cold that day and the feel of his skin, the way his mouth had blossomed into warmth against mine. Then I was angry with myself, wondering why I had to fall for the impossible ones like Jonathan Markway and Mr Stoker, one at sea and the other in London – and probably married, into the bargain. Why couldn't I take a fancy to someone like Jack Louvain, I asked myself, who was not only available, but also kind. But I knew enough to realise that desire ought to work two ways, and Jack carried no torch for me.

My ponderings were shattered by a sudden rattling at the door. Bella hastily covered herself, while I slipped a shawl over my nightgown and tied it at the waist. Magnus Firth came in, reeking of stale beer and tobacco fumes, and said he was going to bed, but I saw the way he looked at Bella and how she hardened and withdrew. In that moment I hated him so much I wished him in his grave.

But my ill-wishing was banished by Cousin Martha and the boys coming in on Magnus's heels, all of them flushed and talkative with drink. At once, I made my excuses and went up to my room.

Nine

Next morning, after putting in a couple of hours at the studio, I went back to my room to wash and change. I pinned up my hair, shone my good pair of boots, and put on my best summer dress, a yellow and white striped cotton that was well suited to the weather. It was a beautiful morning, full of glittering light and the cries of seabirds, a morning to lift the soul and banish any lingering megrims from the night before.

Something good was in the offing, I felt sure of it. My decision to act had come at the right time, just as the summer visitors were starting to arrive in appreciable numbers. Kitchens would be busy, chambermaids would be needed, I would no doubt have to choose between half a dozen jobs, and this was simply the first step. As soon as I was established somewhere, I would look for other lodgings. Full of optimism, I started with the kitchens of the Royal Hotel, just above us on the crown of the west cliff, but despite my efforts before the mirror someone remembered me as one of the girls who came hawking fish, and I was turned away with a contemptuous smirk.

A blow so early in the day dented my confidence severely. From there on, I was rather more circumspect, but even though the hotels were smaller and attitudes and answers varied, the story was often the same: they'd already taken on their extra staff, and I was too late. I trailed up Whitby's hills and down again, silently cursing the fates, my fish-selling expertise, and the red hair which made me so memorable. A little straw bonnet was no disguise at all.

Weary and dispirited, by mid-afternoon I was making my way back to the Cragg, aware that I had not yet covered half the ground but knowing the rest would have to wait for another day. Trudging up Cliff Lane, I noticed a tall figure some distance ahead, strolling along in the generally aimless manner of a summer visitor. The set of the shoulders alerted me, brought up my head and narrowed my eyes in an eager search for detail. I knew that red beard, that well-built frame, that broad-brimmed hat –

'Mr Stoker!' I cried breathlessly, waving as he turned. I had the immense satisfaction of seeing a similar delight as he recognised me, as he swept off his hat and came striding down the hill with arms outstretched in greeting.

'Damaris Sterne! How wonderful to see you!' His smile embraced me, and for a moment as he grasped my hands I thought he would catch me up and spin me round, as he had done once before; he didn't, but I was still giddy at the thought, and found myself laughing as we exchanged the more usual civilities.

'Are you busy?' he demanded, pressing my arm, 'or will you have tea with me? Do say you will, I've been looking for you ever since I arrived!'

'And how long's that?'

He consulted his pocket-watch. 'Oh, at least two hours!'

Laughing again, I suddenly thought of my grandmother and how unladylike she would say I was; but

Mr Stoker hardly seemed to mind my unrestrained amusement. In fact I suspected him of encouraging it, since he barely stopped talking all the way to the tea-shop on Skinner Street and seemed to be enjoying a thoroughly boyish sense of freedom. He wanted to know how I was and what I'd been doing since last we met, but even as I struggled to frame an acceptable reply he was telling me what a long winter it had been in London, exhausting in spite of the successful season they'd been enjoying at the Lyceum.

'But it's so good to be here,' he said warmly, 'I feel better already! I needed a holiday – or at least everyone's been telling me that,' he added with a grin. 'To be honest, I think I was driving them all mad, and they just wanted to be rid of me for a while!'

I wondered who 'they' were exactly, but he gave me no chance to ask. As I faced him across the tea table I thought his light, jesting manner probably disguised a lot of truth, and although the beard covered much of his mouth and jaw it seemed to me he was thinner. There were shadows I'd not noticed before, and a nervous tic below his right eye of which he seemed unaware. I wanted to smooth it away with my fingertips, but it was hardly the thing to do in public; anyway, my hands were never my best feature. Even in crocheted cotton gloves I was conscious of wanting to hide them.

'I'm supposed to be on a walking holiday,' he confided, 'using Scarborough as a base. I've been in touch – sent lyrical cards to all – but they can't get in touch with me here, and that's the beauty of it!'

'You're in hiding, then?' I whispered, making a joke of it, but I wondered why it mattered so much.

'I am,' he said seriously. 'I've had enough of them all. Florence as well as Irving and the rest.'

112

'Florence?' But I hardly needed to ask.

'My wife,' he said bleakly. His gaze met mine and held it, revealing a darkness quite at variance with the laughter of only moments ago. Disturbed by it I had to look away.

Mistaking the reason, his hand sought mine, found my fingers under the table and gently squeezed them. 'I'm sorry. I didn't want to deceive you.'

'That's all right,' I said, forcing a smile to cover my disappointment. 'I knew you had to be married – too nice not to be!'

Under the table, my fingers were almost crushed. 'Does that mean we might still be friends?'

'Oh, I should think so,' I said lightly, disengaging my hand and reaching for the teapot. Excitement made me nervous, and it was a long time since I'd presided at a properly laid table with pretty china and silver teaspoons. Nevertheless, I managed to pour without spilling a drop, and passed the cup across with a hand that was shaking only slightly. 'How long are you planning to stay?'

'I don't know – a few days, a few weeks, who knows?'

'You should stay for the summer,' I said decisively, reaching for the scones. 'It would do you good.'

'Perhaps I will – I've been considering it. Do you know of a place I could stay? For more than a night or two, I mean. I'd need a cottage, something like that – somewhere quiet where I could do some writing. That's essential.'

I didn't know of anywhere, but thought Jack Louvain might; there was also the local paper, and an office near Whitby Town station which advertised properties to let. He wanted me to go with him, but I knew Jack would be busy and I was reluctant to intrude with matters like that. Besides, I hadn't been home all day.

'But you'll meet me later, I hope? We'll have supper together, like last time?'

So I said yes, of course I would; but with the feeling that something rather more than supper had been agreed, I arranged to meet him later in the gardens above the Cragg.

I was nervous and wished very much for something different to put on that evening, but had nothing as flattering as the clothes I'd been wearing. So I set the iron to heat, some water to boil and, having refreshed my dress, hung it to air by the open window in my room. Then I turned my attention to myself. When Bella came bounding up the stairs I was brushing my hair, trying, without much success, to persuade the thick curls into ringlets. She saw at once what I was after, and took the brush and comb from me.

Frowning in concentration, she worked on the ringlets then looped them all in a skein of hair, anchoring both sides with tortoiseshell combs. 'There we are,' she said, smiling: 'looks a treat now, Damsy.'

As I thanked her and turned to examine my dress, she said: 'So where're you going then, what're you getting done up for?'

I tried very hard to keep the excitement out of my voice, to sound more amazed by the coincidence than impressed by Mr Stoker's interest. 'Well, you'll never guess who I bumped into on my way back here. My gentleman friend – the one who helped Jack Louvain on the day of the storm – you know, when he was trying to photograph the wrecks.'

'No,' she said quickly, compressing her lips, 'I don't remember.'

'Yes, you do,' I insisted sharply. 'There haven't been that many gentlemen in my life. If you recall, he treated me to supper.'

'Oh, *that* gentleman – the one who kissed you good-night and had you sighing for weeks. D'you know, for a minute there, I thought you meant young Markway.'

She used his name like a knife under the ribs, and for a moment I couldn't speak.

'You see,' she went on, 'the last I heard, young Jonathan was the one you wanted – so much, you were going to have to leave here and get a job, just so he wouldn't be ashamed to be *seen* with you!'

With that she flung herself out of the room. Furious, I was hard on her heels. 'I never said that! Just what d'you think you're getting at?'

'Nothing,' she said bitterly from the stairs. 'But just remember – the ones with money are the worst, especially when they're hunting for bargains!'

Before I could answer, she was down the stairs and away. And with that, *I* slammed the door, so hard it rattled the windows and my dress fell in a heap on the floor.

The joyousness of that meeting on Cliff Lane was wellnigh destroyed. I could not believe that a few hours could make such a difference, that I could have been so delighted by that moment of mutual recognition, yet be going to meet him now on leaden feet. Bella's parting shot was bad enough, but the fact that he was married gave it credence, and made a travesty of what should have been innocent enjoyment.

I made an effort to be lighthearted and thought I was succeeding until we were settled at our table in the White Horse. But with the order given, Mr Stoker went straight to the heart of the matter and asked why I was so ill at ease. 'Is it the fact that I'm married – does it offend you so much?'

'No,' I declared, which was mostly true. What continued to bother me was the ugly light Bella had cast over everything – my motives and his intentions – but because I couldn't tell him that, I said my evening out had caused trouble with the people I lodged with.

He frowned for a moment, then said: 'But not with the young man you mentioned last time we were here? The one with a gorgon for a mother.'

I shook my head, astonished that he should remember Jonathan and the troubles I'd had then. 'No – no, he's been gone since before Easter. That's the problem,' I said with affected lightness: 'all the likeliest lads go off to sea, and leave their womenfolk at home.'

'And you don't want that?'

'Not if I can help it,' I said pertly, and he laughed and squeezed my hand.

I could tell he didn't quite know when to take me seriously, often mistaking a wry observation for jest, and a teasing joke for gospel truth. But there again he told stories that were impossible for me to judge, relating bits of theatrical gossip over the roast and household names over the pudding that had me sitting there with jaw agape. I gasped and laughed at his quick character sketches of royalty and politicians, the plays they'd attended, things they'd done and said; laughed even more at his backstage tales of practical jokes and near-disasters, often rescued at the last minute by his own intervention.

If his stories of the rich and famous sometimes seemed incredible, they were also great fun, but as the evening progressed he became more serious, and from the tone of our conversation I began to realise that the demands of his work in London had increased. Quite apart from daytime responsibilities, he was at the theatre every night, ironing out problems, charming important patrons, even organising supper parties, so that his precious Mr Irving might relax amongst friends after a performance. He was rarely home before two in the morning, and sometimes, depending on the company, it could be daybreak as he left to walk down the Strand. It was part of his job, but even I could see that the job was wearing him down.

'You needed to get away,' I said with sympathy.

'Oh, yes,' he agreed with feeling, 'I've known that for months. I was hoping to get away at Easter, but it simply wasn't possible. And then – well, I'd finally had enough the other night. Told Irving what I thought about his behaviour and my working hours – I said I was due some time off, that I was taking it as of that moment, and wasn't sure when I'd be back. He said I should be careful – I might not have a job to come back to. That was when I walked out,' he confessed. 'I didn't even bother answering him. I went home, packed my things, and got the train the following morning. Best thing I ever did.'

He grinned then, like a schoolboy playing truant, but when I said: 'Good for you, Mr Stoker!' he remonstrated with me, saying that it made him feel old, so I must call him Bram, as did all his friends in the theatre. And he would call me Damaris, which was such a delightful, old-fashioned name. I agreed it was old-fashioned, and said that was why I didn't like it, but he said the *maris* part of it reminded him of the sea, and suddenly, after that, I didn't mind at all. Hearing my name on his lips made it seem special, somehow, softer and prettier than it had ever sounded before.

After the candlelit interior of the White Horse, we were surprised to discover that twilight was still lingering outdoors. It was an hour when Whitby was at its most peaceful and relaxed, and it seemed to me as we strolled up Kirkgate that my friend had done well to return. There was a compliment in it, somehow, that brought a smile to my lips. Seeing it, he offered a penny for my thoughts, but I was bold enough to say they were worth far more than that.

'Well, I confess freely,' he said with a sidelong smile, 'that I've been thinking of you all winter. Stealing glimpses of you in your fishergirl's garb –'

'You haven't!' I protested. 'Not those photographs Mr Louvain sent you?'

'The very same!' He reached into an inside pocket and brought out the wistful one, the one I'd always liked best, and his grey eyes danced as they surveyed me, blushing and giggling and thankful of the dusk.

But as we passed the Duke of York he wanted to take a look at Collier's Hope, where the Russian ship had foundered. I told him the schooner had been sold and broken up long ago, her ballast of silver sand dispersed to the sea. We stood for a while looking out beyond the piers, beyond the lighthouses, and I was intensely aware of him then, not just his physical presence, but a deeper sense of intimacy between us, as though we'd known each other always. I had a sense of that quiet moment being a necessary pause between what had gone before, and what was yet to be. But then he moved and turned, and it was gone.

As we climbed back up to the pier, I asked whether he'd found the accommodation he was looking for.

'No, the office you mentioned was closing. But your friend the photographer said he knew of several places out of town – empty farm cottages done up for the summer, that sort of thing. He said he would tell you where they were, so you could take me to look at one or two tomorrow. That is,' he added, 'if you're able to.'

'Yes, of course,' I said blithely, disregarding my need to find a job. All at once it didn't seem nearly so important.

This time we managed the Church Stairs with ease. As we neared the top, my companion gazed up at the homely outline of the church, with its short square tower and shallow roof. After a moment, he simply took my hand and squeezed it. Then he turned to look back – and saw the view, that tremendous sweep of sea and sand and cliffs stretching away into the distance of Kettleness. The sun had gone down, but across the cliffs there was still a golden haze gilding the waves far below us and casting the town into smoky shadow. Down there it was almost night, while up here we were bathed in the afterglow, feeling like angels with all of heaven as our domain.

'And you say you want to leave *this*?' he asked.

I shook my head. 'Only if I must . . .'

He wanted to know whether I had ever been away before, and I found myself telling him about my first position, miles inland, and that desire I'd had to come back to the sea. Sympathetically, he patted my hand and tucked it into the crook of his arm, and we moved on, taking the cliff path through the churchyard.

'I miss the sea,' he confessed. 'When I was a child we lived on the coast near Dublin, in a house overlooking the bay. My room was at the top – I could see for miles. Never tired of watching the sky and the weather – and all those ships on their separate journeys. When I was ill and couldn't go out, I used to make up stories about them . . .'

If I'd imagined a life of ease in a grand house, it

surprised me to find that his father had been a civil servant, holding a relatively modest position at Dublin Castle. Abraham Stoker, for whom Bram was named, was now dead, but I gathered he'd been a plain man of quiet beliefs, whereas his mother Charlotte was lively and held strong opinions. Brought up in the west of Ireland, she came from a rather more colourful family in which it seemed there were as many rogues and rebels as upstanding supporters of the crown. I liked the sound of her, and was intrigued to discover later that Charlotte was also twenty years younger than her husband, and that the same gap existed between her son and me. It was the kind of precedent that seemed to lessen the difference, or at least made it acceptable.

It was clear that Bram still revered his mother. She it was who had bullied and cajoled her five sons into doing well, who had insisted on educating them regardless of cost.

'I suppose I'm a bit of a failure by comparison with my brothers,' he said wryly. 'After Trinity I had a spell at Dublin Castle myself, but it bored me to tears. I'd always fancied something a bit more colourful – a writer or an actor, something like that – but the old man got me into the civil service and I had to eat, after all ... Ma wasn't keen on my flinging it all up to come to London and work for Irving, but I dare say she thought it preferable to having a son on the stage! I don't know how she'd feel if I should abandon everything now ... But still,' he added, 'she knows the writing's important to me – she's always been rather keen on that.'

His mother's opinion was evidently important to him, and he went on to say that she was proud of the comprehensive legal guide he'd had published before leaving Dublin Castle. And so was he – it made him feel that his time at the Castle had not been wasted – but she enjoyed his short stories, too, especially the mysterious ones which had appeared some years ago in publications like the *Shamrock*. His chief regret was that he hadn't had time, since, to write anything of note.

It seemed he was hoping to put that right while he was here in Whitby, and I found that intriguing; but for the time being I was more interested in what Florence thought. 'And what about your wife?' I said.

Out of the gathering darkness there came a little bark of laughter. 'Oh, I don't think she thinks much of adventure stories and suchlike! No, so long as Florence has her friends, her busy social round, and a good allowance, she's happy.'

As we paused on the cliffs above the little crescent of Saltwick Bay, I tried to imagine their married life, and failed. 'Didn't she mind you coming away on holiday without her?'

'I think she was more relieved than anything,' he said dismissively. 'She's been telling me for ages that I should take some time off.'

I thought about that for a while, and wondered why a wife would encourage her husband to holiday without her. It seemed a most unusual arrangement. I wondered whether she loved him at all, but found my thoughts expressing themselves contrariwise. 'Do you love her?' I whispered cautiously, part-hoping my words would be lost against the sighing of the waves below.

I felt him turn towards me, felt a tightening of the tension between us; then he looked away, out to sea, where there was a faint, pale rim of light on the horizon. 'Love her? But of course I do,' he said drily, 'she's my wife, the mother of my son.'

Of course. He loved them both so much that he needed to escape from them, needed to come back to

Whitby where the sea met the sky, where even on a night like this there was a fresh breeze along the cliffs. Suddenly chilled and more than a little confused, I moved away. The cliffs here were far from safe, and it was too dark to go on. It was time to turn back, to cut inland. We walked in silence for a while, me slightly ahead, showing the way along a field path edged with swags of fading blossom.

After a moment or two he came up beside me, laughing a little. 'Damaris, don't hurry away. You're like a ghost, flitting ahead in the darkness, impossible for me to catch.' So I took a deep breath and slowed even more, while he captured my hand and then, encouraged, slipped an arm around my waist to keep me close along that narrow path. I was very conscious of his touch, its weight and firmness, so very different from Jonathan's. As we walked I could feel the movement of his thigh against my hip, slightly awkward because of the difference in height and stride, but unexpectedly exciting; by the time we reached the stile my peevishness was forgotten.

The wooden steps were high, and to climb them I had to gather up my skirts. I was quite capable, but he insisted on going first and helping me across. I paused at the top, smiling – and thus enjoyed the novel sensation of being lifted down. Strong hands at my waist, a momentary helplessness, being held against him as he set me on my feet again – these things were so new, I could have been charmed by them alone. But this was a man I liked, a man I found attractive, a man who liked me. His touch left me feeling weak and breathless.

Perhaps my smile was too wide, or my eyes, like his, were shining too bright; perhaps too, he was remembering the first time and that unexpected flare of passion. As he bent his head towards me, I raised myself on tiptoe to meet his kiss, and this time we came together hungrily. His tongue invaded my mouth with warm, shocking intimacy, and at once it felt like falling, or diving too deep beneath the waves – I no longer knew who I was or where, whether I was on my head or my heels, or even, for a moment, with whom. When we parted at last, I was afraid to let go, head spinning, ears ringing, lips burning, while he leaned against the stile, drawing me with him as he sank down on to the step. With arms around each other we paused to draw breath, rescued each other's hats from the grass beneath our feet, and then, suddenly, mutually, began to laugh. It was part delight in those sensations but mostly astonishment, I think, that we could have abandoned ourselves so thoroughly.

Ten

There were stars and a young crescent moon hanging over the abbey, making a discernible reflection in the pool before it. At night, enhanced by its clifftop position, the place had an eerie beauty, and although I often thought it bleaker by day, most visitors found the ruins romantic. Bram was no exception. As we approached he seemed entranced by the sight of the great east end, intact with its tiers of lancet windows and Gothic turrets to either side.

From the road it looked far more substantial than it really was, and since I was jealous of his attention I made an attempt to impress by telling him the place was haunted by a white lady, thought to be the Lady Hilda, a Northumbrian princess who had founded the abbey in the seventh century. 'You see, it wasn't just for men,' I informed him. 'In those days everybody lived together – men, women and children – and Lady Hilda ruled over them all. They do say she can be seen sometimes, looking out of one of the upper windows . . .'

'Do you believe in ghosts?' he asked, giving my shoulders an affectionate squeeze.

I took a moment to reply. 'Mm, well, not during the day – I'm not so sure in the dark!'

'Nor me,' he said, glancing up at the great Gothic arches. 'Can we go in?'

'I don't think so – the gate's bound to be locked by now. Anyway, there's nothing much to see,' I said, a shade desperately, since I could tell he'd made up his mind to find some means of entry. 'This is practically all there is. The rest fell down years ago.'

'But I want to go in.'

'Tomorrow –'

'It won't be the same tomorrow,' he said implacably. 'Come on now, Damaris, you live here, surely you know how to get in.' He kissed my forehead, but it was more in coercion than blessing.

He was right, I did know, and my heart quickened as I studied the best approach. The gate was high and locked, and the wall too smooth to lend itself to climbers in good leather shoes; but back along the road, by the pool which had once been the abbey's fish-pond, there was a place where it was possible to gain access to a meadow, and from there to climb a much lower post-and-rail fence into the abbey grounds.

'You know, this is private property,' I whispered. 'If we get caught, we could be prosecuted!'

'That's a fallacy, Damaris. We could only be prosecuted for criminal damage, and as we're merely looking . . .'

'But what if we get caught?'

'We won't,' he said confidently. 'Trust me.'

Oddly enough, I did, even though it was more along the lines of trusting him to get us out of trouble once we were in it. His grey linen jacket was dark enough to blend into the landscape, while my pale dress made me feel extremely vulnerable. With anxious giggles as we squeezed through the hedge, I worried about being seen by some curious farm worker or vigilant night-watchman, and Bram's lighthearted suggestion that I could pretend to be the Lady Hilda had me smothering horrified laughter. In

125

the next moment I was smothering curses too, as the hawthorn caught first my sleeve and then my finger as I struggled to be free.

'Be still now,' Bram said softly, working carefully to release the material without tearing it. 'There – I think the sleeve's all right. How about you?'

'Fine – I just stabbed myself, that's all. It's nothing, just bleeding a bit – only I don't want it to spoil my dress . . .'

'Here –' But even as he produced a handkerchief, he raised my hand to his mouth and sucked the blood away. The feel of his tongue against my index finger was another shock, astonishingly intimate, as though he was touching me in secret places, exploring and caressing like a lover. I felt myself blushing and pulled back, but he kept hold of my wrist and neatly wrapped the clean handkerchief around the offending finger. 'There,' he murmured, 'your dress saved and not a drop spilled.'

Did he know? The way he looked, I thought he must; thought he would surely kiss me again, and was disappointed when he did not. Instead he took my hand and helped me over the next fence before striding purposefully across the open stretch of grass before the abbey. Admiring his nerve but fearful of it, I clung to his side for safety. He gazed up at those towering walls, stark against the starlit sky, entered the roofless choir and paced its length like an archbishop; he ran his hands around vast sandstone piers, then pulled me with him to investigate the darker arcades of the north aisle and transept. The southern side of the abbey church was completely open – cloisters, aisles and towers were gone, ruined by wind and weather, then stolen piecemeal over the centuries for building work elsewhere.

Remains of more recent falls were still in evidence here and there, blurred by the silhouettes of shrubs and stunted trees; in sheltered corners, clumps of scented pinks had found a home. Following their elusive fragrance down the nave, I stood beneath the carved arch of the old west doorway, and found tiny flowers nodding in profusion all around. Below lay the parish church and below that, unseen from here, the harbour. Through a faint haze I could see the glow of lights over on the west cliff, the outline of the Crescent where Bram was staying and, nearby, the Cragg.

He came up behind me, breathing deeply, to lay an unexpectedly gentle hand on my shoulder. As his arms enfolded me, I sighed and leaned against him, and we stood there for some time, looking out across the town. I found I liked that sense of strength and protection, the feeling that he cared; it was almost fatherly, and I'd missed that. Having it now made me want to hold on at any price. And I liked his smell, a reassuring blend of soap and cigars and maleness, which after a while made me turn to bury my face against his shirt front and rub my cheek against his beard.

All at once I was shivery with anticipation, and so was he. His masculinity excited me, the firmness of his lips, the rough texture of his beard against my skin, the strong fingers holding and exploring my body with wonderful unfamiliarity. His touch could not have been less like a woman's, and that sharpened my desire even more. I even encouraged him with caresses of my own, sighing with pleasure as he unfastened my bodice, and making no objection when he raised me a little to sit on a smooth stone ledge. Above the knee my thighs were bare, and on pushing back my petticoats he seemed astonished to discover no further impediments. I gasped at his touch, even parted my legs obligingly, so he must have thought me well experienced in such adventures. But if he was suddenly hasty, I was lamentably ignorant, so it was disconcerting then to discover awkwardness where I'd expected an easy end to my virginity.

I was evidently possessed of a maidenhead that did not intend to give way at the first attempt. Clinging to his shoulders, I gritted my teeth. The pain and difficulty were more than I'd bargained for; I cried out sharply and with a smothered exclamation he held me tight, breathing hard against my neck. As we kissed I felt his eagerness and rejoiced in it, surprised by a rapidly mounting pleasure that went far beyond anything I'd experienced before. But at the last moment, just as I was learning the rhythm, he moaned and shuddered and quickly withdrew. The act was over, the union broken. I couldn't help myself; I clung to him and burst into tears.

Gasping, sweating, swallowing hard, he held me close, then turned and drew me across his lap, holding me like a child. He patted my shoulder and kissed my wet cheek, thankfully saying nothing until I was calmer. But once he'd recovered himself I think he hardly knew what to make of me. The apparently innocent girl had turned into a woman of some experience, offering eager and practised encouragement; then, unexpectedly, she'd revealed herself as a virgin, complete with blood and pain and tears. The handkerchief that had staunched my torn finger was used again to wipe the streaks from my thighs. At his exclamations of dismay I wanted to say I'd suffered far worse, but it was seductive, being fussed over, so I hid my face instead.

'If I'd known . . .' he declared, then shook his head in bemusement. 'Why didn't you tell me?'

For answer I reached up and pressed my cheek

passionately to his. 'I wanted you to love me,' I whispered, and the truth of it astonished me. I had no regrets, and no sense of betrayal, only a sense of having made a decision, and taken something for myself. Nevertheless, there was a lump in my throat as I added: 'I wanted you to be the first.'

Something between a sigh and a groan escaped him as he hugged me tight. 'Oh, Damaris, my dear – I don't deserve gifts like that . . .'

Desire had been enhanced by more than one forbidden thrill as we explored the ruins together, but at the height of passion I'd forgotten where we were. Now I felt a superstitious dread, as though God and the Lady Hilda might strike us down for desecration of holy ground. And it seemed Bram was equally anxious to leave, even though he assured me that such ruins were no longer part of the Church, and hadn't been for several hundred years.

When I returned to the Cragg it was well after midnight and the house was quiet. I crept up the stairs in stockinged feet, dreading the appearance of Bella, who would have sensed the change in me immediately and demanded to know every detail of my night out. What's more, she would have cast contempt on it, and I couldn't have borne that. I felt adult at last, and immensely superior, as though I'd been let into an enormous secret, vouchsafed to only a few.

I thought I wouldn't sleep, but I did, like a babe, and woke feeling cheerful and gloriously alive. I did my work at the studio, picked up Jack's note, and returned to the Cragg to wash and change and eat a breakfast of fried bread and bacon. Only a sliver of bacon, mind, and that done to a crisp, which occasioned a whining note of apology from Cousin Martha that there were no eggs or kippers to go with it. But it was nothing new and I cared not a jot. For once, food was not important.

Minutes later I was hurrying to meet my lover. He was waiting for me in the gardens on the west cliff, clear grey eyes sparkling as they lit upon me, hands crushing my fingers for a long moment as we met. I felt breathless with joy.

'Did you sleep well?'

'Oh, *yes* . . .'

'Me too.' His smile broadened into a conspiratorial grin, and he turned to indicate a neatly wrapped parcel on the seat behind him. 'I happened to mention that I was going out walking for the day, so the lady at the hotel insisted on making up some sandwiches for me. Enough to sink the fleet! I thought we could share them, and maybe buy a bottle of ginger beer somewhere along the way?'

Touched by his enthusiasm, I nodded eagerly. 'Of course – where do you want to start?' I showed him Jack's note, which named half a dozen cottages, most of them a little way out of town, and explained the relative locations.

'The sea,' he said longingly. 'If just one of them has a view of the sea, then that's the one I want.'

'In that case,' I said, 'we'll start at Dunsley and work back.'

It was about three miles, a pleasant walk along the beach towards Sandsend, then under the new railway and inland via a steep cart-track to the group of farms and cottages overlooking the densely wooded Mulgrave estate which stretched deep inland along a narrow valley. When we found the cottage, it turned out to be one of a row of three and had no view to speak of, so we shook our heads and moved on. With Mulgrave Castle behind us we kept roughly parallel to the cliffs until we came to Newholm, which was a little more substantial and had the advantage of being a mile closer to Whitby. Although not quite as high as Dunsley, there were some excellent views, and I found myself hoping that Bram would find what he wanted here. But we had such difficulty finding the cottage, being directed down every road but the right one, we nearly gave up, thinking Jack Louvain must have made some mistake. Then we found it, some distance from the village, a low, solitary little place built into the hillside, with limewashed walls and a pantiled roof, and, at the bottom of the garden, a leaning, wind-blown hedge.

My eyes took in the sheltered hollow with its view of the sea beyond. It certainly looked pleasing; I hoped the interior was as good. 'Well,' I said, 'this might do.'

'It might indeed,' he agreed softly. 'I wonder who has the key?'

We made enquiries at the farm we'd passed earlier, while I kept my interest discreet as the farmer's wife came down to open up for us. There were only two rooms, stone-flagged, with a scullery attached and a privy outside. The place had been decently furnished with a high brass bed, chest of drawers and wash-stand in the far room, while in the other stood a scrubbed kitchen table with benches and a high-backed oak settle. Folding screens pushed back to disclose a narrow, old-fashioned box-bed set into an alcove by the chimney, and a side table, which looked as though it might do duty as a desk, stood under the window. There was a pair of wheel-back chairs beside the range, and a row of utensils hanging from the high mantelpiece. Everything was neat and clean, if smelling noticeably of damp.

The place had been empty all winter, the woman said; there was less work to be had on the land these days, people were leaving, setting up in town, working in manufactories and shipyards, and there was nothing to be done with these old properties but let them out to visitors. She sniffed disapprovingly – obviously not the owner – while Bram raised an eyebrow and suddenly became very much the London gentleman instead of the easygoing character he'd been only minutes ago.

He turned to me. 'Hm, well, I'm not so sure after all, my dear. Did you say your uncle had a property to let at Robin Hood's Bay?'

'He has several,' I said drily, fixing my eyes on the distant horizon; 'all with fine sea views.'

'Oh, this is a good cottage here, sir,' the woman interjected, 'very sheltered from the worst weather, as you'd know if you were here in the wintertime. I can have milk delivered for you every day – and fresh bread. Meals too, sir, if you're on your own.'

He pulled at his beard and seemed to be considering, while I wanted to laugh for I knew his mind was made up. Eventually, he said: 'That depends – I'm a writer, so I'd prefer not to be disturbed.'

'Whatever you say, sir – it's entirely up to you. The service is there if you want it.'

'Good. Well, I rather think I'll take the place. I must confess, it's the view that's decided me.' He turned from the window and smiled. 'So how do we settle the arrangements?'

She directed him to the agency in town, and while Bram gave her his card and said he would take the cottage for a month, the woman – who introduced herself as Mrs Newbold – agreed to air the rooms, light a fire in the range, and have everything ready for him to move in by noon the next day. There was something ordained about it, I thought, as though contracts had been signed and possession taken already. And as though something personal and more profound was about to be settled between the two of us.

When Mrs Newbold had gone we didn't hurry away but sat on a bench by the wall in order to congratulate ourselves. It seemed right to celebrate with our picnic lunch, so we opened the bottles of ginger beer and laughingly toasted each other as though with champagne. I shivered pleasurably as bubbles ran down my chin and Bram wiped them away, his touch intensifying memories of the night before. I loved his hands. To me they were beautiful, clean and well-shaped, with long fingers and rounded nails; the only noticeable blemish was a dark-stained callus on his middle finger where he held his pen, and I was fascinated even by that. I remember watching him unwrap the parcel, and wishing that he were unwrapping me.

He caught my eye and grinned as he handed me a sandwich of ham and mustard in crusty white bread; it was delicious, but I was so aware of him it was difficult to eat. I tried to study the distant horizon, but then he studied me until we both began to laugh. The food was barely half eaten when he took my hand and led me through the hollow of the garden to a spot beyond the hedge. Well hidden from any prying eyes, we fell back into long, dry grass that was more like a hayfield, scented with meadow flowers and the salty tang of the sea. It was then that he touched me, stroking my face and throat like a blind man, and running his hands – those beautiful hands – over my arms and shoulders as though needing to assure himself that I was real. It was as if the night before had been no more than a taste, a sample of what pleasures we might enjoy, should we be given time and opportunity to proceed.

Beneath the disguise of his beard and moustache, he had a full, rather sensual mouth and strong white teeth that fascinated me. I bent to kiss him and the light teasing was abandoned for a grip which brought me down on top of him, for a playful exchange of lovebites and kisses which soon demanded satisfaction. We were hampered by layers of clothing, yet nothing was removed; consumed by inner fires, we managed to perform the most intimate of acts out there on that grassy slope, too satisfied afterwards to feel any kind of shame. Fortunately that neglected spot was too removed to be seen from the beach or railway, and the chance of human eyes peering down on us in shocked surprise was negligible; at least, that's what we told each other afterwards. And afterwards, when he was calm and relaxed and almost asleep, he sighed deeply and told me with a smile in his voice that it was the best picnic he'd ever had.

Nothing was said that day about my moving into the cottage, yet I had an instinct about it, strong enough to prompt me to sort out my belongings when I returned to the Cragg. The books, I think, were what brought Jonathan to the forefront of my mind again. Ever since my argument with Bella I'd been pushing him away, refusing to entertain the possibility that I was betraying anything. After all, what was there to betray? Attraction, liking, minutes of tongue-tied conversation on largely neutral subjects – shipping, trade, weather, books, the finer points of seamanship and navigation – and a kiss, of course, which I knew full well was rather more than casual.

But I didn't want it to be important. I didn't want Jonathan to be important, I'd never wanted that. I didn't want him, no matter how good-looking he was. He was nineteen, or perhaps twenty, with years to serve before he could call himself Master, before he could afford to marry and settle down. Always provided he wanted to marry me. Always provided he survived and his mother didn't make his life a misery for even thinking of marrying someone like me. Well, I'd settled the matter now, once and for all. He wouldn't want to marry another man's mistress, which saved me from torturing myself on the subject.

All the same, beneath my sense of satisfaction, I had a bad conscience.

Early next morning I washed a few things, put them out in the yard to dry, then went upstairs to pack all but immediate necessities. Bella came up to my room in the midst of it and knew at once what I was doing.

'I see you've made up your mind, then.' At my cursory nod, she said, 'So, did you get a job, or are you moving in with him?'

I took a deep breath. 'Neither, yet. But I will be leaving in the next day or two – I don't think I can stay here any longer, Bella, do you?'

'I suppose not,' she said with a sigh of deep resignation. 'All I can say is, I hope it's worth it. I hope he treats you like you deserve, and not like –' She broke off, compressing her full lips into a thin line of disaproval. 'Well, you know what I think of men . . .'

When I looked up a moment later, she'd gone. So few words, yet they had the ring of finality. All at once I was seized by great pangs of guilt, and for a moment I wanted to hurry downstairs, put my arms around Bella and say sorry, it doesn't have to be like this, we could still be friends no matter what. But as I turned towards the door it came to me that whatever had been between us before was over. And even if I was sorry, I knew I couldn't wait to get away. So

I didn't go after her, didn't say the comforting words I should perhaps have said; and, from that moment on, made sure I kept out of her way.

Eleven

Two days later, when Bram had moved in, unpacked, and filled the little cottage with his presence, he asked me to stay with him. I felt a great surge of happiness and relief, but tried, even as I agreed, to make it clear that while I liked him tremendously, I didn't imagine myself in love, and expected nothing from him beyond his respect. Nevertheless, I was determined to have that. I treasured the idea of a month at the cottage as a holiday away from normal, everyday life – as I'm sure he did – while making clear from the start that my work at the studio had to come first. Not only was it necessary for me financially, it was part of my independence and self-respect. As was my decision to cook and care for him in return for my bed and board. Once those terms were understood, I went back to the Cragg for my box.

Envisaging difficulties, I said I preferred to go alone, and with Lizzie's help moved my things only as far as the studio. Jack Louvain said nothing when I arrived, but his disapproval was obvious. Very briefly, and studying my new gloves as I told him, I explained that I'd accepted a job as temporary housekeeper to Mr Stoker while he was on holiday, and needed to leave my box at the studio for a little while until it could be picked up. There was a long

137

and rather uncomfortable silence before Jack said in a very controlled voice that he hoped I knew what I was doing, and hadn't leapt out of the frying pan into the fire. When I dared to look up he was frowning at his list of appointments.

'But I couldn't stay with the Firths any longer . . .'

'I know that,' he said curtly. 'I just don't want you to let me down at a time when I need you most. And you'd better get that box moved as soon as you can – it's in the way.'

Feeling that I had fallen several notches in his estimation, I promised fervently not to let him down. Initially, I tried to keep to the hours I'd been used to, which were mostly in the early morning, but I saw quickly that life with Bram was not going to permit that. His habits had been formed by the theatre, by years of late suppers and convivial discussions which often went on into the early hours. As a consequence, he was wide awake at midnight while I was nodding, and fast asleep at 6 a.m., when I was generally on my way to work. And there was too the fact that he enjoyed being out at night, while the rest of the world was abed. So I spoke to Jack Louvain, explaining that it would be better for me to work after the studio closed in the evening, and after that the days began to fall into a pattern which suited everyone.

The weather, which had been dry and warm, turned hot by the end of that first week in June, bringing with it a crushing stillness barely stirred by our proximity to the sea. Looking out each morning, we saw a hazy bank of fog hovering mysteriously just a mile or so offshore. It lurked out there for days on end, waiting to curl in during the hottest part of the day on currents of air that were cold and clammy as a dead man's hand.

I'd been in town, shopping, the day the first

outriders swept in low across the still surface of the sea, white wraiths snaking up the east cliff to engulf the fortifications of church and abbey. It happened every year, sometimes day after day for a week; but that sudden siege was alarming enough to catch the breath, to make even townsfolk stand and gape in the middle of a busy morning, as harbour, bridge and river were claimed within minutes. Bram, waiting for me on the pier, gazed across the water in astonishment, transfixed as a great python of mist swirled at his feet.

We were perhaps fifty yards apart. As the mist enveloped him I saw him turn, and, afraid we might lose each other, I hurried to his side through the blanket of fog, grasping his arm as he turned eagerly to me. 'Did you see it?' he demanded. 'Did you see the mist?'

'Sea-fret,' I corrected him, 'it's called a sea-fret . . .'

But for the moment he was less interested in local etymology than in the phenomenon he'd just witnessed. 'Never,' he swore, 'have I seen anything like that. Marvellous, quite marvellous – I must get back, write it down . . .'

I grinned then, amused by his enthusiasm, glad to be free of that momentary alarm. We made our way through the fog and down to the beach, with the intention of walking back along the sands towards Newholm. To our left the cliffs had resisted that stealthy invasion, and it was less dense as we left the town and harbour behind. Somewhere above us the sun was shining, turning the mist to a milky, translucent shroud. Once past the Saloon we were isolated, veiled from public view, able to skip and hop – turn somersaults if we wanted! – along the firm, damp sands at the edge of the sea. I took off my shoes and ran for sheer joy, teasing Bram until he removed collar and tie, boots and socks, and dropped them in my shopping basket as he caught up with me. Laughing, linking hands, kissing, we frolicked like children while foam came surging round our ankles, wave upon gentle wave, where, incredibly, it seemed, the *Mary and Agnes* had been driven ashore by powerful seas.

All the signs were gone now; but we guessed the spot, reflecting on the day that had brought us together. Terns and oystercatchers flapped away as we slowed to a stroll, picking up shells and bits of jet, progressing through a private Eden of dew-drenched, gossamer warmth. Our shared awareness was intense; we stopped and kissed, wanting to make love there and then while every sense was at its peak, but we were neither brave enough nor mad enough then for that. In the end need drove us away from the beach, up the steep and narrow track that led back towards Newholm and the cottage.

We passed beneath the ghostly iron girders of the railway bridge, climbed further, and suddenly had the odd experience of walking out of the mist as one might walk through a doorway. Behind us, in hot, dazzling sunlight, stood the edge of the cliff, while beyond it floated a mass of fluffy white cloud, hiding sand and sea, everything bar the clifftops of Kettle-ness on the one hand, and the skeletal ruins of the abbey on the other.

Held by the magic, we stood and gazed at that shifting featherbed of cloud, while bees hummed amongst the gorse and butterflies fluttered all around. I was suddenly aware of the heat of the sun, my thin cotton dress clinging damply to my skin. I looked at Bram and his beard was jewelled with minute drops, a lock of hair hanging over his right eye. Touching lightly, we continued on our way. A short while later we were entering the cottage, peeling off damp clothes between hungry kisses, not even bothering to close the door before falling on to the bed and into each other's arms.

Afterwards, when I was feeling satisfied and sleepy and smiling like a cat at the very idea of being in bed at that time of day, he lit a cigarette, releasing spirals of blue smoke into a golden beam of sunlight. As I sniffed pleasurably at the scent of tobacco, he asked whether I minded him smoking. I didn't mind at all, and said so; but then there came a stab of pain as he said somewhat smugly: 'Florence hates it – I couldn't do this at home. In fact, if I were at home, I wouldn't be doing *any* of these things – I wouldn't be smoking, I wouldn't be in bed, and I certainly wouldn't have been making love ...'

'With me, you mean,' I added with forced lightness, ignoring the oblique compliment as well as the reference to his wife.

'No,' he corrected, 'I mean I wouldn't have been making love.'

'But of course you wouldn't,' I answered sharply, digging him in the ribs before making a rapid exit. 'At this hour of the day you'd have been at the theatre, *working* ...'

He laughed at that and said I was impudent – and maybe I was, but I wanted him to see me, Damaris Sterne, not some convenient and malleable substitute for Florence. If I punctured his ideas from time to time, and tried to deflect those comparisons with his wife, then it did him good, I think. It made for what I considered to be more honest dealings between us.

Quite what he made of my attitude, I'm not sure. I know what Bella would have said, but I didn't feel like a whore, and didn't imagine Bram saw me in that light. Perhaps he regarded such freedoms as part of local culture and custom, or thought himself singularly lucky in meeting someone like me, a girl who didn't mind sharing herself completely with a stranger, a married man to boot. Perhaps he thought I was mad. Most likely, with all the problems he'd left behind, he was simply reluctant to question the situation too deeply. But I knew there were problems back in London, even though they were rarely mentioned.

As for me, I was happy to accept things as they were, questioning nothing for the moment. In a way I suppose Bram and I were both escaping from intolerable situations, and like all escapees we were drunk on freedom, intoxicated by all the silly things we had in common, by a physical and emotional closeness that neither of us had experienced before. Certainly, during those first few days I discovered great pleasure in living for the moment, and was determined to relegate guilt, like my upright relatives, to the far corners of my mind.

My existence seemed to be touched by a kind of magic, and I became as enchanted with the life we were living as I was with Bram. It was like a game to me, exciting, full of treats and thrills and laughter. Time had no meaning, and I felt like a child playing truant from school, one being aided and abetted by a fond and over-indulgent parent. When I said this to him, he only laughed and provided me with more, a ride on the train down to Scarborough, afternoon tea at a pretty tea-shop by the castle, a visit to the revue at the theatre.

He looked after me very well indeed. It seemed there was never any shortage of money, and he liked to buy presents. In Scarborough he happily ordered what almost amounted to a new wardrobe for me, serviceable items as well as pretty dresses. And we wanted them quickly, he said; by the end of the week, if they pleased, and here was another five pounds to hurry things through. Impressed and delighted, I tried not to gape.

But when my pretty things were delivered, I couldn't see them on, except in bits, because we had only a small looking-glass. So then he booked a room at the Royal Hotel on the west cliff, where we went in a pony trap, complete with luggage, and all for the pleasure of trying on my new things before a tall pier glass. Several blouses, a good skirt and jacket, two sprigged cotton dresses with frills caught up at the back, as well as a more formal gown in pale green silk. That gown was so beautiful I could barely speak – the most luxurious thing I'd ever possessed. Even the underclothes were pretty, trimmed with more lace and bows than I'd ever seen.

Taking off his coat and shoes, Bram stretched out on the bed to watch me. I was used to wearing a corset, but refused the drawers on the grounds that I'd never known any woman who wore them, other than a doctor's wife I'd worked for, and I judged her habits none too clean. I said I was happier without and, from his quirky smile, I gathered Bram was pleased for me to stay that way. But in spite of my reluctance he was keen for me to try out some of the rouge and eyeshadow and face-powder we'd bought.

His experience in the theatre had made him skilful with make-up and he was able to show me how to apply it. 'There, you see ...' He knelt before me while I tried not to giggle and blink, gently applying colour to my eyelids, lips and cheeks. 'You don't need much,' he said softly, 'you're not going on stage ... Just a little to enhance your natural beauty ... And then, if you pin your hair like *this*, to one side ...'

I wasn't prepared to believe it, but he was right. The hairstyle was new, sophisticated; the rouge accentuated the shape of my mouth, making it fuller, somehow, and prettier, while the blue-green shadow brought out the colour of my eyes. With a dusting of powder to disguise my freckled cheeks, and a little lamp-black applied to my lashes, I barely recognised myself; it seemed strange that a man should have effected that transformation, so quickly and so easily. As I gazed wide-eyed at his reflection behind mine in the glass, he smiled in confirmation, and for the first time I was willing to believe that when Bram called me beautiful, he meant it.

The stark formality of evening dress suited him, complementing his fine physique and providing a foil for the whispering pale green silk of my gown. As he said, we were well matched, and what with his red beard and my red hair, we made a fine-looking couple. Going down for dinner, I felt as though we'd been transported to another world, Bram's world, where all was beauty and illusion and nothing was quite what it seemed. I was no longer Damaris Sterne, sometime fishergirl and domestic servant; I felt like a leading lady in my shimmering green silk, playing a part and loving it, delighted to be having our evening meal in the grand dining room below. It was a glimpse of Whitby I'd never experienced before, a world of wealth and ease and pleasure, of grand rooms with chandeliers, orchestras playing, elegant ladies, gentlemen in evening dress, a world of wine and compliments and food dramatically presented. It was dazzling, and even though I tried hard to seem composed I could not entirely suppress my sense of awe and delight. Bram smiled so much it made his eyes shine, and every time I looked at him he was gazing at me with pride and affection, which for some reason brought a lump to my throat and made it difficult to speak.

Wanting to hold the moment, I clung to his hand

instead, and it was as though he were saying the moment was fine, it could last, it could grow, it wasn't all illusion and pretence. But there was no escaping the fact that our liaison was illicit, and the need for secrecy gave everything an added edge. Whenever we were in Whitby, one of Bram's chief concerns was that of being recognised by some old acquaintance or patron of the Lyceum. There were times when I felt he sailed close to the wind on purpose, for the sake of enjoying the risk, although for discretion's sake on this occasion he'd registered under a pseudonym. However, that was only because the *Whitby Gazette* published weekly lists of visitors to the town, and he was reluctant to advertise his presence in such a way. Fortunately, his friends the du Mauriers, who were regular visitors in the summer, rarely took up residence before July, when everyone came with children and servants for a month by the sea.

After luncheon the following day, we took a stroll down to the Saloon, built, Bram remarked with a sly smile, like some miniature German *schloss* cut into the rock of the west cliff. Later we took tea while listening to a band playing Viennese music. The excursion was largely for my benefit, since I wanted an excuse to wear one of my pretty cotton dresses and flourish a parasol like all the fine ladies; but in truth the afternoon was not a success. Bram seemed happy enough behind a newspaper, occasionally peering at the world from beneath the brim of his panama, but if I'd felt safely cocooned inside the hotel, out there on the esplanade I felt vulnerable. Not just to any passing relations, but at any moment, it seemed, Isa Firth or one of my rivals from the fish market might look down from the clifftop and recognise me by my hair. All in all I was more relieved than sorry when we left.

I think Bram was as glad as I was to return home and embrace the security of our little cottage. He could relax there and be himself, collarless, with sleeves rolled up, chewing on a cigar or the end of a pen, asking questions of me while I cooked or cleaned or ironed. After we'd eaten, we'd relax for a while, and generally, if he'd been writing, he would join me in the garden and we'd drink lemonade or ginger beer, or feed each other the tiny red fruits of strawberries I'd discovered on the sunny side of the wall.

Our days were much the same; it was a sunlit, timeless world, where nothing seemed to matter. I fell into a habit of retiring outdoors in the afternoon, to lie in the shade with a book or yesterday's newspaper to hand. It was such luxury to be able to read when and if I wanted, that I no longer felt obliged to cram in words like a starving man. Sometimes, drugged by an afternoon's love-making, I would gaze idly out to sea while Bram dozed; I could please myself, and that knowledge was part of my enjoyment. I loved the garden, loved its wild, neglected air, the overgrown hedge and collapsed drystone wall, with its clumps of thyme and sea-pinks and valerian. I loved the scents and colours and sounds, the buzz of insects and the distant murmur of the sea, but it seemed no more permanent than a hoard of fairy-tale treasure. I knew I must appreciate it, since it might well disappear with the next shower of rain.

Perhaps that awareness was true for Bram as well. He too loved the cottage, but he said I was the one who made him happy, the only one who could make him feel that life held some hope. It seemed a strange thing to say, but he wouldn't explain. As time passed, however, I began to realise how erratic his moods could be, veering between optimism and uncertainty, benevolent good humour and a kind of absent-minded melancholy I found difficult to comprehend.

Loving him seemed to help; in fact sometimes it was the only way I could bring him back from those bleak abstractions. I would hold him and caress him like a child until the mood broke, until he turned to me like a lover, stripping off my clothes and taking me to bed. In physical pleasure the black moods would be banished and forgotten.

The intensity of our encounters astonished me, as did the craving for more. I might have preferred to dismiss my experience with Bella as being of no account, but whether I knew it then or not, loving Bella had helped to open my mind and taught my body to respond; and in the sensual world Bram and I were creating for ourselves, right or wrong seemed to have no existence.

Certain practical considerations entered in, of course, and, besotted though we were, we tried not to invite trouble. We were mostly discreet in our dealings with the outside world, and careful when we made love. I employed methods Bella had sworn by, such as standing up, washing carefully, using a vinegar sponge. I believed in them at the time because they had obviously worked for her, and although Bram was less convinced, he did his utmost to protect me. In sane moments I even appreciated his care, although there were times at the moment of climax when, contrarily, I longed for him to let go, to give me his heart and soul in the moment I gave him mine. In this respect, however, he'd been well tutored by his wife. Florence had borne their only child within the first year of marriage, had had a difficult time with the birth and afterwards, and had ultimately vowed never to go through that appalling experience again. I gathered that her chief method of prevention was to close her bedroom door, or, when her husband cajoled and pleaded, to lie as cold and unresponsive as a dead thing, so that his requests became less pressing and far less frequent. And yet he loved her, even then I knew it. It hurt me, because I was young and I wanted him to love me. I wanted to be the only one. I didn't understand then about love and passion and the various accommodations of marriage.

For he was a passionate man, deeply so beneath that urbane and practical exterior, with a nature often as generous as his features had always suggested. But it grieved me to discover that he disliked his own looks, that he thought himself ugly, with a jaw and brow too heavy and a mouth too full for masculine beauty. It was nonsense, of course. Classical ideals were all very well, I said, but who wanted to kiss a cold bronze statue, or make love to a description in a book? I certainly did not. Pushing aside my own private ideals, I told him I preferred a man of flesh and blood with kind hands and a generous smile, to any tight-lipped portrait of perfection.

But he did not agree with me. So what was handsome? I asked, and for answer he described the kind of looks his friend Irving possessed, slender, fine-boned, aristocratic. At that I had to restrain a rude remark. Henry Irving was no more aristocratic than I was, and I found that I was beginning to dislike him almost as much as I disliked the prissy Florence. I wondered whether either of them knew Bram as well as I did, or cared for him a quarter as much.

Twelve

Although seasonable, the long hot days were enervating and seemingly endless. The sun rose before four and shone through a dazzling haze of heat until well after eight in the evening, when the moon appeared to transform the golden dusk into a silvery twilight. Even when the weather was misty the nights were illumined by a pale, mysterious bloom. It was like walking through a dream. Everyday places were eerily unreal, recognisable but different, heightened and distorted by that strange diffusion of light.

Round about ten o'clock, after several hours at his makeshift desk, Bram was always keen to be out, to walk and talk and explore, to loiter along the staiths watching the boats and the tides, the moon rising over the cliffs. Sometimes he came early to the studio and talked to Jack if he happened to be in, but most often he would arrange to meet me in the churchyard, where a public bench caught the last of the long summer twilight. From there, as the moon grew larger and brighter with each succeeding night, we explored Whitby together.

If at first I found it strange, I soon came to enjoy that nocturnal existence; it was so much pleasanter after the overpowering heat of the day. Before midnight there were generally plenty of visitors about, enjoying the cooler air, and the popular walks between Whitby and the outlying villages were often thronged with groups of well-dressed young people, their eager and excited voices carrying far on the still night air. Moonlight walks seemed to be quite the fashion, and – judging by the excess of squealing laughter – so was playing the fool.

'What on earth's the matter with them?' I asked of Bram, as we observed one such group passing over the bridge at Ruswarp, their going accompanied by anguished howls and moans, and shrieks that would have put a harpy to shame. 'The noise they're making, you'd think Old Goosey was after them.'

'I imagine they're telling ghost stories,' he said with a grin, 'frightening each other silly and enjoying every minute of it. Anyway, who's Old Goosey? Ghost or goblin? Man or gander?'

'He was a man,' I explained, 'whose ghost walks as a goose . . .' In the midst of Bram's sudden merriment I saw the joke for myself, but eventually, when pressed, I managed to tell the tale of Old Goosey, a local man who'd earned his nickname over a wager, and then lost his life because of it.

'Many years ago, when times were hard, he bet a wealthy man that he could eat an entire goose in one sitting. The test took place at one of the local inns, before a great crowd of people, and bets were running high. He lost the first time, having managed all but the rump; but won the next round by starting at that end and finishing the rest. So he was Goosey ever after, and a popular man, until he came to grief over a similar wager a few months later. He won that time, but as he left the inn somewhat worse for wear, he was struck down on the way home, his money stolen, and his body thrown into the Esk.

'His assailant was never brought to justice – so you

see, that's why his ghost walks along the riverside, searching for the man who killed him . . .'

'But surely not as a goose,' Bram protested, 'that's too ridiculous!'

'No, it isn't – that was his punishment, don't you see? Even though he was murdered, he invited it, in a way. It came about because of his greed and gluttony, and for that he was condemned to take on the form of a goose –'

'Poetic justice?'

'Yes, I think so. I believe that, don't you?'

'I don't know . . .'

Bram said we were getting into the realms of metaphysics, but that was a word beyond me then. I knew I believed in the existence of good and evil, and just occasionally the idea of divine retribution could frighten me rigid, although the lane which ran along the gentle watermeadows beside the Esk was hardly the place to be afraid. There were cows in broad pastures, behind hedges full of dog rose and honeysuckle; great trees dipped their branches in a river moving with summer slowness down to the dam at Ruswarp, where moonlight revealed a string of rowing boats tied up beneath the trees. During the day the village was welcoming, and the railway station by the bridge made it a place that was popular with picnickers, from families with children and elderly aunts to serious walkers who began and ended their rambles along that gentle stretch of water.

On the far bank, however, downriver from the weir, where the land rose steeply above the Esk, lay the densely wooded ravine of Cock Mill Woods, which had a very different reputation. Amongst summer visitors who knew nothing of its history it was regarded as a place of great beauty, where a waterfall tumbled some forty feet over huge rocks before rushing away to join the main stream further down. It was one thing to admire nature on a summer's day, however, and quite another at night. I was interested to note that the noisy group which had crossed the Ruswarp bridge earlier kept to the road and passed quickly through the ravine towards Whitby with barely a pause for shrieks and shivers. Not that I blamed them; it was very dark just there and I was equally keen to keep moving.

Bram sensed my fear and wanted to know the cause of it. He would not be put off, and urged me to tell the story there and then, threatening to go no further until I did. So we stopped on the bridge over the beck, where patches of dappled moonlight revealed rocks and rushing water below. On either side a mass of trees stood tall and still and black, an occasional whispering of leaves or undergrowth prickling my spine with apprehension and alarm.

In the woods somewhere above us lay the ancient mill with its great waterwheel, and the old cockpit which gave the place its name. I thought it likely that both had been there since the days when the abbey owned everything along Whitby strand, but it was just far enough away and sufficiently hidden to be ignored by authority. In the old days, the mill was known as a place of ill-repute, the haunt of smugglers and dice-players and loose women, a place where vast amounts of money changed hands, where salt and silks and fine wines were hidden in secret caves, and where men fought to the death over insults and ill-judged wagers. Then, at the time of the wars with France, the ravine became a hideout for seamen escaping the press-gang. Few of His Majesty's bully-boys would risk body and soul in a place like that.

If we'd been in possession of a lantern, I'm sure Bram would have insisted on taking the steep way through the woods, in spite of those tales of death and disaster and of people disappearing, never to be seen again. With all the connotations of gambling and cruelty and blood lust, the place had an evil reputation, and local tales that the Gentleman in Black attended the dice games and cock fights were commonplace. It was said that he was wont to stand amongst the crowd, more avid than the rest, stamping his feet, urging and inciting the worst excesses; and, if anyone happened to be trodden on or grasped by him, the marks remained, deep in the flesh, like the brands of a cloven hoof.

Bram shivered at that, then laughed softly, as though half ashamed of such foolishness. He pulled me closer and tried to persuade me into the woods, but at night, just there, the idea of hell opening up from some hidden crevice seemed all too real. I wanted to leave, and for once my insistence was stronger than his desire. I couldn't wait to climb the bank and be free of that sense of oppression.

If Bram encouraged me to relate local folk-tales, he also liked to scare me with the kind of stories he shared with his London friends. I often envisaged them backstage at the Lyceum, after everyone else had gone home – the great theatre, vast and empty, echoing with ghostly voices, while Bram, with Irving and their novelist friend, Hall Caine, relaxed with brandy and cigars after a comfortable supper in the old Beefsteak Room. It was a room backstage, once the venue for a theatrical dining club, that Bram had discovered and opened up during Irving's first season there; as he described it, the oak panelling and beamed ceiling gave the place the look of a medieval hall, complete with suits of armour, a huge open fireplace, and old portraits of famous actors looking down from the walls. Sometimes, he said, it was almost possible to feel their presence late at night, when the place was quiet; and to imagine the ghosts of other great performers still lingering on the stage . . .

The three men vied with each other in collecting and exchanging strange stories and superstitions, weird events to be related after midnight when the fires burned low and other guests had gone in search of cabs to see them home. Although the tales I could tell seemed tame by comparison, Bram appeared to savour them, often asking me to repeat a story next day so he could be sure of getting it right.

As a rule we were out most nights, becoming more than a little moonstruck, I think, as we walked and talked and found secluded places to picnic on whatever food I'd brought. It was surprising to me how quickly the spontaneity of those walks developed into ritual. Bram liked to tramp across the moors, but even if we'd been out in the afternoon I soon discovered that he had to walk at night, that he could not stay in, and if he did, he rarely slept. He survived on cat-naps, almost as though he were afraid of missing something or wasting precious time. Restless, almost voracious at times, he seemed as hungry for love as he was for knowledge, taking chances and tempting fate in ways that often left me breathless.

We toured Whitby with a thoroughness that would have put most visitors to shame, while I plumbed the depths of memory for stories to keep him entertained. I told him of wafts and hobs, witches and wisemen, empty houses and haunted yards. The Old Hall on Bagdale boasted the fearful presence of a headless Cavalier, while another old house nearby regularly showed lights moving in the empty upper storeys; I'd heard that a grey lady walked the cobbled steps of Union Road, and down a yard between Baxtergate and New Quay moved a ghostly whaling captain, the air around him cold as the Greenland seas.

Down by the harbour, we watched brigs and barquentines being unloaded in the long summer dusk, and spoke of seagoing mysteries, of deserted ships come upon far out at sea, with the wheel lashed, or dinner set in the cabin and not a soul on board. I told him of the Dutch sea-captain my brother knew, who swore he'd conversed with the ship's mate in the wheelhouse one night, only to find that the man had been killed in a brawl ashore several hours previously. The story made me shiver even in the telling.

Over the bridge, in the narrow curve of Low Lane where the explorer James Cook had spent the winters of his youth, ancient alehouses and taverns with seedy reputations slouched before sober, straight-faced Georgian buildings. There, overlooking the harbour, where the penny-hedge was erected every year in penance for a medieval murder, it seemed the past was all around us, history and legend blending into one. There, I found it easy to imagine a cluster of shadows, darker than the rest, taking on shape and evil intent; flickering pinpoints of fire, which might have been no more than ill-tended gaslights, could so easily have been the eyes of the barghest, the spectral hound with eyes like burning coals which was said to haunt these footpaths. I could remember times, especially on winter's nights, when Bella and I had frightened ourselves silly, skittering home like rabbits because we thought we'd heard something following us, or seen great eyes staring from the darkness of one of the yards.

'But the worst thing is to *hear* it,' I whispered, peering anxiously into the depths of alleys and doorways as we passed. 'It howls and shrieks under the windows of those about to die. *He's heard the howl of the barghest*, folks say when somebody looks not long for this world.'

'Like the wail of the banshee,' Bram murmured, moving just as softly through the shadows, 'which they talk about in Ireland . . .'

As we came into Southgate, I told him about the bargheist coach, another ghostly phenomenon, which was known to career along past the abbey, through the churchyard and across the graves, plunging over the cliff and into the foaming sea below. 'It always appears after the burial of some local mariner – it comes to pluck him out of the earth, you see, in order to return him to the deep, where he truly belongs . . .'

'You mean all those grand memorials to dead seafarers are just tombstones over empty graves?' he asked, giving me a sidelong look as we crossed the road by Markways' chandlery.

'But of course,' I said earnestly, guiding him to the right, preferring to be challenged on folklore than about Jonathan and the people I'd once worked for.

We passed the warehouses and repair-yards, and from Southgate took the hearse road, the route taken by grand funerals, since the old donkey road beside the Church Stairs was too steep for decorum, and only ordinary folk went on foot to church, carrying the coffin between them up the steps. In some of the old townships, I told him, there were still torchlit processions, although the practice was declining; in Robin Hood's Bay, wine and sugar-biscuits were served beforehand, and woe betide the relatives if they forgot to invite someone, for no one would come to a funeral 'unbidden', and the grudge would be carried for life.

At mention of my old home, Bram asked why we hadn't been there, why didn't I take him? I was forced to explain that if he was afraid of being recognised by people in Whitby, I was equally keen not to be seen with him in Bay. 'People might *talk*,' I said, 'but if they don't actually see me with anyone, I can always deny it.'

'That's like sticking your head in the sand!'

'So – is it any different to what you're doing?' I asked.

It took a moment for him to answer. 'No,' he said slowly, 'I suppose not . . .'

Saltwick was not much more than a mile away, and the moon was up, so we continued in that direction. The little cove looked magical, sheltered and pretty, dark waves touched with silver as they rolled gently to the shore. It was hard to believe the place had once been a hive of industry, much less the scene of fierce battles during the time of the press-gang. Several rough paths led down to where the remains of an old jetty made it a good place for swimming during the day, but the cliffs were dangerous and honeycombed with holes from the long-dead alum works. More recently, a lively trade in smuggling was said to be conducted from there, which made another good reason for keeping away after dark. Nevertheless, having clambered up and down those cliffs innumerable times, I felt I knew them well enough, and on such a bright night did not seriously expect to run into smugglers.

The tide was on the ebb as we descended to the beach, but we found a smooth dry ledge where we could sit and eat the picnic supper I'd brought, of soft bread and a crumbly local cheese, with pickles and ham and a fresh-dressed crab. For too long I'd lived on a diet of oats and fish and poverty, and it pleased me that Bram relished good food and took such delight in my enjoyment of every meal. He liked me to feed him things, licking my fingers one

157

by one; and then he would feed me, popping choice items into my mouth like a parent with a baby bird, watching me eat and drink with avid interest, kissing my mouth and making love to me amongst the debris of a meal.

He was relaxed and sensual then, breathing in the scent of my hair and skin, caressing me with tender affection. I quickly learned his ways, and was generally happy to accommodate them. That night we'd barely finished eating when he reached for me, pushing back my skirts to caress my warm, bare legs. There was no need for him to say what he wanted; I found his eagerness contagious, and moments later we were feverishly seeking the best way of making love in that deserted but far from comfortable place. There was shingle underfoot and the sand was wet; we tried one way and then another, almost gave up from laughing so much, and then his mouth was warm again on mine, his tongue licking at lips and teeth, and suddenly we were serious and in need of satisfaction. With a moan of desire he turned me around, against the rocky ledge, and lifted my skirts from behind. I felt him probing between my thighs, and a moment later he was deep inside me, filling me completely, thrusting hard against my womb in a coupling that forced the breath from my body. It was painful, even a little alarming, since I could neither move nor protest; but it was undeniably exciting too, and I came to climax almost as he did. Only as sense returned did I become aware of the painful imprint of his teeth in the curve of my neck, and a stinging in hands and face where I'd grazed myself against the rock.

Unaware, Bram took me in his arms with fierce affection, rubbing his cheek against mine until a wincing cry brought the grazes to his notice. At once he was full of apology and regret, licking blood and grit from my cheek and palms, kissing the place where his teeth had marked my neck. 'I'm sorry,' he whispered again, but somehow it was too much, and his attempts to console were disturbing.

Not knowing what to think, I found it easier to banish unease with activity. Springing up, I began to strip off my clothes. 'Can you swim?' I challenged, laughing at his astonishment. 'Race you to the Nab!'

As he struggled to his feet I ran into the sea, striking out at once before the shock could halt me. I swam across to the Black Nab and paused to catch my breath, pushing back the hair from my face as Bram swiftly crossed the intervening distance with smooth, powerful strokes. He was an excellent swimmer and I was impressed, but equally determined not to show it. As he reached for me I laughed and eluded him, slipping back through the water to cross the little bay. But as I turned to look, the sky was already paler, the moon fading as it dipped towards the horizon. Everything was still and silent in those moments before dawn, and I knew it was time to leave, before some passing fisherman caught sight of us playing the fool, or before an early and less understanding visitor reported us for worse.

'You look like a mermaid,' Bram said, coming up beside me and shaking water out of his eyes.

'In that case, you must be Neptune!' I retorted, tweaking the red-gold hairs on his chest.

For that he pinched me, and chased me back to the shore, where we stood laughing and gasping with cold and effort. In the dawn light he looked magnificent, dangerous, less a sea god than an early Viking raider. Watching water dripping from his muscular frame suddenly I wanted him again, had to kiss him, touch him, press my body to his until his arousal matched mine. He entered me then with an extraordinary ease and coolness that excited us both, making love with slow and satisfying concentration. It seemed to go on for ever, until I locked my ankles around his waist to urge him on, and he flooded me once more in a long and shattering climax.

Afterwards, relaxed and limp, I felt myself collapsing like a rag doll. Sleep tugged as we lay against each other on that rocky ledge, until gradually I became aware that it was fully light and the sun was coming up. Across the eastern sea, almost like a benediction, a glorious sunrise turned everything to molten gold, shimmering so that we could barely look.

But we gazed transfixed until the sun rose clear of the horizon, until that brilliant light left us both concerned by the prospect of discovery. I should have swum again to cleanse myself, but there was no time to linger and I was reluctant to break the bond between us. For once I wanted to hold him to me and never let him go. It was a foolishly sentimental notion and part of me knew it; but if my skin was salty it was mostly warm and dry. I told myself it was silly to get wet again.

Thirteen

The mornings were glorious, with a blue, misty haze over the sea that spread upriver like a magic spell. The hedgerows were in full green leaf, with great creamy fronds of meadowsweet and cow parsley edging fields and footpaths across the cliffs. Below the Saloon the sands sported a brightly painted crop of bathing machines, and young children in pinafores appeared daily to dig trenches and build castles with all the dedication of apprentice engineers.

Around the harbour, naked urchins dived in and out of the water, while life and work went on as usual. Steam tugs towed barques and brigantines in and out with every tide, and cobles went out fishing. Every time I was in town, I scanned streets and quays for familiar faces, not with any particular fear or apprehension, but I was well aware that my time with Bram was precious, that I was hugging it to me and didn't want it spoiled or besmirched by any ill-judged comments. In short, I didn't want to have to defend the indefensible.

But I was growing rapidly more attached to him, and this was borne in upon me one Saturday afternoon, as we were coming up to midsummer's day. It was particularly hot, and I was helping Jack Louvain with an important photographic appointment at a big house near Dunsley. We'd agreed to

161

meet outside the pub at Newholm, and when I arrived I half expected to find Jack inside, enjoying a pint; but like the red-faced boy he'd employed to carry equipment up from town, he was drinking a cup of water from the village pump.

'It's water for me as well,' he said wryly. 'Clients don't care for the reek of ale – especially those who summon photographers to their houses!'

When we arrived, the family were just finishing a picnic lunch under awnings in the garden. It was a benefit in one way, since everyone looked replete and good-tempered, but it necessitated much straightening and cleaning up before we could begin. Mothers tugged and wiped until the little ones were tidy and clean-faced, while the grandmother fussed over the seating arrangements: who should have precedence next to her husband – it was his birthday, after all – and which child should sit on whose knee.

Biting back an urge to interfere, I turned my attention elsewhere. The design of the house was plain in the extreme, but the enclosed rear garden was a delight of arches and arbours, swagged with trailing ivy and heavy-headed roses. Through tall windows that opened into a sitting room I could see carpets and easy chairs, polished tables, pretty ornaments and a pianoforte decked with photographs. They were beautiful things, but it was what they represented that struck me so forcefully. Bram's home with Florence must be like that, not just a little two-roomed cottage with a tiny scullery and a stone floor. All at once I was seized by shame and envy and a sense of despair. Bram could never give up such surroundings for the bare simplicity of what we shared at Newholm, and yet, almost without realising it, I'd become used to playing house with him and wanted it to continue.

At this time of year it was fine – *charming* was the

word he used – but it couldn't possibly compete with servants and a house in London, especially in the depths of winter. I was fooling myself if I thought it could.

With a forceful nudge, Jack muttered under his breath, 'Get them into some kind of order, for heaven's sake – we can't have the tallest and the shortest stood together, no matter what Grandmama says about age and precedence. And get that child on to somebody's knee before it falls over and starts screaming. Otherwise we'll still be here at midnight.'

I was glad to do as I was bidden. My thoughts were pointless and painful, so I thrust them aside and organised the children instead. Jack and I worked together with reasonable efficiency until the pictures were taken and he was satisfied, and then, having consumed plates of cake and welcome glasses of lemonade, we gathered up the equipment and made our farewells. We'd been out for hours and I thought we would go straight back to Whitby, but he said the light was just at that interesting point; and anyway, he had some extra plates from the sitting which were just begging to be used.

The lad he'd brought with him was dragging his feet, and I was feeling the strain of the afternoon, but Jack was adamant. So we made our way down to the beach at Upgang, where the old Mulgrave Castle Inn, with tiled roof askew and chimneys leaning, stood perched on the very edge of the cliff, catching the evening light against a darker sky behind. From below there was a wildness and drama about the place, as if it were defying the elements still, and, more than that, hiding within its walls the dutiable kegs and silks of days gone by. But although the old smugglers' rendezvous had been closed as a public house for a year or more, I suspected it was still used by certain of the fishermen for short periods at dark

163

of the moon. Its dubious reputation hung on, as it might cling to an old rogue until the day of his death. But all it needed was one more winter, one more ferocious storm to undermine the shale, one more prolonged period of frost, and the old inn would be no more.

Jack managed to get a picture from the beach before the incoming tide made the angle impossible, and, having climbed back up, was insisting on a pose from me when I saw Bram coming down from the direction of Newholm. He was happy to find us, happier still to watch Jack working with me, and insisted on knowing all the technical and artistic details involved in the taking of such a photograph. Being tired and hungry and somewhat cast down after my afternoon at Dunsley, I was not best pleased; all I wanted was to go home and have him make love to me.

I fidgeted unhappily, while Jack seemed intent on explaining everything to his new pupil, even to the extent of letting him view me – upside down, of course – through the camera's great fish-eye lens. With an intelligent audience he wanted to show off, and started talking about composition and the art of making pictures with a camera. I might not have been there, despite being the subject of the picture. Gritting my teeth, I moved here and there as requested, while the two men fussed over shadows and focus and the angle of my limbs against the weathered walls of the inn. But my misery produced frowns and Jack wanted wistfulness for this photograph, so I had to straighten my face and think about something I was longing for, like passionate kisses for tea, and strawberries and cream for supper.

Since there was no need for me to be at the studio, next day Bram and I went out for our customary walk rather earlier than usual. It was a beautiful evening, very still, and most of the way from Newholm we could see the walls of church and abbey catching the last of the sun, while the sea was reflecting the sky. By the time we reached the east cliff the light had gone, and a high tide was filling the harbour; the Sunday visitors were leaving, while groups of old mariners were discussing the weather, as always, and saying the extraordinary heat couldn't last. In search of solitude, we walked to the far end of the graveyard to rest on Bram's favourite seat, watching fishing cobles and a small schooner going out between the piers.

We were soon reduced to shadows in the dusk, deeper tones of grey against the ranks of upright stones. Voices, snatches of music reached us from below, but all was peace around us, as though we were ghosts of ourselves already. The strangest feeling seemed to have a hold on me. I couldn't have lifted a finger to dispel it, but after a while, Bram broke the stillness with a long sigh that brought us both back to life.

'Coming up here,' he murmured, 'it seems to happen every time ... there's something extraordinary about this place ...' His accent, which was rarely noticeable, always became more pronounced when he was stirred, and in that moment it was rich and undisguised. 'It draws me ... makes me want to stay...'

Hearing the longing, wanting to respond, I was almost afraid to speak. 'Then stay,' I whispered lightly, pressing myself to his side.

'I wish I could.' Turning, he slipped an arm around the back of the seat and drew me closer. 'At this moment, it's what I want more than anything in the world.'

I could scarcely breathe. 'Do you?'

He brushed strands of hair away from my neck, and gazed at me with longing. 'You know I do. This place and you – what more could I ask? You've given me so much, and I want you all the time. I think I've wanted you more than any other woman in my life . . .'

My heart raced. It was what I longed to hear, but that mention of other women brought his wife immediately to mind. Afterwards I could have cursed, but the words were out before I could stop them. 'More than Florence?'

With a sudden grimace, he released me. 'Oh yes,' he said tersely, rising to his feet, 'even more than Florence.'

Furious with myself, wishing I was older, wiser, more tactful – or at the very least that I could learn to simper and keep my mouth shut – I watched in despair while he left my side.

A short distance away, across the path, an old table tomb stood close to the cliff edge, a reminder of others that were no longer there. It was a dangerous spot, but tempting, and Bram paused there often at sunset, leaning against the tomb and smoking his cigarettes while waiting for me to leave the studio. He stood there now, a dark silhouette, locked into the mystery of his own private world, while I watched from the bench, wishing he would talk to me, explain things to me, tell me what he wanted, what he really planned to do. Most of all, I wished I had the courage to ask.

I watched him, trying to read his mood from the set of his shoulders. After a minute or so he relaxed and turned and beckoned me towards him. 'You're very young still, aren't you?' he murmured, kissing my forehead. 'I tend to forget that.'

I'd have preferred him to say I was impudent, since that at least implied a certain crude wisdom; in this case to be young was to be ignorant, and I was too often aware of that. Feeling vulnerable, I perched on the edge of the tomb in silence and looked out across the harbour. Some distance below us was the East Pier and the pale strip of Collier's Hope; to the left stood Tate Hill and the short stretch of Henrietta Street.

'It must have been a grand place to live, once upon a time,' he said musingly, following my eyes and studying the uneven line of houses below. The street had been built as a fashionable extension to Kirkgate in the time of the third King George, on a ledge known as the Haggerlythe, but now it was better known for its wooden smokehouses and oak-smoked herrings. Catching a drift of the aroma, Bram added drily: 'But I'd have thought the view was wasted on a load of old kippers, wouldn't you?'

'Well, at least kippers can swim!' I joked, glad of his change of mood. Playing up to it, pointing to the gap between cliff and pier, I started to tell him about the collapse of Henrietta Street into the harbour. 'It used to continue right along the Haggerlythe – as far as the steps there. Except in those days the gap wasn't as wide.'

I had a strong memory of being plucked from my bed in the dark, clutched to my mother's bosom as she ran out of our house on the Cragg. There were yells and screams and raised voices, torches blazing across the harbour, the sound of thunder...

On a deep breath, I said: 'It happened one night when I was a child, not long before Christmas. There came a great rumbling and roaring, and half the cliff disappeared into the sea. The far end of the street went first, taking most of the houses with it. The noise and the shaking were terrifying – just like an earthquake – we felt it across the harbour. Everybody turned out to see what was happening. They thought the whole cliff was going. It was dreadful,' I assured him, even though my own memories were somewhat limited, 'like the last trumpet-call, they say, with chasms opening up, entire houses cracking and sliding down the cliff, huge chunks of rock and shale tumbling down, and worst of all when the graveyard fell away! – coffins coming down like rain from above! All the coffins smashed open along the Haggerlythe and on the Scaur. They say it was hard to tell bones and skulls from *haggomsteeans* amongst the rocks.'

He'd been gazing in awe down the cliff, but as ever at mention of a dialect word, his attention came back to me. 'What are they?'

'Oh, magical stones, lucky stones – the ones with perfect round holes in, that you nail to the doorpost to keep evil spirits away. You find them on the Scaur, along with giants' teeth and cannon balls,' I said with airy unconcern. 'You know, the ones you call ammonites. But for ages you'd find skulls and bones and human teeth as well.'

'Teeth?' With a little grunt of amazement he reached into his pocket for notebook and pencil, squinting to write in the semi-darkness, muttering something about fossils, and death and resurrection, while I peered over his shoulder and grinned. It was a fact of life that both cliffs were unstable, and every winter brought small falls and new threats of collapse. But the way I viewed things, people who fancied such extraordinary views – either in death or in life – had to be prepared to pay the price.

'In the end, though,' I went on, as certain other gruesome facts returned to mind, 'the sea washed everything away. Which was just as well, since most of the collapsed graves were from the cholera burial ground. Furthest from the church, and nearest the sea – no wonder folks didn't want to clear them up.'

At the mention of cholera, he slowly looked around and put away his notebook. 'In Ireland,' he said heavily, 'they had a terrible epidemic when my mother was young. Whole families died of it in Sligo. In one house close by, Ma said there was a little girl left alone. They could hear her crying piteously, and she begged to be allowed to help – but the poor child died in her arms soon afterwards.'

'And was your mother all right?' I asked, awed by such courage. Whenever he spoke of her, Bram made his mother sound like a woman after my own heart, one with red blood in her veins and an independent spirit. I liked the sound of Charlotte Stoker, and was always eager to hear more.

He said she'd suffered no ill-effects, but that was probably because his grandmother was the kind who swore cleanliness was next to godliness, and boiled and fumigated everything. Ma always said she was too young then to think seriously of dying. But I know she was frightened of the coffin-maker – he made her flesh crawl, she said. He used to pound on the door of their house, asking did they have bodies to bury, and if not, did they want to be measured up for a decent set of matching coffins. If they paid him now, this terrible old rogue told them, he'd see they got the best of everything.

'They begged him to go away and not to call again, but he kept on. Eventually, Ma hung out the window and said if he came again she'd throw something at him, and it wouldn't be money! But he did come, so out went a great jugful of slops on his head – the man was furious! Shook his fist and said that if she died within the hour, he'd make sure she didn't have so much as a box to be buried in. So Ma said she wouldn't care anyway, and slammed the window shut. He didn't come again. It was the looters came next, she said – and they were much more frightening. At first they took only small items from empty houses nearby – mostly food, clothing and money – understandable, in a way, when so many were so poor. But as each day went by they were becoming bolder, arriving in gangs and with handcarts – clearing whole houses of everything, from clocks and paintings to chairs and kitchen crockery, and swigging whiskey as they went. Not just men, but women as well, wild-eyed, avaricious, even mad – capable of anything.

'Ma's family barricaded themselves in and kept a lookout, but by then they were becoming slightly mad themselves. It was July and the weather was hot, they'd very little food left in the house apart from flour and beans, and hardly any fuel with which to cook them. They were afraid to go out for fear of being stricken by the cholera or attacked by thieves, too frightened to sleep except in snatches – and it seemed these lawless gangs were now set to break in and murder them for the sake of a few sticks of furniture!

'They were terrified, you understand – all of them, terrified for their lives. Then ... well, something happened, and they realised they had to leave, no matter what.'

Pausing, he sat quite still for a moment. Sensing his tension, impatient to hear the rest, I stared at his profile in the gathering darkness. He was gazing across the harbour, obviously uncertain whether to reveal the details. 'Ma never mentioned this,' he confessed at last, feeling for his cigarette case. 'One of my uncles told me – he was much younger, and saw it happen.'

Lighting up, drawing deep, Bram released a cloud of pale smoke into the sultry night. 'A gang of looters tried to break in. It was probably a concerted attempt, with two or three attacking different parts of the house. Anyway, one tried to climb in through the skylight over the front door, and Ma was so terrified, she swung an axe at him and chopped off his hand. I don't know whether she meant to, or whether it was just a question of trying to beat him off, but that's what she did. The man's screams were horrific. Before he fell back,' Bram murmured huskily, 'he just hung there, staring, while his blood spurted all over her face and clothes.'

Stunned into silence, I could only gape at him, while he seemed an impossible distance away, beyond the harbour, beyond the present, in a time and place that belonged to neither of us.

Fourteen

Sickened and disturbed, I tried to shut out the image of a man wedged fast and screaming, his arteries gushing. It gave the young Charlotte Stoker a grim, different image, one of fierce and ruthless determination. Suddenly, I was less sure of her, and uncertain of her son.

'Did he die?' I asked faintly.

'Who – the looter?' Bram stood up. 'I don't know – possibly. Probably, yes – I doubt there'd have been medical attention.'

'They got away? Your mother's family, I mean.'

'What? Oh, yes. Grabbed a few things and escaped before daybreak. Had a bad time of it, trying to reach their relatives in Ballina, but yes, they got away . . .'

He took a step or two away from me, a shadow in the darkness, illumined by the glowing point of his cigarette. I shivered, feeling the gruesomeness of his tale as something real and close, far more so than the collapse of the graveyard, which I'd witnessed as a young child but knew mainly second-hand.

In response, he turned and said, 'But they were lawless times, Damaris, and I expect things weren't much better here. Frightened people do horrific things.'

I nodded, aware that his mother's story gave Tate Hill Pier and the Church Stairs a fresh significance.

'Here,' I said tersely, trying to suppress the shudder in my voice, 'they ferried the bodies of cholera victims across the harbour, at night, so they didn't have to carry them through town. Even so, they had to bring them up the 199 steps to be buried, and they're supposed to have buried at least one of them alive.'

'How was that?' he asked, startled.

'They said they felt him struggling as they dragged his coffin up the steps, but didn't stop to open it because *he was already nailed down*. Can you believe it?'

'Yes,' he said quietly, as I hunched and pulled a face, 'the awful thing is that I can . . .'

I tried to shrug it off; but the phrase 'nailed down' conjured up other stories I'd heard, of murderers and malefactors – and suicides too – who were literally 'nailed' to their coffins and the ground by oak or hawthorn stakes.

'According to Old Uncle Thaddeus,' I said, 'all those who could not rest easy in their graves – whose souls belonged to the devil rather than the saints – were interred near unmarked crossroads out on the moors. Or buried with a stake through the breast, to stop them breaking free of the grave and *coming again*, to find the living.'

'Here?' Bram whispered in response, gazing at me with awed and glowing eyes. 'Malefactors were staked *here*?'

'So they say. Before our time,' I hastened to assure him, 'but yes, they were staked. Some had their legs and ankles bound with rope or chains to stop them walking. Some had their heads chopped off.'

'They were *decapitated*? You mean, to stop them rising again – as a ritual, not as a punishment?' As I nodded, he grasped my arm quite painfully and asked: 'When was this, do you know? *How* do you know? Are we talking about living memory, or centuries past?'

But that was a difficult question and his avidity scared me even more than the subject itself. As he paced up and down, alarmingly close to the sheer drop below, I clung to my perch on the edge of the tomb. Nervously I explained about Old Uncle Thaddeus and his interest in local history and folklore. He'd published several small books and articles, and such facts as I remembered were culled from items I'd heard or read as a child, clandestinely, since Grandmother professed disapproval of such macabre tales. 'I should think it was all long ago,' I said, 'but there's bound to be copies of Old Uncle's books in the library – you could look them up.'

He promised he would, and paused for a moment more to look out over the water. Chilled and longing to be gone, I slipped off the cold stone and took his arm, persuading him back to the path.

He turned towards me then. 'Tell me,' he said with low intensity, 'have you ever heard of vampires?'

All at once, as my breath caught in my throat, the moon appeared, rising fast and huge like a monstrous face behind the abbey. For a few seconds it looked horribly capable of swallowing cliff, church and graveyard, including ourselves, without so much as a hiccup. Startled, awe-struck, we watched it rise clear of the horizon, miraculously shrinking until its great yellow smile ceased to threaten and became no more than a distant smirk of amusement.

It was an omen, I thought with the frantic racing of my heart, a warning. The significance escaped me but I was fearfully aware of it, like great eyes staring down at us from the sky; like the eyes of God, I thought in a moment of panic, remembering the homilies of childhood. The embroidered sampler, THOU GOD SEEST ME, complete with cyclops eye, had always scared me most of all. I wondered whether there would indeed be a Day of Judgment when all would be called to account, a time when the dead would rise up to answer the charges before them, before being cast back down the cliff to eternal damnation.

Standing there, surrounded by tombstones, picturing skeletons and decaying bodies bursting forth from their graves, I had a moment of paralysing fear. I clung to Bram's arm and he turned to me, eyes glittering in the moonlight.

'There's no need for alarm,' he said softly, 'it's only the moon ...'

But I thought he regarded me strangely. He cupped my chin in his hand and moved to kiss me, licking at my lower lip, lightly drawing its fullness between his teeth. It was something he often did, something I'd grown used to and even welcomed in the midst of an afternoon's gentle love-making, but I was unsure of it now, half afraid that he would try to take me here, under the full moon, in the shadow of one of the tombs. Apprehensive, uneasy, I wanted to walk away but his embrace was overwhelming; he furled my lip with his thumb and bent to taste the soft flesh within. As I responded to him I felt the sharp nip and sting of his teeth.

Shocked, I struggled in his embrace, but he held me to him, apologising, kissing me more gently, then whispering that he loved me, he wanted to be part of me, wanted me to be part of him. Wiping my mouth, feeling the place with my tongue, I said shakily I didn't care to be loved like that, and would thank him not to do it again. But as we left the graveyard and its strangeness behind, I began to wonder what was happening to us, whether the moon was exerting her strange power as she did upon the tides, and turning us both into lunatics.

*

Fired by what I'd told him about Old Uncle's published works, he went to the subscription library on Pier Road the following morning and borrowed several books by different authors. That afternoon, instead of going out as he usually did while I hung out the laundry, he spent his time reading, dipping into various local histories and travel books, and making notes.

He seemed intrigued by the idea of the dead walking, not just unquiet spirits, but physical bodies rising from the grave to 'come again'. As he browsed through the volumes he wondered aloud where such beliefs originated, while my mind, conditioned by the previous night's talk of plague and premature burial, came up with one of the worst of childhood's tales, made all the more terrifying by the fact that it was a well-known family story and probably true.

At the end of the last century, the young and unmarried Alicia Sterne had died suddenly, of no obvious cause except that her heart had simply stopped beating. That was mysterious enough in itself, but she remained unaltered. On the day appointed for her funeral, while the house was full of relatives and friends gathered for the interment, the undertaker refused to close the coffin. He insisted that the Doctor be recalled, that another examination be made to certify death, since her glossy fair hair, rosy lips and cheeks, and bright, wide-open blue eyes looked so terrifyingly alive. The Doctor, it was said, had pierced her heart to be certain; and the word that had been whispered ever since, and always silenced, was that which Bram had used: *vampire*. The tale was repeated, mostly at wakes and vigils, and children had terrified each other with it down the years, until poor Alicia Sterne had passed into legend, and her grave in the old churchyard above Bay was given a wide berth.

Bram wanted to go at once and find it, but, as I said, the cemetery was scattered with Sterne family graves, and I didn't have the first idea where to start looking. Nevertheless, when he met me that night after work, his footsteps led inexorably in that direction, over the tops of the moors with the glittering sea beyond. But Bay was further than he realised, and the last train back was long past, so, thankfully, we turned for home. In spite of the distance, it would have been more sensible to return by road, but Bram, being in possession of a local map, was set on taking the shorter but steeper way, by the old monks' trod which led down through Cock Mill Woods.

I was just as set against the idea, even though it was a clear night and almost as bright as day in the open; but Bram dared and teased and persuaded until eventually, against my better judgement, I gave in. Faced with the woods I tried not to think of what might be lying in wait for us, but from the open moors down to the river was a descent of over a mile, the blackness of the path illumined by dappled and shimmering pools of moonlight, blue-white and brilliant under the looming trees.

Everything was distorted, every footfall uncertain, every stride like stepping through water. The old paved way was not wide enough for us to go safely side by side, and we were blinkered by the darkness, aware of each other only as voices moving down and away through wavering pools of light. At first Bram went ahead to protect me, but with a better view of the steps he let me go in front. He was happy enough to talk, whereas I was too afraid of falling, and too terrified to give more than monosyllabic replies.

The woods and the falling streams, he said, reminded him of the German forests he'd visited the year before with Ellen and Irving. I begged him sharply to tell me no more of his gruesome tales, but of course he did. His favourite, *Carmilla*, had been written by the editor of the newspaper for which Bram had once penned theatrical reviews, and he said it as though I should understand how normal it was to invent such stories, as though really there was nothing to fear. It did nothing for my courage and in fact made me feel lamentably ignorant, as though he knew everything and everyone and I knew nothing at all.

I tried to close my ears but there was a rhythm to his words that matched every descending footfall, and a hypnotic quality in his voice which seemed to resonate through the woods. In the rustling darkness, he told the story of a well-born young woman, the only child of an elderly father, whose friends and neighbours lived many miles distant. They found the arrival at their castle of a cultured lady in a state of distress something of a welcome diversion, and although the girl and her father knew nothing about their visitor, the mysterious Carmilla was cared for and befriended from the beginning.

She stayed on at the castle in the forest, while the impressionable young heroine fell rapidly under her spell. But in spite of her beauty and those lustrous eyes, the girl was aware of an element of revulsion, especially when overwhelmed by one of Carmilla's ardent embraces. The grand lady could be as forceful and suffocating as she was passionate; there were kisses and caresses, and the languid, sensual gestures of an experienced, voluptuous woman. The girl was disconcerted, Bram said, but she was steadily being seduced; and in her heart, in spite of herself, she longed to respond . . .

'*Desire and loathing strangely mixed,*' he quoted, and I pictured it at once. Friendship, beauty, sensuality, the attraction of knowing one is loved and desired, accompanied by a strong sense of dismay. Even, ultimately, revulsion. I understood those feelings, but it was disturbing to hear them expressed by Bram. At Carmilla's name I even found myself picturing Bella's face and form, at every step half expecting her to be lying in wait for me with bared teeth.

'Then the courtship,' Bram went on in that insistent tone, 'began to subtly change. In the midst of this romance there came disturbing dreams; the girl was feeling lethargic, melancholy, dimly in love with death. The beautiful Countess Carmilla was as fiendish and unnatural as she was seductive, using vampiric arts to mesmerise the girl, to visit her at night, to possess her youth and beauty, to drain her very life . . .'

I had the feeling he was aroused by the story and wanted some kind of response from me, but I was too scared to protest. I sped down the worn and broken pathway as fast as I dared, trying not to think of old ghosts as we came down past the mill and the falls, nor to worry about nameless horrors lying in wait under the bridge below.

As last the worst was behind us, and I began to catch my breath, but as the trees thinned and we came down to the smooth-flowing river, he said chillingly, 'You see, Damaris, love will have its sacrifices, and there's no sacrifice without blood.'

'What on earth do you mean by that?' I demanded, breath still heaving, but braver now that I could see light reflected off the water.

'Well, I'm merely quoting,' he said, lengthening his stride as I stepped out towards the bridge at Ruswarp: 'it's a line from the story that always stuck in my mind. But it's true, don't you think?' And he went on to expand about love and marriage and the sacrifice of a woman's virginity, about birth and death, and the ultimate sacrifice of friends laying down their lives for each other.

I'd come to feel thoroughly chastened, when he said: 'And what about the greatest sacrifice of all? The Blood of Christ, which we drink as wine? Or actual blood, come to that, if you happen to be Catholic.'

In spite of what I liked to call my unbelief, I thought I detected a whiff of blasphemy there which justified an outraged protest. I suppose fear added force to my words, but they were barely out before Bram caught at my arm. He pulled me round to face him then, his breath coming hard enough for me to realise that he was angry too.

'I never thought of you as small-minded, Damaris. Young, yes – insufficiently educated, yes, but never ignorant, never petty. Don't you understand? I'm not trying to upset you. This is a matter that interests and intrigues me – blood is the essence of life itself, that's why we fear to see it spilled. That's why it's so precious to us, so mystical, so *significant*.

'Doesn't it mean anything,' he asked more softly, touching my face and throat, 'that you gave your virginity to me – *gave* it,' he repeated, 'to me, a stranger? I couldn't have *taken* it, knowing – it was far too precious a gift. You said you wanted me to love you – and I have, I do. I've shared things with you,' he whispered earnestly, 'that have never been shared with anyone else . . .'

So then I felt ashamed for having given myself so lightly, and for such unconsidered reasons; at the time, evidently, it had meant more to him than to me, and now I was hurting him by failing to understand the gift he was bestowing in return.

'You hold my secret self,' he murmured, 'so please hold it safe . . .'

I promised to try, even though I couldn't help

feeling somewhat unequal to the burden. His philosophising made me uncomfortable at times, and though I tried to view it calmly, I had the suspicion he was a little too intrigued by the significance of life-blood and bloodshed, and the mystical idea of marriage.

That night we reached home before cock-crow and, after a few hours' sleep, it was easy to dismiss my unease as the product of fatigue. Bram was generally up and dressed before me, with the fire lit and kettle bubbling on the hob, and that morning was no exception. When I went through into the kitchen he was at his desk, writing and smoking a cigarette, with a mug of tea at his elbow. As he reached up to kiss me I told myself that there was nothing wrong with him or the world beyond the window, he was imaginative, that was all, intrigued by aspects of life that most people never thought about. Never had *time* to think about, if truth be told.

When he went outside, I took the opportunity to look at the notes he was making. Open on the desk was an old book with a strange title: *An Account of the Principalities of Wallachia and Moldavia*, written by a man who had once been the British Consul in Bucharest. I glanced at a page or two, and it seemed to be an account of the times when Catholic and Orthodox princes were at war with each other as well as the Ottoman Turks, when it was difficult for any overlord to keep his territory for long.

Bloodthirsty days, and they'd caught Bram's imagination, I could tell from the notes he'd made. I don't know why, but my tongue went straight to the place inside my lip where he'd drawn blood the night before; and then I went back into the bedroom, opening my collar to view the purple bruises of lovebites on neck and breast.

181

Fifteen

Although I spent little time in Whitby, I kept a lookout for people I knew while shopping or going to the studio in the evening. Mostly to duck down a side-street, but there were times when face-to-face meetings were unavoidable, and since leaving the Cragg it was curious to note the various reactions. As Bella's friend I'd been more or less accepted, without too much overt interest in my background; but word had evidently spread that I was 'housekeeping' for a London gentleman, and that seemed to have whetted more than a few appetites. Suddenly, women who were neighbours of the Firths – women like Mrs Penny, the coalman's wife, Sarah Blyth the seamstress, and Betsy Cullen who lodged across the yard – were eager to stop me in the street and ask how I was getting along. Previously, who I was and where I came from had never – or rarely – been mentioned, but now they wanted to know about the Sternes, what had brought me to the Cragg originally, and what I thought of my new job. What was it like looking after a rich foreigner like that? Was he very demanding? Did he like good plain cooking or demand fancy dishes, and was he difficult to please? And with the questions came the sly smiles or avid looks. What they really wanted to know, of course, was whether I was sleeping with him, and what he was like in bed; whether, in fact, he was very different from other men, working men, the kind of men they were used to.

I thought he probably was, even though I had no other experience to go on, and that awareness was beginning to worry me. Unable to say so, I tried not to colour under those searching eyes, and said only that he was kind and easy enough to work for. They took in my clothes, pretty and sweet-scented, and, with a twist of the lips, drew their own conclusions. It was uncomfortable to know that they would carry those conclusions away and repeat them to whoever would listen, but there was nothing I could do about that. I found it more difficult to be told that Bella was like a lost soul without me.

Ironically, the one person I wanted to see was Bella, and she seemed to have disappeared. It wasn't that I imagined she would know the answers, but in explaining things to her, I thought I might understand them a little better myself. Even so, as I made the bed and tidied things away I wondered what she would make of Bram and his curious stories, what she would say to our moonlight rambles. I was afraid she might pour scorn on them.

If it shamed me, still I lacked the courage to go to the Cragg and knock on the door. I'd looked out for her before in order to avoid a meeting, but now, wherever I went, I searched for her face in vain. I even made a point of passing the fish stalls, but she wasn't there, and I didn't want to speak to Cousin Martha, not even to ask after Bella. It was ridiculous: she was the only friend I had, certainly the only one with whom I could discuss such personal matters, and I'd turned my back on her.

That anxiety took the edge off everything, including my good humour, and since I couldn't explain to Bram I put it down to the oppressive heat, a feeling of exhaustion and the fact that our midnight walks were not what I was used to. But he was offended when I turned away from him, by what he saw as my rejection, becoming moody and abstracted in ways he hadn't been before. He'd always been prone to impulse, even in the midst of his writing, and often, after a lengthy period of concentration, would abruptly stand up, grab his soft, broad-brimmed hat and linen jacket, and call to me to come out for a walk. Now he stopped asking me to go with him and went alone.

I felt wounded by that, and doubly anxious. For several days there was tension between us, but as I recall, towards the end of June, there was heat and tension everywhere. Landwards, the sky had turned a sickly shade of yellow, like a smothering blanket which obscured the sun and muffled every breeze. Even the fog lurked far out to sea, as though unable to penetrate the barrier. The nights, which until the solstice had been so clear and invigorating, were humid, and the waning moon was no more than a shrouded lantern over the sea.

Things came to a head in ways that I could not have foreseen. It had been a stifling day and the evening was no cooler. Bram called for me at the studio about half-past nine, stopping to talk to Jack in the doorway while I completed the last of the cabinet prints and switched off the gas hob. The little back room stank of chemicals and glue, and I couldn't wait to get outside. Removing my overall, I hurriedly washed and tidied myself before the sliver of mirror above the sink. A moment later I was ready to go, but the bridge was open, and one of the paddle tugs was going through, belching sparks and smoke as it towed in a large barquentine laden with timber.

Jack detested the tugs, and as usual complained about the noise and smoke, while Bram, predictably, responded that he'd rather cross the Atlantic by steamer any day. Their conversation expanded into a friendly argument on the relative merits of steam and sail, while I found myself in the background, listening, suddenly beset by memories of Jonathan. Like Bella, he'd been absent from my thoughts during these last unreal weeks, but just then his presence seemed so strong, I half expected to see him passing by. I wondered what he would think if he saw Bram and me together, and unconsciously stepped back into shadow; and then I remembered what Jack had said when I left the Cragg: *be sure you're not exchanging the frying pan for the fire*. At the time, the excitement of being desired and cared for by a man of age and experience had far outweighed the risks involved. Now, it seemed, I was in danger of feeling the burns.

The vessels went through, the open bridge swung back into place, and the crowd started to move across, but the surge had thinned to the more usual level of evening strollers before Bram was ready to leave. Like myself, he seemed to be examining every passing face, and in the meantime I could feel trickles of perspiration running down inside my bodice.

Although I would have preferred to head straight home, Bram was in one of his stubborn moods. He'd been out on the pier in search of a breeze and wanted to take a turn on the east cliff for the same reason. I thought the effort of climbing the Church Stairs seemed out of proportion to any possible benefit but he wouldn't listen.

Over Kettleness, the afterglow of sunset was blood-red against a louring sky, becoming more dramatic as we climbed. There was a dark pall of smoke hanging over the harbour, and the sultry atmosphere was threatening; I could feel it like a tight band around my forehead. Taking the steps slowly, pausing on the coffin-rests, I said again that we should head for home, but Bram wanted to press on.

'Not a breath of air,' I said mutinously as we reached the top, needing no ancient weather prophets to tell me we were in for a storm.

'There'll be a breeze out on the headland.'

'In that case,' I persisted, 'what was wrong with the west cliff? Why couldn't we catch the breeze over there, instead of trailing right up here for it?'

As I followed him, dragging my feet, he turned and gave vent to words that cut me. 'If you don't want to be here, then for goodness' sake go home. Do what you want, Damaris, I'm not here to stop you. Only please don't whine.'

'I'm not,' I protested, but I could hear the injured note in my voice which bore a worrying reminder of Cousin Martha. Clearing my throat, I tried to sound as though his sharpness didn't matter. 'It's just that it's so hot, and I'm sure we're going to have a storm. I'd rather get home before it starts.'

Ignoring that, taking my arm, he led me to our usual spot. As I expected, he chose the tomb in preference to the seat, and, leaning against the stone, looked out to sea. Even here, there was only a slightly cooler breath, a stirring of the air that was more a waft than a breeze. The twilight was sinking fast, leaving no more than an angry glow low down in the west. Everything was darker than usual; even the sea looked black, while the squat grey shape of the church was barely visible against the sky.

With an exaggerated sigh I looked around, then turned my eyes on Bram, seeing tension in the set of his shoulders. He lit a cigarette and smoked ruminatively, while I wondered why things were going so sadly adrift. With nothing much else to do, I hoisted myself up and tucked my feet under me, absently tracing the remains of lettering on the stone's upper face. Salt winds had scoured almost all but a solitary name, *Lucy*, and the month and year of her demise; except even the year was in question, since the last two numerals were hard to define.

We'd speculated before on her age and identity, from time to time adding pieces to a background that had become almost as fanciful as that of the young heroine in *Carmilla*. In one of his lighter moods a few nights ago, Bram had put everything together and informed me that Lucy had been a spoiled and adored young woman, very beautiful, with several suitors vying for her hand. Tragically, she'd fallen ill with consumption, and in just a few short weeks had wasted away . . .

In this story, her grief-stricken suitors carried her coffin in torchlit procession all the way through Whitby, while her best friend followed behind, carrying Lucy's gloves and a wreath of thornless roses, pink and white to symbolise her youth and purity. 'Except,' Bram had then added, 'one of the stems bore a single thorn, which stabbed her finger, so a trail of blood was left all the way up the steps and into the churchyard . . .' At that point, having introduced the Whitby barghest as a threat to the friend, he had to summon another character to deal with it. This aristocratic and somewhat daunting figure owed much to the German count who had solved the problem of Carmilla. He was to come by ship from one of the Baltic ports, arriving in a fearful storm . . .

Round and round the letters of Lucy's name, my finger went on tracing; then suddenly Bram turned and spoke, and, soft though it was, his voice startled me.

'Did I tell you I finally deciphered Lucy's date of death? It was the other evening, while you were at the studio.' He turned and struck a match over the stone, moving it around in an attempt to clarify the date. But the old-fashioned scoops and whorls had been expanded and distorted by the weather, and I could no more decipher it now than at any other time. The match burned away and he let it drop to light another, but it was no use. He sighed. 'That's a shame. The sun was really low and bright, and just as I happened to look down, I saw the date – either 1852 or '32 –'

'I don't think it can be '52,' I said as the second match went out, 'it's too near the edge of the cliff –'

'I know. It has to be '32. The year of the epidemic.' He paused for a moment, then said: 'I'm afraid our poor dear Lucy may be one of your cholera victims . . .'

'Not *mine*,' I said, recoiling at the suggestion. Nevertheless, the fact that she'd been buried in style, at such an unusual distance from the church, did give credence to the suggestion. It seemed so obvious, suddenly, I wondered how we'd failed to work it out before. I slipped down from the tomb as revulsion shuddered through me, but Bram seemed not to notice, seemed not to feel appalled, as I did, that we'd been weaving fantasies around a poor girl dead of the cholera some fifty years before.

'Well,' he said, matter-of-factly, 'I wouldn't have made the connection, if you hadn't told me about the collapse of the old burial ground. She must have been on the landward edge of it. I wonder,' he added, glancing round, 'whether any more survived the fall?'

I shook my head, preferring to think of all that sickness and contagion being long gone, absorbed and cleansed by the sea. In the gathering darkness I wanted to be gone myself, preferably to a place of lights and laughter, where we could forget this morbid preoccupation with death. But when I suggested returning to town Bram was adamant as ever, urging that we walk along the cliffs and back by the abbey, as we'd done so many times before. I agreed, but with a singular lack of grace.

We'd gone some distance when he turned to me and said, 'By the way, I think I should tell you something.'

We both stopped. It was dark by then, even up there, and hard for me to read his face, but I was struck by apprehension. 'Tell me what?'

'I went for a walk on the pier this evening –' He looked up and I caught the glow of his eyes; then as I nodded, willing him to go on, he said abruptly: 'I bumped into George du Maurier's wife.'

'Here already? But they never come before July –'

'She's here with a friend,' he explained. 'George and the children are still in London. Of course, she was very surprised to see me,' he continued ironically, 'wanted to know where I was staying, what I'd been doing for the past few weeks, that sort of thing. Everyone's missed me in London, apparently, rumours have been flying, and – or so she said – Florence is getting very tight-lipped about my absence.'

I was suddenly tight-lipped myself. 'I see. And what did you say to that?'

He gave a little bark of laughter. 'Well, I tried to pass it off, said I couldn't think why, when everyone knew I was on a walking holiday in Yorkshire and couldn't be contacted. So then, for heaven's sake, she wanted to know when I would be back in London – I felt like telling her to mind her own damned business!' he admitted angrily. 'Anyway, I managed to hold my tongue and said I hadn't made any definite plans yet . . .'

At my little moan of dismay, he turned to me and said harshly, 'What am I going to do?'

In the thick air I found it difficult to breathe. What was he going to do? The dread of this moment had been at the back of my mind, but we'd never discussed it. No doubt Mrs du Maurier, whose husband was famous even in Whitby, for his writing and his *Punch* cartoons, would send a jolly little note to Mrs Stoker, saying not to worry, her husband was found, and would be returning any day now . . . *Such a joke! We've so enjoyed the tease, pretending we all thought Bram had disappeared, that he'd walked out on home and job and family, when all the time he was on a walking holiday in Yorkshire – what a lark!* . . . And Florence, what would she do? Treat it as a lark – pretend to Bram, even, that it was all a silly misunderstanding, and make a great fuss of him once he was back home?

A well-bred lady, I thought, might well do that. It would certainly save a great deal of unpleasantness and difficult explanations all round. In Florence's place, though, I would be livid – mad enough to discover his whereabouts, if only to get him back to London so I could kick him out again.

But Bram – what did he want?

'Well,' I said sensibly, while trying to distance myself from the pain and dismay, 'you knew this might happen. We've had four weeks together – perhaps it's time to give in with grace.'

But he denied that at once. 'No, never. I won't give in. I won't go back.' He grasped my shoulder, kissed my hair and my face, found my mouth and crushed it under his. 'How could I ever live without you,' he whispered fiercely, 'when I can't get enough of you now? I want you all the time!'

I wanted him too, and with a touch of desperation at the thought of losing him, but it seemed we'd reached the end of the line. I'd hoped against hope, but never seriously expected him to give up his life in London. All that talk of staying in Whitby and writing for a living was little more than fantasy, and the practical side of my nature resented being teased by promises that were never going to be fulfilled. So I tried to counteract his wilder claims with more serious issues. Every time he said he would stay, I asked him to tell me what he would do instead, how he would support his wife and child in London, if he was living with me in Whitby.

'I'll find a way.'

'But you've always said how extravagant she is,' I said reasonably, hurrying to catch up as he strode away from me in the dark. 'What will you do if Florence gets into debt? She's your wife – you're responsible for her. And what about Noel? Don't you care about him?'

Suddenly he stopped and tore at his hair. 'Damaris!' he cried, 'for the sake of God! Just leave it be! Let me worry about Florence, will you? Anyway, why should you care about her – or my son, for that matter? What are they to you?'

'I don't care!' I shouted at him, feeling tears spring to my eyes and hoping he couldn't see. 'Why should I? But I do care about you – and I won't have you making foolish promises you can't keep, and raising my hopes, and then going away, and – and – *leaving* me. I just won't!'

'I've no intentions of leaving you. I've told you – I'm staying here, in Whitby. I'm *not* going back to London!'

'But you *love* Florence, you know you do, it's no good saying –'

'Do you want me to leave?' he demanded. 'Are you sick of me, too?'

'Of course not!' I yelled, sobbing for sheer frustration. 'I love you!'

We stood apart, glaring at each other through the darkness; and then he came to me, and cautiously took me in his arms. He was shaking with emotion: it seemed to extend from his brow to his feet, and yet he held me away from him, as though afraid to do more than touch his forehead to mine. 'I know and I'm sorry,' he murmured. 'Forgive me, my love – I'm not myself this evening.'

I took a deep breath. 'We should go back –'

'No – let's walk a little further.'

We did, hand in hand, his fingers crushing mine. It was a measure of my distraction that I paid no attention to where we were. Did I love him? I imagined I must, since I'd said so, but that declaration had astonished me as much as Bram. And yet he said he knew. And was sorry. For what? For his anger, or because I loved him? My head was bursting with hope and despair, with a riot of questions and blank-alley solutions, until I had to risk putting one of them into words. 'Perhaps,' I began tentatively, 'if you really feel you can't bear to leave Whitby, then –'

'It's not that. London's the problem, Damaris – I don't want to go back to London.'

I felt that like a knife to the breast, and was extremely thankful I'd put Whitby in place of myself. That way I'd saved us both from embarrassment. But it was wounding to realise that his sense of anger and loathing was so much stronger than the love he professed for me. Initially I was too upset to wonder why, too upset to notice anything very much, except that we were walking and I was thankful for it. I was even thankful for the dark, although as sense returned I realised that Saltwick Bay was long behind us and we were some distance along the cliffs. Flashes of light over the horizon warned that it would be wise to go no further, and by mutual consent we stopped and turned and began to retrace our steps.

With London on my mind I found myself considering Florence. She was a beautiful woman and apparently had many admirers; I wondered whether she'd become involved with one of them, whether in fact she had taken another man to her bed and that was at the heart of Bram's dilemma.

It would have explained a great deal, and I was using it to settle my mind when he said unexpectedly: 'The problem is that Emma du Maurier will now write to George, and even if she doesn't immediately write to Florence as well, George will no doubt mention it to Irving. In fact,' Bram added with what seemed unwarranted harshness, 'I wouldn't put it past George to go round to the Lyceum with the express purpose of relaying such information – it's the sort of thing he'd find amusing . . .'

'Why should it matter?'

'Why? Because at the moment they don't know where I am. Irving doesn't know. I told you – I was supposed to be away for a week or ten days, but he hasn't been able to contact me for almost a month! In all this time,' he added, circling my shoulders and pulling me close to his side while we walked, 'I've been safe, in control of my own destiny. I've been here with you, Damaris, and not one of them has been able to touch me! Loving you,' he added earnestly, 'has saved me . . .'

'From what?' I asked faintly, but as I slowed and stopped, Bram bent his head to kiss me, cupping my jaw in his hand. 'From myself,' he confessed against my mouth. Confused, even a little alarmed by that strange mood, I backed away.

I set off along the path, but he caught at my arm. 'Please,' he whispered passionately, 'don't walk away from me. I can't bear that. I love you. If I could marry you, I'd do it tomorrow. I can't live without you. You've freed me, given me back my life, made me see what love is. I can't go back to that other existence – it's false, artificial, an illusion, no better than one of Irving's plays. And I'm just an onlooker, don't you see? I can't touch anything –' His voice broke on a note of distress and he turned away, shaking his head. As I reached out to comfort him, he said again, harshly: 'I can't *touch* anyone, do you understand that? Everything is forbidden to me. I can't even hold my *wife* . . .'

His pain overrode my own. I didn't understand, but I heard the words *marry you* and *can't live without you* and responded at once. He couldn't marry me, but he wanted to: that was the main thing. I felt a great surge of love and gratitude and, in that moment, would have willingly laid down my life for him. I hugged him fiercely and reassuringly, while his mouth sought mine and we kissed with such intensity that I was dizzy. For a moment he broke to gaze down at me, to caress my throat and jaw, and then he was rubbing his thumb over my chin and lower lip, forcing it down, biting into it, thrusting his tongue so deep into my mouth I could hardly breathe. I felt the stinging flow of blood and heard the plea to bite into his lip. I struggled but he held me fast, breathing hard as he forced his mouth on mine again.

The bitter-sweet metallic taste of blood filled my mouth. I realised he'd bitten hard into his own lip, so that his blood and mine were flowing together. For several moments, as sheet lightning lit up the horizon, it seemed we were melded together in shock; and then as I coughed and swallowed and retched, he picked me up as easily as though I'd been a child, and set me down on a grassy slope.

'You're mine now,' he whispered soothingly, kissing and caressing me gently, 'and I'm yours, always and for ever. I'm part of you, just as you'll always be part of me – nothing and no one can change that.'

As I shuddered and drew back, thunder muttered not far away. He was keen to make love, but I wanted none of that. Pushing myself free, I dabbed at my lip and scrambled to my feet, about to render a verbal lashing, when the sound of other voices halted me in mid-breath.

I listened hard, trying to determine how close they were, and suddenly, as odd words became clear, I realised that I knew them. My lips froze, my hand gestured Bram to be silent; Bella and her father were coming this way.

I strained to hear what was being said, knowing Bella was raging yet striving to suppress it, while her father was trying to ignore and outpace her words. We were already some yards from the path, but as Bram stood up I gripped his arm and dragged him with me behind a patch of bushes. 'I know them,' I hissed, 'so for heaven's sake be quiet!'

Although they were still some way off, their voices carried; Magnus's voice, raised in protest, rivalled the approaching thunder. 'You're daft – touched by the moon, you silly little bitch! Now get on home if ye canna leave me be – I've work to do!'

'I won't – not till you promise to leave her alone!' There came a low, unintelligible growl of words, followed by Bella's voice, raised to a shriek: 'You bastard! I'll kill you! You're evil, rotten, spawn of the devil – how does God ever let you *live*?'

Lightning flashed, brighter now, and Bram's eyes glittered at me through the darkness; then, closer, came a yell of rage, followed by shrieks and curses. A scuffle was going on, out there on the cliff, but we could see nothing.

There was a deep rumble of thunder; then all went quiet, and that was worst of all. I could feel the pulse thumping in my throat, and Bram's grip, almost crushing my wrist. A sudden torrent of abuse from Bella set us both breathing again; Magnus barked some retort, and I could feel the sweat standing out on my skin. On the tail of another rumble I thought I heard something else – a cry, a scream, perhaps – a moment or so later, but it seemed far off and I couldn't be certain.

I stood up then, trying to make out where they were, what was happening, but though I peered hard enough to make my eyes ache, I could see nothing. The sky lit up, but succeeded only in blinding me, so I stumbled in darkness down to the path and, with Bram on my heels, set off in pursuit.

We were both rocked by the ferocity of that argument, fearful of the outcome as much as the imminent storm. But more than anything else I was frightened for Bella, and Bram seemed to understand that. We hurried along, watching the cliff edge, scanning the path as best we could. The wind sprang up, a sudden gale off the sea, accompanied by cracks and flashes overhead and huge, thumping spots of rain. Within moments we were drenched, battered and blinded by the downpour, deafened by the noise.

We seemed an impossible distance from home, but another sheet of light showed the Black Nab, and a marionette figure ahead in the rain. It had to be Bella, it could be no one else. The sight urged us on. We caught another glimpse of her across Abbey Plain, and then, with a stitch in my side, I begged Bram to ease up. I'd had some idea of catching up, talking, finding out what happened, but I abandoned it. I knew she was safe, that was enough. I preferred not to think about Magnus.

At the top of Kirkgate Bram barely hesitated, dragging me straight into the Duke of York, where the Russian seamen had been welcomed the year before. I dare say we must have looked equally in need as we stood on the threshold. It was already after midnight and the landlord was on the verge of closing, but he produced a towel with which to effect some brief repairs, and a bottle from under the bar. With little more than a raised eyebrow, he handed over two generous measures of the best French cognac instead of the drinks we had ordered. Bram was mystified until I nudged him and said to ask no questions.

We sat in silence, not looking at each other, too battered to speak. But with the brandy stinging my swollen lip, I realised what Magnus Firth and Bella were doing up there on the cliffs, and on a night with no moon. The relief was so warming, I had to restrain a smile. While the boys took out the coble and provided an alibi for Magnus, he and Bella would have been making their way to one of the hidden coves between Saltwick and Bay, to meet a boat, probably one of the Dutch coopers, bearing a lucrative cargo of gin and tobacco but no customs clearance. The dutiable goods would no doubt be hidden somewhere in the cliffs to wait for transport inland on some other dark night – or at least that would have been the plan.

The storm might have changed things, but Magnus Firth wouldn't be dead, not when the devil looked after his own. Knowing him, I imagined he was still there, sheltering in a cave somewhere below the path, while he waited for the boat.

Sixteen

For some time, Bram had been pestering me about Robin Hood's Bay and against my better judgement I had agreed to go with him the next day. After our soaking on the cliffs, however, and the hours we'd spent talking before a revived kitchen fire, I'd imagined he would have preferred to postpone the visit. But the rain had stopped before we went to bed, and when we woke the sun was shining. Bram's mood, I felt, was much the same. It was as though the events of the night before had never occurred. Up early, cooking breakfast, he said it was a shame to waste such a glorious day, and, since I was just as eager to put those disturbances behind us, I pinned a smile on my face as I stood before the mirror and prepared myself to face a difficult few hours in Bay.

Some time later we were passing through town again, and once more taking the path along the cliffs. I was glad we'd breakfasted well. There was a searching wind blowing in from the sea, ruffling the waves far below and the heather above, reminding me that I'd walked this way too often before on an empty stomach, particularly the previous winter. From the twin headlands of Robin Hood's Bay ahead, right round to Saltwick Nab and Kettleness behind us, the seas were busy with billowing sails, pink and buff and brown, skimming their way northwards to the Tees or tacking down to Scarborough or the Humber, or even to the Thames. The sea was there alongside us, impossible to ignore, and even though most of the time we pretended to be studying the style of sails and rigging, hazarding where the ships were bound, what they might be carrying, I'm sure we were both thinking about the night before.

I'd told Bram about the Firths as we were drying out before the fire, hesitating at first over the worst details, simply because I couldn't find words to describe what Magnus did to his daughters. It was Bram who used the word *violation*, and that seemed to express everything. He was appalled, but somehow less shocked than I'd imagined he would be; he was even able to explain why Magnus Firth had never approached me, and why Bella was being passed over for her younger sister, Lizzie. It was a regrettable fact, he said, that some men preferred young girls. But for a man to violate his own daughters was truly unforgivable. In that light, Bella's rage – even the worst of her curses – had become understandable, a matter for sympathy. Nevertheless, he'd wondered, as had I, what incident might have prompted it . . .

We kept on towards Bay, coming out on to the road below Bank Top. The descent was steep as it swept down from there, but just as it seemed the road could become no steeper without being vertical, the chimney-pots and red roof-tiles of Baytown appeared, apparently growing out of gorse and grass at the very edge of the cliff. Gulls wheeled and hovered above the rooftops, while the cobbled road fell more steeply, to become a street of shops and houses, with footpaths leading off to either side.

It felt strange to be back home again, but I knew Bram would appreciate the miniature streets and tiny, cheek-by-jowl houses that made up Baytown. To me it was still the hidden, secret place of childhood, a maze of delights and constant surprises, of sunny, south-facing windows and back walls hunched against the cliffs and the weather; a place of hide-and-seek games and catch-me-if-you-can. In part at least. But where houses clung together for protection, the inhabitants were close neighbours indeed, and, while they might have prided themselves on being staid and upright citizens, not all were above listening to gossip. For that very reason I'd been apprehensive about going there, especially with Bram. The word would go round that young Damaris Sterne had been seen in company with a gentleman, and somewhere a connection would be made with Newholm and housekeeping. Before the day was over, no doubt Old Uncle Thaddeus would have had his worst suspicions confirmed.

But for all Bram's concern about being seen with me, that morning he gave no sign of it. He was ready to be charmed by Baytown, by what he called its ancient and romantic character, and insisted on seeing everything. I led him into the maze, past high stone walls and whitewashed cottages, up steps and through archways to all the surprise views I remembered. A mass of rooflines, a curving expanse of sea dotted with ships and fishing boats, all appeared in their minute variations like a series of framed pictures. It was a place popular with photographers and artists alike, particularly watercolourists, who seemed to enjoy setting up their easels in the least convenient spots.

Like every other visitor, Bram wanted to know why, when Robin Hood was supposed to be an outlaw of forests more than a hundred miles inland, he had given his name to this place on the coast. So I told him the forests were vast in ancient times, and anyway, the legendary outlaw had been summoned by the Abbot of Whitby to assist against a persistent band of Viking raiders. Robin and his men had defeated the raiders and earned not only a royal pardon but the right to reside by the sea at Bay, which place then took on his name to distinguish it from the older township, inland at Fyling. Nearby were the mounds known as Robin Hood's Butts, where his men had practised their archery.

With a teasing grin, Bram said the story was just about unlikely enough to be true; I was glad it appealed to him, but couldn't enjoy his good humour. I was too concerned about whom we might meet, and the closer we came to the Wayfoot, the more my anxiety increased. We passed the shops and the lifeboat house, and paused where the cobbled street became solid rock to provide a natural slipway into the sea. The tide was just on the ebb, beach and rocks were still well covered, but within the hour we would be able to walk along at the foot of the cliffs, searching for fossils and shells. It was the sort of thing visitors did, the sort of thing we could do without being remarked upon.

But Bram had different ideas. First of all, having spotted the Bay Hotel standing squarely on its rock overlooking the beach, he dismissed my objections and insisted on going in for coffee and hot buttered scones; and then, while perusing the scene from that vantage point, suggested we might hire a boat for an hour or so. It was something else summer visitors did, but local people didn't, and I felt very conspicuous approaching old Fred Poskitt and asking would he take us out for a trip on the water. Nevertheless, having decided to assume the role of local guide, I'd have felt worse letting Bram make the enquiries. As it was, I had to undergo old Fred's exclamations as to my sudden reappearance, all the enquiries regarding my health and present situation, and whether I'd been to see Mr Thaddeus. Of course I had to say I intended calling on him later, adding that I'd been very busy doing two or three jobs that summer which left me little time for visiting.

All the time I was silently cursing Bram, who was winking at me from behind Fred's back, but as the old man pulled away from the beach, he was soon distracted by the view. Mainly hidden from landward, Baytown made a pretty sight from the sea. I turned to look from time to time, although having no parasol I had to pull down the brim of my bonnet to shade my eyes. With my eyes half shut against the sun, I was aware that Fred was glancing behind occasionally, in the manner of all oarsmen; but then he looked, and looked again, and although his rhythm barely changed, we were both aware that something untoward was happening. Gulls were wheeling over a particular spot, their raucous cries drawing our attention to a group of three cobles between us and the skyline.

'Summat caught in t'nets, I'll be bound.' He rowed on, while Bram and I stared at the distant fishermen. Sunlight dancing off the waves made it impossible to see what had brought them together. 'Storm last night,' Fred declared, 'so't could be owt – bit o'wreckage, most like . . .'

We both nodded sagely. Bram and I had been talking earlier about tides and currents, about that southerly sweep from Whitby, and the knack wreckage had, within a few short hours, of fetching up in the Bay. Dragging my eyes off the sea, I asked about the quality and quantity of salmon being caught that season, and managed to keep on the subject of fish and fishing for another few minutes. After that, I could endure it no longer, and made the increasingly choppy motion of the waves an excuse for asking him to return to the shore.

The three cobles were ahead of us, and by the time we beached I felt genuinely sick. I had a horrible suspicion as to that fouling of the salmon nets, and, from his glance at me, so did Bram. We saw people gathering by the Wayfoot, and an ominous shape laid out on the slip.

'Drowned man,' old Fred muttered flatly, as he grounded the boat and helped us ashore. Dread leapt to my throat. The worst thing was trying to pretend we did not know who it was. But I had to look, I had to be sure. No good leaving it to Bram, who would have kept me behind him out of a misplaced sense of chivalry. He'd never set eyes on Magnus Firth, and I wanted to be certain.

It seemed to take an eternity to cross the beach. I felt my boots crunching on sand and shells, I felt the squelch of seaweed underfoot, but could not take my eyes from that group by the slipway. The gulls, determined and beady-eyed scavengers, were already alighting and taking a bold interest in the dead thing lying there.

Ghastly and somehow shrunken, his body looked so much smaller than I remembered, more like that of a dead seal than a man. But then I drew closer and saw his face, blanched, bloodless, streaked with weed and mucus, and marked by strange purple lines. From nose to mouth and between the brows, they made a hideous caricature of his face; but it was him, no doubt of that. Besides, I recognised his Whitby gansey, as would others too. Where so many drowned, the patterns were specific, to make identification easier.

I felt no grief for him, but had a light-headed moment of unreality in which I seemed to be looking down on everything from a great distance. I saw one of the herring gulls, a massive adult with a beak like bamboo, stride purposefully forward between the seaboots to take several vicious, darting pecks at the head before being kicked away by one of the fishermen. But others took its place, until someone dragged a tarpaulin across to cover the body.

Giddiness was replaced by horror, and as my gorge rose I had to turn aside to be sick. Bram was solicitous where I would have preferred to be ignored, but fortunately a constable from the police station arrived, distracting everyone's attention. Fred Poskitt took pity, and said we should go before officialdom started asking questions no one could answer; otherwise, we'd be there for the rest of the day. Needing no second prompt, I thanked him and made for the slip.

Left to himself, Bram would have lingered, returned to the hotel, most probably, and watched the proceedings from the bar. I thought it morbid, but he said he was curious to see how they did things in Bay; adding, with a wry downturn of the lips, that his friend Irving would have been fascinated. When in Paris, he liked to visit the morgue, to study the facial expressions of the dead.

Revolted, I strode away up the bank, needing distance and fresh air. There was a shop halfway, where I bought a quarter of mint imperials to sweeten my mouth; and then we continued together towards the station. We heard a train arriving with a swish of steam; it departed, chuntering, and a few minutes later the road was busy with a lively throng of visitors. I longed to tell them to avoid the beach, but as Bram said, for many the discovery of a dead body would be no more than extra excitement, something they could enjoy reading about over breakfast the next day. It was nothing personal to them, nothing to get upset about – except as a reminder, perhaps, that death waits for everyone, and sometimes in unexpected places.

He was probably right, but I kept wondering why I felt so weak about the middle, as though the breath had been punched out of me. After all, I'd feared Magnus Firth, even hated him a lot of the time; I might even have been forgiven for being pleased at his death. But I was not so much as relieved; indeed, I felt shocked, more fearful than ever. I might have started to fool myself that the storm and that violent argument were part of a nightmare, but seeing Magnus Firth dead on the beach proved otherwise.

Suddenly, Bram gave a muffled exclamation and said something I barely caught until it was too late. He stopped, while I turned and glanced back in confusion, to see him smiling and raising his hat to two elegant ladies of middle years, in pastel dresses and pretty hats. The elder of the two was a regular visitor to Whitby, and I recognised her at once as the wife of Mr du Maurier, the artist. In the very same moment, to my dismay, she cast her eyes over me. I felt naked, seen through, judged and found wanting, and knew that no matter what Bram said or did to cover the situation, this woman would not believe him. In one glance she had seen what she wanted to see, and needed no further proof.

I think he sensed it as well as I did. For form's sake, however, he performed a belated introduction, as though I meant nothing to him, was merely the daughter of people with whom he was staying. Conscious of my bruised lip, I forced a smile and tipped the brim of my bonnet against the sun, while Bram went on to explain in sepulchral tones the tragedy we had just witnessed on the beach.

'Most unfortunate, really, as Miss Sterne offered to be my guide today, and – well, it's been a little bit upsetting for her. So I'm escorting her back to Whitby.'

He did it very well, making me sound like the sheltered child of doting parents, but I fear Mrs du Maurier was too much a woman of the world to be convinced. By the time they were ready to move on, having agreed to explore Bay's tiny squares and footpaths before taking luncheon at the hotel, I was rigid with tension. As Bram raised his hat in farewell, I could see the band of sweat around his forehead. I wanted to clutch him, hang on to his arm, have him circle my waist in a declaration of unity, but instead we had to turn uphill and walk on, keeping a foot or more apart.

'Would you credit it,' he muttered under his breath, 'meeting those two *again*? Do you think they believed a word?'

I shook my head, unable to speak for a sudden fit of hysteria which insisted on breaking out every time I met his glance, or thought of the ordeal we had just been through. Not that it was funny in the least – indeed, the laughter felt very close to tears. It was cured, however, by another shock. As bad luck would have it, Bram was just buying our tickets for the train back to Whitby when I noticed a tall, white-haired gentleman in grey crossing the station fore-court.

Old Uncle Thaddeus.

With a frantic signal to Bram, I dived for the barrier. Fortunately, the ticket collector let me through on to the platform, where Bram, looking mystified, joined me a moment later. Just in time I was able to explain and issue hasty instructions; as Old Uncle Thaddeus appeared, I slipped into the ladies' waiting room until I heard the train chugging up the incline from Scarborough. I peered out, judging the moment when he would be too occupied in finding a free compartment to notice me boarding at the far end in Third Class. I dared not join Bram for fear of being spotted.

On disembarking at West Cliff station, again I hung back, wanting to be sure that Old Uncle was well on his way into Whitby before I headed along the road in the opposite direction. Bram was waiting for me on a public bench about a hundred yards away, considerably more cheerful than when we'd parted. He was delighted to have met the head of the family at last, and travelled with him on the train. Not only had he travelled in the same compartment, he had even engaged Old Uncle in conversation about his book on local history and folklore.

'He reminds me of Tennyson with that beard and those features,' he said warmly, 'and a little of the American poet Walt Whitman – although with those eyes, I swear he looks fiercer than either.'

'He's like an old Viking chief,' I said tersely. 'And he knows it. He should be wearing a horned helmet, never mind a top hat.'

Bram laughed at the picture, which made me smile too and went some way towards curing the alarms we'd both experienced that morning. On the way back to Newholm we even congratulated ourselves on our handling of one difficult situation – Old Uncle Thaddeus – and told each other that with regard to Mrs du Maurier there was absolutely no reason why she should doubt Bram's story, or the impression he had been at pains to put across. I don't suppose we were convinced by that, but we said it anyway. There seemed little more to be said about the body on the beach.

That night it seemed we had to take the way through the fields to Ruswarp, across the river, then along the riverbank past the haunted woods of Glen Esk and

Cock Mill. They were as eerie as ever, with sudden cracks and sighs in the darkness all around us. I clung to Bram's side, almost pushing him along; but even as I sighed with relief at leaving the woods behind, he insisted on taking a detour up to the abbey. Upset, I begged him not to go, but he could not be happy without spending a few minutes near that great ruin, or amongst the dead of the east cliff.

We took the hearse road, but somehow fetched up by Tate Hill, where a funeral procession was gathering. Dozens of fishermen in their woollen ganseys and great leather seaboots were awaiting the arrival of the coffin, although when it came it was more like a stretcher, carried by four closely shrouded figures. I was confused, but when I looked, I saw that the body was that of Magnus Firth, slumped exactly as we had seen him on the slipway that morning. A blubbery, bloodless corpse, with those indelible lines on his face. And Bram was saying to me: 'Is it the blood? The blood that makes the life? Davy Jones has taken his . . .'

He kept on and on repeating those words. And all the while I was begging him to hush as we followed the procession up the 199 steps, pausing, as the bearers paused, at every long flat coffin rest.

'Rest – rest? He'll never rest,' Bram whispered in my ear. 'They'll have to stake him down . . .'

The church was dark, not a glimmer of light to guide us or speed the departing soul. By fitful moonlight the procession ringed the ancient building, then moved out on to the cliff, to the very edge of the graveyard, where the vastness of the open sea beyond seemed endless and eternal. As we stood there gazing at the distant horizon, a great black hole appeared at our feet, the shrouded figures took hold of the body, swung it three times, and dropped it into the grave with a sickening thud.

All at once there came an ominous rumbling, a shaking of the ground like an earthquake. As we turned in panic, it seemed the whole cliff was collapsing, but from the shadow of the ruins careered a massive old coach drawn by six black horses, plumes tossing in the moonlight, mouths flecked with foam, hooves pounding through the graveyard. They came to a snorting, rearing halt, leaving a path down which came several figures in dripping oilskins. I smelt the dank smell of the sea as they circled the open grave; then, with the dead man walking between them, they returned to the coach. Moments later, the horses were off again and that sinister conveyance was thundering and rattling all the way down Church Stairs, to turn at the bottom along Haggerlythe. As we peered down from the graveyard, it plunged on, beyond the end of the street and over the cliff, to be lost in the foam below . . .

I felt myself falling with it, screamed out loud and awoke with shock. Those fearful images leapt at me from the darkness, so large and real and vivid I could not believe they were just a nightmare. Bram reached out to hold me and I fought him off; then all at once I was clinging to him like a child, trembling and whimpering in his arms.

'Tell me,' he whispered, 'tell me what it was . . .'

With returning sense I did, and in the telling recognised events from the day before, mixed with fear and anxiety and Old Uncle's old folk-tales. Aware of nothing more until late morning, I woke feeling thick-headed and confused. Then the dream came back to me like a thump in the chest, and at once I remembered Magnus Firth and his fall from the cliffs.

'You mean his murder,' Bram responded tersely when I said as much. Having woken him, my nightmare had kept him from sleeping again. He was edgy and there were shadows beneath his eyes. A crumpled pile of notepaper gave evidence of several restless hours spent working, but again, when I dared to mention it, I was wrong. 'Letters,' he said. 'I spent most of the night trying to write letters, and thinking of what I ought to do for the best.'

'What you ought to *do*?' I repeated in alarm, envisaging policemen, gaols and judges, Bella on trial for her life.

'*Yes*. I can't just sit here, like a rabbit in a trap, waiting for something to happen. Florence, at least, deserves an explanation.'

Weak with relief, I sank into the nearest chair and tried to stop a tremulous smile from broadening too far.

By the time I went down to the studio, news of the discovery of Magnus Firth's body was all over Whitby; and of course Jack had heard about it and was full of speculation. It took a vast effort of will to appear surprised, while I dreaded what might come next. I'd not been there long, however, when Isa Firth walked in, and it was a measure of my anxiety that I was more fearful than annoyed by her presence. That she carried a torch for Jack was something I had known for a while, and it pleased me to think it was not reciprocated. Under normal circumstances I would have been gratified to see Isa looking grim and a little red about the eyes, but this was different. Obviously, she had been called home from Middlesbrough.

I made a fuss of finding my knives and brushes, lighting the gas ring and mixing the glue, while steeling myself to offer condolences. As far as I knew, Magnus Firth's death was still a mystery, so it was all right to ask questions about what had happened, and how and when.

'Well, how can anyone know?' Jack said. 'He went out Monday night and was found Tuesday morning at Bay – drowned. He may have been caught in that sudden storm we had – anything could have happened.'

Very true, I thought, keeping my face turned away. 'I suppose he was out fishing?'

There was a pause, and when I dared to look at Bella's twin she was frowning and twisting her fingers into knots. 'No, the lads were out in the boat. He was on foot. On his way to, er, Saltwick, I think, to meet a friend.'

'Not a smuggling friend, by any chance?'

'For God's sake,' Jack hissed, glancing at the open window as though coastguards might be lurking outside, 'it's no joking matter!'

'And I didn't mean it to be. Don't forget,' I said, 'that I lived under his roof for almost a year. I know his habits, his comings and goings, just as well as Isa.' I turned back to her and forced the next question to my lips. 'Was he on his own?'

Again, she glanced down at her fingers. 'Yes.'

She knows Bella was with him, I thought; or, if she doesn't, she's guessed. Suddenly, the fact that Bella was not alone, that someone else shared my knowledge – even her sister Isa – lifted a tremendous burden. Isa might be sly and vindictive, but she was still Bella's twin, still a Firth, and she knew better than most what the whole family had suffered under her father's hand. 'Well, then,' I said softly, 'I dare say anything could have happened along those cliffs in the dark. Especially in that storm.'

'Aye, that's what I keep thinking.' As her voice cracked, her eyes reddened even more. Embarrassed, she turned away. 'Well, I'd better be going – Mam's on her own and she's upset. Thanks, Mr Louvain, for your help.'

'That's all right, Isa. Call in any time.'

'What about Bella?' I asked, my voice sharper than I intended. 'How's she? And the others?'

Isa shrugged. 'Lost without him,' she said with bitter irony, and for the first time I sympathised, knowing what she meant. They'd all hated their father, I knew that; but with him gone their lives had no direction.

Seventeen

Bram's moods had been unpredictable for some time, but with the posting of his letters home he became edgier than ever. One morning a couple of days after the storm, I took the opportunity of his absence to go through his desk. I felt ashamed of myself, but my curiosity was intolerable. He'd written to both Florence and his mother, I knew that, and I felt there might be copies, or even odd pages left from those I'd seen stuffed into the kitchen fire.

In his hasty writing were several loose sheets and my hopes were raised at first, only to be dashed as I realised they were notes on local folklore, or the beginnings of stories. One, with a first-person narrative, seemed quite extensive, and something about it caught my attention. I started reading, but for some reason it had been cut up. My frustration was intensified by the abrupt termination of each page and the lack of continuity between them. Nothing made sense. Crossly, I searched for more, until, on the point of giving up, I had the wit to connect a dried-up pot of paste at the back of the drawer with the odd pieces of manuscript. At once I examined a stack of books on the window ledge, and there, between novels and those volumes he'd borrowed from Whitby library, was a bound notebook with marbled covers, its pages bulging with the missing pieces of the story.

I thought it a most peculiar method of putting anything together but, surprisingly, it seemed to work. The story concerned a trio of friends, two men and a woman, travelling abroad on the Continent. To me, the narrator was Bram and, in spite of some obvious differences, I was able to recognise in the other two characters elements of Irving and Ellen Terry, and also the general circumstances of the tale, which seemed to take place in a fortified town in Germany. Nuremburg, I guessed, from the way he had described it to me previously. But in all the anecdotes, I recalled no mention of any grisly accidents in the torture chamber, although he had certainly described his visit there, together with the hideous items of persuasion ranged about the walls.

These were described in detail in the story – racks and boots, spiked chairs and beds to break the bones – but the worst item of all was the crudely shaped Iron Virgin, in whose embrace lay certain death. Complete with eye-slits and grinning mouth, this massive, bell-shaped figure had a hinged door, which could only be hauled open by ropes and pulleys. On the inside were long metal spikes, two to penetrate the eyes, and two beneath to pierce the heart and vitals. At the time of describing it to me, Bram had told how poor Ellen Terry, suddenly overcome by the horror of the thing, had gone to sit down, then with a shriek of alarm jumped up again, jabbed by the rusty spikes of a torture chair. Only her dress was damaged, but even so she had been upset and eager to leave. Irving, Bram said, had laughed about it; and then, oblivious as ever, he'd insisted on a minute examination of every instrument on show.

From all Bram had told me, I could imagine the man being exactly like the character in the story, brushing off all attempts to dissuade him, all concerns for his well-being, in his determination to find out *what it felt like* to stand in the shoes of a victim. And he would laugh – I could almost hear it – at the ropes and pulleys required to hold open the door, at the encrusted stains on those iron spikes within.

If the story was too realistic for comfort, the ending was gruesome. It left me feeling shaken, even alarmed by the darker recesses of Bram's imagination. I felt he'd used the story to illustrate some of the worst aspects of Irving's character: inflated pride and self-importance, coldness, insensitivity, and the heedless cruelty that can conceive of no possible retribution. I didn't know what Irving had done to Bram personally, but it seemed to me that he'd made him pay for his sins in the harshest possible way. In fact there were such strong elements of revenge in the tale that I found myself hoping I never had cause to disappoint him.

With a shudder I closed the notebook and pushed it back into place. But in my haste I disturbed the volume on Wallachia and Moldavia, and slips of paper, covered in Bram's scribbled notes, fell out as I tried to arrange things more neatly. I glanced at the names of those medieval princes, bloodthirsty rulers of a violent region, to whom instruments of torture would have been no more than playthings in the struggle for power. One who seemed to have written his name in blood was a Wallachian voivode who went by the name of Dracula. He had favoured impalement, on a grand scale, as a method of disposing of his enemies. It was said he was seeking revenge for the deaths of his father and elder brother.

I saw that Bram had underlined the word *revenge*.

That evening when I went down to the studio, Jack

told me that an inquest into Magnus Firth's death was to be held the next afternoon in Baytown. The news produced a strange effect on me. I felt compelled to be there, to witness the inquiry, yet I dreaded its conclusions. Most of all I dreaded seeing Bella, coming face to face with her, having to meet her eyes. I felt sure she would know what I knew, and that in some strange way it would damage us both.

In the end Bram and I decided to travel down separately, and to attend the inquest in similar fashion. I could go as a friend and distant relative, while Bram as a summer visitor was entitled to have a natural curiosity, having been there when the body was brought ashore. Even so we were both apprehensive. Bram elected to walk over in the morning, and to lunch at the Bay Hotel before making his way to where the inquest was to be held. I decided to go by train, and was so sick with nerves I could eat no more than a slice of bread beforehand.

In Whitby, inquests on the drowned were generally held in the nearest and most convenient public house, but so many bodies were washed up in Bay that there was a special place on the hillside at the edge of town, a low stone building that did double duty as a mortuary chapel and Coroner's Room. It was known throughout Bay as the Dead House and, though I'd always been familiar with the place, I approached it now with trepidation, all the while keeping a lookout for Bram and Old Uncle Thaddeus, who as a distant relative of the grieving widow, and pillar of the local community, was bound to attend. I was wearing one of my old summer dresses and a large pleated cotton bonnet of local style which had the advantage of hiding all my hair and most of my face. I did not want to advertise

216

my presence, or find myself in awkward conversation afterwards with any member of the family.

Judging the time with care, I waited until I saw Bella and Isa and the two older boys go in with Cousin Martha, and then joined a small group of older women sitting on public benches at the rear of the hall. Douglas and Ronnie sat with bowed heads as though in church, while Isa was looking round surreptitiously, but I could see Bella staring stonily ahead. She was wearing a severe black dress and matching cotton bonnet which lent her an air of rectitude. She was not looking at the coffin, and I didn't want to look either, but found I couldn't help myself. My eyes were drawn to it again and again, and every time, with the cry of seabirds overhead, I kept seeing that great herring gull, determined to peck at eyes and forehead.

Jumbled impressions of anger and darkness and the approaching storm invaded my head as I sat there waiting in the silence. Perhaps, after reading that short story and those notes of Bram's, I had vengeful motives on my mind, but I could not forget Bella's curses, nor that furious threat to kill her father.

I breathed deeply, fending off the memory. An accident, I told myself; it had to have been an accident.

A shadow loomed in the open doorway; I glanced up and saw Bram removing his soft-brimmed hat as he sat at the end of a row halfway down the hall. A moment later Old Uncle Thaddeus came in, attracting all eyes. He nodded to Bram and took a seat nearby. Someone coughed. A stray waft of air brought in the scent of new-mown hay from outside, and just as I wondered how much longer we would have to wait, a gentleman in a black frock coat entered briskly, set down his top hat and his papers on the table, and opened the proceedings without further ado.

I was surprised by the informality. The Coroner addressed the family, summed up the inquiries already made, asked questions of the local constable about the finding of the body, the coastguard about the tides, and Cousin Martha, Bella and the boys about the dead man's movements on the night he disappeared. Cousin Martha said that Magnus had left the house that evening apparently to do some line fishing from Saltwick Nab; but, when questioned, she confessed that her husband had been involved with smuggling in the past, and that his journey that night might have had nothing at all to do with fishing.

The Coroner's voice took on a particular gentleness when addressing Bella, and in a quavering response she admitted following her father through town – how my heart stopped at that! – as he'd forgotten his supper and she was trying to catch up with him. But she'd been caught in the storm near the abbey and lost sight of him in the torrential rain. She said she'd been frightened for him but had been forced to seek shelter, raising the alarm next morning when he failed to return home . . .

I let out a long, slow breath but dared not look up. We'd heard those violent exchanges: could it be that no one else had? But no one came forward and the Coroner did not press the case much further. In his summing up, he said that the possibility of Magnus Firth being involved with illegal activities at Saltwick Bay – such as the landing of contraband goods from Dutch or French boats – could not be ruled out. There was a possibility that he might have argued with one of these dangerous characters, and might even have met his death violently – but there was no evidence for that. The strongest likelihood was that on such a night, caught in the sudden storm, Magnus Firth had simply slipped and fallen to his death. And that, the Coroner said, was as close to the truth as anyone was ever likely to get. He felt, therefore, that he must record a verdict of accidental death.

For a moment I couldn't breathe. I looked at Bella, but she was just as rigid as before. Douglas took her arm and seemed to pull her to her feet as everyone stood while the Coroner left. Bram waited while other people moved to the door, and I followed him out. No one appeared to notice me, not even Old Uncle Thaddeus, who stopped beside the coffin to speak to Douglas and Cousin Martha. They were discussing the funeral, which was to take place in Whitby, and as I paused close by I heard Old Uncle making sure there were sufficient funds with which to bury Cousin Martha's husband. Bella and Isa walked out with their younger brother, taking the steps to the Wayfoot with Bram's tall figure just a few yards behind.

I wanted to speak to one or other of them, even to express the briefest and most conventional of condolences, but Bram and Old Uncle Thaddeus were somehow in the way. Instead I walked on to the Square, and stood for a moment or two looking at the tiny house where I'd spent most of my childhood. When I reached the station Bram was on the platform but so were several other people. He raised his hat to me and we kept the distance of mere acquaintances until our destination was reached. Even then, with West Cliff station behind us, we refrained from discussing the inquest until there was no chance of being overheard.

The following day replies came to two of Bram's letters, replies that were evidently not what he had hoped for. He sighed so much while reading them that I told him he was blowing up a gale, which raised a smile of sorts and made it possible for me to ask him who had written, and what had been said.

Unfortunately, the one from his mother in Dublin was hurtful as well as a severe disappointment. 'She's written so much herself,' he commented bitterly, 'that I thought she would understand my ambitions.' Sorting the pages, he read out sufficient of it for me to understand that Charlotte Stoker was calling her favourite son a fool and telling him to pull himself together before he ruined his life completely. I could hear the note of stern impatience in her voice – or was it Bram's voice, impatient with her? – as the words were read aloud. 'This kind of impulsiveness will be your downfall' was a phrase that stood out, while the letter went on to remind him of previous instances of foolishness, not least when he had married that girl Florence Balcombe without a proper engagement – and what her parents were thinking of to allow it, Charlotte could not imagine, except that they had even less money than the Stokers, and considered Bram to be some kind of prize. A delusion that must have been catching, she maintained, since he promptly gave up secure employment at Dublin Castle in order to become manager to a strolling player!

A few lines further on, he turned to me with all the pain and anger of a small boy. 'What is it about mothers,' he demanded, 'that they know so well how to hurt?' A moment later he added bleakly, in answer to his own question: 'Although, I have to say, she never thought much of either Florence or Irving, and made no effort to hide it.'

For a woman of such ruthless opinions, her reaction seemed mild. To my mind, the two of them were fortunate to escape with no more than bad reports, and Bram with a written castigation; but I did wonder what she would think of me, if we should ever chance to meet.

None of this boded well, however, and I was soon as cast down as Bram. I hardly dared ask about the other letter, and apart from telling me that it was from his friend Hall Caine, he said no more. In all that he had quoted, I felt conspicuous only by my absence, and I began to suspect that in sharing his plans to leave London and retire to Whitby as a writer, Bram had not mentioned me at all. With that realisation my heart sank further. Our future together was rapidly slipping away, while Bram made no effort, spoke no word, to make me think otherwise. He did not even look at me, perched on my stool by the kitchen table, but preferred to sit tensely by his desk, smoking one cigarette after another, as he stared from the window.

Paralysed by misery, I sat in silence. After a while I forced myself to move, but although it was sunny outside it was also blustery, and the wind made me shiver. Even the garden looked beaten. Somewhere below, hidden by a fold of the hillside, a train chugged along the line to Sandsend, puffs of smoke rising like signals to remind us both of the world beyond. For the past month we had managed to pretend that reality did not exist, but now it was pressing in on every side.

Panic clutched, and for a moment I could have fled from there. Then I turned to see Bram watching me from the window, his expression so precisely reflecting my feelings that I ached for him. That he was also balanced insecurely, between two very different worlds, was suddenly clear to me; I knew I had to fight for him, using every weapon I had. Why should I feel sorry for his wife, I asked myself deliberately; what was she to me? Not even his mother felt sympathy for her – a sense of duty, perhaps, but no real pity or affection. And an abandoned Florence would hardly be allowed to starve: she had too many well-connected friends and admirers. I had but one, and I needed him.

Lifting my chin, I forced a smile and went indoors, twining my arms around his neck and rubbing my cheek against his. The letters in their envelopes were on the desk before him, but although I dearly longed to read them for myself, I picked them up boldly and skimmed them on to the kitchen table. 'Take no notice,' I murmured against his mouth. 'What do they know? They don't understand . . .'

Whereas I did, of course; or at least that was what I was trying to suggest. That I knew him better than anyone else, knew his literary ambitions as well as his sexual inclinations, and was prepared to assist in one and satisfy the other. I was barely nineteen years old and thought I was so clever, so worldly-wise. I had learned that the sexual instinct could override many others, including the sense of right and wrong; I had learned that it could cross social and family barriers, and exist between members of the same sex; and I suspected it could also destroy those whose desires were constantly thwarted. If Florence was determined to spurn him, then Bram needed me. With me he did not need to pretend; with me he could be himself.

Determined to prove the point, like some old-style courtesan I loosened his tie and slipped my hand inside his shirt, teasing him with little nips and butterfly kisses as I worked my way downwards. My intention was to seduce him into bed where we could both enjoy the pleasures of the afternoon, but although he responded, he made no move to rise. Instead, he made it clear that I was to carry on,

222

and pushed me down on to my knees before him.

For the first time I felt like the whore that Bella thought I was.

Eighteen

In the past, a bit of teasing with mouth and teeth had been enough to arouse him. It was part of a game to which I'd imagined we both knew the rules. So far, and no further. But this time his arousal was slow, and he would not allow me to give up. I would have abandoned the game, but he made me carry on to the end. There were no words, no endearments, just a terrible intensity, and that final, choking conclusion.

Afterwards, he simply let go of me. I collapsed like a doll at his feet, then crawled aside to hide my face in my skirt. I expected some gesture of tenderness then, but he offered nothing. No comfort, no assistance, no apologies. His breathing was ragged for a while, then the chair legs scraped on the stone floor, and a moment or so later he said he was going out for a walk. I heard the door close. When he'd gone, I finally gave way to tears.

I felt shamed by what had taken place, and couldn't imagine he felt anything more than contempt for me. That scoured my pride as well as my affections. I blamed myself, and wept some more; but at last I managed to pull myself together sufficiently to wash my face and mend the fire. Then I filled up the water boiler so that I could take a bath.

Thinking things over, I turned to look for Bram's

letters in the hope of reading them, but even in his haste he'd remembered to pick them up, and their absence was like another insult. I told myself I hated him; but then it came on to rain. At first I was pleased, but the rain continued steadily and heavily, and after an hour I was worrying about him being out on the moors alone, envisaging him not only soaked to the skin, but slipping down some hidden ravine, injured and helpless.

It was a grim evening, but although there was no need for me to be at the studio, I was sorry not to have work as a distraction. I paced the kitchen, peered anxiously from the window, and kept trying to estimate how much time had elapsed since Bram's abrupt departure. Finally, I set about preparing our Saturday meal of rabbit stew. I wasn't hungry, but it was something with which to occupy myself; and anyway, when Bram did come home – and I told myself he would, of course he would, my imagination was simply working to excess – he would need something to eat. Curiously, in extremity I did all the things a good Baytown wife would do. And when I'd bathed, I even sat down to wait.

Darkness closed in early, and when he still failed to come home I began to feel afraid. What if he really was injured? Whom should I contact? I didn't even know in which direction he'd gone. Watching from the window I found myself thinking of Florence, for the first time sympathising with her, since I could imagine her sitting alone, as I was doing, wondering where Bram was, whether he was safe, and whether she would ever see him again. She must have done that every night for the past few weeks, I thought, feeling wicked and remorseful and in receipt of my just deserts. And what of the boy, Noel? Did he miss his father at tea-time, when Bram was usually home to play for an hour while Florence entertained her friends? Even now, was he praying for his return?

It was unbearable. I was so exhausted I went to lie down. I didn't imagine I would sleep, but some time later I was disturbed by movement and a light in my eyes. Confused, squinting, only half awake, I saw Bram at the edge of the bed, turning to give a sheepish smile as he undressed. As he leaned towards me I caught the powerful odours of beer and tobacco, and even in my confused state I realised he'd been carousing somewhere while I'd been waiting for hours, not only torturing myself over the rights and wrongs of our relationship, but about whether he was alive or dead.

'Where have you *been*?'

'I know, I'm sorry, it's late, but I bumped into Jack Louvain, and –'

'You've been at the studio all this time?'

'Oh no, not at all – been around town, in a few of the pubs, talking to some of the fishermen. Marvellous fellows, I must say –'

'But I thought you'd gone out for a *walk*,' I protested, scarcely able to credit such callousness, scarcely able to enunciate the words. 'I thought –'

'Yes, but it started to rain, and I could see it was set in for the night, so I came back through town, and that was when I bumped into Jack. He suggested we have a drink together, and well, you know, time just disappeared . . .'

Grabbing the patchwork quilt I did not so much turn over as fling myself away from him. I was so furious, I could feel my heart pounding and eyes pricking, but I would not let him see.

'Oh, come on, Damaris,' he said, as though the fault was mine, 'don't be peevish – one evening, that's all. I've said I'm sorry, but a man needs a bit of male company sometimes, you know.'

'That's got nothing to do with it,' I ground out between gritted teeth. 'I was worried about you. I thought –' Unable to say what I'd thought, I finished resentfully: 'Anyway, I made your supper – it's on the hearth.'

For answer he reached out to caress my shoulder. I thought he was going to find his ruined meal, but a moment later he was leaning across the bed and pulling me towards him. 'I'd rather have you,' he murmured huskily, sliding a hand under the bedclothes and feeling for my breast.

I was upset and he'd clearly been drinking; nevertheless, a variety of reasons told me not to object too strongly. Unwilling to drive him away again, I responded with a sulky kind of acceptance when he said he was sorry for what had happened earlier. I wanted to be loved and reassured, but even as I tried to draw him down beside me, he stripped the covers back and pushed my thighs apart. It was not at all what I had in mind, but after a moment or two I could see that he was going to fail. I murmured something to the effect that it didn't matter, and raised my arms to embrace him, but he forced them up, above my head, and with a sudden bitter groan turned to my naked breasts, sucking at them and biting in anguished frustration. Since I was not in the least aroused, the pain of this assault was not alleviated by any kind of pleasure. He bit again, harder, and it was like being stabbed. With a convulsive jerk I cried out and threw him off, kicking him as I rolled away and covered myself up.

It sobered him and he muttered an apology. I calmed down eventually, clinging to the far edge of the bed, persuaded to stay by a chilly sense of exhaustion and his fervent promises to leave me alone.

I must have slept, since dreams brought me to the

surface again. Erotic dreams in which I was being caressed by a faceless but persuasive seducer. Faceless because he was behind me, his mouth against my neck and the curve of my shoulder, his member hard and nudging rhythmically at the gap between my thighs. Then dreams became reality, and I was half giving myself up to this sleepy, sensual exploration, until that slow approach became a more serious offensive against unfamiliar places. One hand took hold of my throat and jaw, while the other grasped at the waist. He forced his way into me with short, sharp, ferocious thrusts. Tearing pain twitched every nerve-end, paralysing, turning everything to panic. I fought, bit, thrashed, in order to breathe, in order to be rid of him; but I felt impaled, pierced to the vitals, my shrieks reduced to a strangled protest. Within moments he was done, the gasping release of his climax scoring the agony of my humiliation.

I hated him. In retrospect there was a certain satisfaction in having bitten his forearm deep enough to draw blood, and elbowed him so hard in the stomach that he doubled up in pain. But that did not answer my disgust at what he'd done, nor my sense of shame that I'd acquiesced to such an extent beforehand that he felt entitled to go on treating me like a whore. This time he did not apologise, but simply shook his head and murmured: 'I didn't mean to do that.'

Hurt and angry though I was, part of me believed him. But I could no longer lie there beside him. Shivering, I retreated to the kitchen. My whole body ached. I felt used and soiled and in need of privacy. Streaks of blood indicated the loss of another kind of virginity, not one I had been aware of, but a violation, even so. Had I been alone, I would have drawn some water in order to wash myself and soothe my hurts, but day was dawning and the sea was waiting at the foot of the hill. I felt I needed its purification and reached for an old cotton dress, one I wore about the house. It slipped on easily over nothing at all. Taking a towel and a shawl, I walked out, leaving the door wedged open on the flagstones.

It was less than a mile down to the beach at Upgang, and I walked it blindly, with no thought except to plunge into the cold, cleansing waves. The tide was high, showing no more than a few yards of firm, dark sand; shivering in the chill, I discarded my things behind a rock and dashed into the grey water, striking out at once with strokes that took me far from the shore within minutes. The cold was numbing and I embraced it willingly, but my attempt to outrun pain was foolish, with the currents sweeping down from Kettleness and out into the North Sea. As the sun came up beneath a low ceiling of cloud, I realised how far out I was, rising and falling on a long swell, and how far down towards Whitby. The windows of the Saloon were glinting in the sunrise; beneath, the brightly coloured bathing machines were drawn up under the cliff, and suddenly all that I had ever envied and despised about the elegant and exclusive west cliff was very dear to me.

I felt the hot, bubbling rise of panic and quelled it fiercely, forced myself to discipline every breath and make every stroke count. As I turned for shore the distance looked impossible; more than once the ebbing tide seemed to be taking me further out. Swimming steadily and aiming for the railway bridge at Upgang, I knew the currents would probably bring me ashore nearer to the Saloon, but I dared not let them sweep me past the piers – or even close to town. Half drowned and naked on a Sunday morning at the beginning of the holiday season really would cause a scandal. I could almost see the faces of the pious on their way to early service at St Mary's, breathing hard as they climbed our local Hill of Difficulty with its 199 steps, staggering a little at the news, rushing to find a vantage point to see this naked young woman dead on the Scaur. Would they rush to cover me up? Would they think my death accidental or deliberate? Would they believe anyone could be so brazen as to swim without a stitch of clothing – or so stupid as to go out on an ebb tide? Such an event might even make headlines in the *Whitby Gazette*.

Ridiculous thoughts, but they kept my panic at bay. Oddly enough, I did not think about Bram until I was almost within reach of the shore, when every breath was like a knife wound, and the effort of swimming made my limbs feel like lead. I did not know how long I'd been in the water, but thought about an hour, an hour in which some people would be up and about, no matter what day of the week it was. I was glad that, it being Sunday, no cobles were out fishing and no collier-brigs unloading from the beach. Faced with death my nudity had been an amusement but, within reach of safety, all at once I was anxious not to be seen. I swore to myself that I would never, ever, swim again without a costume of some kind, be it only a shift between me and a charge of indecency.

My trailing limbs touched bottom not far from the Saloon. Keeping just within my own depth I summoned enough reserves to paddle my way along the beach until I was nearer the trestle bridge, perhaps two or three hundred yards, but the gap between sea and cliff had widened considerably. Desperate, incoherent, I swore and cursed with every rasping breath. Where was Bram, for God's sake? A man with the Royal Humane Society's medal for lifesaving should have been on the beach looking for me, ready to summon the lifeboat, if necessary. Where was he? Did he not care at all? Was everything a sham?

When I had the sense finally to give in, and allowed myself to roll ashore, I sloshed and scraped amongst sand and shells, barely able to lift my body out of the foam. But anger gave me the impetus to cross the intervening distance to my clothes. Trembling with cold and shock, I dragged on my dress, covered myself with the shawl, and sat down to recover. I thought I'd never manage the walk home, but after a while I was startled into action by the whistle of the early morning train, and its rumbling, rattling progress across the narrow ravine behind me.

The day was cloudy, yet my skin was tight with salt and my throat parched. I felt like a castaway, and my thoughts, which had of necessity been concerned with survival, turned all too soon to the disaster of last night. Shame possessed me, but I was sad too at the loss of something that had been precious. I'd loved him, really loved him, in spite of all my clever talk in the beginning. There'd been no need to explain myself, or worry what he thought, since he seemed always to accept me as I was, and to be just as easy with me, even though I didn't always understand him. Why did he have to spoil it? Together, we'd enjoyed so much; love as much as luxury, fun and excitement as well as the unexpected pleasures of domesticity. But I should have known, I told myself bitterly, that good fortune like that was never destined to be mine, especially when it involved another woman's husband.

And yet on the heels of that bitterness came the inevitable protest, the feeling that life was being grossly unfair, that surely I deserved some kind of happiness, and, if only I tried hard enough, it could

231

be mine. Could it be with Bram, though? Did I want it to be with a man who was not only married, but who used me in such a way?

I wasn't sure. Suddenly I wasn't sure about anything: about his love for me or my love for him, whether he enjoyed inflicting pain, or was just excited by the idea of blood, by its colour and taste and the living flesh from which it sprang. If I was honest with myself, he was beginning to frighten me, he was causing pain and disgust as well as pleasure, and I recoiled from thinking what else he might do if we stayed together. All the same, I was even more afraid of what might happen to me if we parted.

I felt it would be wise to talk to him, not be too impulsive. I didn't want to jump again from the frying pan into the fire. So with the sense that I'd made a very grown-up decision, I brushed the sand off my skin and tried to untangle my hair, sticky with salt and grit like skeins of drying seaweed. Fresh water loomed large on my list of immediate desires, to drink first, and then to wash in; and when my hair was clean and curling in the sun like soft red feathers, Bram would sit with me in the garden to brush it dry. He loved my hair, loved its luxuriant length and weight, loved to coil it around his fingers, pin it up, pull it down, wrap it sensuously around my neck; with his mouth against my skin he would tell me how very beautiful I was, how much he needed my love and understanding, how he would willingly promise me anything, if only I would stay . . .

Blind to all else, and thoroughly enraptured by my own imaginings, I saw nothing until I entered the garden, until I was faced by a strange-looking man with a vast, domed forehead and long, auburn hair. He was very thin and exceedingly well dressed. In his skeletal fingers he held a yellow silk handkerchief, one that might have been perfumed, since he shook it at me rather like someone fending off an unwashed beggar.

'No, I'm afraid you can't go in,' he said peremptorily as I approached the door. His arm, barring the entrance, tried to turn me away.

'But,' I protested, 'I live here –' Although I stood my ground, alarm and anger made me shrill. 'Who are you? Where's Bram?' I tried to push past him, to get to the window, but the thin man with the frighteningly dark eyes was stronger than he looked. 'What's happened – where is he? Bram!'

There was movement within, and voices, Bram's raised as he wrenched open the door. 'For heaven's sake, Tom, let her in!'

I wanted to fly into his arms, but something held me still. He reached for me and whispered, 'Where in God's name have you been? I was worried.'

'But not enough,' I said, drawing back, 'to come looking for me!'

His face contorted with sudden anger. Turning away, he glanced back over his shoulder into the shadowy kitchen, and I became aware then of another presence, a dark shape moving in my direction, with pale hands and patrician features. An unaccountable but chilling impression of power set me trembling again, and all at once I knew that just a short while ago I had been very close to drowning. The superficial warmth which had touched me on my walk home vanished, leaving the deep cold of the sea in my bones.

In a silent plea for Bram's hearty warmth and vigour, I leaned on his arm. A voice I hardly recognised as my own said feebly: 'I went down to the beach – to swim –'

'So I see,' he acknowledged, giving me no chance

to explain. He touched my hair with a certain dismay, which ordinarily, between the two of us, would not have mattered. But in front of these people – these friends of his with their fine clothes and perfumed handkerchiefs – the gesture held an intimation of criticism, of shame at my appearance. It cut deep and, as I drew back, he said with quick apology, 'I'm glad, though, to see you safe. I was just leaving the house to look for you when Tom and Irving turned up. Of all people – and at such an unearthly hour!' I could see then that he was agitated, and the nerve which had been a feature of the last few days was again jumping beneath his eye.

Tom – Thomas Hall Caine – forced a smile to his small mouth as Bram took my arm and led me indoors. He presented me to the shadowy presence within, a tall figure who turned slowly, and with maximum effect, to reveal shrewd, deep-set eyes and a thin smile that seemed to assess everything about me in one unhurried glance. His dark, slightly greying hair was worn long, and while the black frock coat and striped trousers would not have been amiss at Morning Service, the silk bow and richly embroidered waistcoat were perhaps a little too flamboyant for Whitby in the forenoon. But Henry Irving was as famous as royalty and could wear whatever he pleased, even the togs of a fisherman, if he should be so inclined, and still be thought no more than eccentric.

I have perhaps never been so aware of standing at a disadvantage. When meeting total strangers, both before and since, I have been brave, foolhardy, and sometimes even brazen; I've been cowed, shamed and furious, but never have I been so ill-equipped to meet a foe.

And he was a foe, no mistake about that. A man who could look me over in such extremity, and dismiss me with no more than a slightly raised eyebrow of surprise, was never likely to be on my side. That he regarded me as a member of the serving classes, and thus beneath notice, was obvious. It struck me afterwards that had I been dressed as a fisherlass and standing on the pier, then at least I would have been accorded some status as an object of interest; but as a skinny, scuffed, untidy kitchen maid I was apparently less than nothing in his eyes.

The truly infuriating thing, however, was that he had so little depth of sympathy with Bram, who was, after all, supposed to be his friend as well as a valued colleague. He was not willing even to scratch the surface of this situation to discover what was going on, or why it had all come about. Conversely, my own intuition was so heightened, I felt the conflicting power of unspoken agreements and manipulations, like the tug of currents and the battering of waves. But, having survived the earlier battle, I was aware that I was not best placed to win this infinitely more dangerous one.

Nineteen

It was clear that Irving was irritated by my interruption. To his credit, in that moment Bram displayed more concern for me than I expected. My dishevelled appearance, together with my terse explanation, had evidently registered, and with a brief apology he ushered me through to the bedroom and closed the door. I turned to him, babbling incoherently about the sea and the Saloon, about my nakedness and fear of drowning, about the awfulness of coming back to find his friends at the cottage, ready to kidnap him back to London. Holding me tight, he murmured soothingly and told me not to worry, he was going nowhere.

But if I looked exhausted and dishevelled, so did he. His hair and beard, once so short and well groomed, had been neglected recently, giving him a rakish appearance which had increased considerably after a sleepless night. And although he was wearing a jacket, he had evidently dressed quickly since he was minus a collar and tie. He was so far from being himself I was afraid of what might yet be agreed, and let him go reluctantly. A few minutes later, perched on the edge of the bed while forcing down a revolting combination of brandy and water, which he insisted I drink, I realised Bram had dropped something: a letter written in violet ink on pale yellow notepaper.

It was expensive and scented – jasmine, I think – and closely written on both sides in a neat, upright hand. My nose wrinkled suspiciously at the scent, but my elation at the signature was short-lived, since it was only one page of a letter from Florence, and what there was made me curl with embarrassment.

On a previous page, she must have been accusing him of taking her away from home and family in order to bring her to London – at the point, I judged, when Irving had bought the lease on the Lyceum, and suddenly offered Bram a job.

'We did not even have a honeymoon,' Florence wrote. 'Instead, you gave all your time and attention to your lord and master, abandoning me in the depths of winter, to fend for myself in London. And I was expecting your child! What did you care whether I was frightened or homesick or feeling wretched? You were never there!' Even allowing for some exaggeration, there was a horrible ring of truth to that, and I found myself feeling sorry for that girl – no older than myself – who had been lonely and friendless in a strange city. But Florence had not gone under. Over the years she'd learned to survive, and it seemed there had been some consolation in their social connections. 'I've learned to settle for what I have,' she went on: 'a comfortable home in which to entertain, interesting friends, and a moderately satisfying life of my own . . .'

She made it clear that she would cling by tooth and nail to what she had. Florence did not see why it should be disrupted, why she should be made to suffer in order that Bram might indulge a whim. If he wanted to write, let him write at home – she might even see more of him – and if he must have a mistress to indulge his carnal tastes, why not in

Kensington? All she asked was that he observe the conventions.

Carnal tastes! I might have pulled a face at that the other day, but not any more. Instead, I found myself wondering at the truth behind their marriage. He said she refused him – well, if that was true, *why* did she? And if he wouldn't force her, then why would he force me? Pondering the answer to that, feeling its bitter taste, I was distracted by the men's voices, Bram's unmistakable tones deeper and heavier than usual, Hall Caine's lightly accented, and, dominating both, Irving's rich, well-modulated voice, busy propounding who-knows-what irrefutable solution to the present dilemma.

I longed to know what they were saying, but my skin was itching and prickling with salt. Bram had brought in some water for me, so I stripped off to sponge myself clean from top to toe, trying not to wince at the bruises. There was little I could do about my hair, so I swept it up with combs, donning a skirt and blouse that I hoped was more in line with the Sternes of Robin Hood's Bay than the half-drowned kitchen wench who had greeted them earlier. Peering in the glass, noting the blue-grey shadows under my eyes, I dusted my face with powder, my lips and cheeks with a hint of rouge, and was pleased with the effect. I was intending to surprise them all by marching into the kitchen, when, with a gust of wind, I heard the outer door open and close, and the heavy murmur of men's voices ceased.

Peering between the curtains, I saw Hall Caine leaving, but as I furrowed my brow, conversation in the kitchen resumed. Then I heard my name mentioned, and despite the old adage about eavesdroppers never hearing good of themselves, I paused at that with my hand on the iron sneck. The old door had a triangle of ventilation holes at eye level, and from there I had a good view of the room beyond, of Bram with his back to me, seated beside his make-shift desk, and Irving with hands locked behind him, standing before the fire. From the silence and Irving's poised, predatory stance, I gathered that questions had been asked and he was waiting for the answers. With the outer door shut there wasn't much light at that end of the kitchen, and he looked pale and bloodless in the shadows, insubstantial as a photograph, a black and white figure shifting slightly against the cast-iron range and glowing coals behind. Yet his presence filled the room to overflowing. If this man were behind me at Cock Mill, I thought with a shiver, and happened to grasp my arm, I'd be looking for the marks of a cloven hoof . . .

By contrast, Bram was sunk in gloom, chin in hand, elbow on the desk. When he spoke I could feel his misery. 'I know, I know,' he said at last. 'I do understand – I just don't know what you want me to say.'

'But surely,' Irving intoned, 'you must have thought of these things?'

'Of course. The problem is, I've given my prom-ise.'

'And are you not *obliged*, my dear chap, to honour other promises previously given?' The voice was velvet, but the eyes probed and devoured. 'Hmm? To me, if you recall – not to mention to poor dear Florence, who is beside herself with anxiety.'

'Oh, for God's sake, Irving, let's leave Florence out of this, shall we? It's no use invoking her name, when you know as well as I do that you and she have been at daggers drawn ever since I brought her to England as my bride!'

In spite of what I'd just read, the depth of Bram's bitterness shook me; but I was glad to see that Irving had the grace to look discomfited. He turned away slightly, and, as he thought himself unobserved, I could see how carefully he watched and judged his quarry, how he shifted viewpoint but remained in charge; above all, how he tempered his performance to suit the situation. Now, turning back, he looked hurt, and managed to sound even more so.

'My dear chap, please understand that Florence and I drew up terms and came to truce long ago. She and I have learned to respect each other, just as we now respect each other's needs, and the time you spend with each of us.'

It was said simply and reasonably, as though they had every right to divide him up between them. Furious at that, I felt my fists curl and had to turn away. There was a rumble of disagreement from Bram; when I looked he had abandoned the safety of his desk and was running fingers through his hair in a distraught kind of way. 'Florence has her own life,' he said curtly, 'as you well know. She hardly needs me, except as part of the scenery.'

'Well, I beg to disagree there,' Irving said, with what seemed to me his first ounce of real sincerity. 'She says she loves you, and in that respect I believe her ... I know she can be difficult, Bram, but she is a woman, after all, and which of us can begin to understand the workings of a woman's mind?' He shook his head, and for the first time looked away, into the darker recesses of the kitchen. 'You're lucky, you know – at least your Florence has learned to be accommodating. In my opinion, most of them are destructively and certifiably mad. Look at Tommy, for goodness' sake – Rossetti I was almost able to understand, but this – this *child* he's involved with now. Blackmailing him, for heaven's sake, at the age of thirteen!'

The great actor paced the width of the hearth, looking genuinely angry and bemused. 'What is it about young girls, Bram? One can hardly call it innocence when they're up to sordid little tricks like that!'

I was still trying to work out what he meant about Hall Caine and blackmail, when he paused to look at Bram again. 'And this one,' he said quietly, 'that you're involved with – is she blackmailing you?'

For a solitary moment which seemed to stretch on and on, I felt my life was suspended. Even the blood paused in my veins, only to pound afresh with Bram's indignant denial. I fell back against the wall, barely able to hold myself up.

A scatter of rain against the window brought me to my senses; when the brief flurry passed I opened the casement, gulping at the damp, chilly air. How could this man, knowing nothing, suspect such a thing of me? I felt like a child, wounded, ignorant and helpless, and wanted to hurt him in return. I had visions of abandoning him on the cliffs at dark of the moon, or far out at sea in a small boat; but Bram always spoke of Irving's enormous nerve and courage, and, anyway, I found it daunting enough to think of him travelling all those miles – apparently overnight and presumably after a performance on stage in London – simply to see Bram face to face. That spoke of great stamina and determination. And friendship? But Hall Caine – why had he come? As Florence's emissary, I imagined, although I wouldn't have trusted a man with eyes like that. But perhaps she had no idea about the thirteen-year-old black-mailer? No doubt ladies were protected from such unsavoury details.

Suddenly, I was so cold by the open window, my teeth were chattering. I didn't want to hear any more, but as I dragged a shawl around my shoulders I was drawn back to my position by the door. In the next room Irving was doing his best to persuade

241

Bram that Whitby was just a backwater, picturesque perhaps, but nowhere near big enough for a man of talent and ambition. There was no scope, no cultural life, no —

'Don't you think I've had enough of cultural life in the last eight years?' Bram interjected. 'That's all I have had. There's been no room to breathe, to expand, even to *think*, for heaven's sake. Here at least I'm able to be myself – no one knows me, no one expects anything from me, and that's more of a relief than you can ever know.'

'Relief?' the other man echoed, with just a suggestion of contempt in his tone. 'You mean the relief of stepping off-stage, removing the make-up, taking a brief respite? Well, that's fine, my dear chap, as long as you remember that we need demands and expectations to draw out the best in us. Without expectations we merely exist, we do not *strive* – and without the striving, what are we? Animals, creatures, what you will – if we do not strive, we are not *men*.'

'I have striven, Irving – you know that. You, above all, have had my *best* . . .'

His voice was muffled but the emotion was clear. I saw that he had moved to sit beside the range, and that Irving was in the other chair, leaning towards him. 'I know,' he said, so softly that I had to strain to hear, 'and that is why our partnership has been so successful – because we have *both* given our best, and at all times. We've never stinted, never short-changed. We've worked harder in the last eight years than most men work in a lifetime – and we've *succeeded*, Bram. And why? Because you and I – *you and I, Bram* – have led, bullied and cajoled the best company in London. More than that, we've *made* them the best company. I beg of you – now we're established, don't let me down.'

It seemed he was poised for a long time, not moving, just waiting for a reply.

Bram sighed and shifted and shook his head. 'That's just it,' he burst out at last, 'you are established now, the Lyceum has a reputation second to none, and because of that you've been able to attract the best people – accountants, secretaries, press agents – to do all the jobs I used to perform single-handedly. You can afford to commission your own plays, and even to employ writers to straighten out the old ones. You don't need me, Irving, any more than Florence does. If I thought you did, I wouldn't have –'

Irving threw up his hands. 'Oh, my dear chap, you couldn't be more in error! It doesn't matter who or what I can afford! No one can edit a play like you – no one sees the essence of a plot as you do, and I swear no one else has your flair for pace and timing and the perfect dramatic impact . . .'

Well, I thought sardonically, you should know . . . But I believed him, anyway, and thought Bram would too. I was astonished when he denied it. 'Use Tom,' he declared, 'he's better.'

'No. No, no – you miss my point. Hall Caine is a fine fellow and a perfectly competent novelist, but he lacks the quality I'm speaking of. How can I describe it, except as a question of rapport? You and I have it, but with other people, I spend so much time explaining what I mean and what I want, it's generally quicker to do it myself! Anyway, with whom should I air my ideas but you?'

He had such fire, such sincerity, it was impossible not to be moved by those claims. Even I was convinced. When he reached out a hand and said: 'I can't do it by myself, old chap, I need you,' I expected Bram to be inspired, to offer emotional thanks for the honour and the vote of confidence. I was almost ready to give him up in such a cause. But I was not prepared for the force with which Bram flung himself out of the chair and across the room. Expecting the door to fly open I cringed against the wall. When I dared to look he was leaning forward over the desk, his face contorted; I could hear him taking harsh, rasping breaths that shook me almost as much as they racked him. Eventually, with great effort, he brought himself under control and said to Irving, 'And is that *all* I am to you? We were *friends*, once.'

There was such agony of emotion in those few words that I had to jam my fingers into my mouth so as not to make a sound. Knowledge ripped through me like a butcher's knife. He wasn't afraid of *London* – it was *Irving*, Irving he was running from, hiding from, battling with in the secret recesses of his mind. Irving who made his heart pound and lungs heave, who could wring that effort from him and edge his voice with such distress.

As he came out of the shadows, I saw concern in the older man's eyes, and heard it, thankfully, in his voice: 'I hope we are still – I hope we will be, always . . .'

Bram took a deep breath and steadied himself, but I could see the glint of tears on his cheek. 'That's been my hope too – but you know, latterly –' He broke off, shook his head, unable to go on.

'I know. I'm sorry. It's been my fault. We must set things right – make a return to our old style – what do you say?' Irving asked with a charming, almost puckish smile. Again he reached out, but this time Bram did not flinch away. At Irving's touch he turned and, with a single, wordless exclamation, they embraced.

The gesture was as brief as it was emotional, but the intimacy – even to Bram's lack of embarrassment as he dried his eyes afterwards – spoke of a closeness between the two that I could not have suspected. I felt shocked, jealous, excluded. I wanted to tear open the door, knock Irving out of the way, and enfold Bram in my own protective arms. But then I wanted to shake him too, to bring him back from tears and the marshy depths of sentiment to his former position of anger and resistance. I wanted him to stand firm.

Irving's voice was like silk. 'You've had a difficult time of it, I know, and I feel dreadfully responsible. The thing is, you have such a genius for organisation, you make everything look easy. I tend to forget how much is involved. In future, you must remind me.'

In future! He speaks, I thought furiously, as though all were settled, as though only his wishes were of any account, as though there had never been any real question as to the ultimate decision. No doubt he was accustomed to achieving his own ends, and to using whatever means came to hand, from cold professional discipline to this warm cloak of sympathy and charm. I willed Bram to reject that, to withdraw from the actor's seductive aura. But although he continued to voice words of protest, they lacked conviction. Somehow, in Irving's embrace, he had lost that wonderful vibrancy which had been so much a part of him, had become clumsy and slow, even physically diminished, as though the very marrow was being sucked from his bones.

Twenty

I had been so sure that Bram was in love with me, that it was possible to ensnare him with passion while his cold-hearted wife stood no chance at all. But standing there, clinging to the door, spying on my lover with the man who had ruled his life for the past ten years, I knew with absolute certainty that my rival was not Florence Stoker. By comparison with Henry Irving, Florence was almost incidental, and Bram's truancy with me was no more than an escapade that might linger in the mind, but sooner or later would be forgotten.

I felt crushed, ground underfoot, while he was locked in conversation, unaware. Despite his protests and explanations – about the fascination of Whitby, its extraordinary character and folklore, the writing he had been doing since his arrival – I knew an acknowledgement had been made, and because of that, Irving was prepared to listen. For a while at least. It was when Bram started to talk about me that I wanted to kill him. I felt he had no right to discuss me with anyone else, least of all Irving, even though he described me in such fulsome terms, I barely recognised myself. On his lips, I sounded like some paragon of new womanhood whose growth had roots in a distant, almost mythical past, leading a life as fascinating as anything portrayed in the stories he wrote. All nonsense, but even though I could not imagine Irving believing a word of it, such excess angered and embarrassed me.

Unable to eavesdrop a moment longer, I had to act. With no idea what I was about to say, I picked up the letter, unlatched the door and strode into the kitchen. They both turned, momentarily dumb-founded, and the effect gave me courage.

'By the way,' I announced to Bram, handing him the sheet of scented yellow paper, 'you dropped this.'

He stared at it, and then at me, before reaching into his pocket for the rest. Obviously taken aback, he seemed to struggle for words before saying abruptly: 'We'll talk later.'

'Why can't we talk now?' I demanded, my voice high with nerves.

Irving's timing was smooth, and I could feel his eyes taking in the changed details of my appearance and demeanour. 'We shall soon disturb you no longer,' he said with a slight, courtier-like bow. 'Hall Caine is merely changing our bookings for the return journey.'

I turned on him. 'And is that for two people, Mr Irving, or three?'

The challenge startled him, but, as if on cue, Hall Caine made his entrance, and my question remained unanswered. Then, as though by arrangement, Bram was immediately involved in conversation and I found myself ushered outside, into the garden. Henry Irving was the kind of man who concentrated absolutely upon the person he was with, and, having been forced to elevate me somewhat in the scheme of things, his attitude had changed considerably. Despite my antipathy, it was hard not to be aware of his charm. Or his looks. For he was tall and fine-boned and graceful, as handsome in the flesh as

Bram had described and far more striking than any photograph. He also possessed the actor's ability to use every asset to full effect.

I could feel the attraction he exerted, as well as a stronger element of repulsion. Even so, when he spoke it was hard not to be seduced. His voice was gentle, persuasive, reasonable in the extreme; if specific words failed to register, I imagine it was because I heard the message loud and clear: give up the fight, release Bram, let him return to his own kind. I tried to refute that, not because I thought Bram loved me more than he loved either Irving or Florence, but because I knew he had another side, other talents that were in grave danger of being bled dry by Irving's monumental selfishness and conceit.

It was a rearguard action at best, and in the end he overcame my resistance by the simple trick of taking me into his confidence. And the subject he chose was debt. Assessing correctly that a poor young woman would understand the horror of that, the obligations and the implications of owing money to the wrong people, he told me that Florence had always lived beyond her means, and not even Bram knew how heavily she had spent on refurbishing their new house. He had no reserves with which to pay her debts, but while he, Irving, was willing to settle the problem, he had to have Bram at the theatre. 'And please believe me,' he said, his voice deep with sincerity, 'I do need him. Bram is good at what he does. Very good. Do you think I would be here, begging for his return, if I could make do with anyone else? The Lyceum has been in chaos since he left.'

'Then treat him with respect, Mr Irving,' I retorted sharply. 'Not like you did before – and not like some flunkey you can replace at any time!'

With rueful laughter he acknowledged the rebuke.

'Yes, indeed, it's been a much-needed lesson – rest assured, I shall not forget! However, Miss Sterne, there are things you would do well to remember. Particularly this nonsense of his about writing for a living – which is all very well if your name happens to be Charles Dickens or even Thomas Hall Caine, turning out pot-boilers to capture the public imagination. But who knows Bram Stoker? If he had some kind of private income it might be feasible to retire to the country and do as you suggest, but he hasn't, you know – not a penny. He cannot afford this folly, my dear – believe me, he cannot.'

Sufficient doubt was introduced to dampen my convictions; and when, in a last-ditch attempt to hold on to something that had, in effect, already been torn away, I said I would accompany Bram to London, that too was dismissed as unwise.

'It wouldn't do, my dear, to take Florence's words at face value. For the moment she needs him, and is therefore prepared to say anything to get him back. But she could make things very difficult for Bram – and for you too. Besides, it wouldn't do him any good to be reminded of so many impractical plans, and promises hastily given – he would only be dissatisfied and unhappy. In these instances, I always think it's best to make the break complete, don't you?'

His arrogance appalled me. I wasn't an *instance*, for heaven's sake, I was a human being, and this was my life he was talking about. *And what about me?* I wanted to yell at him. *When Bram's returned to his old life and everything's back to normal for you, what do I do?* But something – pride, perhaps – held it back. That was my problem, to be dealt with later. In the meantime I was angry, and with the sense that nothing now could make things worse, I turned on him before he could walk away.

'Come now, Mr Irving, why hide behind Florence's skirts? You've got that poor woman where you want her – I'm the one you're not sure of, the one who might be too much of a challenge. Truth is, you don't want me getting in the way. You're just a tiny bit afraid I might have a hold on Bram, aren't you? That I might prove awkward, not know my place – that I might actually be a serious rival!'

He assumed a convincingly bemused expression. 'I don't understand what you're suggesting, Miss Sterne.'

'I'm not suggesting anything – I'm telling you I know your game. You're a cheat and a blood-sucker, Mr Irving – you can't bear to think of there being so much as a *drop* left over for anyone else, not even for Bram himself. Well, let me tell you, Mr Bloody Irving, you can have him – after all I've seen and heard today, I don't want him. I don't want a man who's willing to be used like that – or who uses me as a substitute for the thing he can't have!'

I wish I could recall a wonderful, resounding silence after that outburst, but by the time I'd finished I was trembling so violently with rage that I was aware of nothing but a need to get away. I stumbled towards the house, but ran blindly into Bram, who'd heard every word and was desperate to hold and deny and explain –

'Leave me be!' I cried, beating him off. 'I don't want to talk to you – I don't even want to *see* you! You disgust me. Get your books and your clothes and your fancy friends and just *get away* from here – back to London, back to where I can't see you. Go!'

He made some protest as I broke free, then caught up as I struggled with the gate, grabbed my arm and shook me before I could escape. 'Don't, Damaris, listen to me – don't be so foolish!' Harshly, he cried: 'It wasn't like that! Believe me!'

'No? So what was it like? What was it all about?'

'A mistake! It wasn't –'

'Oh, let go of me – I don't want to hear it! *Let go!*'

'Not until you promise to stay away from the sea.'

Laughter sprang from somewhere, a crazy, hysterical sound. 'Oh, don't flatter yourself!' I cried, with a violent effort shaking myself free. 'I've had one brush with death this morning – you needn't think I'd risk another. Not on your account, anyway!'

'So where are you going?'

'Out. For a walk. Alone. Just be gone when I get back!'

His arms dropped in defeat. 'You don't understand – it isn't what you think. There are things I have to do in London, which might take a while, but –' He broke off and took a deep, shuddering breath. 'I love you, and I want to return –'

'Don't,' I said harshly. 'I never want to see you again.'

Between rage and pain, I thought my heart would break. I fumbled my way through the gate and up the hill. When I turned he was still there, following me with his eyes. Just at that moment the sun broke through and caught him in a noose of light. His beard was like a flame, and I was tempted, fleetingly, to run to him, to be forgiven and held in his arms; but then I saw Irving behind him, poised and waiting, like the Gentleman in Black.

It was the middle of summer but I was terribly cold. I banked up the fire as though winter stood on the threshold, and drank cup after cup of black, sweet tea. I couldn't eat and I couldn't sleep. My mind kept going over everything, from the night I'd first given myself to him at the abbey, to those more recent moments before the storm. I'd wanted freedom, enjoyment, no responsibilities on either side. No

251

wonder, I thought, that with so much on offer he'd felt entitled to take everything, to possess me entirely and in every way possible, with hands and mouth, tongue and teeth, body and soul. He'd bitten into my flesh and tasted my blood; naked, he had covered me until our sweat intermingled and became one, until, at the last, he had succeded in penetrating me in every way. It was as though he'd striven to fill me with the essence of himself, in order to make me his own.

There was something frightening in the idea of such possessiveness, about moments of such physical and spiritual intensity. I didn't understand that need, but the more I dwelt on it, the more I pitied him. If Irving was the one he truly wanted, then it seemed to me that Bram was doomed to misery. Irving would tempt him constantly, giving only a little here and there, a look, a touch, a brief caress of approval, even an embrace where necessary. But that would be it. To give more would be to relinquish an important element of his power. And it seemed to me that Florence was using similar weapons.

Of course I didn't come to these conclusions immediately – I pored over the problem for years, returning to it again and again like an obscure mathematical equation, adding bits of information here and there, working at it until gradually a sense and a balance began to emerge. Sadly, to begin with I didn't understand at all, and dwelt on it to the exclusion of all else. I examined everything from every angle, and then went over it all again. I wanted to see where I'd gone wrong, whether anything I might have said or done would have altered the outcome. To do that, I felt I had to understand Bram, so I thought about him more than anyone else. Bella, I knew, would have called me an idiot, a dreamer, a time-waster, while urging me to get busy and forget him. But that was the difference between us. When the crisis came for her, she lashed out in pain and ended by killing someone. I preferred to waste time in doing nothing.

And waste time I did. The food I had prepared for us the night before stood untouched on the hearth. As I remember, it stood untouched for several days. Every time I looked at that pot of rabbit stew, my stomach threatened revolt. Unable to clear it away, I closed my eyes to it and survived on what was left in the larder: stale bread, a few eggs, some cheese. It was not until Mrs Newbold came down from the farm to ask why I hadn't collected the milk that I was surprised into more rational thought.

I was puzzled to discover that three days had gone past, while I had no recollection of having moved out of the kitchen or of going to bed. When I opened the door to the other room, everything seemed undisturbed; I looked down, and realised I was wearing the same clothes, now stained and crumpled, that I'd donned so hurriedly on the morning of Bram's departure. It was fortunate that Mrs Newbold had gone by then, because with that realisation I finally burst into tears. I wept for hours, wept until exhaustion claimed me, and then I slept on the bed we had shared, all night and well into the next day.

I woke with a sense of panic, suddenly aware that I should have been at the studio, that Jack would have been wondering where I was, furious to have been let down again when he'd warned me so strongly before. I looked at my clothes, raised a hand to my hair, and knew I could do nothing until I'd bathed and changed my appearance. The matted curls took so long to separate and comb that in the end, frustrated, I chopped off great hanks. By the time I had neatened the ends, several inches had gone and my hair was barely shoulder-length, but it felt better and I had no regrets.

I had to re-light the kitchen fire, and the water took some time to heat; while I was waiting I cleaned the cottage, stripped the bed of its linen, and threw out the mouldy, festering mess in the pot. After the shocks of that day, after the blankness and exhaustion and the torment that followed, a dull anger took hold of me. It gave impetus to my actions and, for a while at least, banished the lethargy of grief.

The side table with the two drawers which had been used as a desk was noticeably tidy, free of its usual collection of books and papers and pencils. I ran a duster over it, and then sat in Bram's chair, spreading out hands and arms in a kind of embrace, an attempt to conjure his presence from the things he had touched. But grief threatened, and I stood up at once, fighting off those useless tears. Almost as an afterthought I looked in the drawer, and found an open box of writing paper with envelopes and sealing wax. The topmost envelope, sealed with wax and penned in Bram's usual quick scrawl, was addressed to me.

My hands shook and something fell out as I unfolded the sheet of paper inside. *Please, Damaris, if you have loved me at all, look after yourself. The rent is paid until the end of August, and the enclosed should keep the wolf from the door – take it to one of the banks in town. If you need more, write to me at the Lyceum. Forgive me. My love – always – Bram.*

The first sentence held me. *If you have loved me at all* ... Oh, yes, I'd loved him, there was no doubt of that. Between tense fingers, the sheet crumpled. The enclosure, fallen to the desk, was a narrower slip, written and signed by Bram, but with the address of Coutts Bank printed at the top. For a long moment it seemed incomprehensible, but then it dawned on me that this was a cheque for £100, that it represented money he wanted me to have.

I sat there for some considerable time, just staring at the cheque. Had the amount been less, or in sovereigns, I think I might indeed have felt like a whore, being paid for services rendered. But because the cheque was so unfamiliar, because it did not *feel* like money and yet was so plainly valuable, I had no thought of destroying it. The enormity of the sum seemed almost mythical, even though I remembered Bram saying that leading players in the London theatre were earning upwards of £50 for one week's work. Just a pound to me was luxury, and I could manage on half that. All that money seemed ridiculous, excessive. Why had he left all that? To ease his conscience? To ensure my future?

I don't think it crossed my mind at the time that this money must have come, one way or another, from Irving. If it had, I would have burned it. I saw it then as Bram's money, Bram's gift, and, increasingly as time went by, as tangible evidence that he had cared for me.

But I was mystified, even a little afraid of that piece of paper, so I thrust it back into the envelope to be dealt with later. I hurried through my ablutions, dried my hair before the fire, and dressed myself for the studio.

Walking into town felt very strange. Knowing that for the first time I would not be meeting Bram after work, I felt bereft and anxious. I wondered what to say about his sudden departure and hoped Jack would understand my absence. As it turned out, my anxieties were unnecessary. When I reached the studio I discovered I no longer had a job.

Jack was apologetic, even sensitive in that he closed the inner door so that we could talk in private. I suspected Isa Firth was in the back room, probably helping out during my absence, but it was a shock to hear that Jack had employed her in my place.

'Understand, Damaris,' he said heavily, detaining me when I would have walked out without a word, 'I warned you before. I told you I had to have help, that I couldn't be let down again, but I haven't seen you for almost a week. You sent no word at all. I didn't know whether you were indisposed or just disinclined to come in – what was I to do? Why didn't you send a message through your friend Mr Stoker?' He drew breath at that, managing to look sardonic and disapproving at the same time; then, with what seemed a regretful sigh, he added: 'Isa needs this job, you see. Because of her father's death, she's looking after the family now.'

'Why?' I asked, feeling stabbed by the betrayal. 'What's wrong with Bella? She's always looked after them.'

'I don't know, I haven't see her – although Isa says she's taken it badly. Mind you,' he added with an expressive shrug, 'I understand she was always her father's favourite . . .'

'Yes – yes, she was,' I heard myself saying, although my lips were stiff with irony and disbelief. Jack's explanation might have been reasonable, but it didn't seem so to me. I'd imagined there was liking and a certain respect between us, yet he'd allowed himself to be manoeuvred into this situation by Isa Firth. She had taken immediate advantage of my absence, working on Jack until she got what she wanted – which was to be close to him. I couldn't bear to tell him why I'd been absent, that my friend Mr Stoker – and, after all, he was Jack's friend too – had gone back to London, and I was now alone and jobless. I took some satisfaction in thinking that since Jack had dismissed me, he must find out certain things for himself.

256

Apart from the cheque – which didn't seem to count – I had my wages from the last few weeks, some loose change in my purse, and thankfully no rent to pay. Even so, my work at the studio had been enjoyable, and I knew I would miss it. Jack too, although it pained me to admit it, especially when he'd shown himself so faithless.

I was about to leave when the door to the back room opened and Isa appeared. Jack turned and acknowledged her, then turned again to me. Behind his back, Isa smirked. In the circumstances it was like an obscene gesture. Wanting to rattle her teeth, I gritted mine and walked out.

Twenty-one

I had to see Bella. We were both grieving, both in need of sympathy, and I thought that mutual feeling might break down any lingering remnants of guilt on my part and pride on hers. But she was not at home. Lizzie was playing with her youngest sister in the yard, and when I asked said gruffly that her mother was out and Bella was at the pub. Discouraged by the news, I stayed with them for a few minutes, finding Lizzie as reticent as ever but somehow less hostile. Ever since that dreadful afternoon in the winter she'd done her best to ignore me; but while I talked to her, it struck me that although she still looked away she was no longer fearful. Not of me, anyway.

Wondering what to say about her father's disappearance, I tried to approach the subject tactfully, skirting round it as best I could, only to receive the kind of blunt reply that reminded me of her sister.

'He's dead,' she said flatly, 'and Bella says good riddance to bad rubbish.' And with that she grabbed the little one's hand and went inside.

Feeling thoroughly snubbed, I rose from my knees, dusted off my skirt and tried to think what to do. More than ever it seemed important to speak to Bella, even though I was reluctant to go searching for her in the pubs and taverns of the west side. Her old haunts had included several in the vicinity of Pier Road, so I tried each in turn, feeling strangely self-conscious and out of place. Men who once might have glanced and smiled in recognition now looked at me suspiciously as I poked my head round corners, disturbing games of dominoes and shove-ha'penny with my enquiries. Peering over walls of gansey-clad shoulders, I wondered where all the familiar faces were, and was uncomfortably aware that in a very short space of time things had changed. And for the worse, it seemed.

Backs were turned, I was no longer recognised, atmospheres were no longer welcoming. Or so it seemed to me then. In retrospect, I think the change was in me, not so much in my clothes but in the way I spoke and walked and held myself. Somehow, since leaving the Cragg I'd left behind the attitude and personality of a fisherlass. I had absorbed part of Bram's outlook instead. Or perhaps there was something in him that echoed the Sternes and Old Uncle Thaddeus, something that called forth a similar response in me. It was disturbing, but I could not escape the fact that my month with Bram had brought about some subtle alterations, not least in the way I viewed things. The old Neptune inn, one room almost invisible through a thick fug of smoke, was no longer a cosy refuge from the harbour winds, it was a choking hole where fishermen smoked foul-smelling tobacco and grumbled about the weather, market prices, and the ugly engines of the new steam trawlers. These trawlers raked up immature fish, they said, disturbing the spawn, maiming and mauling good fish until it was unfit for the table; they flooded the markets with rubbish and destroyed decent prices . . .

But I'd heard those conversations so often before I could have supplied the dialogue for both sides. It had always been better in the old days, when they were lads, or before the Dutchmen came; better somewhere else, with somebody else at the helm. Modern times were no good; nothing was right these days, not even the quality of stuff for making nets and pots. Once I had been sympathetic; once I'd been as dependent on every catch as they were, as the Firths had been. But now Magnus was gone, and I needed to speak to his daughter.

Impatiently I turned my back on the Neptune, and continued to the Three Snakes, so-called because of the emblem of three ammonites set into the wall outside, and when she wasn't there, went next door into the Star. It was a place of black beams, tanned walls and ancient barrels, of spittoons and sawdust and the odour of an old sailing ship, which, in spite of the dirt, was probably why it had always appealed to me.

Nevertheless, it had never been among Bella's favourites, so I was surprised to hear her voice and laughter from one of the back rooms. When I looked in, a little nervously, I was astonished to see her perched on the lap of a brawny young seaman, not local: that I could tell from both speech and attire. Dutch, I thought, and at once Magnus's smuggling contacts sprang to mind. Was this man one of them? Surely not, I reasoned; Bella would never be so stupid. Even so, her behaviour seemed shocking to me, simply because it was so far out of character. Her long hair was loose over her shoulders, and her throat was bare to the top of her breasts. I supposed she was drunk, but although I'd seen her drunk before, never had I known her be so free with a man, or so encouraging. His hands were all over her, and she did not seem to mind; and, when he pressed his mouth to hers, she did not push him away.

To my mind, it was just as well they were in a dark

corner, or the landlord would have turned them out. Approaching the table, I said stiffly: 'Bella, may I sit down? I need to talk to you.'

As she recognised me, there was a momentary flicker of guilt in her rich brown eyes, and then, as she slapped away those wandering hands, there came the frown of suspicion and disbelief. 'Well, what's up with you,' she said gruffly, 'coming in here on your own, after all this time? Where's your fancy man?'

'He's gone,' I said abruptly, taking a seat across the table. 'Anyway, I heard about your father. I just wanted to say I'm sorry.'

'Oh, aye – what for?' she demanded, her mouth narrowing. 'He was no friend to you.'

'Nor you, as I recall.' I held her gaze and let the words linger between us. 'I meant I'm sorry he's – gone. It must be difficult for you.'

'Aye, well –' She glanced away. 'We're managing.'

'That's not what I heard from Jack Louvain. Isa's taken my job – on the basis, as far as I can gather, that she needs it more than I do, especially now she's come home to look after the family –'

'Now just a minute!' Bella declared, striking the table. 'I look after the family – you ought to know that! And the way I heard, you walked out on the job and left Jack high and dry!'

'I did not!'

'But you will not leave me,' the Dutchman laughed, pulling Bella down again and planting a kiss on her bare neck. 'We have an agreement, yes?'

'Yes, later,' she agreed, grappling hands like tentacles while struggling to speak to me.

'Later, I go to my ship. Our agreement,' he insisted, 'is for now. So now we go, yes?'

He was a good-looking young man, clean, with a ready smile and a twinkle in his light blue eyes, yet

261

Bella looked on him with distaste. 'Aye, all right,' she said wearily, draining her tot of gin and rising from the table. 'Look,' she turned to me with a quick, apologetic glance, 'I've got to go with this lad – I've promised him, and you know what they're like. I won't be long, though. D'you want to wait for me?'

'Yes, all right,' I said hesitantly. 'Where? The pier?' I rose to follow them out, and the young Dutchman – who was surely more enthusiastic than serious – slipped an arm around my waist and drew me towards him.

'So, Bella – maybe I have your friend as well?'

He was laughing, but Bella dragged him away. 'You couldn't afford her,' she said with an edge to her voice.

Not until they'd gone, until I'd watched them turn the corner into Pier Lane to climb the steps to the Cragg, did I realise what he meant, what the agreement was, and what was about to take place between them. As the truth dawned I felt slow and stupid and angry – with myself for not realising at once, with Bella for lowering herself to that level, and yes – for including me in the same sisterhood. That felt like an insult, because I was different, Bram and I were different, we'd shared something –

What? I asked the question of myself, but could almost hear Bella's voice enunciating the words. What had we shared that was so special? He went when he'd had enough, just the same. No good saying it wasn't for money, either, because money – a very great deal of it – had been left behind for me as a sop to his conscience. I'd been used and paid, just as Bella would be in the next half-hour. In my case, the difference was in the length of time we'd spent together, probably no more than that.

I tried to be tough, just like Bella, but even tough

thoughts hurt. I discovered very quickly that calling myself every kind of fool made no difference at all. I told myself I hated him, but I ached with loneliness, still wanted to be with him, still longed to hear his voice, whether brisk in hearty greeting or soft and lilting with love. Even the twilight reminded me unbearably of our walks together, and I wondered whether I would ever again look up at the east cliff without expecting to see him waiting there. Everywhere, things were in their usual places, yet not the same. If I had looked with new eyes while showing the town to Bram, discovering in the process a pride and knowledge I hardly knew I possessed, in his aftermath everything had changed again. It was as though the vibrancy had gone, leaving no more than a lifeless shell, a trick of the eye, a shabby stage-set for actors who were playing to a different tune.

A few visitors were strolling along the harbourside, but they were mainly men; more were out along the pier, watching the movement of fishing boats on the horizon and a couple of sailing ships anchored off the bell-buoy, waiting to come in with the tide. There was the usual group of older men at Coffee House End, solving the world's problems, and women and girls hanging about the Battery, most of them gossiping, knitting socks and ganseys, enjoying the fine evening while waiting for husbands and brothers to return. But for the first time that mundane scene seemed less than innocent. I was aware of those on the very edge of the group, who might have been chatting, but whose eyes were on every passing male. Standing provocatively, with hips pushed out, necks and ankles well exposed, they were poised to catch the most fleeting interest. Amongst them I recognised a couple of girls who lodged near Jack's studio but who posed regularly for someone else, and, as I watched, they attached themselves to a pair of fashionable young men who were evidently heading back into town.

There was nothing new in it, I'd known plenty of girls talk men into having their photographs taken at the end of the pier, and then go off with them afterwards for a drink in one of the local taverns. But somehow, before, it had always seemed no more than a laugh, a way of getting visitors to part with their money. I'd never done it myself, preferring a small gratuity any day to lewd suggestions and wandering hands. As far as I knew, Bella had been of the same mind, and we'd sneered at the other girls for fools, never thinking – well, I didn't – of further transactions taking place.

But they did, of course, with monotonous regularity; and knowing made all the difference. I thought of Bella suffering attentions that must remind her of her father, who surely would have killed her for going with another man. Instead, either by accident or provocation, she'd killed him. As a consequence – and with what irony! – she was now entertaining men for money in order to keep the family together, whereas before she'd entertained her father in order to keep the peace.

And meanwhile Isa had taken my job.

If I could have swapped the twins, persuaded Jack to take Bella and installed Isa at the Three Snakes as a kind of public convenience – always providing her knees could have been prised apart – I might have been a happier woman that night. As it was, I watched and waited for Bella until it was almost dark, and when she did not come I returned alone to Newholm and the empty cottage.

The following morning I went into town again, this time to take my cheque to the bank. Not to turn it into cash, but to keep it safe against the day when I might need it. Knowing very little about bankers or banking, I went to Chapman's on Low Lane. I'd heard they were Quakers, committed to fair dealing, and besides, Jack Louvain banked there and I'd never heard him complain.

Nevertheless, it was a nerve-racking exercise. With no previous experience, I had only the vaguest idea how to go about the business of the cheque, and the hushed interior with clerks on high stools made me glad of my new blouse and skirt. These gave me a veneer of confidence at least. A clerk came to the counter and peered at me from over his pince-nez. He bade me good morning and asked what he might do for me, so I handed him the note and said I wished to open an account.

He seemed to stare at it for longer than was necessary, and I thought there was a moment of question or surprise, although it's been my experience since that bank clerks and cashiers are rarely surprised by money, in whatever form it appears. Perhaps it was the fact that I was a new customer, young and female, fiddling nervously with gloves and shopping basket. He informed me that I would have to open an account first, before the bank could accept the cheque; and that I would not be able to draw against it until it had cleared.

'Cleared?'

'Until it has been established, miss, whether the signatory has sufficient funds in his account at –' Somewhat ostentatiously, I thought, he peered at the cheque again – 'yes, at Coutts Bank.'

I felt the colour rise to my cheeks. I hadn't thought of that! What if Bram's open-handed generosity failed to match the truth of his situation? From what Irving had said, that seemed all too possible. What a fool I was! I swallowed hard and said, rather faintly, 'Yes, I see,' while wanting to snatch back the note and run. But there was no chance of that. The clerk had my cheque for £100 and was determined to keep it on his side of the counter. Even more alarming, he wanted to introduce me to the assistant manager, who, he said, would take down all my details for the opening of this new account.

But why bother, I felt like saying, if the cheque is worthless? With that thought denting my confidence even further, I had to go through what seemed a pointless rigmarole – and pay out good coin into the bargain – just to open the account. The assistant manager – Mr Richardson, a kind-eyed, quietly spoken man – asked what I thought were a lot of questions about this sum of money, not how I'd come by it, but what I wanted to do with it once the cheque had cleared. It was rather a large sum, he said, to be left idle, and went on to suggest that I might like to consider investing part of it for higher returns.

I hesitated, wanting to respond in a positive way, yet too unsure of myself. He waited, then suggested gently that I should think about it for a while, and then we could talk later. I seized on that gratefully. Only as he saw me to the door did he remark upon my name, and ask whether I was closely related to the late Damaris Sterne of Robin Hood's Bay.

Relieved that the ordeal was almost over, I replied at once. 'Yes,' I said, 'she was my grandmother.'

'I thought so,' he smiled. 'I remember you when you were a small girl, visiting my mother at Bank Top. She was Rachel Sterne before she married – do you remember her?'

I froze. For a fleeting moment I had a clear picture of old Aunt Rachel, in a shiny black dress and elaborate white lace cap, wielding a stick as she ordered the servants about from her invalid chair beside the fire. She'd been a ferocious old lady who'd terrified me; I could not imagine this softly spoken, middle-aged man as her son.

My surprise must have shown, because he said: 'Mother suffered a lot, but she always appreciated your grandmother's visits.'

That surprised me again, since I could not imagine the old lady appreciating anything, much less the visits of a poor relation. But I thanked him anyway. Then Old Uncle Thaddeus sprang to mind, and I was alarmed at the thought of him knowing my business.

My new friend – or I should say, relation – must have been adept at reading his clients' faces. Before I could frame the words, he was assuring me of the bank's discretion, and a level of confidentiality which equalled that of medicine and the law. So I crossed the threshold into Low Lane feeling much lighter and more confident, and it was not until later, when I was going over the entire interview for the second or third time, that I started to dwell on the possibility of the cheque being worthless.

In bed that night I felt angry for worrying, telling myself that it was not possible to lose something which I'd never possessed; but the idea of that £100, and even more, the possibility of making it grow into larger amounts, was exciting. If I could not have the security of marriage or the protection of a man who loved me – and it seemed to me then that I'd forfeited both – I told myself I'd better find my own hedge against the future. Money was a form of protection in itself; it was also an escape route and a means towards other ends. I fell asleep making plans, each more grandiose than the last, and all dependent on the backing and growth of that unexpected farewell gift. It stopped me thinking of the man who'd given the money, and where it must have come from.

*

In the clear light of day, however, it seemed more practical to concentrate on finding some temporary work. The Penzancemen were beginning to arrive, in large, two-masted fishing luggers which – with the Peterhead boats a little later – came every summer to fish the great shoals of herring feeding off the coast. From late June to early October the Scots and Cornish boats anchored inshore during the day, and fished at night, their riding lights like glow-worms in the dark, bobbing here and there across the horizon. They were a welcome sight, not just for the pretty view they presented offshore, but for their numbers and the trade they brought. They filled the harbour when they came in on Saturdays, the crews shopped for supplies and slaked unquenchable thirsts in quayside taverns, worshipped in local churches, and drew fisherlasses from Scotland and Northumberland to deal with the fish they caught. The lasses followed the shoals of herring down the coast and worked the summer from port to port, taking board and lodgings with local families. On their heels in August came the regular holiday visitors to Whitby, train-loads of day-trippers as well as the wealthier families with retinues of servants.

With holiday accommodation at a premium, I considered taking in a couple of lodgers, but was reluctant to offend Mrs Newbold by breaking some rule of occupancy. Nevertheless, it was a good time to go looking for work as a waitress or housemaid, so again I prepared to do the rounds of hotels and boarding-houses on the west cliff. This time I was successful in obtaining a position at a small hotel, where one of the young chambermaids had suddenly walked out. I soon discovered why – the housekeeper was a tyrant, scarcely more civil to guests than she was to staff. But I'd suffered worse, and my weeks of rest and good food had replenished both stamina and resilience.

I had the feeling it pleased this sour-faced woman to have young and pretty girls slaving over menial tasks, since she seemed determined to make the job more difficult than was necessary. But if the hours were long and the rules petty, at least an aching back took my mind off a severely bruised and battered heart; and there was an added bonus in such long hours, in that I was generally too exhausted to think at the end of the day. I would fall into bed about sunset, and rise just after five to be at work for six o'clock, when the morning rounds of cleaning, tidying and bed-making would begin. All the upstairs rooms had to be done, including corridors, lavatories and bathrooms; afternoons were devoted mainly to sorting linen, mending, and ironing, and I was free to go home by five in the evening. I earned ten shillings a week plus breakfasts and dinners. Tea I took at home.

More to the point, I had no need to break into Bram's cheque, which cleared, thankfully, within ten days. All the ideas I'd had in the winter, when money was short, were suddenly within my grasp but, for a little while at least, my nerve wavered. When Mr Richardson asked what I would do, I said I was not yet ready to do anything; I needed to think and plan. Approving of that, he gave me some ideas to think about. Inevitably, the ones I favoured were those to do with shipping.

Twenty-two

I woke, about half-past four it must have been, to a bedroom flooded with light. Awake and alert, with my heart pounding crazily, I was suddenly aware that my plans were likely to come to nothing. In all this time I hadn't thought of it, but I should have had my monthly visitation at least a week before Bram left.

Trying not to panic, I told myself that the shock of his departure – never mind anything else – was enough to stagger the most reliable cycle, and mine had rarely been that in recent times. During the previous winter, cold and constant hunger had played havoc with everything, and I hadn't had so much as a show for three months. Then, when it did come, it came like a spring flood when the snows have melted and the moon is full, and I was afraid to leave the house for a week. I told myself that the opposites of too much food and self-indulgence were bound to have similar effect, and – completely ignoring my relationship with Bram – that it was foolish to worry. But all the time it was there in the back of my mind, colouring everything I did, taking the edge off every plan I made.

Waiting, wondering, it was difficult to be sure of anything, and I could only guess at being two to three weeks overdue. At the hotel I ran up and down stairs, and worked so hard I earned a stiff smile of approval from the housekeeper. Nothing helped, however. Beside myself with anxiety, and afraid to confide in anyone else, I had just decided to go looking for Bella when she turned up one evening at the cottage.

She apologised for having missed me by the pier as though it were yesterday, and then complained that the cottage was too well hidden, it had taken her an age to find. She seemed determined to criticise but I could tell she was impressed, especially when I suggested sitting outside in the garden, and then served cake and glasses of lemonade on a small tray. I wondered why she'd come, what it was she wanted, but all she would say was that she had to get out of the house, and was sick of the local pubs. Sick of men and booze, I judged privately, since she looked haggard, even in the soft evening light. Her eyes had that feverishness which spoke of desperation and too little sleep, and I had the feeling she'd not rested for a long time. Despite having so much on my mind I wanted to comfort her, offer sympathy, ask what on earth she was doing, going with men for money, when she detested men so much. I longed to confide in her, but found myself asking banal questions and uttering the most mundane of comments. Having put a seal on my tongue in respect of her father's death, it was as though I'd lost the power to break it.

Eventually my banal questions led Bella to ask me about Bram and, almost before I realised, I found myself telling her I thought he'd left me with a child.

There was a horrified silence, in which she stared at me open-mouthed; and then she raged and railed, for all the world like an outraged parent. A moment later she was hugging me and kissing me and saying she was sorry. Sorry for everything, I think, but then I was sorry too.

'You could try a half pint o'gin and a hot tub,' she said, casting a critical eye over me. 'It's been known to work if you're not too far gone. In the meantime I'll have a word with Nan Mills – she'll see you right, don't you worry.'

'In what way, though?' I asked dubiously. Nan Mills lived at the top of the Cragg, and was the local midwife as well as being renowned for her 'herbal remedies', specifically for female complaints; all very well, but other, less salubrious things were attributed to her, always in whispers, and generally behind closed doors.

'Nay, not that!' Bella assured me, as though she'd divined my thoughts. 'I meant her special *mixture* – tastes foul,' she added with a shudder, 'but it'd shift an army. I know – I've had some. And more than once, so don't look so gawpy.'

Foolish I might have looked; stupid certainly I felt. Things were coming out that I'd never known about Bella, that she'd never even hinted at; although from the way she'd lived perhaps I should have guessed. I found myself wondering whether the horror of recent experience had reduced all else to the level of minor transgressions, so that none of it seemed so bad any more, not even touting for custom in local pubs. But that was only one of the things I would have liked to ask. With everything bubbling at the forefront of my mind, I was almost afraid to open my mouth for fear of letting out the wrong thing.

Looking for a safe subject I asked about the family, and she told me the lads were still fishing, although it was harder on their own and she didn't know how they'd manage in the winter. Or if they'd manage at all. Douglas, the eldest, was talking about shipping as crew aboard a collier or timber ship, or maybe even finding a berth on one of these new steamships out of the Tees. He just wanted to get away, and his brother with him. She didn't blame them, and nor did I. Whatever they did, we both knew would be no harder than fishing, and could not be more brutal than life with Magnus Firth. The independence he'd clung to and held out like a carrot to the boys was barely more than a myth, when against the value of owning their own coble must be set the sheer precariousness of such a life, and the fact that alone, without their father, their chances of survival were even less.

At mention of Magnus there was a small silence, and then I found I couldn't avoid the subject any longer. Clearing my throat, I asked awkwardly: 'About your dad, Bella – what really happened that night?'

She stiffened and looked away from me, out to sea, at all the sails, large and small, between us and the horizon. Then, with a shrug, she said, 'Well, like I told them at the inquest, he was off to meet somebody at Saltwick – smuggling, I dare say, you know what he was like. There was a storm blew up – I think he got caught in it, and either missed his way and fell, or part of the cliff collapsed. If you think about it, really, it's the only thing that could have happened . . .'

It was all so plausible. 'And did they search the cliffs?'

'Aye, they did. But like I said to the constable, when he asked me did he have any enemies, I said my father had nowt else but. And that's true, as you well know. They'd have better asked, did he have any friends . . .'

Silence stretched between us. Longing for her to confide in me, tell me the truth, I asked then whether

273

the police had suspected anything remotely untoward. Whether in spite of the verdict they'd thought
Magnus's death had been anything other than accidental.

She turned to me and moved her lips in what was
more a grimace than a smile. 'Nay, Damsy, I don't
think so.'

For a moment – just for a fleeting moment – I
almost said: 'You were lucky then, weren't you?' But
even as the words were forming on my lips I felt
them stiffen into silence. She didn't want to tell me.
And if she knew that I knew, was there not a
possibility that she might see me as a threat? I told
myself that it was an unworthy thought. But I kept it
to myself, nevertheless.

Bella brought gin for me next day, which was my
afternoon off, and together we heated the water and
prepared the bath. For at least two hours that
evening I soaked and sweated and protested as Bella
kept the heat up and the gin flowing. Red as a boiled
lobster and as maudlin as Cousin Martha at her
worst, I was finally allowed out, weak and dizzy, to
stagger to my bed. The night passed in a drunken
haze of spinning lamps and window frames, and I
remember being very sick several times. Bella stayed
the night and I was vaguely aware of her in the bed
beside me, but that was all. Nothing happened,
except I had a monstrous hangover next morning,
and spent most of the day in the outside privy.

Only after I'd recovered from that foolishness did I
start to think more clearly. If I really was carrying
Bram's child – and that doom-laden thought was
beginning to outweigh everything else – then it was
time to start making plans. Bella's confident asser-
tions about gin and herbal mixtures sounded as
reliable as her preventive measures, which had been
considerably less than effective. I was beginning to

274

realise that other people's advice was not always a substitute for good sense, and for too long I had not been utilising mine.

As I discarded false hope, it seemed my choices were bleak. Abandoned, with a child to care for, it would be all too easy to fall back on the Firths, sliding into the habit of joining Bella in places like the Neptune and the Three Snakes as she touted for business. If that idea made me flinch, I turned abruptly from the thought of leaving any child of mine with the likes of Cousin Martha, to be dosed with gin every time the poor mite cried. That seemed infinitely worse. The best I could do would be to swallow my pride and throw myself on Bram's generosity, and trust that he would be willing to continue his support.

It was a gamble, but the alternatives were far riskier. There was no point in being hasty. As he'd said I could, I wrote to him at the Lyceum, not to mention my condition but to thank him for the cheque, which I assured him was now safely invested at the bank. He'd always said that he took his holidays in August, and I ventured to suggest that he might spare me a day or two to talk things over. It was important, I wrote, and I needed a quick reply – a simple yes, or no, would do.

He would be busy, I said to myself as July wore on, as I hurried home each day to look for his reply. I even took to asking Mrs Newbold, when we met, whether any letters for me had been delivered to the farm; but that was a dangerous exercise, as she was already looking on me with suspicion in her eyes. At the end of the month she started reminding me that the rent had barely four weeks left to run, and, when I said loftily that I would continue to pay if she would but advise me of the sum required, she snapped back that the agreement had been with the

London gentleman, Mr Stoker. If he required the cottage for another month or more, then that would be acceptable, but the owners would not thank her, Mrs Newbold, for letting out their property to some chit of a girl who was no better than she should be.

Stung, I retorted: 'We'll soon see about that!' while my face flamed with guilt and fury. I flounced off in the direction of the cottage to write another letter to Bram, this one tersely phrased, to the effect that I needed his agreement to keep the roof over my head. A week later, all discretion was abandoned, my phrases to the point. I was expecting his child, I said, and didn't know what to do; would he please contact me at once.

I thought a reply would come by return, but when nothing came by the end of the week, I was forced to reach the conclusion that he had no intention of contacting me.

I felt hollow. Well over a year had passed since I'd walked out on Old Uncle Thaddeus, and, instead of improving, my situation was infinitely worse than it had been then. I was carrying a child, my job was uncertain, and it seemed I was about to be turned out on the streets. Disgust overwhelmed me. I was ashamed of my own blind foolishness, and angry too. I even suspected that Old Uncle was right and I was wrong. Had I been possessed of the right degree of humility, I could have gone to him and apologised; I might even have begged his help. But I was both too proud and too ashamed for that, and, more importantly, didn't trust him not to come up with some means of punishment specifically designed to break my will. Instead, feeling desperate, I went to see Bella, and Bella went to see Nan Mills.

That was the worst mistake I ever made. It was nearly the last, too, but by then fear and recklessness had mastered good sense. Before I met that appointment, however, I went to the bank on Low Lane to speak to Mr Richardson about investments. While I was there I mentioned to him my problem about the cottage, and managed to imply that the owners' agent was having difficulty accepting a young woman as a responsible tenant, and that my previous guarantor was no longer in a position to help. Although it was not my intention at the time to play the part of a weak, defenceless and misjudged woman, that aura must have been clinging about me. I could not help but notice the speed and concern with which Mr Richardson prepared to spring to my aid, and before our interview was over he had noted all details and was making arrangements to pay the next month's rent from my account.

'But I shall have to find fresh accommodation before the end of September anyway,' I told him, 'and a new job, I'm afraid. What I'm doing now is purely temporary.'

'And what are you doing now, my dear?'

I mentioned the Misses Sterne at Fylingthorpe and explained that I'd been trained as a ladies' maid, which calling I'd followed until my grandmother's last illness called me back to Bay. Since then, I said, a combination of fortune and misfortune had led me to my present position at the hotel, which was as temporary assistant to the housekeeper. The claim was inflated and a risk of sorts, since he could have checked up; but I had the feeling he liked me too much for that. There was no need to fake emotion as I went on to tell him I thought it was time for me to leave Whitby and start afresh elsewhere.

But I had plans for the future, I said, and with regard to my £100 I wanted it investing at once, in something with a chance of good return. At that Mr Richardson raised his eyebrows and asked whether I understood the risks involved; his advice to me would be to start small, and build up to the point where I could afford to lose a little. But I cut him off, and with a tight smile said I wanted to invest all my money in shipping. I was prepared to spread the risk over two or three local owners who were always advertising shares in Baltic and North Sea cargoes, but I would like one of the ships to be the *Lillian*. Whether from sentiment or superstition – or simply as an antidote to my own sense of recklessness – I felt the need to hold on to something, and Jonathan Markway, aboard his 'good seaboat', was the safest image I had.

'It's a gamble, I know, but less so at this time of year. And anyway,' I added coquettishly as I gathered my things and prepared to leave, 'don't you think we come from a long line of gamblers in Bay? My father and grandfather gambled with their lives – and lost. This, after all, is only money . . .'

On that piece of heresy I left, emotions high and my heart beating so frantically I thought it would burst. It was a fine, warm afternoon, and the bridge was busy with townsfolk and visitors, all having some reason for crossing from one side of the harbour to the other. Ladies with parasols jostled elbows with Scottish fisherlasses in headscarves and greasy aprons; smart young men in blazers dodged between elderly couples and invalids in bathchairs. Seamen and shipbuilders, coastguards and harbour officials, were all going about their business that afternoon quite unconscious of the reckless young woman in their midst, who had persuaded herself that the stakes were high enough to warrant risking all for a future free of shame and poverty.

With Jonathan on my mind, I was startled, walking through town, by the glimpse of a young man's reflection in a glass window. He looked so much like

278

him, for a moment I was stopped in my tracks, torn between apprehension and a rush of foolish longings. But then he moved and, when I saw his face, the resemblance to Jonathan was slight, mainly a combination of youth and colouring, of curly dark hair and tanned skin, which seemed so prevalent amongst the Cornish fishermen.

Offshore, the Cornish luggers were idling at anchor in the heat of the afternoon; watching them, I found myself wishing I could turn back the clock. Jonathan's occupation, which had seemed such a drawback to begin with, now seemed no problem at all. I could even see advantages in being married to such a man. With the feeling that I'd give anything to start afresh, I wondered where he was, whether he still thought of me, and, laceratingly, what he would think if he knew what I'd been up to, the state I was in as a result.

Reluctantly, I went back to the cottage. I knew I should eat, but there was no fire and it was too much trouble to light. Instead I cut a piece of cheese and buttered some bread, slaking my thirst with a glass of water. Why hadn't Bram replied to my letters? He'd written so much, surely he could spare me a few lines? Like the thud of a steam hammer the questions banged at me as I looked at his desk, his chair, his view from the window. But none of the answers made sense. Even if my letters to him had gone adrift, I felt if he loved me at all he would have written anyway, just to ask how I was faring without him.

But that was always the point where emotion took over from logic, when I had trouble controlling my grief. I swear, if I'd had any intimation that I still mattered to him, that there was some chance of his continuing to care what happened to me, then I would not have gone ahead with what I was about to do. But with no word at all, I felt I had no choice. Life was hard enough alone, but with a young child, ostracised and unprotected, not even £100 would take me very far. At the end of it, I could see nothing more clearly than the workhouse, and I was too proud to contemplate that.

At sunset I picked up the few things I'd been asked to bring, together with a sum of money, and set off for the Cragg. Bella met me at the top of Cliff Lane – no more than a stone's throw from where Bram and I had first kissed all those months ago – and we went along together from there. It wasn't far, but as soon as we were out of sight of the road we stopped to drink from the bottle she'd brought. The neat gin tasted oily and perfumed and made me want to vomit, probably from nerves as much as recent memory: it took an effort of will to keep it down. The second swig was easier, the third I barely noticed apart from a lingering shudder as we arrived at Nan Mills's house and knocked at the door.

The house, like so many on the Cragg, was tall and narrow, tucked into the cliff between neighbouring roofs and walls, somehow managing to give an impression of solitude and secrecy amidst that rookery of homes and workshops and lodgings. As on my previous visit I was impressed by its cleanliness in an area that was generally poor and often less than cared-for. Even the outside walls were recently whitewashed, giving a cool blue tinge to the warm summer shadows and providing a foil to pots of flowers and herbs ranged along the window ledge. Inside, it reminded me of my grandmother's house at Bay, with scrubbed stone floors and white deal tables, an array of pewter plates and utensils on painted shelves in the kitchen. It was hard to imagine anything illegal going on in such a place.

Despite the warm evening, a small fire was

burning and a kettle steamed gently on the hob. Nan Mills in her white cap and apron reminded me of the children's nurse at my first place of work, and I wondered if that was what she'd been, and why she was called 'Nan'. But if she sought to give an impression of uniformed efficiency, better that than the smiling, slovenly, half-drunken carelessness of a Cousin Martha.

She'd been pleasant enough a couple of days previously, when it was just a question of asking questions and conducting a brief examination to confirm what I already suspected, although her tone had changed once she understood what was wanted. Even then she'd been keen to assure me that the operation was simple; the only problem being that we had to be discreet. If she agreed to do it, then I must swear not to implicate her under any circumstances. This had been said as much to Bella as to me. Now, grimly, with the door shut and the kitchen lamps lit, she asked whether I'd brought the money. I had, and in the collection of coins I tipped out of my purse lay the equivalent of three weeks' wages. I suspected that Nan Mills charged as much as she felt her clients could afford, and was thankful I'd not told Bella about the cheque.

She took one of the lamps and indicated that we should follow her up the circular staircase to the floor above, where a small back room was closely curtained against prying eyes. There was a long table, such as might be found in any good kitchen, with layers of newspaper spread over it, and a wooden chair and wash-stand to one side.

To my surprise, having expected a bed, I was asked to climb on to the table and lie down with my knees up. Nan folded back my skirts and placed a thick wad of paper beneath me, then turned aside to wash her hands. She told me to spread my knees wide, and, when I hesitated, became impatient. 'Come on now, we don't want to be here all night.' The hands that pushed my knees apart adjusted the set of my ankles, and then moved in from there. To my intense discomfort and embarrassment, she placed one hand on my abdomen while pushing the other inside me, feeling and probing with fingers that had no respect for my tender parts. On that unforgiving table I felt naked and exposed, just like a goose at Christmas subject to the prize-fighting fists of the cook. Bella was seated on a chair, head down and chewing her fingernails, obviously preferring not to watch. I didn't blame her at all. Trying not to wince, I bit my lip instead, all the while fearful of what I could feel but could not see. It seemed a nonsense to be told to relax, but at last, as Nan withdrew her hand I heaved a great sigh of relief, my ignorance thinking the whole thing was over.

But as I moved she stayed me with a dry laugh. 'Nay, lass – we haven't started yet.'

From a cupboard in the wash-stand she took out a slim leather bundle and unwrapped it. My heart leapt with fear as I saw scissors and a thin knife, and long metal instruments that looked like meat skewers, or flexible crochet hooks. Bella shook her head and reached for the gin. This time I almost snatched the bottle out of her hand, took one hefty swig and then another, the thought of sick hangovers infinitely preferable to the ordeal I was about to go through.

Fear made it worse, of course. And being threatened. Nan Mills made it terrifyingly clear that if she was to perform the operation safely, I must keep very still indeed. She had to find the neck of the womb and insert a probe in order to pierce the membrane; she did not want to pierce me by mistake, she said, just because I was stupid enough to wriggle at the wrong moment.

Putting the gin aside, Bella took my hands instead. I was intensely thankful for that, as I was shaking so badly I began to be afraid that a sudden twitch might kill me. Nan arranged my knees to her satisfaction, then felt inside me again, all the while telling me to push out, not clench up. The next moment I felt something graze me deep inside, something at once sore and sharp that prompted an involuntary clenching of every muscle. Bella gripped tight, but, even as I whimpered with fear, it was over, the hand was sliding out and my stretched and bruised parts were miraculously flexing back into place.

While I lay there in a haze of gin and dizzy relief, with tears pouring down my face, Nan Mills issued instructions I was incapable of taking in. Then she took her instruments and went downstairs.

Bella helped me up and wiped my face. 'We've to go down – there's some medicine she wants you to take.'

I groaned at that but was beyond protest. My legs felt like twine and just as likely to wrap around one another, but with Bella's assistance I managed the stairs. Nan was pouring boiling water into a cup, and I thought gratefully of tea. But it was a herbal tea, a spicy, slightly bitter drink of raspberry leaves and ginger, that she said would help the action of the womb. I was to take it three times a day for a week, and must expect a heavy flow of blood.

Feeling dizzy and confused, I clutched the packet she gave me, and found that we were outside in the darkness. Bella put her arm around me and suggested going back to her house until I felt better, but I suspected I might feel worse before that happened, and anyway, I couldn't bear the thought of the chaos and the children – or of Isa's prying eyes. I wanted peace and quiet, a measure of order and cleanliness, and, most of all, what I had come to think of as my own bed.

Fresh air sobered me, and in spite of everything we managed a reasonably steady progress back to Newholm. Bella insisted on staying overnight and I was glad of that; the bleeding had started and we were both apprehensive, not knowing what to expect. Next morning I felt weak and unwell, but elected to go to work as usual, and, having lately impressed the housekeeper with my diligence, was able to gain a little forbearance for my malady. I said it was something I'd eaten, which gave me an excuse for frequent visits to the privy, where at least I could sit down for a few minutes. By mid-afternoon, however, although the bleeding had stopped, I had pains in my stomach and back and was beginning to feel light-headed. One of the other girls took over the ironing and made me sit down in the linen room. Not long afterwards I keeled over in a swoon, and came to on the floor.

The housekeeper was not pleased by the inconvenience, but, after issuing several dire threats and warnings about taking time off for illness, finally gave me permission to go home. By then I was feeling too ill to care. For a while I sat on a public bench on the west cliff, wondering whether to go looking for Bella who had gone home that morning, or to carry on to Newholm. In spite of the distance the latter seemed easier, certainly more straightforward, if only I could keep on putting one foot in front of the other. How I managed to cover those two miles I'll never know, but after many stops along the way I staggered down the path and into the cottage.

I remember going into the scullery and pumping water into the ewer. I remember it being too heavy for me to lift, and feeling distraught because I knew I had a fever and needed plenty to drink. Everything hurt and my ears were buzzing and all I wanted to do was lie down and shut my eyes, but I had to have that water. I drank some, poured some more away, then lurched across the kitchen with it. In the bedroom, shivering violently, I started to undress, but was suddenly seized by agonising pains. Nausea gripped, then came the urge to evacuate, so powerful it was all I could do to get to the privy and sit there through spasms of agony, groaning and gasping for breath, convinced that I was dying.

And without Bella, I would have died. Not quite then, perhaps, and certainly not from the pain alone, but I could not have survived the ensuing fever without constant care and attention. Although my memory of the next few days is unclear, I know Bella arrived at the cottage not much more than an hour or so after me. She said she'd been worried all day, and after waiting near the hotel about the time I should have left, finally plucked up courage to call at the tradesmen's door and ask for me. When she heard the tale from one of the kitchen maids, she set off for Newholm at once, running most of the way.

I owe her my life for the way she looked after me, for cleaning me up and putting me to bed, for nursing me so well and so unfailingly through the delirium that followed. The fever kept me in its grip for days, with endless dreams of water and falling, of bloody wounds and accusing fingers, hissing snakes and erotic visions that turned into nightmares of rape and impalement and dead men walking. Amidst the parched desert of my agony I had moments of clarity in which I recognised Bella, anxious and hollow-eyed as she bent over me, feeding me water from a spoon, or wiping the sweat from my face and breast. Then I would drift away again and be terrified, surrounded by pale, drowned faces with seaweed hair and sightless eyes, or black-clad devils with pitchforks, prodding me back into the flames.

But it wasn't the devil who had me in his grip, nor even Henry Irving at his most sinister. It was, in effect, childbed fever, which had snatched my mother's life away, and came so close to taking mine.

Twenty-three

That summer was the last I spent in Whitby. Looking back, certain moments stand out vividly, moments that had nothing to do with Bram, except that that summer everything had something to do with him; yet when I think of it now, even our involvement was like an echo of something that had its origins before I was born.

I remember standing on the bridge, watching the fisherlasses along the quay, knives and fish flashing in the sun as they worked the great troughs of silver herring, gutting and packing so fast their hands were impossible to follow. They were cheerful, confident, a joy to watch in their short-sleeved, bright woollen jumpers, with arms and faces bronzed by the sun. Their voices carried across the water, the accents of the Scottish girls reminding me of my mother, bringing a lump of longing and loneliness to my throat that was underlined by my loss of Bram. In need of comfort and reassurance, I remember wondering whether that young woman who was my mother would have understood the anguish of my predicament, or castigated me for its foolishness.

I hoped she might understand; after all, she had fallen in love with my father who, like Bram, belonged to a different class, educated, property-owning, used to a life of ease far above the impoverished existence she'd known as a girl. On the face of it at least. The realities may have been closer than either side liked to admit, but even in households where cash was tight and income heavily committed, there were degrees of pride and gentility, accepted codes of behaviour that people clung to in spite of everything. Grandmother certainly did, and I can imagine my father as a young man burning to rebel, longing to flout all domestic rules and restrictions, particularly after finishing a long and disciplined apprenticeship at sea. He'd met a beautiful girl and fallen in love; and, like some medieval knight, was determined to rescue her from a life of brutal work and poverty, no matter what anyone else had to say.

There must have been opposition, although, if his nature was anything like my own, opposition was probably the thing to harden him. I'd always believed in crossing barriers and breaking conventions, which was why I felt such sympathy with my young and wayward parents and longed to emulate them. A least that was how it seemed at the time. Now, all these years later, I wonder whether it was simply a matter of loneliness and deprivation, of trying to get close to my mother and father by imitating their experiences, their codes of behaviour, their ways of life.

Being young, however, I did not see the pitfalls. The eagerness which led me to embrace life with the Firths swung like a pendulum to land me in the arms of a married man twenty years my senior. There's no doubt that I was dazzled, in love, passionately enthralled; but it strikes me now that I was also looking for a father's love, that I wanted the luxury of being spoiled and cared for, the sense of comfort and protection only an older man could provide. I trusted Bram more because of who and what he was. But that only made the betrayal worse.

Looking back, it still seems strange to me that my brush with death should have been so similar to my mother's. Common enough, some might say, in women of child-bearing years, with nothing so strange about it, except in the recovery. Nevertheless, it was an experience which affected me profoundly, leaving me feeling intensely vulnerable and as though I should waste no more time on hopeless causes.

I knew I was lucky to have survived that fever. In my mother's case, with a stillbirth following so closely upon the shock of my father's death at sea, it's possible she lost the will to fight; but there again, perhaps she simply lacked a nurse with Bella's skill and determination. And that was extraordinary in itself. Even though Bella seemed to have spent half her life supervising her mother's confinements, or nursing the younger children through measles and whooping cough, and the older ones through injuries with fish-hooks and knives, I never thought of her as a nurse. So much had been done from necessity, and so much was resented, I could hardly credit being the recipient of such voluntary dedication. We had been friends, yes, and in many ways very close indeed, but I believe now that there was more to her actions than that – certainly far more than I was capable of understanding at the time.

Afterwards, when I was recovered enough to be aware of how ill I'd been, how close to death I'd stood, but still feeling weak and very much afraid, she kept thanking me for getting better, for pulling through, simply for *living*. Reasons which seem so obvious now – that I was the life saved, the debt paid for the one taken – were then misunderstood. I thought she meant that my survival was important to her future. God forgive me, but I thought she was intent on binding us together, and that scared me. Things had changed dramatically since Magnus's death – Isa had returned and was taking over, the boys were planning to leave home, and Bella was no longer needed to stand guard between her father and the rest. She was released from her post, freer than she had ever been in her life before. The trouble was, she had no thought beyond the morrow and did not know what to do with herself. And I thought she was relying on me to provide her with a new role.

I'd had my moments of thinking it might have been easier to die, but with survival came euphoria and a desire for freedom. Alive and aware of it, I was intensely grateful for what Bella had done for me, it was just that I could not envisage the future with her by my side. I wanted to, I tried to, but in truth I wanted freedom more. So I was burdened by guilt as much as gratitude, and wondered how on earth I could ever discharge my debt.

A decision was required more quickly than I could have imagined. Mr Richardson wrote from the bank to say that one of his father's far-flung relatives from Bay, a widow who was also one of his clients, had contacted him regarding a new companion. Her present young lady would shortly be leaving to be married, and Mrs Addison wanted another Baytown girl, because to her they were always like a breath of home. She was getting on in years and wanted someone about the place who was young and fit and cheerful, and preferably with a modicum of good sense. Mr Richardson stated that in his opinion I fitted the requirements very well, and that if I would call to see him, we could discuss the situation further.

It was two weeks after the fever and I was still

convalescent, still had Bella looking after me. Although she went home regularly and often stayed the night there, she spent most of her time with me, and on the whole looked and sounded better than in all the time I'd known her. I couldn't pay her, I had very little cash left and most of that went on food, but I gave her items of clothing she coveted: a pretty shawl Bram had bought me, some mother-of-pearl buttons and a lace collar, a bonnet that suited her. When she asked how I could afford to stay on at the cottage, I explained that Bram had paid the rent and left me a few pounds when he went back to London. I hadn't told her about Mr Richardson or the bank, so the letter when it arrived presented something of a problem.

I would have liked to share the excitement, since it was exactly the kind of job I'd always wanted. For me it was a way out, a way forward, a reason for leaving Whitby behind with all its attendant problems, and while I sat there in the garden, pondering the situation with the letter in my hand, Bella hovered nearby, anxious to know what it was about. In the end I told her a version of the truth, that Mr Richardson was a relative, and that I'd approached him with regard to references.

'Do you want to go away?'

'Well, I can't stay here, can I? The rent runs out soon, so I'll have to find work of some sort – and accommodation. I know it's not ideal, but for the moment the easiest solution is to find a living-in job.'

At that she looked crestfallen, like a child whose only toy has been taken away. I must confess I was irritated, since she knew we were living there on borrowed time. Perhaps it was the illness, but anger and peevishness came to me easily then, and I said crossly: 'You could do the same, you know. You always said you wished you could work in the kitchens of a big house, and now's your chance. Why don't you?'

'Maybe I will,' she said defensively, but from the look in her eyes I knew she wouldn't. I also knew I'd hurt her.

Next day we went into Whitby together on the carrier's cart from Newholm, which was something of a novelty for both of us. While I went to my interview at the bank, Bella did the shopping in town, and we arranged to meet an hour later by the station for a lift back. I fully expected Bella to return with me, but she managed to deflate my excitement and self-satisfaction by handing me the shopping and announcing flatly that she was going home. It was obvious, she said, that I could manage on my own now, whereas she'd just been home and her mother was begging her to return.

'It's no use, I've got to go back,' she said. 'They can't manage without me, and Isa's driving everybody mad.'

I was stunned, but didn't doubt her for a minute. When I stopped to think, the only surprise was that she'd managed to stay away so long. Cousin Martha had been leaning on Bella for years, using her, confiding in her, having all her faults and foibles catered to by a daughter whose tongue might be harsh and crude at times, but whose feelings were tender and could be manipulated. The other one, Isa, for all her mincing manners, was hard as flint underneath. She would cater to no one, least of all her mother. For that very reason Isa was the best person to be in charge in that household, and I felt that Bella should let well alone.

'Don't go,' I said vehemently. 'You'll regret it, you know you will.' Just a few yards from the station was a domestic employment agency that I'd been intending to use, and in my eagerness I took Bella's arm and urged her towards it. 'Go now,' I said, 'and see what they've got. Bright girls can do well. You could get to be a cook in a few years...'

But she dug in her heels and refused. 'Nay, Mam needs me,' she said stubbornly. I had the feeling she was readily setting herself against me and my suggestions and I wanted to shake her, but she would not be shifted. I was upset too, because once more our friendship was faltering, and on similar grounds to the last time. I wanted to take a chance and be adventurous, while she kept finding excuses not to cross the threshold.

I found it hard, going back to Newholm alone. I missed Bella's company, and knew that I would soon have to say goodbye. Not just to her, but to the cottage I'd shared with Bram. To my surprise, it pained me to think of leaving. Nevertheless, with the future in mind, I worked hard at regaining my strength, eating more, and walking a little further each day.

As soon as I was able to walk back and forth into town, I called to see Bella. The way we'd parted made me apprehensive, but she was all right and things seemed much as they'd always been, except that the house and its atmosphere were noticeably lighter. When I ventured to remark on it, however, it seemed the cause was not the spiritual one I'd imagined, but the simple fact that the windows had been cleaned for the first time in years. That made me chuckle, and when Bella asked what I'd thought was the reason we both started laughing crazily, almost to the point of hysteria when I said I thought it was to do with her father. The fact that he was not there any more, that his reign of terror was over because he was dead, was hardly a matter for amusement, but we laughed anyway, and our laughter released something, his ghost perhaps, making it possible for us to part as friends.

To Mr Richardson I was Miss Sterne, and always would be, but I felt my new employer might prefer to address me more informally; anyway, it seemed a good time to implement something that had been on my mind for a while. So, on leaving Whitby for Kingston upon Hull, I made the decision to change my name. Damaris was not only out of fashion in the modern world, it carried too many sad associations. The new me was embracing a fresh start, looking to the future, and I wanted a name to express that, a name that was short and up to date.

Marie seemed just right, not only a close derivative of my baptismal name, but one I happened to like. And so did Mrs Addison. She commented on it when we met, and used my new name ever after. I had no difficulty responding to it, just as I had no difficulty with Mrs Addison.

She turned out to be the kindest, jolliest old lady I ever had the pleasure of knowing, and my time with her was one of the best periods of my life, lacking any sort of unhappy complication. I found the other servants as pleasant in their own way as the mistress of the house, which was large, well equipped, and in the heart of town. The late master, Captain Addison, had begun his life as a mariner, become the owner of several ships engaged in the Baltic trade, and ended as a major shareholder in a new, expanding shipping company. His death, some ten years previously, had left the family with a healthy business and considerable assets.

There were four sons, referred to by Mrs Addison as her 'boys', who were in fact men old enough to be my father. She adored them and their families, presiding over gatherings at birthdays and Christmas like some benevolent, matriarchal despot, and, because they adored her in return, they indulged that idea, which made for smooth running all round. She treated me more like a daughter than a paid companion, and certainly encouraged the broadening of my education. There was an extensive library which I was allowed to use in my time off, and a collection of maps and charts which fascinated me. Mrs Addison said it was a treat to know the place could still be useful, and often joined me there. That winter, before the library fire, we had some wonderfully illuminating conversations in which she told me of her travels as a young woman, and how she and her husband had worked together to get started in the shipping business. Life had been hard, but they'd been diligent – and lucky in a business which involved some powerful elements of chance. That led us to talk about my parents, and how things might have been for them had my father lived a normal span.

Mrs Addison understood my conflicting feelings about ships and the sea, and even led me to believe that if I could have travelled as she had, then I would have been less fearful. 'The sea's a destructive power,' she said, 'no doubt of that. And no one with sense ever loses their fear of it entirely. But at least if you've faced it, if you've been on deck in the midst of a storm when disaster looms on every side, and seen how the little ship shakes off the last wave and climbs to the top of the next, how the Master uses every ounce of wit and experience to keep her going forward with her head into the weather – well, then, my dear,' she added with a kind but confident smile, 'then you'll start to understand some of the skill involved, and, as a consequence, that most ships survive, most of the time. The devil doesn't have it all his own way!'

It was easy to grow fond of Mrs Addison, and by comparison with everything else I'd done, looking after her was a pampered existence. In that atmosphere Bram's memory faded a little, and the emotional wounds began to heal. As Marie Sterne, I had few real demands, little to worry about, and every meal provided. The weight I'd lost through being ill was quickly regained, and after that my slender frame gradually filled out. Within the year I hardly knew myself, while Mrs Addison kept telling me how pretty I'd become, and insisted on dressing me accordingly.

I was fortunate in other ways too. The instructions I'd left with Mr Richardson were tempered by his own good sense, and the result proved satisfactory for both of us. We invested mainly in the exporting of coal and pig-iron, and the importing of timber from Russia and Scandinavia; also cork from Spain and grain from the Black Sea ports. It was solid and unexciting stuff but provided reliable returns, which were sometimes enlivened by additional part-cargoes of luxury goods: coffee, tobacco and silks from Constantinople, antique statuary from Piraeus and Taranto, furs and gemstones from St Petersburg.

But if my new life put Bram in the background, it often brought Jonathan to mind. All that talk of ships and the sea, all that studying of maritime trade, kept him very much before me. As I pondered my investments I would wonder where he was, what he was doing. Still working for the same Whitby owners, I imagined, but after a season of poor earnings from the 'good seaboat', Mr Richardson persuaded me to stop chasing her, there were better prospects in view. Not long after that the brigantine was sold, and I felt sad at that. The *Lillian* had always reminded me of Jonathan, of the times I saw him in his room at the top of the house on Southgate, head bent over books or a chart, or raised to view the array of ships on the Bell Shoal. I tried not to think of him looking for me as he'd promised he would, talking to people around the harbour, asking questions. I knew Bella wouldn't tell him anything, she'd promised not to tell anyone my whereabouts, not Jack Louvain and especially not Jonathan, but there were plenty more who'd be willing to gossip about 'the London gentleman' – and Jack could have furnished his name, if pressed.

For a long time it shamed me to think of Jonathan hearing those things. Not so much the truth of what I'd done in living with Bram at the cottage, although that was bad enough, but how it must seem to other eyes, how it would be interpreted and embellished in the telling. And when he heard, Jonathan would feel foolish, as though he'd been taken in by a wanton hussy who was clearly no better than his mother had maintained, and probably much worse. I hated to think of that.

During that first winter especially, when I was almost sure of him being at home in Whitby, it was a weight on my conscience. There were even times, late at night, when I worried about Mr Richardson finding out, and, in a state of shock, telling Mrs Addison that she was harbouring a woman of ill-repute, who was fit only for the nearest house of correction. But whatever was happening in Whitby, there were no repercussions in Hull. Life went on as before and eventually the worst of my anxieties faded.

Once in a while it occurred to me that Jonathan's ship might put into Hull and I might bump into him one day in the street, but it seemed a remote possibility and I didn't worry too much about that.

Which was just as well, since there were ships aplenty in the town docks, masts topping even the tallest buildings and bowsprits jutting proudly, all within a few minutes' walk of the house. My errands and shopping trips on Mrs Addison's behalf were generally a few minutes longer because of the time I spent identifying cargoes and interpreting conversations shouted across the quays.

It was a busy, cosmopolitan port with two faces, an ancient, medieval town on the River Hull, with narrow lanes and decrepit, timber-framed houses, and an affluent modern city of broad streets and imposing buildings which looked to the vast and swift-flowing Humber. It was a clearing house for goods from the industrial heartlands to the rest of the world, and a receiver of raw materials from abroad. I was there for three years and took to the place from the beginning; I felt invigorated by its atmosphere, by that sense of movement and purpose and confidence, and I was equally fascinated by the everyday detail of the Addisons' family business.

The two younger sons were based in London, while the older pair were more directly involved with running the ships from Hull, and called two or three times a week for luncheon with their mother. I kept quiet and listened, and in addition read everything I could about home, middle and foreign-going trade, agreements with colonies and foreign powers, transport of goods, bills of lading, freight rates and charter parties. In my own way, and without realising it, I became quite knowledgeable, and in the meantime my own small investments were increasing steadily.

My interests were regarded as something of a joke in the beginning. Not by Mrs Addison, I'm glad to say – she'd been brought up in Baytown, she knew the reputation its women had for shrewdness, and set about educating me accordingly. I think she wanted to prove to her sons that the legendary tales she told could still be true, even in an age where men of wealth and position expected their womenfolk to be idle and frivolous – and I was equally determined to vindicate her faith in me.

Even after years of retirement, I felt she could have run much of the business single-handed. She still had her contacts, old colleagues of Captain Addison who had remained her friends, and her 'at home' days were always busy, mostly with semi-retired gentlemen callers, which she regarded as being delightfully scandalous. It was at one of her more formal soirées that I met Henry Lindsey. He was a business acquaintance of the Addison brothers, and if I was aware of his interested glances from the beginning, I have to say that his were not the only ones.

After the first few months, when I'd more or less recovered from the trials of Whitby, I began to realise that I was attractive to men of a certain age; but since most of them were married, and I was far from willing to be impressed, I took no notice. As time went on, however, and I gained in confidence, I began to use their interests and intelligence for my own ends. Always modestly, always discreetly, so that no one could say I was flirting or teasing or making overtures; nor, more importantly, that I was garnering information. But I was. And making decisions. My nest-egg was growing, and I wanted it to grow even more. I wanted to be my own mistress, and never be dependent again.

Henry Lindsey was less gullible than his peers, and more observant than most. Since he had never been one to underestimate women, it took him no time at all to figure out what I was doing, and at first, he confessed, he thought the Addisons were using me as some kind of spy. Determined to find out the truth, he pursued me over several visits, until he was reassured that my interests in shipping and cargo rates were purely selfish. Oddly enough, I think he admired that. He was certainly amused. My resistance on other fronts intrigued him, and then became something of a challenge. After all, he was an extremely eligible widower, childless, and not more than three or four years over forty. I think he wanted me to be impressed by his attentions, and the fact that I was not made a dent in his pride.

But then he left suddenly, and afterwards, to my surprise, I found I missed the battle of wits. By comparison the others were not much of a challenge, but he had a certain style that appealed to me. From our conversations I knew he was a native of King's Lynn in Norfolk, but his connections in Hull were increasingly important, hence his dealings with the Addisons. The main part of his business, however, was as a broker with the Baltic Exchange in London, and although the idea of London still sent pangs of anguish through my heart, at least the business of the Exchange was something I was beginning to understand.

It was several weeks before he returned to Mrs Addison's drawing room, but he was obviously pleased to see me, and I was sufficiently charmed by that to abandon my habitual defensiveness. Telling myself that it would be churlish to ignore him, I sat with Mr Lindsey for quite a while that evening, and discovered that I liked the way his mind worked even when we were not crossing swords. He had wit and good humour, and, although his colouring and features were unremarkable, I found them quite pleasing. Certainly, he was nothing like Bram, and that was a bonus.

I liked Henry Lindsey, admired him, enjoyed his company – and yes, I was flattered by his interest in me, by the fact that he invariably singled me out when he came to pay his respects to Mrs Addison. Over a period of about a year I saw him perhaps once or twice a month, and he never forgot to ask me, teasingly, how my sixty-fourths were doing. It was his way of referring to the part-shares in ships and their cargoes that were being bought and sold on my behalf by Mr Richardson. I always said they were doing well, which generally they were, whereupon he would tap his nose and threaten to steal me away from the Addisons.

'Do you know, my dear,' old Mrs Addison said to me one day when he'd gone, 'I really do think he means it.'

She was right, he did. As winter gave way to spring, Henry Lindsey set about courting me with determination, in a charming, old-fashioned way that won Mrs Addison's favour at once, and made me feel both honoured and valued. At Easter, he called almost every day for a fortnight, bringing primroses and early violets, scented boxes of Turkish delight, a journal or two as well as the latest novel; and ultimately, as a joking reference to my maritime passions, an old copy he'd found of Nathaniel Bowditch's *Practical Navigator*. I was aware of his sense of humour, but I think that piece of evidence endeared him to me more than anything else. And I must say it was exciting to be courted in such a way, to know that I had a suitor, and a most respectable one at that. He was an excellent prospect, far better than a young woman in my position could expect, and as I went up to bed that night with Nathaniel Bowditch under my arm, I couldn't help thinking how pleased my grandmother would have been, if she'd known.

Henry kissed me first of all one afternoon in Mrs Addison's library, but although it was a tender moment, I was aware of stronger desires burning away in the background. And not only on his part. In the warmth of his embrace I felt myself responding, bending into him before awareness caught me and made me flustered. I backed away, blushing, while he was obviously charmed by what he took for virginal modesty, and that embarrassed me even more.

I felt confused. For a long time, after the emotional and physical tolls of Whitby, there'd been nothing much left in me beyond a desire for survival. My sexual needs were so diminished I'd imagined them gone for good; and as for affection, I'd wanted nothing and no one. My girlish fancies about men had been destroyed. I'd ceased to expect love and tenderness, much less a romantic courtship with marriage as the conclusion, so what was happening with Henry was rather a surprise.

The next evening, he told me he would have to return to London in a few days, and might not be able to visit again for some time. Part of me was relieved, because in anticipating the next step I felt in need of time to adjust; even so, disappointment struck hard. The time we'd spent together had been enjoyable, and I knew I would miss him. A moment later, he took my hand and said he had something to ask me, something important that he hoped I could answer before he went away. The approach was hardly original, nor was the question entirely unexpected, but I was overwhelmed. In response I found myself blushing and stammering like a schoolgirl, as though his proposal was the one thing in life I needed to make me happy; yet in reality I was unsure of myself, and little short of terrified of what might happen if he were to find out about Bram.

But I accepted, of course I did. I could do no other. And at least Mrs Addison was genuinely thrilled, like a mother in the way she clucked and fussed over the forthcoming arrangements. I disappointed her by insisting on a quiet wedding – she would have asked a hundred guests and willingly footed the bill – but in truth there were so few people to invite on either side, it seemed a nonsense to make a fuss. Nevertheless, I wrote to Bella and to Mr Richardson, and, at Mrs Addison's prompting, I penned a line to Old Uncle Thaddeus too, mainly to let him know that I'd managed to save myself from perdition after all, despite those early indications to the contrary.

But if he was surprised, I was astonished when he volunteered to come to the wedding and give me away. He said I was still his brother's granddaughter and my grandmother's namesake, no matter what I called myself now, and he would not shame me or the Sternes of Robin Hood's Bay by letting me pretend that I had no family. Reading those sentiments I was ridiculously touched; even more so when he arrived at the house, immaculately groomed and as hawk-like as ever.

'I was glad to hear from you,' he confessed, reaching out to clasp my hands. 'It was about time . . .' He stood back, while those penetrating blue eyes took in everything about me. 'You've grown up,' he said at last, decisively, 'and you seem to be blooming, praise God. That pleases me – there was a period when I was concerned . . .'

He didn't say more. He didn't need to. Meeting that glance I had a vision of Magnus Firth's body on the beach, and the inquest at the Dead House. He'd probably seen me there, while letting me think I'd remained unnoticed. He probably knew about Bram, too. Remembering all my sins and shortcomings, I could scarcely believe I'd been forgiven, and yet the head of the Sterne family was here, ready to give me away in marriage to Mr Henry Lindsey, ship-broker

303

and member of London's Baltic Exchange. I had a speechless moment, thinking he might be about to tell all, but then I decided that even Old Uncle Thaddeus might be feeling impressed by how well I'd done. That dispelled the fear.

I was married in the summer of 1890, which was the summer Bram finally returned to Whitby. Whatever the reason, I tried not to question it. I was not there, and anyway, he was not alone. He came with his wife and nine-year-old son; and he came in August with everyone else, all the artists and writers who were making Whitby famous then. George du Maurier even penned a little cartoon of the family Stoker, which I happened to see in *Punch* when Henry and I returned from our honeymoon in the Lake District. It cut me to the heart to recognise the house and gardens which were the setting for that cleverly observed cartoon, and of course I knew Bram at once. I have it still. There he is in the sketch, tall, long-legged, leaning forward in a wicker chair, soft, broad-brimmed hat shading his face as he watches his son; even the beard is sketched to perfection. The little boy, Noel, in his sailor suit, is trying to attract his mother's attention, but she is reading a book and does not wish to be disturbed.

'*Little boys,*' Florence says sternly, '*should be seen and not heard.*'

'*Yes, Mamma,*' the poor child retorts, '*but you don't even look at me . . .*'

Twenty-four

A successful marriage, I believe, is generally based on compromise, and – particularly for a woman – the adjustment of romantic ideals to reality. Since my romantic ideals had taken something of a battering in Whitby, I told myself that this time I was using my head, not my heart, and, if I was not in love when I married, at least I had the benefit of fewer illusions. Nevertheless, I had some, and they caused trouble enough.

Thankfully, the question of my virginity never arose. Although I worried about it before the wedding, Henry did not appear to wonder about my previous history and I was never called upon to explain. But that first night I was as nervous and apprehensive as any virgin bride. Apart from a few kisses and restrained embraces, Henry and I were strangers to each other, and, although I wanted to be with him, I'd long ago lost the innocent enthusiasm that prompted my response to Bram. Henry was different, less hesitant, more practised somehow, lacking that strange combination of intensity and emotion that gave birth to such passion in Bram. He had none of Bram's sensuality, or even his perversity, which always gave an edge of danger to our encounters.

But if Henry was predictable, he was also considerate. He had no desire to hurt me, rather the reverse; and, if he failed to set my world on fire, at least we managed to achieve a level of satisfaction in the marriage bed that Bram and Florence would have envied. Unfortunately, our early days in London were less equable, largely because there were so many adjustments to make on other fronts.

Henry had been married before, and his home had been furnished by his first wife, which made me feel like a visitor or an employee when the mistress is absent, unsure of my welcome as well as my duties. He found it difficult to understand my feelings, and regarded my requests for change as a criticism of the dead. He was hurt, I was hurt, and the fact that his household had been run very efficiently by a pleasant and capable housekeeper for the previous two years made everything so much more difficult to handle. I had nothing to do. He thought I should enjoy that, but I had been brought up to different expectations, and to be a lady of leisure was not one of them.

I was bored, and no assurance that I would have plenty to do once the children came along was enough to cure my hunger for activity. Also, despite the stomach-churning reaction whenever I thought of it, I was afraid that one day not so idle curiosity might lead me to the Lyceum on the Strand, and that if Bram and I were to meet again, even by chance, no good would transpire. I was less afraid of passionate embraces than of furious rows as I gave vent to my sense of injury and injustice, the kind of scene that might even erupt into violence. In five years I'd forgiven him very little, least of all for ignoring my letters. And the fact remained that when Irving crooked his finger, Bram went running, so I hated

Irving too. I didn't think I could ever bear to see the man again, not even upon a stage.

I needed distractions. So, while making small changes throughout the house, I pleaded for something more challenging to do, an opportunity, perhaps, to put my burgeoning financial knowledge to good use. But that was tantamount to asking for a job – unthinkable as far as Henry was concerned. It soon became clear to me that my interests in the shipping world were acceptable only as an eccentric kind of hobby, and that was a severe blow, since I was proud of my achievements. I had been vain enough to think that Henry had married me for my wits as much as my looks and apparent good health.

During one heated exchange I dared to say so, which provoked an angry retort. He said that, amongst other reasons, he'd chosen me as a suitable mother for his children, but as we'd been married for almost a year, he supposed he was bound for disappointment again. The accusation stopped the breath in my throat. I felt despised for my failure, and was bitterly hurt; doubly so because I felt inadequate as well as guilty, as though I'd cheated him by injuring myself before we even met. I was already beginning to fear that Nan Mills, or the fever I had endured afterwards, had somehow ended my chances of bearing children.

It would have been easy then to slip into melancholy or self-pity, and indeed I suffered both for a while, until anger and self-respect came to my rescue. Unwittingly, I'd married Henry Lindsey under some kind of false pretence, yet in a way he'd managed to deceive me too, so perhaps we were even. We'd both married selfishly, trusting the other to provide what we most wanted from life, and we were both disappointed. We were very different people. He was neat, precise, methodical, and his days were planned from dawn to dusk. His clocks, which at first fascinated me and then drove me almost to distraction with their ticking and striking, symbolised so much about his life, whereas I'd spent almost twenty of my twenty-four years with the sun as my only timepiece.

By comparison I must have seemed careless, unreliable, pleasure-loving, and I often thought he liked to see me that way, fitting the mould of the frivolous young bride, making him quite the man to be envied by his contemporaries. That irritated me, because it was not an image I cared for, but it was one of the problems caused by the difference in our ages, and was difficult to overcome. Henry would persist in treating me like a child, and seemed unable or unwilling to grasp the idea that I wanted his care and appreciated his protection, but did not need him to think for me. I was perfectly capable of doing that for myself.

During my time with Mrs Addison I'd found that interests which had been just out of reach were suddenly within my grasp, and, allied to a schoolgirl talent for figures and the keeping of simple accounts, I'd discovered a whole new world, a world that challenged and delighted me. With my £100 I'd opened the door on the world of risk and invest-ment, and with no more than a little knowledge had entered it enthusiastically. Inevitably there were losses, but with advice and guidance I'd done quite well at a time when many others with more experi-ence were going to the wall. The 1880s and early '90s were not a good time for industry, which meant a thin time for shipping too, but I'd stuck to my instincts and been lucky – I'd even been fortunate in what I thought of as my 'sentimental' shares. Invested because of Jonathan, most had done well, and I kept hoping that he did too. Knowledge and experience were often necessary and always desirable, but where the sea was concerned, it paid to remember the unpredictable element of luck.

I listened to Mr Richardson, and while he tended to be modest about his advice, I knew he had a seaman's heart inside that banker's exterior, that he summed up a lot about the day ahead while crossing Whitby harbour bridge each morning. In short, I trusted him, and after a while he came to trust my instincts too. Between us we made a good team, and in less than five years Bram's £100 had grown far beyond my first imaginings. Nothing was truly predictable, ever, but I knew that, if necessary, within a month or six weeks I could have raised something between £700 and £1,000.

With regard to Bram, one thing pleased me in spite of everything, since it was a poke in the eye for Irving. He was writing, and writing well. His first full-length work of fiction had been published about the time that Henry and I were married, but I'd had a copy of *The Snake's Pass* in my possession for well over a year before I could bring myself to read it. Somehow it brought him too close by half, worse than having him in the room with me. Reading his words, his story about a wealthy young Englishman travelling in the west of Ireland, was almost like being inside his head, experiencing his thoughts and emotions, especially with regard to the girl. And although she was nothing like me, except in her youth and station, I couldn't help equating the two of us, just as I drew parallels between the young man and Bram. But he'd written an excellent tale of mystery and suspense, so evocative of life in Ireland that I was reminded of the stories he used to tell when we were together, not just about his mother, but of his own journeys undertaken as a young man with the Irish judiciary. At times I could almost hear his voice, that soft lilt which was always more pronounced when he was talking about Ireland. Often, sitting there reading alone, I felt I was drawing the essence of him from the page and into my mind. It was unsettling, to say the least. And I found myself wondering whether he'd gone to Whitby in that summer of 1890 in the hope of finding me again, to tell me about the book and his success.

Whichever, it was too late, and had been for a long time. I found it in my heart to wish him well, if only to justify my faith in his talent as a writer. Fate had decreed other paths for me, had brought me closer, in a way, to the Sternes and what they would have wished my future to be. But without Bram's cheque I might never have met Mr Richardson or the Addisons, and without them, how would I have met Henry?

The mere fact that I dwelt on these things was an indication of how unhappy and frustrated I was at that time. And how often Bram was on my mind. His cheque had changed my life, there was no doubt, and as a consequence I was on the way to becoming a wealthy woman in my own right. But I preferred to forget that Irving's money was most probably behind that gift, and I tended to ignore the efforts I'd put into making it grow. Instead, in my unsettled state, I thought rather too often of what might have been, and found myself questioning acutely the point of wealth and idleness.

On one trip north, while Henry saw to business with the sons, I called on my old employer for a short visit. She sensed at once that something was wrong, and swiftly drew out the superficial problems. After an hour or so in Mrs Addison's company I felt brighter and much more confident. As she remarked, my 'legacy' might easily have been frittered away, but I'd not only acted sensibly by

310

placing it with Mr Richardson, I'd worked hard at learning the principles of investment, and had subsequently made my own fortune. There was no need for me to feel unworthy of my husband; on the contrary, she said, he should feel proud of me. Regarding the matter of children, that was a matter for a Higher Authority; I should cease worrying at once, she said, and concentrate on other things. Children would come along, all in good time.

Privately, I was not so sure; but I appreciated her advice, her comments, and most of all the simple fact of her faith in me. It gave me courage to speak to Henry of a plan I'd been contemplating for some time. When we returned home, I gathered my courage and said I wanted to go away for a while, not as a protest, but as a means of broadening my experience. He had travelled in his youth, but I had barely moved the length of the country. I had money, and was happy to pay my own way if he would allow me to go in company with a maid, or even a maid and manservant for protection. My proposals dumbfounded him – and, I must admit, they scared me too – but whereas I'd expected anger and outrage, after a time, he agreed. With just one stipulation: that he should come with me. He thought he might arrange things with colleagues at the Exchange, and – as long as we took no longer than three months – leave the business in their hands.

I was overjoyed.

The idea of the tour was inspired by my investments as much as those conversations with Mrs Addison, and having bought many a sixty-fourth share of cargo travelling from the Tyne to Tallinn or from Taganrog back to the Tees, I wanted to see for myself how things were done. The old Whitby colliers were still plying their trade up and down the coast and across the North Sea, and there were plenty of grain ships creaking back under sail from the Mediterranean. That was how I wanted to travel. I felt it was time I faced my childhood fears. I tried to explain but poor Henry was appalled. He begged me to go for something more modern, one of the new steamships catering for passengers, not some old hulk that might sink without trace in the first storm we encountered.

I was just as appalled by his remark, which seemed to suggest that we shipped cargoes in vessels that were unseaworthy – so he was forced to take it back. Eventually we compromised by booking passage at the beginning of May aboard a well-seasoned, but not old, sailing vessel bound from the Tyne to St Petersburg. Everything was done through the Addisons, and with a young shipmaster who often had his wife travelling with him. On this voyage he left her at home and gave us his cabin, which was no doubt the biggest and best but still very cramped. Nevertheless, we made ourselves at home aboard the *Bonny Lass*, and sailed with the tide a little after midnight.

Excited and apprehensive, I found it difficult to sleep that first night. As the gentle motion of the river gave way to the more boisterous action of the open sea, I thought I might prove to be a poor sailor, but by morning the queasiness had passed, and with bright weather ahead and a following breeze, the little brig fairly skimmed over the waves. I never lost a slight apprehension, but I think I fell in love from that moment, with the sea, with ships, with that sense of being at one with the elements. As sails were reefed and unfurled, as the wind cracked in the shrouds, I understood at last what had enthralled the men of my family from the beginning.

On a surge of sympathetic feeling, I thought

particularly of Jonathan Markway and wondered how he was faring, whether he'd gained his Master's ticket yet, and the command which had been so important to him. I hoped so: he deserved that. And with my eyes on the Master and Mate I even wished, rather foolishly, that he was aboard this ship, so we could have talked. In admiring their alertness and skill and experience, I felt I was admiring and understanding him.

Although Henry and I spent most of our time either lying down or pacing the tiny afterdeck, trying not to get in the way, I was too intrigued by what was going on to mind any discomfort or inconvenience. We were fortunate with the weather, having good-speed westerlies and very little rain, but Henry was not enthralled. Nor was he a very good sailor. He was irritated by the coal dust which kept appearing everywhere, in spite of the efforts of the crew, and particularly upset when his pale grey gloves were ruined, even though I'd warned him to wear black. By contrast, I found I loved every minute and even managed to be amused by my own irritations, which in truth were minor compared to some I'd known, especially when I'd lived with the Firths.

I remembered those days well, when sand and fish-scales clung to everything, and the old house reeked of smoke and bait and mussel shells. Having avoided eating fish for years, I was forced to contemplate it again aboard ship. We had fresh cod, caught on a long line, served baked for dinner with potatoes and beans, then there was fish pie, pickled herrings, and kippers from the stores. For a change the cook served smoked German sausage and beans, and we managed to have eggs for breakfast. That, as Henry bemoaned on more than one occasion, was just the beginning of our gastronomic privations. But

313

in spite of the food – or even because of it – I enjoyed that bracing voyage across the North Sea and through the Skagerrak. It thrilled me to be sailing those cold blue seas on a bright May morning, to see the soaring mountains of Scandinavia, the tiny islands and deep inlets from where our ancient forebears had set sail in their dragon-headed longships, to raid the gentler coasts of England.

There was an element of romance about the distant past, called into being by an invigorating present. Longships had raided our coasts time without number, destroying Whitby's first abbey, killing and burning the surrounding settlements before those fierce warriors had been seduced by the rich farmlands, taken the women to wife, and paved the way for peace. Such thoughts reminded me of Bay and Old Uncle Thaddeus, his fascination with the Viking invasions of more than a thousand years ago, the dialect and folk-tales which were a survival from those days, and the old beliefs that were only now beginning to give way to the modern world.

That voyage across the Baltic Sea to St Petersburg was but the first leg of our journey, and if Henry was pleased to be on dry land again, I was less so, finding the scale of the Russian city daunting. The buildings were breathtaking, beautiful but huge, the streets as broad as an entire village at home, and even the system of waterways on which the city was built seemed to me a giant's creation. I could not understand it, since the people were of normal size, although Henry supposed it was Peter the Great's way of impressing the rest of Europe with his riches and power; and we must not forget, he said, that Russia's western capital reflected the vastness of the continent beyond.

The very idea struck a chill into my soul, and I was relieved that in planning our itinerary from the Baltic to the Black Sea, of the two routes open to us, we had not chosen the Russian one from St Petersburg to Moscow, and Moscow down to the Crimea. It sounded simple until one studied the map and saw the endless distances involved, the apparent lack of relief in the form of mountains or great cities. Instead, we had chosen to stay with our ship during the short journey to Narva where it would be loading a return cargo of timber. From there we left the ship to travel overland through part of the great forests which supplied our needs, down to the ancient port of Tallinn, which had a special significance for me. Henry and I climbed the rocky heights of the old town to look down on the sheltering bay, with the great Gulf of Finland beyond. Somewhere out there, beneath the grey seas, lay the wreck of the *Merlin*, lost in a violent spring storm when I was just a child. With the wreckage were the bones of my father and grandfather, and seven crew.

Henry made enquiries for me, and for that I will always be grateful. He discovered the area where the *Merlin* had foundered, a submerged skein of rocks not unlike Whitby's Scaur, where many other ships had also come to grief. It was not accessible from landward, but I bought a wreath of flowers and, when we took ship for Stettin, as we passed the spot I cast the flowers out upon the waves. They floated like a lifebuoy, which at once seemed dreadfully ironic and made me weep and wish I hadn't done it; but Henry understood and let me cry. We stood there on the afterdeck, clinging to the ratlines and watching the little wreath of flowers grow smaller and smaller, and we talked about love and death, about my family and his, and even a little about his first wife which, in an odd sort of way, helped my grief.

*

In Stettin we disembarked again, and began the first stage of our overland journey through Europe. I mention it now, not just because it came at an important time in my life, but because of the strange coincidences which revealed themselves later. While Henry and I boarded our train to Berlin, and continued southwards from there via the ancient cities of Dresden, Prague and Vienna, unknown to me, Bram was busily working on a novel which had had its beginnings in Whitby. While he was writing about Jonathan Harker crossing Europe at the beginning of May, I was making that journey with Henry. By the end of that month we were following the River Danube south from Vienna, through what is known as the Carpathian Gate at Bratislava, and travelling by steamer down to the twin cities of Buda and Pest. But where Bram sent Harker across the Hungarian plains, and up into the Carpathian mountains at Bistritz, we continued in a southerly direction, via Belgrade.

That much-disputed city had a certain battered charm, particularly the citadel with its domes and minarets, narrow streets and Moorish bazaars, standing high on a great rock above the town. The lower town was less ancient and more European, but from the safe distance of our steamer its buildings resembled nothing so much as the ragged camp of a surrounding army laying siege to the hated foreigner above. Belgrade had been fought over for centuries and it was easy to see why. From the east, the city was so positioned that it held the key to Hungary in the north, and to protect that half of their empire the Austrians had fought long and hard to oust the Turks, which they'd only succeeded in doing some twenty-five years before. Since then, it had become the capital of an independent state, Serbia, but we sensed such hostility and oppression there we were uneasy, and glad to move on.

Reading the guidebooks, I was startled to come across the name of Dracula. The bloodthirsty Wallachian prince whose history Bram had noted in Whitby seemed something of a local hero, and it felt strange indeed to find those echoes so far from home. The brooding, snow-capped peaks of the Transylvanian Alps loomed ahead of us, and the great River Danube was squeezed through a narrow, winding gap, into fifty miles of violent cataracts which ended near Orsova in Romania, at a place called the Iron Gate. It was wild, stormy country, and, the river being in flood, we were forced to leave our steam launch for an overland journey by carriage. Some years later, reading Bram's account of Harker's journey through the mountains, I was reminded of those days and shivered at the uncanny similarities. We were anxious and apprehensive too, dependent as we were on the surly mountain people, and traversing roads which hardly justified being classified as tracks. With much relief we left that oppressive region and put the fortifications of the Iron Gate behind us. Thereafter, with the Carpathians to the north, and the Balkan ranges to the south, the valley broadened into a flat but marshy and fertile plain.

The weather was at once milder, and, as we moved further south, great stretches of pale green wheat were rippling in the breeze. It did my heart good to see a familiar crop, to be away from the vast, oppressive heartland of continental Europe, and to be heading for the sea and open skies. A sense of recognition assailed us, growing stronger with each passing mile. We were both aware of feeling safer. Henry had been subdued, and I felt as though I had been withstanding some nameless threat, but with the prospect of the sea before us, albeit a less salty expanse than we were used to, we were as excited as children on a day trip to the coast.

There was also a sense of satisfaction for me, in that I had travelled with one cargo, seen another growing in the great forests of northern Europe, and yet another – wheat – was beginning to ripen before our eyes as we sailed on towards the great delta where the Danube entered the Black Sea. Meandering through the wheatlands, the river continued to broaden until it became a mile, two miles wide, like a sea itself, dotted with islands, busy with traffic of every description, from simple dhows and fishing boats to the most modern of yachts and steamers.

From Galatz, Henry and I took yet another ship for Odessa and the Crimea. We both wanted to see Sebastopol and Balaclava before turning back and, having contacted the Addisons' agent, we embarked aboard a grain ship in Taganrog for the journey home. In the Russian ports Henry was horrified to see women doing all the manual work, but I reminded him sharply that women were still doing back-breaking physical work in England, at pitheads as well as on farms and in factories, and no one complained about that. He saw the point and conceded it, although I suppose, to be fair, he had little conception of that style of life. I rarely mentioned the Firths to him, and never the circumstances in which I'd lived and worked in Whitby.

If nothing else, our journey had been one of enlightenment. He often said, drily, that it had been a practical lesson, akin to the reading of *Pilgrim's Progress*; but when we arrived in Constantinople his endurance was wearing thin. He managed to persuade me to abandon cargo ships in favour of something more conventional, and we transferred to a hotel for several days of sightseeing before picking up a passenger steamer to take us on to Piraeus. After all our privations – and we had endured many in the previous six weeks – it was good to have some basic comforts in the way of good food and bathing facilities. Henry, who had been so stoical, was suddenly cheerful and relaxed, so thankful to be in acceptable circumstances again, he was ready to give me the moon had I asked for it. All I wanted was the chance to work for him, which was perhaps a shade more difficult, but he was even willing to grant me that. As a consequence we were both immensely happy, drawn closer by our shared experiences. Reluctant to let go, we took another month to get home.

Henry may well have believed that I would not work for long, because either pregnancy or boredom would intervene, but I was so pleased with myself, so full of satisfaction at all we'd overcome and managed to achieve, I found it hard to believe anything could dent my happiness, let alone puncture it. We had agreed on where I would work, how many hours, and what I would do, and every morning we set off to Henry's office in the city.

Most of his work was done elsewhere, either at the Baltic Exchange or in meeting other brokers and agents at various hostelries and coffee-houses nearby. The City being such a male preserve, that was perhaps the most taxing part, and although the public houses were not exclusive clubs, the men who frequented them liked to think they were. To begin with, my appearance – albeit in sober grey and black – shocked them, and that first week I found myself so uncomfortable that if I'd been less determined I would have surely given up. I kept telling myself that working on the fish market was worse, that a woman who had sailed on a Whitby collier, and travelled all the way through eastern Europe, ought not to be afraid of civilised men in an English city. But some could be very hostile indeed. Wherever I went I was either stared at or pointedly ignored, while the men to whom I was introduced talked at me or around me, sat in silence or made some excuse to stand up and move away. At first, Henry was embarrassed too, but we'd made a bargain in Constantinople and he was determined to see that we both stuck by it.

There were one or two seriously unpleasant moments, in which Henry was cut dead by men he'd regarded as friends, but at last the situation settled down sufficiently for me to be accepted as one of Leadenhall Street's minor eccentricities. I could not enter the Exchange, of course, because I was not a member, but I was able to involve myself in most other aspects of the business of buying and selling, new ships, old ships, cargo space and cargoes. If the Addisons were surprised at my addition to the London office, old Mrs Addison was delighted. She wrote a glowing letter to Henry, praising his shrewdness and pioneering spirit, which brought forth a wry smile, but as I settled down he became happier and, as I began to pull my weight, I think he even started to be proud of me. His praise might have been reluctant at first, but it was genuine, and that for me was the very pinnacle of satisfaction. I had proved myself to him. I felt then that I could go on to prove myself to his contemporaries.

That was when I received my first communication from Isa Firth.

Twenty-five

Mystified by the handwriting, which was so much
more precise than Bella's unformed scrawl, and far
less elegant than Mr Richardson's, I wondered who
else would write to me from Whitby. Inside was a
single sheet of notepaper, folded around an
unmounted photograph. I didn't need to peer too
closely at the couple in the centre of the picture, the
naked man and woman making love amongst the
rocks, to know who they were. After the first split
second of shock I even knew when and where it had
been taken.

I slipped it straight back into the envelope, as
though hiding the evidence would obliterate it.
Thankfully I was breakfasting alone that morning,
but even so it was a while before the panic subsided.
I dared not read the note, nor take the photograph
out again to examine it, in case someone came into
the room. Like a criminal I slipped upstairs to be
alone, but not before borrowing a magnifying glass
from the study. Although even without the glass I
could recognise my own face quite clearly, catching
the light from the rising sun. With my head thrown
back, arms clinging to my lover, legs hooked around
his naked haunches, it seemed I was urging him on
to greater endeavours – which may well have been
the case. With the glass, however, details were even

more distinct – our clothes on the rocks, the remains of a picnic, the foam of the incoming tide – all somehow suggesting other hungers, other surges. What could not be seen, because his head was turned away, was the face of the man so obviously pleasuring me, but his back was beautifully defined from head to heel, so well he was almost moving in that captured moment, muscles rippling in the low, revealing light.

It was a shockingly beautiful picture, so good it might have been posed. Except I knew how natural it was, how stolen, how long Jack Louvain must have watched and waited amongst the rocks at Saltwick Bay before he pressed the shutter . . .

And that was when I had to rush to the wash-stand, in order to vomit my shock and disgust. It was a while before I stopped shaking, before I could be sure the nausea was over. I sponged my face with water from the ewer, and sat down by the window to read what was written.

Cutting aside the fact that Isa Firth and I had never had anything of any moment to say to each other, that letter must have been the chattiest blackmail note ever written. She must really have enjoyed conveying the bad news; I even sensed a relish to the bitterness that came off the page.

News, tone, content, were all shocking. One blow came hard on another until I hardly knew what to do, what to think. Jack Louvain was dead. On top of the blackmail photograph, I could barely take this in, and had to read the details over and over again. Jack Louvain had had a nasty accident on the cliffs at Upgang in the summer, when he had slipped and broken his leg. The leg had subsequently refused to set properly, which meant that it had to be amputated; but then the wound wouldn't heal, gangrene had set in, and despite several operations and a long stay in hospital, Jack had died a month ago.

Isa had apparently been housekeeping for him for some time before he died, as well as working in the shop, and in the course of sorting out his possessions had come across some very interesting photographs that Jack seemed not to have published. She felt it was a shame to leave them languishing in a drawer, as she was having to find money to erect a suitable stone to Jack's memory. As I'd been such a friend of Jack's, she thought I might like to buy this photograph of myself, and so help contribute to keeping his memory alive.

My initial reaction was that the death and suffering of a peeping Tom were well deserved. But hard on the heels of that came disbelief, a conviction that none of it was true, bar Isa Firth's poking and prying, and her wicked desire to stir up the past and ruin my life. But then grief for an old friend overtook me; Jack wasn't old enough to die, he couldn't be dead, he –

But he was, he had to be – Isa wouldn't, *couldn't*, make up something like that, it was too easy to check. Anyway, his death, true or not, was incidental to the facts, and the facts were that Isa Firth had somehow found prints or a photographic plate of Bram and me making love one early morning at Saltwick during that summer of '86. I couldn't help wondering whether she knew who he was, or had other photographs which showed his face, because he would have been a prime target for blackmail. That thought made me quake, made me want to rush out of the house at once and straight to the Lyceum. I was so badly shocked, I needed the support of someone who knew and understood, someone who could give advice without making moral judgements.

The temptation was almost overwhelming. I might

even have done it, except that some quirk of fate sent Henry back to the house that morning. An accident on the main line just outside King's Cross meant that trains were indefinitely delayed, so he had telegraphed the Addisons to postpone his trip to Hull. If he was surprised to see me still at home, there was pleasure too. He loved me, trusted me – more than that, he'd risked his own professional reputation in order to satisfy my desire to work in his field. I could not betray that trust in any way, least of all by contacting Bram. I would have to face this problem alone.

That first letter with the photograph did not mention a specific sum, only that Isa would appreciate a reply with some indication that I understood and was willing to make a charitable contribution towards Mr Louvain's memorial stone. She made it sound like a shrine, which to her it probably was, something to be cleaned and polished and genuflected to. Something to give her empty life a focus. I even had an image of her in my mind, kneeling at a little prie-dieu with Jack's picture nailed above it.

It was a sickening thought. Every time I thought of the photograph – I didn't need to look at it – I found myself hating with a passion I would not have believed possible. I wished for something violently dramatic to happen to Isa, such as the braining smack of a winch hook as she passed the shipyards at the bottom of Southgate, the terrible splintering crash of a load of timber giving way, or a bolting dray-horse to knock her down and pulverise her underfoot.

Despite those ill-wishes, I wrote a civil enough reply saying I understood the situation very well, and how much did she expect? Her reply mentioned £50, which was outrageous, so I responded with a curt demand for the plate as well as every print in her possession. In the letter which followed, Isa dropped the charade, threatening to post a copy of the photograph to my husband if I did not forward the money before the end of the month.

I knew Isa too well to doubt her word. Anyway, she wasn't doing this just for the money, but out of envy and wickedness, to hurt me. No doubt Bella had told her about my marriage to a wealthy man, and that would have rankled, especially in the light of her unrequited passion for Jack. I found myself wondering whether he'd left a will, and if so, who had inherited his photographs. They were part of his business, after all. But if his accident and subsequent death had been the darkest of thunderclouds to Isa, then those photographs must have been like finding a crock of gold at the foot of the rainbow. I wondered how many the crock contained, and whether all had been taken on the same occasion.

At one time I would have sworn Jack Louvain was incapable of such behaviour, but Isa's letters knocked all such certainty out of me. I was ready to believe anything, and I trusted no one. Instead of sending money through the post, I would have liked to go to Whitby to throttle the truth out of Isa, but the work I'd fought so hard to do made it impossible. Henry was away for several days in Hull, which at least gave me time to compose myself, but he had started to count on me, to use me, and as a result the business was picking up again after our extended leave in the summer. The challenge was just what I'd prayed for; I could not abandon everything on a whim. So, although it grieved me sorely, I took money from my own account in five-pound notes and posted it to Isa's new address.

Next day I wrote to Bella, an apparently general, chatty letter, asking for all the news since it was so long since I'd heard anything from anyone in Whitby; at the same time I sent a note to Mr Richardson, asking him to take out a year's subscription to the *Whitby Gazette* for me. It was something I should have thought of before, since it would give me an official version of local events, with enough gossip to be read between the lines. After some years in which the past had begun to lose its hold on me, suddenly it was on my heels again with a vengeance. I needed to know what was going on in Whitby, and from as many sources as possible.

After that, Bella wrote from time to time, largely because I kept up the correspondence and refused to let it lapse again. I learned that Lizzie and the youngest sister Meggie – who had been no more than seven or eight years old when I lived with them – were both in service, the two eldest boys were doing all right at sea, and only Davey and young Magnus were still at home. Davey was the bright one, Bella said, he wanted to join the railway company, so they were hoping to keep him at school until he was fourteen. Magnus was a willing bairn, but a bit slow, so there wasn't much point in sending him to school when he hated it so much. Their mother still liked her tot of gin, but with most of the bairns off her hands and lodgers bringing in money, she was a lot happier. Especially now that Isa had a place of her own. In the end she'd done quite well out of what Mr Louvain left her . . .

She rarely mentioned herself, and for a long time I just assumed that Bella was doing what she'd always done, helping her mother in the house. Except that she was twenty-seven years old and most women of her age were married with children, while those of the fishing community in Whitby were generally baiting lines and selling fish as well as raising a family. Remembering how hard we'd worked that winter I'd lived with them, and for so little reward, I did ask myself how Bella was managing to survive; it wasn't until the following spring, however, that I discovered the truth – from the *Gazette*.

Amongst the usual court reports on cases of common assault, brawling and drunkenness, I read that Bella had been charged with soliciting in Pier Road, drunk and disorderly conduct, and abusive behaviour towards the arresting officer. I was appalled. It wasn't headline news; such incidents were common and usually reported with brevity. The case was proved, however, and even though it was her first time before the court, Bella was fined and sentenced to seven days in gaol. Her claim that she was unable to pay the fine was met with an alternative – another seven days inside.

Horrified, I tried to work out how long had elapsed since the case had appeared before the magistrates, and whether the sentence was still being served. I wrote at once to Mr Richardson, asking him to check up, and to pay the fine for Bella if she had more than a day left to serve. What he must have thought, I don't know; by way of explanation I said only that she had been good to me once, and I could not bear to think of her being in prison and in need. It was a brief understatement but it was true.

As things turned out it was too late to pay the fine: Bella was being released even as Mr Richardson made his enquiries. Nevertheless, it marked the beginning of another stage in our relationship, one where I started watching Bella from a distance, watching like a mother with a backward child. Watching with arms outstretched, all the time praying for good sense, but worrying just the same. It seemed to me there was no logic to Bella's behaviour. I could understand why a girl who had been so badly used by her father would find it hard to trust men, or to have much faith in the estate of marriage; I could even see that she might prefer the company and love of women. But I was too naive still to understand how someone who hated sex could do it for money. Not when the money could have been earned in other ways.

I would have liked to put the past behind me, cut myself free, live totally in the present with Henry and our brokerage business in London, but Whitby kept intruding on different levels. I found myself involved in more and more business that was Whitby based, and in a sense that was gratifying, but it kept my thoughts focused where I would have preferred them not to be. I came to expect the letters, twice or three times a year, from Isa, but although I expected them they still produced the same sense of revulsion and fury.

And yet I must confess to feeling a certain perverse satisfaction. I don't know why. Perhaps Isa became my hair shirt, part of my penance for that affair with Bram. I suppose that sense of guilt might have lessened over the years, except for my inability to have children; and there again, my guilt and regret were further complicated by the knowledge that I was less stricken by that failure than Henry. He was the one to whom children were important; I just felt bad at not being able to provide them.

In some strange way, although I hated it, paying Isa made me feel better. Just as keeping an eye on Bella relieved a different sense of guilt. I saw them as two sides of a coin, facing in opposite directions, hardly aware of each other as separate entities. If they'd become friendlier for a time after Magnus's death, it was clear that all pretence had evaporated with Bella's first conviction for soliciting. Isa was sly and secretive, and so disapproving she could have put a Puritan to shame – which made me wonder whether Bella got drunk deliberately and accosted policemen partly to annoy her sister.

Aside from my concerns in Whitby, Henry and I had ten years together that were in many ways both challenging and fulfilling. Whatever sadness or regret we harboured was mostly buried in the business, which as the '90s wore on, increased tremendously. After the first few years we didn't talk about having children, and he seemed to accept that my chief interests were always going to be outside the home, in the movement of shipping and trade. We both worked hard, and I took every opportunity to travel on business, whether by train to Hull, or by ship across the North Sea. Sometimes Henry came with me, but more often I travelled alone. Living in Hampstead, I found myself languishing for fresh sea breezes and the hustle and bustle of the docks; I tried to persuade Henry to move, but he liked being high above London, and in sight of the Heath.

Sometimes I thought about Bram, and envied that house he'd talked about, overlooking the river. But to have lived in Chelsea would have put us too close for comfort; and I was thankful that my husband's cultural tastes ran more to operetta and light comedy than the type of high drama presented by Irving at the Lyceum. Every time we ventured into theatre-land I was very much aware that this was Bram's world, a world of fame and first nights, of champagne suppers and titled friends. It made Whitby, and all we'd shared ten years ago, seem very small beer indeed.

In the summer of '95 I thought about Bram a good deal, since it seemed he and his friends were rarely out of the news. Oscar Wilde, who had once been in love with Florence, was convicted on charges of gross indecency and sent to gaol, while in the same week Irving's brand of high drama – not to mention his largess – paid off in the form of a knighthood. He was the first actor ever to be honoured in that way, but I could not be pleased. Indeed I felt contemptuous of Irving and sorry for Wilde, which was perhaps contrary of me, so I kept my opinions to myself. Nevertheless, I did wonder how Bram felt about the situation. It seemed to me that one had been elevated by reverence and an over-emphasis on dignity and drama, while the other had been trampled underfoot for daring to mock current morals and manners.

And what about Florence, and Wilde's poor wife? How did *they* feel about it?

But it seemed a long way from the world I inhabited with Henry, and their concerns were not mine. Bram faded from my mind for a while, until just after my thirtieth birthday, when he made himself felt once more. Ironically, it was a time when I was feeling pleasantly mature and in control. Business was improving noticeably, and I knew it was more than just a trend; much of it was to do with my efforts, and the pursuit of instincts which rarely seemed to let me down. I was pleased with myself, perhaps even a little smug; if I'd had detractors, I knew I had admirers too, and not all were based on business. There were plenty of lingering glances to tell me I was still a desirable woman, in spite of the severely tailored outfits I wore to the office. Henry often smiled about my weekday clothes, saying I looked like a redoubtable schoolmarm in my greys and browns, but in fact I liked them: not only did they suit my face and figure, I felt they were a good foil for the flamboyance of my hair. But for Henry's sake, when we were at home, I wore my hair loose and the softly coloured silks he preferred. I wore them mainly to please him, and if they didn't always have the effect I desired, I told myself it was because he was working too hard; we both were; we needed a holiday.

That Saturday morning, in the early summer of '97, was the sort to put holidays in mind: bright and sunny, with the promise of more to come. I walked into my favourite bookshop on Heath Street, and noticed the assistant unwrapping a parcel. The yellow-bound books attracted my attention. I was about to ask what they were, when I saw the author's name in red on the cover: *Bram Stoker*.

It was a shock. Invariably, whenever I saw his name in a journal or newspaper, it was like being thrust straight into his presence: time and distance were inconsequential. That day, with trembling fingers I reached out for a book and, turning it over, read the title: *Dracula*.

The title chilled me even then, before I knew what it was about.

I had the book wrapped and sealed and stowed away at home until I knew that Henry would be gone for a couple of days. When I settled down to read that book, I wanted to be alone. A week later my opportunity arose. It was the beginning of June, just eleven years since that summer we'd been together, and the weather in London now was just as hot if considerably less salubrious. The noise of iron-shod hooves and wheels, the stink of horses, stables, privies, smoke – the taste of sulphur in the air, the yellow sky over the Heath – all combined to make Henry urge me to take time off, to travel with him to King's Lynn, where he had some urgent family business. I had solid enough reasons to refuse, since we had business pressing on Leadenhall Street, but the heat was such that I almost regretted it.

When I got home from the office that evening, I

peeled off my clothes and took a bath, and then, wearing a light robe, I ordered my dinner on a tray upstairs. It was something I did often when Henry was away. I liked my privacy to relax, and the large well-proportioned room at the rear of the house was a place where I'd been able to express my own taste in comfortable furniture. There were long windows and a balcony overlooking a walled garden, with trees and an orchard to provide a screen, and long muslin curtains which drifted slightly on the evening breeze.

On opening the book I was bewitched from the very beginning, travelling across Europe with the young solicitor, Jonathan Harker – marvelling at the name, even seeing young Jonathan Markway's face in the description before me – eating strange food with him, hearing strange voices, seeing the fortified medieval towns and the vast, oppressive landscape. When he took the carriage from Bistritz I was there, lurching over mountain passes, hearing the wind and the wolves and the music of the night. My heart leapt in my breast: I knew what it was like. But the author took me further than that, I could hear his voice as he whispered in my ear – *my* ear, no one else's – drawing word-pictures against the darkness, making me fear the advent of Jonathan's host and what strangeness he might find when he arrived at his destination. He put ice in my veins and a chill down my spine as he brought me to the threshold of the castle, and face to face with the mysterious Count Dracula.

Despite the chill there was a strange attraction. The Count was proud of an aristocratic past, yet so attentive and solicitous, so childishly innocent in his eagerness to learn how things were done in England, that one felt drawn to him even while wondering at

332

his purpose. But then, as Jonathan's lonely imprison-
ment in the castle became clearer and the Count's
nocturnal existence ever more sinister, unease deep-
ened to flesh-crawling fear. There was a nightmarish
quality about him, a more-than-real horror in the
way he cloaked himself to crawl like a lizard, *face
down*, down the massive castle wall, leaving his
young guest in a terror of speculation as to what
manner of creature detained him.

In an attempt to discover more, the young man
went exploring, and against the Count's advice was
foolish enough to fall asleep on a couch in the
moonlight, to be woken a little while later by three
voluptuous young women, two dark and one fair,
who seemed to have designs on him as a lover. They
viewed and flirted and laughed coquettishly; one
crept up on him while he pretended to be asleep,
bent over his recumbent form to look and sigh and
lick her glistening red lips in anticipation of the kiss
she would bestow. There was something so disturbingly erotic about the description that I found myself
inadvertently warming in response. I was breathless,
tantalised, horrified – yet as they crept closer, red
mouths agape, I almost wanted the women to
succeed. On the brink of fulfilment, the Count's
sudden appearance, his banishment of the women,
that cry of his: 'This man belongs to me!' was at once
a relief and a disappointment, as though the ultimate
in forbidden pleasure had just been denied.

Dreadful enough, but behind that was something
else, something that amounted almost to recognition.
In that moment of languorous ecstasy, the young
man – Jonathan in the book, Bram in my interpretation – was waiting to be pleasured by a beautiful
woman. Ready and willing to give himself up to her,
his pleasure was stopped on the point of fulfilment,
forbidden by the mysterious Count who banished all

three women, and claimed the man for his own. Snatching him back to a place of safety, he even spoke of love ...

I found that disturbing. Nevertheless, I read on through the evening, lost to all else bar a need to light the lamps. Then I was startled by a sudden breeze as darkness fell, a shivering of the curtains, and the erratic fluttering of a great moth around the room which terrified me. Some time later, my maid's light tapping at the door made me jump again with fright, but I couldn't give up the book. Unlike poor, foolish Lucy – our Lucy of the clifftop grave! – I made sure the doors and windows were securely locked before I climbed into bed, with heavy winter curtains shut close against the moonlight.

The graveyard scenes in Hampstead were extraordinarily vivid, reminiscent of nights Bram and I had spent together in Whitby, but far more chilling in their depiction of death and decay. I no longer frequented burial grounds, and had never been in the local cemetery, but his setting for Lucy's tomb might have been chosen deliberately, as though he knew I lived close by. I was frightened, as much by the memories his novel evoked as by the subject matter; he brought everything up close, stirred me yet made me shiver at the words he used, the pictures he created.

I winced and squirmed at the staking of poor Lucy, and wondered who was the life-model for that light, flirtatious girl, the one who could not make up her mind which of her many suitors she wanted to marry, and, as a consequence I felt, paid for it very heavily. Was it Florence with all her admirers? Was she the tease, the one who infuriated him, the one Bram really wanted to hammer into the ground? The other girl, her friend Mina, was a different and far more complex figure. As a representative of New

Womanhood, she should, I felt, have had my approval; but she was too good to be entirely true, more like some wished-for mother-sister-wife, pure, sensible and innately good. But distinctly untouchable. The only time I was able to sympathise with Mina, really put myself in her place, was after she married Jonathan Harker, when the Count came and took her while her husband lay sleeping beside them. Not only fed from her, but held her face to his breast and made her feed from him. That was real. That was shocking. That was something I could recognise.

The air in the room was warm, but still I shivered under a shawl, and did not put out the lamp until I was certain the sun was up.

The brilliance of the novel made me want to write to him at once. His depiction of Whitby was so clear I found myself choked with longing, for the place, for the time we'd been happy there – even, painfully, for him. Surely Bram could not have written so well unless he too remembered fondly, and that thought was almost my undoing. I had to remind myself that more than a decade had passed since he and I had been in Whitby together, that he'd used me, and used me badly, before obeying Irving's command to return to London. Since then, we'd become different people, leading different lives. Even so, I had to force myself to the office that day, to surround myself with work and people lest I give way to temptation.

I found it necessary to count my advantages, to remind myself of all the good things Henry and I shared, that were not worth putting at risk just because of an extraordinary piece of fiction. But amongst all the questions that sprang to mind, one that kept recurring was to do with Jonathan. I could not help wondering why Bram had used that name – even the surname, Harker, was so close to Markway that I felt it was deliberate. To my knowledge they'd never met, and yet the physical description was close enough to make me wonder. Like the matter of Hampstead and Lucy's tomb, there were too many connections – it was almost as though he was trying to tell me something. Or was he just fulfilling, in print, a fantasy that had begun in Whitby eleven years previously, with talk of a young man he'd never even met, shipwrecks and folk-tales, strange books and stories woven around a tomb on the cliff?

I read *Dracula* again, and with the second reading I found myself even more aware of the sexual themes, and very much disturbed by those echoes from the past. Red lips, white teeth – kisses, blood, sensuality, a sense of excitement and fear – most of all I was disturbed by a sense of *possession*, with the exchange and mingling of blood. Not just latterly, in that darkly erotic scene between Mina and the Count, but earlier, with the transfusions, when Van Helsing was trying to save Lucy's life, when the men who had courted Lucy, and with whom she had flirted so outrageously in the beginning, were invited to take turns to donate their blood to her. At that, I felt a shocking sense of licence, as though Bram had allowed each of these men to possess Lucy in a moral and sexual sense. Perhaps my response was not what was intended, but I could not help remembering Bram's belief that the mingling of blood was more truly binding than any marriage, that it made two people one in a way that was eternal and indissoluble.

As once before, in Whitby, I had a sense of desire and fantasy being played out on the page. Once the Count had lost the whiteness of age and took on the appearance of a younger man, he reminded me most strongly of Irving. I could sense his presence in the background, like that of Irving that day at the cottage, when I saw him behind Bram, moving through the shadows. The truth was hidden by veils and shrouded in darkness, yet Bram had painted a portrait of great power and ruthlessness: a character both urbane and menacing. Irving could have portrayed him to perfection.

Eventually, when I'd distanced myself a little from the shock of it, I wondered whether that was part of the idea: to dramatise the novel and have Irving play the vampire on stage. If so, there were some subtle ironies involved, but it pleased me to think of Bram being aware of them, utilising them, taking a form of revenge in print for the use that had been made of him.

If anything, the insights gained by that second reading were even more disturbing, but they were more of the mind than the emotions, and thus more controllable. So I did not write, but endeavoured instead to retain my poise while searching for published reviews. I felt naked, exposed, more than a little afraid of what I might find, and wondered tremblingly how Bram must feel, awaiting a professional response to his book. What would people think? Would they see what I saw, or were my eyes keener because of what we'd been to each other, and what I knew of him?

The reviews I found were mostly favourable, far too bland to be aware of any secret undercurrents, which in one way was an enormous relief. But none expressed the level of enthusiasm I felt the novel deserved, and it was difficult to contain my sense of indignation.

Henry, whose usual reading was more in the nature of history, or travel and exploration, was bemused by what he termed this new fad of mine. Novels were not to his taste, but he wanted to know what it was about this book that had so caught my attention. It was impossible for me to reveal what I knew of the background – or, indeed, that I was personally acquainted with the author – so I had to let him read my copy and accept his opinion without too many questions or protests. He thought the book original, and liked the bits about Whitby, but did not care for the style of presentation – he said it read too much like a series of grotesque events, which, had it not been for the Whitechapel murders of a few years before, he would have found totally unbelievable.

That was an alarming new slant, one I'd not considered. The murders had occurred a couple of years before we were married, and the murderer, still uncaught, had been styled 'Jack the Ripper' by the popular press. Suddenly I wondered whether he too had played his part in the conception of Bram's novel, if *Dracula* and the character of the Count were some kind of fantastical explanation for what had happened. But there had been so many rumours at the time, I even wondered whether, with his social connections, Bram might have been privy to secret information about those murders in Whitechapel in '88.

Twenty-six

The period which followed was unsettling. I made some expensive mistakes that summer, which Henry had to underwrite; then old Mrs Addison died in November, after a short illness, which necessitated a sad journey to Hull. She'd been a kind and generous woman who celebrated life through her friends and family, and Henry and I were both upset by her death. Also, for a while, we wondered whether it would change any part of our dealings with the Addison brothers. As it transpired, things went on much as before, but I was particularly aware of her absence. I'd been fond of her; she'd been a woman I liked and respected, someone who'd done many of the things I wanted to do, and could therefore be relied upon to offer encouragement rather than pursed lips. I knew I would miss her.

Then, just before Christmas, I heard Bella was up before the magistrates again. As a persistent offender she was not fined this time, but sentenced to fourteen days, and there was nothing I could do to help. I kept imagining her in some cold cell on Christmas Day, eating thin prison fare while in Hampstead Henry and I feasted on roast goose and apple sauce. More accurately, I should say the roast goose was on the table – I was too distracted to eat much, and Henry was irritated by my mood, so it was a somewhat miserable holiday. The new year did not begin well, either. Severe weather in home trade waters sent costs spiralling upwards, while news of floods and shipwrecks increased the sense of gloom. By mid-February, however, when things were beginning to improve on the shipping front, the evening papers were full of a fresh disaster, but fortunately one that involved no loss of life.

In the early hours of the morning there had been a massive fire in Southwark, beneath the brick arches of the Chatham and Dover Railway. Stored there was almost all the scenery which had been used by the Lyceum Theatre in the previous twenty years.

The Lyceum's business manager, Mr Bram Stoker, one newspaper reported, arrived post haste from his home in Chelsea, after being summoned by the police. It was a dank, miserable morning, bitterly cold, and the scene at Bear Lane was chaotic, with the narrow street blocked by fire engines, all pumping away at the inferno beneath the arch, trying to contain flames which were threatening neighbouring property as well as the railway lines above. Even at a safe distance the heat was scorching, yet Mr Stoker seemed anxious to get as close as possible, and had to be discouraged by the police.

He was deeply shocked, he said when interviewed; it was impossible to take in the scale of the loss. Yes, they were insured to a certain extent, but the cost of the property was nothing compared to the real loss, that of the time, labour and artistic endeavour which had gone into their creation. Forty-four plays, and twenty-two of those had been great productions – all the scene painters in England, he claimed, working for a whole year, could not restore the scenery alone, and the cost to Sir Henry Irving was even greater than that – he had lost the bulk of his repertoire.

Reading the report, I hardly knew whether to laugh or cry. I remembered Bram telling me all those years before that major productions were hugely expensive to stage, and that when a play closed after a long run and the scenery was struck, it was always stored against future requirements. In that way, popular draws could be set up again at short notice and no extra cost. They were an extremely important part of an actor-manager's stock-in-trade. They were, in fact, his life-blood. Without them, he was finished.

I should have been ready to gloat. Part of me wanted to, but I couldn't. I kept thinking of Bram and the ending of his novel; and somehow, because I'd identified Irving with the Count, I felt the destruction of one was connected to the mortal blow delivered to the other. It was a distinctly uncomfortable thought, which then made me wonder whether this catastrophe was entirely accidental. Perhaps it had been partly engineered. Such suspicions did not make for restful nights, and I found myself examining every report twice over, as though secrets were hidden in the newsprint like invisible writing, and might suddenly appear by firelight.

I worried what might happen next. I was certain Irving was ruined, both financially and as an actor, and if so, Bram would be without a regular income. I hoped Florence had learned to curb her spendthrift ways, but doubted it, and wondered whether he could earn enough from his writing to keep them both. There were reports that Irving was ill, tours were cancelled, the railway company was suing for compensation for the damage done to its lines by the fire ... Eager to know what was going on there, I kept my eyes and ears open, following the fate of the Lyceum very closely in the months that followed. That summer of '98 the theatre was sold to a consortium, which seemed to indicate that Irving was indeed in trouble, yet he continued to perform there; and then, as the months became a year, then two, with tours of America and the British provinces apparently going on as before, I assumed they'd found other backers and were surviving.

But by the autumn of '99, I had enough to worry about on my own account. War had broken out in South Africa and we were barely able to handle the work it generated. After so many years of industrial and agricultural depression, in which we'd often struggled to find cargoes for the space available, with the war we found ourselves frantically looking for ships to provide transportation for the vast volume of goods and men going overseas.

As the century ended and turned into a new one, we were almost too concerned to notice. Financially we did well, but by the time the war was over in 1902, so many things seemed to have changed. The old Queen had died, and we had a new King who was hardly young; my Henry was fifty-seven and seemed to have aged a great deal, whereas I was barely thirty-five years old and stimulated by survival and success. I felt I was still advancing, still achieving, and that at long last I knew what I was doing. My chief regret was that I could not breach the defences of the Baltic Exchange. Henry's was the name, so I had to rely on him. He was passing much of the work to me, but while I didn't mind that, I did mind what I saw as the regression of our marriage. Somehow, he and I had slipped into a limbo of predictability, in which we rose, breakfasted, travelled to the office, parted, met for luncheon, discussed business matters, wrote reports, sent telegraph messages and returned home again, and that was our life together. A life I'd fought for. I chafed at it, but felt I had no right to complain.

But words and feelings left unexpressed have a

habit of either festering or dying, and although I tried to pretend that nothing had changed, in my heart I was lonely and unhappy. My days were full but there was an emptiness growing inside me that was not satisfied either by Henry or by a social life with Henry's friends. The men had grown used to my business acumen and treated me rather like an honorary man at table, but the women still regarded me as an object of curiosity, or worse, with suspicion, as though my interests were feigned, merely a new way of seducing the opposite sex. Henry said it was because I was still too young and attractive, that if I'd lost my looks or been cursed with a face like a horse, they wouldn't have minded so much; but I said it wouldn't have made any difference, since women who had brains but no looks to speak of were generally pitied, which was just as bad. Pity didn't make for friendship either.

In truth, I had neither time nor interests in common with the wives of Henry's friends. Apart from their children, the younger ones gossiped about parties and the latest fashions; the ones of my own age discussed homes and servants and their husbands' achievements, while the older ones whispered in martyred tones of their ailments. I was hopeless on any of these topics. I liked clothes but not enough to be fashionable, and I had no time for a house in the country. I had no children to brag or complain about, and was not yet of an age, thank God, where health was my sole obsession. I would have liked to enthuse about the building of a new steamship on the Tyne, the excitement of seeing a keel laid, of watching all those men working steadily, busily, competently at a great undertaking. I would have liked to describe my latest journey to St Petersburg, and that sense of trouble seething beneath the gloss and glitter; I would have liked to say –

But what was the use? Not even Henry understood my enthusiasms any more: we were together in name and business only. I would have liked to be honest with him, to say that it was not purely for reasons of business that I travelled abroad, but because I needed to get away, it was essential to my sense of self, to cure the feeling of weight and suffocation that home and work sometimes engendered. But perhaps he knew that anyway; perhaps that was why he made no objections.

In the spring, about a year after the ending of the South African War, I was desperate to get out of London, and, after an exceptionally hard winter, found myself longing for warmth and sun. I tried to persuade Henry to come with me to the Mediterranean, but he preferred the gentler unfolding of an English summer, and anyway had never been keen on shipboard life. So this time he encouraged me to holiday alone, and arranged passage for me, with Alice, my maid, aboard a steamship bound for the Far East. It was one of the Addisons' larger cargo ships, which also carried a handful of passengers. The ship would put into Gibraltar for fresh stores and fuel, also into Valletta and Port Said, before proceeding to Bombay. I'd never been to Egypt, and from Henry's books on travel and exploration, I thought it seemed the most different of Mediterranean countries, and at that time of year promised all the warmth and colour I needed. I instructed Alice to pack the very lightest garments for our stay. We would arrange our return voyage through the Addisons' agent in Cairo.

While travelling with me, Alice's duties were as much those of companion as personal maid, and generally she fulfilled them admirably. We got on well together, but she was not enamoured of long voyages, and often in rough seas would simply take to her cabin for days on end. Then I became the maid, making sure she was comfortable while I spent my time on deck, in a strange way enjoying the remnants of my fear, and all the excitement of a battle against the weather. It was now the journeys that attracted me most, particularly the sea voyages, which I found so invigorating. Something about the movement of a ship, that rolling, plunging motion, the shush of the bow-wave and the lonely cry of the seabirds, gave a sense of flight and freedom. I no longer wondered why my forebears had sailed the oceans; for me, even modern steamships, which lacked much of the spirit and beauty of sail, had a magic that nothing ashore could match.

Most people seem to prefer passenger ships, with all the care and service that goes with them, but from those early days with Henry I found I always preferred the working view from cargo ships. The facilities may have been less refined, but everything was quieter, less formal and, to me at least, far more interesting. Also, times had changed, and by and large the food was better. The Addisons seemed to be good owners who treated their crews fairly and made a decent allowance for victualling. Even so, when travelling in the past I had sometimes taken it upon myself to comment afterwards, since few other people either could or would. The Addisons were probably used to me after all the journeys I'd made across the North Sea and into the Baltic, but I dare say I was something of an irritation to the shipmasters who disliked having even a handful of passengers aboard. Most especially single women. But I tried not to mind that.

We were fortunate on the journey out, since there were five others – two Indian Army officers, a middle-aged lady returning from leave with her unmarried daughter, and a single gentleman of indeterminate years and occupation who kept very much to himself. The rest of us were happy to be sociable. The weather was good once we left the Channel behind, and unexpectedly calm for March, even crossing the Bay of Biscay, for which Alice was profoundly thankful. My only complaint, if complaint it could be, was that I found the other passengers distracting. I was so interested in their lives, in their interest in each other – even to the odd gentleman's unsociability – that I barely had time to notice the ship or even her officers and crew. Which probably meant that they were excellent. Anything less and I would have noticed a great deal.

Of the voyage back, naturally, I remember everything.

Alice and I spent three weeks in Egypt, both of us overwhelmed by a sense of having stepped out of reality and back into biblical times. The main streets of Cairo were the modern anachronism – most other places seemed unchanged since the days of Moses. I'd seen lithographic illustrations of the Sphinx and Pyramids, and even some photographs, but they could not prepare me for the dazzling light and colour of the reality. Nor the smells, which were equally overwhelming at times, and the dust, which got into everything.

In some respects, the mosques and the museums reminded me of Constantinople and that journey I'd made with Henry ten years before. We'd been so close, so happy then, like honeymooners. It seemed a lifetime since, and I was saddened, knowing it could never be recaptured. But those thoughts were too melancholy. As a remedy, I dragged poor Alice everywhere, by carriage, by camel and donkey through the desert, and by dhow along the Nile, until we were both exhausted, freckled, and suffering from a surfeit of tombs and temples and hieroglyphic texts – not to mention the surprising number of men who seemed to want to act as our personal guides.

'But guides to what, ma'am?' Alice muttered darkly, fearing yet again our joint abduction into the white-slave trade. 'Nearest opium den, most like!'

I laughed but fending off that kind of attention had been a strain, even when we were on accompanied tours. The trip had been most enjoyable, but I was ready to go home. On arrival in Cairo we'd been advised that there were two ships leaving Bombay about the same time, and another expected to leave two weeks later. There were berths available on all three. I'd chosen the first one, as the *Holderness* and her master were known to me from London, so when I went into the agent's office in Cairo to confirm, I checked only the date and time we were due to embark at Port Said. It never occurred to me to check anything else.

A young deck apprentice, helping to check stores and sweating profusely in a stiff collar and waistcoat, was on duty by the gangway when we arrived. He organised a crewman to bring our luggage and escorted us to our accommodation amidships.

'Master's ashore just now, ma'am, but I'm sure he'll be pleased to greet you when he returns.'

'Tell him there's no hurry,' I assured him airily. 'I don't need the guided tour – it's only Mrs Lindsey, and he knows I've been aboard before.'

The young man seemed to hesitate, but then he nodded and returned to his duties, while Alice and I set about making ourselves comfortable in cabins which were barely bigger than cupboards. Since everyone else seemed to be occupied, while Alice unpacked I introduced myself to the other passengers, a young woman travelling in company with a much older man, who turned out to be a doctor going home on leave. From her pallid complexion and languid movements I assumed Miss Fenton was returning from India for her health's sake. She was seated beneath an awning on the boat deck, and to be civil I accepted the chair beside her, while the Doctor fetched another.

We made the kind of conversation that strangers make, judging and placing each other while affecting a greater interest in the busy quay. Ship's officers were checking the stores coming aboard, market traders in boats alongside were shouting their wares – boxes of fruit, honey cakes, embroidered hangings – while shoreside officials tried in vain to clear them off. It was a shifting kaleidoscope of colour and noise, and in the midst of it I noticed a man in a peaked cap and linen reefer jacket, carrying a folio of papers beneath his arm. He was dark and tanned and bearded but there was something familiar about him, particularly in the way he moved through the crowd and strode lightly up the gangway towards us.

Miss Fenton said, 'Ah, here comes our gallant Captain . . .'

'Mr Barlow? Surely not –'

'No, no – he was taken ill just before we sailed, and Mr Markway came from another ship to take over.'

But I'd recognised him even before she said his name. 'Markway,' I repeated, feeling as though I'd been winded. 'Of course – I'd forgotten . . .'

Forgotten how he looked and moved, what a pleasure it had always been to see him. He was older now, of course, with a man's weight and breadth in the shoulder, but still with that grace which had so distinguished him as a boy. Both hair and beard were a little too long and curly for neatness, and yet he was as striking as ever. I could not believe that I was seeing him in the flesh after all these years, that he was Master of the ship on which we were travelling.

But if I was astonished and taken aback, I was afraid his reaction might be worse. He was coming towards me, striding up to where his passengers were relaxing, obviously with every intention of greeting this woman he'd been told about, this Mrs Lindsey – *long-standing friend of the owners, so mind your p's and q's* – with absolutely no idea of who she really was. I had to force myself to my feet, to intercept him boldly before there was any chance of embarrassment in front of these idle but interested onlookers.

I must have seemed brash in the extreme as I pinned on a smile and extended my hand, shepherding him towards the side-rail to shield his astonishment. 'Captain Markway – this is a surprise! I was expecting Mr Barlow, but Miss Fenton informs me the poor man has been taken ill – nothing too serious, I hope? – and you're his replacement. I'm Marie Lindsey, by the way. So pleased to meet you –' I shook his hand vigorously and beamed at him – 'and may I say how much I'm looking forward to the voyage!'

The colour which had warmed him drained at once, leaving the skin waxen with shock. His eyes were like jet as they gazed at me in disbelief and something like horror. That I managed to retain my smile while uttering a string of banalities was, I'm sure, a tribute to my years of City trading, but Jonathan Markway did not know that.

'Mrs Lindsey,' he managed at last, executing a stiff little bow, 'I'm – I'm sorry I wasn't here to greet you, but – welcome aboard the *Holderness*! We don't, I'm afraid, have many passenger ship facilities,' he added rather hoarsely, as though suddenly recalling a standard speech, 'so you must expect things to be somewhat basic – but we'll do all in our power to ensure you have a comfortable voyage.'

'Thank you,' I responded sincerely, trying to hold his gaze, to imply something infinitely gentler than the loud, over-confident woman I'd just been playing. But he seemed determined to look elsewhere, and, having cleared his throat and regained his more usual voice, he smiled briefly in the general direction of his other passengers, excused himself, and disappeared inside the accommodation.

Miss Fenton was offended, it seemed, as much by my gushing manner as by Jonathan's brusqueness. Even Dr Graeme, who'd been pleasantly attentive, appeared to regard me dubiously. I resumed my seat, a smile fixed over the vacuum inside. Listening, nodding, uttering inanities, I bore the company for another quarter-hour, then pleaded the heat and went to lie down. When sensibility returned and I was able to think rationally, I suspected I'd set myself a course for disaster with both sides.

Had the *Holderness* been a passenger ship, then Jonathan could have avoided me quite easily. But aboard a cargo ship the accommodation area amidships was not large. It comprised the six passenger cabins and saloon, the officers' and Master's cabins, and wheelhouse and chartroom above. Even if Jonathan did not join us for every meal, he was generally in the saloon at least once a day, and common courtesy demanded that he exchange a few words with each of us. For almost three days I tried hard to place myself in situations where we might have a chance to speak privately, but in such a confined area there were always people about, and – other than a brief acknowledgement of my existence at table – he made no attempt to engage me in conversation. We might have been strangers, except that he never even looked at me.

The situation was awkward and embarrassing; I found it painful too, and all the rationalising in the world could not alter that. Nevertheless, in company I worked hard at maintaining an equable front of smiles and pleasantries – perhaps not quite so brash as I'd pretended to be initially, but certainly bolder and braver than I felt. Alice saw through it very early on and, having missed that initial confrontation, was concerned enough to ask what was wrong. She was tidying my clothes away while I brushed out my hair in readiness for bed; the ship was rolling gently, like the comforting motion of a cradle, and that, combined with her concern, almost unsealed my tongue. I forced myself to look hard in the mirror, to take note of the softer shoulders and fuller breasts, and the traces of little lines – laughter lines, Henry called them – at the corners of eyes and mouth. I was no longer a young girl, I was a mature, responsible woman and, furthermore, Alice's employer. With the past laying siege to my sensibilities, I forced myself to tell her only the barest of truths, which was that the ship's Master and I had known each other long ago in Whitby.

'We were very young – there were no declarations, nothing like that, but I think he would have liked me to be there, waiting for him, when he came back.'

'But you weren't?' she asked, and I had to explain that I'd left Whitby while he was away, to work for the Addisons. 'Well,' she said matter-of-factly, 'he should have come to see you, ma'am, if he was that keen. He shouldn't take it out on you like this, not after all these years. It's not mannerly.'

351

'No, indeed.' I gave a noncommittal smile, unable to say what I thought, which was that Jonathan had not forgiven me for rejecting a future with him in favour of short-term benefits from a much older and richer man. For prostituting myself, in other words, which was how he would have seen my affair with Bram. But I couldn't put it like that to Alice.

She asked slyly, 'Weren't you keen on him?'

'Not keen enough, obviously.'

'Shame, really, him so handsome . . .'

'It might have been – then. Not now, though,' I reminded her firmly. 'In case you've forgotten, Alice – I'm married.'

As I imagined he was, too.

Later, when I was alone, I found myself wondering who he might have married and where he might be living, whether he'd made his home in Whitby or elsewhere; and whether he was happy.

Twenty-seven

As we passed the great delta of the Nile, the sea was milky for scores of miles, the weather calm and hot, with barely enough breeze to fill the sails of a dhow. I noticed several brigs and schooners becalmed as we steamed along, and found myself thinking of Jack Louvain and Bram, standing outside the studio in Whitby, watching the paddle tugs and discussing the relative merits of steam and sail.

To those with no experience of the hardships involved, sail would always be best. But for all the beauty and heart-lifting pleasure of dancing along over a summer sea, even the best of the old ships were cramped and damp below decks, and the worst could be killers of men, as the wrecks around the British coasts could testify. Steamships were different, less beautiful perhaps, but safer, less likely to be forced aground on a lee shore. They kept going in fair weather and foul, their engines providing heat and water and fuel for the galley, making life at sea generally more comfortable. Hard for those who stoked the boilers, but at least they could look forward to a hot meal and a dry bunk at the end of a watch, unlike the old days, when bad weather meant wet clothes for days on end, and meals of cold porridge and hard tack.

Nevertheless, while mentally counting the blessings of progress I was emotionally wishing I'd taken a leaky old barque to Oslo or Copenhagen and worrying about the chances of arriving safely rather than facing three weeks of stiff-lipped embarrassment in the sunny Mediterranean. There was little to do but pace the long wooden foredeck, or sit beneath a canvas awning in company with the spoiled Miss Fenton. Alice did not like her, and had decided to retreat behind her 'dumb servant' mask, which she could do to perfection when necessary, but I felt obliged to be sociable for at least an hour or so each day. My sense of obligation was not helped, however, by the suspicion that she would have shunned my company at once if there had been a better choice.

Dr Graeme was pleasant enough, with a dry, ironic sense of humour – I had the impression he was glad of me to spare him his duties for at least part of the time. He and I often met on our walks around the deck, and he seemed genuinely interested in my connection with shipping and the Addisons. It was something to talk about, other than the weather and life in India. I was reluctant at first, because of the awkwardness between the Master and myself, but then I saw that my business and social position had been accepted as the reason for Jonathan's stiffness towards me. It made me feel less publicly humiliated by his attitude, and I was grateful to Dr Graeme for that.

Away from the humidity of the Nile, we steamed into fresh sea breezes and settled into the kind of shipboard routine which benefited everyone, especially the ship's officers. Most of them seemed happier to be at sea, ready to exchange a quip in passing, or to talk about their families as we ploughed steadily on through the Mediterranean towards home. Within the week, however, those fresh sea breezes had turned into brisk, northwesterly winds, and with the colder air came violent squalls and rougher seas, which soon confined Miss Fenton to her cabin. Poor Alice succumbed shortly afterwards, but I have to admit that for me it was an improvement all round. The weather suited my mood, and there was no more need to be polite. Even Dr Graeme seemed to understand. We passed each other grimly on our walks around the deck.

Next day the temperature dropped again, while driving rain bleached the colour from sea and sky, making the outlook more like the environs of Whitby in winter than the blue Mediterranean I'd come to expect. Perhaps it struck a similar chord with Jonathan, since he managed to address me at breakfast that morning, when he came down from the bridge. I was later than usual, having slept badly, and was eating alone.

Timing the roll, he took his place at the head of the long table and unfurled his napkin. That morning I'd seated myself in Alice's place, almost at the foot, and I was glad of the four places between us. When the steward had taken his order for bacon and eggs, he said gruffly, as though he thought I might resent the information, 'In case you're interested, Mrs Lindsey, we'll be passing the island of Sicily to starboard during the course of today. Not that you'll be able to see much of it, unfortunately.'

'Indeed?' I responded, managing to sound coolly polite while my heart thudded like that of a startled schoolgirl. I wasn't sure whether I was angry or embarrassed or even pleased to be so addressed, whether I should take the opportunity to converse, or just finish my coffee and go. At that point the ship gave a more pronounced roll, and the cruet flew past me like a toboggan on a downhill slope. I grabbed at it before it could cannon over the rim of the table and on to the floor.

'Well fielded,' my companion said with a small smile; but he carefully avoided touching me as I passed it back. 'By the way, the weather's worsening, as I'm sure you're aware, so I'd prefer you to keep off the main deck. In this weather it's not very safe.'

'I'm aware of the dangers,' I retorted, perhaps a little more sharply than I intended, but his attitude felt like an insult, especially when he knew I'd been used to working in far worse conditions as a girl.

His dark eyes met mine, and beneath arched brows I saw a depth of anger there that silenced me. 'Even so,' he said quietly, 'when you go outside, I don't want you venturing below the level of the boat deck.'

'Very well,' I agreed, forcing the words, 'I'll do as you say. Might I ask whether this rule applies to Dr Graeme as well?'

'It applies to all the passengers.'

In the limited confines of a ship, with too little to occupy the mind, it can be surprising what irritates the sensibilities; but later that morning, as the Doctor and I leaned on the boat deck rail and tried to peer through the murk towards Sicily, we agreed that the wind was stronger and the pounding of the waves more pronounced. I was suffering from a dull headache, and my companion had begun to feel queasy. I joked that I would soon be looking after him too; and before the evening meal he'd taken to his bed, and I was serving soup in enamel mugs to three groaning patients.

Later, leaving Alice's cabin, I was startled by the unexpected appearance of a tall figure at the end of the alleyway. 'How are they?' Jonathan asked.

'Feeling dreadful, looking worse – but none sick as yet.'

'Well, that's something. And you, Mrs Lindsey – how are you?'

'More comfortable outdoors,' I replied acidly, 'with fresh air and a view of the horizon.'

There was amusement in his voice as he said: 'I know that shouldn't surprise me – but somehow it does.'

I paused outside the saloon and turned to look at him. 'It shouldn't surprise you at all,' I said with bold reproof. 'In case you've forgotten, Jonathan Markway, you and I come from the same place.'

'I haven't forgotten.'

'And neither have I.'

There was still challenge as he met my gaze, but the anger seemed less. For the first time I felt he was beginning to see me as the woman I was now, rather than the girl he remembered, and that pleased me. As I went in to take my usual place at table, he said, 'Well, then, if you'd care to come up to the bridge for a while, about ten or fifteen minutes after eight, I think we can at least offer you a change of scene.'

Trying to restrain a satisfied smile, I nodded my acceptance. The invitation was not exclusive, I knew that, since the Doctor had been up there two or three times to my knowledge, and so, I gathered, had Miss Fenton, previous to our arrival; but it was the first time that I had been asked, and my only regret was the time of day. Dinner was at six, and by eight o'clock it would be pitch black. But still, it was a beginning.

After dinner I made my round of the invalids again, reluctantly performing the kind of duties that reminded me of my time as a personal servant all those years ago, although for Alice I didn't mind. I waited then until I could be sure the previous watch had been handed over, with the First Mate away to bed and the Third Mate taking his place. Wearing long boots with a jumper and divided skirt for ease and practicality, I made my way to the bridge, hanging on to every hand-hold along the way. Outside, the roar of the sea was almost deafening, and I was glad to reach the glass-enclosed safety of the wheelhouse. Above, on the monkey-island, the shrouded figure of the lookout paced back and forth, while inside the helmsman struggled to keep the wheel steady, and the Master and Third Mate watched the darkness to either side.

Before midnight the first watch was undertaken by the junior officer, but because of his inexperience the Master was generally on hand for safety's sake. 'And in bad weather, at night, when we're so close to land,' Jonathan confessed softly, 'I like to be up here most of the time.'

Somehow, that confession put another dent in his armour. I was touched by it and very much aware of him as he stood close by me on the bridge. After a little while he resumed his routine, pacing back and forth between the windows, checking the course and heading with the helmsman, stepping outside, viewing the darkness in a broad arc from stem to stern, then coming in to pace back and forth again. I looked too, but could see nothing but the rearing of huge white waves either side of the bow, and the phosphorescent glow of foam breaking over the decks. I felt the familiar prickles of alarm, and closed my eyes for a moment. Opening them, looking down, it was easy to see why we passengers had been banned from the main deck; and as the ship took another severe roll, that the weather was getting worse.

The checks on course and heading were done quietly, just audible above the wind and the underlying throb of the engines. I saw a faint, winking light to port at least half a minute after everyone else, a light which turned out to be another steamer heading east. That was all, and yet there was something compulsive about looking for other signs of life in the darkness, especially on a night like this; like searching the heavens for shooting stars, or staring into the fire, late at night, when other, more sensible people were in bed.

I thought I'd been there an hour, maybe a little more, but when the lookout went below to brew up, I was surprised to discover that it was almost eleven. Sipping cautiously at a half-mug of hot, sweet cocoa I smiled suddenly, remembering another time, years ago; and as Jonathan paused by my side, I found myself describing my first sea voyage with Henry aboard a Whitby collier to St Petersburg and Tallinn. I even told him, very briefly, about the *Merlin*.

'I remember,' he said quietly, 'how important that was to you.'

In the darkness, for a moment, his eyes lingered on mine. Then with a frown he moved away, and I thought it was probably time for me to check on my patients before retiring for the night. But as I turned to go, Jonathan insisted on coming down with me to see how the others were faring. After we'd checked each one, he said he hoped that I would be able to see to the ladies while the weather was bad; but if Dr Graeme started vomiting, he'd get one of the stewards to attend to him.

'Really, if I'm looking after Alice and Miss Fenton, I don't mind seeing to Dr Graeme as well –'

'Perhaps not, but I'm sure he'll be less embarrassed by the presence of a steward,' Jonathan insisted, grinning as an unexpected swing forced us both back against the wooden bulkhead. It was an extraordinary feeling, like being on a fairground cake-walk in possession of a body that was alternately heavy as clay and light as air, a crazy, delirious sensation that I couldn't help enjoying even while it scared me half to death. We were standing in the narrow alleyway between the cabins, and as I turned to my door another violent lurch nearly threw me off my feet. Jonathan grabbed my arm, steadying me against his side as I started to giggle helplessly. 'Careful,' he cautioned, 'things are getting dangerous.'

'I know.' But I was laughing and trembling all over. I felt drunk, out of control, almost on the verge of collapse. We seemed to stand there for an age, clinging together while the ship was pitching and rolling and doing its best to throw us off our feet. His hands were firm, and while he was holding me, everything was fine. I didn't want him to let go.

But on the next roll, Jonathan reached for my door, opened it and pulled me inside with him. In that narrow space he could lean one shoulder against the upper bunk while holding the door with the other hand. As he held me steady, there was a long, close moment in which we swayed together like dancers. I felt my breasts grow heavy against him, and the tightening of his muscles as he took my weight; then a sudden lightness, a delicate brushing of his body against mine, the nearness of his face and a parting of lips in anticipation.

'Damaris,' he whispered, and it was like a hungry sigh. But after so many years the name sounded strange to me. As I frowned and took a breath, he shifted his stance, and suddenly the tension was different, the intimacy gone.

'I'm sorry,' he said abruptly, setting himself apart. 'When you get to bed, Mrs Lindsey, wedge yourself in with something – a pillow or spare blanket. And be careful – especially between cabins. Doors can be lethal.' For a moment, in contrast to his speech, he looked wounded, indecisive, his mouth working as I gazed at him. 'Forgive me – I must get back to the bridge.'

With that he was gone.

Like a punctured balloon I felt all the air and lightness leave me. Letting go of the upper bunk I let the ship knock me down into the lower one. Since it promptly threatened to disgorge me on to the deck, I did as Jonathan had recommended and stuffed a blanket under the mattress before lying down fully dressed.

I didn't sleep, or even get much rest. The motion was too distressing, and anyway, I was torn between thwarted desire, guilt at what I desired, and a niggling doubt about whether Jonathan wanted me as much as I wanted him. Whether in fact he wanted me at all. My longings were so strongly physical I could feel my pulse racing, and no matter how wrong that was, how unfair to Henry – how disloyal, betraying, and utterly *adulterous* that made me – I felt my conscience was unlikely to hold in any battle between the two.

That initial skirmish almost took my mind off the storm. It certainly made me forget to be afraid. From time to time I remembered to be concerned about the invalids – well, I was concerned about Alice, and felt a reluctant duty towards the other two. I was up and down half the night, applying cold compresses to fevered brows, and emptying slop buckets before the ship could tip them all over the deck. That was an art in itself, since the bathroom floor was wet, and flushing waste down the lavatory had to be timed, otherwise a gush of seawater could jump back out again. But it took my mind off Jonathan Markway, even if underlying frustration found vent in the colourful fishergirl language I hadn't used for years.

Some time before dawn Alfred, the senior steward, appeared, and after that we managed the worst between us. I felt queasy myself at one stage, but it was no more than a combination of hunger and exhaustion. I had a bowl of kedgeree for breakfast, with a mug of tea, and after that was able to sleep for a while.

Despite the conditions, I needed fresh air as well, but even on the boat deck exercise was arduous as well as dangerous. I confined myself to the area around the accommodation, holding on to the rail as I took a few steps up and down, marvelling at the wildness of the sea as I fought for breath against the wind and spray. The storm and that combination of fear and exhilaration reminded me of Bram and our first meeting; and then, as memory led me down some familiar paths, I caught myself wondering whether that day had been the breaking point where Jonathan and I were concerned. In spite of all the obstacles, our strong mutual attraction could have grown, I was sure, into something more serious. But my meeting with Bram had intervened, radically altering my perceptions. And my life.

Not for the first time I railed against fate, questioning why I'd had to meet such a man, and why I couldn't have been happy to settle down in Bay like the rest of my forebears, with a seafaring husband like Jonathan.

But I'd fought against that idea before I met either of them, and I knew that my feelings for Jonathan had been divided from the start by what he did for a living. I tried to cling to those thoughts, but they slithered away before the more powerful fact that I'd always found him physically attractive. That was what plagued me now, and I even caught myself wondering whether it was some kind of retribution for past shortcomings. I was so tormented, I would have given almost anything for some diversion to distract my mind.

I might have gone up to the bridge, but there was no invitation; anyway, I was held back by the memory of those moments in my cabin. Instead, Jonathan and I met awkwardly in passing, between the cabins and the saloon, or briefly out on deck. I longed to feel his arms steadying me again, but we kept well apart, knuckles showing white as we gripped separate sections of rail. He would ask how I was, in tones that suggested genuine concern, but I was afraid it might be assumed for anxious women passengers, so I said I was fine. I thought he looked very worn. No doubt he thought the same of me.

At last, on the fourth or fifth day, the weather abated. The seas were still violent, but the wind had dropped, which meant everyone could relax suffi-ciently to get cleaned up and take some rest. That afternoon, having intended only to lie down for a while, I slept the sleep of the just. When I awoke, about three hours later, I felt strange and uncertain, and went out on deck for some air. To my amaze-ment, in the westering light I could see mountains, bare, cinnamon-coloured peaks between the grey sea and the misty blue of a late afternoon sky. The vista was so beautiful, and so unexpected, that my eyes blurred with gratitude. Without acknowledging it before, I realised I'd been afraid for days, hardly daring to believe that any of us would see land again.

Hearing a footfall, I blinked and took a deep breath. Jonathan came out on deck and leaned against the rail. 'The Atlas Mountains,' he mur-mured, with a sigh of satisfaction. 'A sight to be thankful for, don't you think, after the last few days?'

His sentiments echoed mine so precisely, they came close to destroying what little self-control I had left. 'Yes,' I answered thickly, fishing in my pocket for a handkerchief. I blew my nose somewhat vigorously, while trying to control emotions that seemed determined to let me down.

After a while, he said hesitantly, 'I was planning to have a drink before dinner in my cabin – I wondered if you might join me? In about half an hour, if that would suit?'

My heart gave such a thud of astonishment that I almost wanted to say no, I couldn't possibly; but I heard myself agreeing, saying yes, that would be fine, I was just about to go indoors and change for dinner. Moments later, in the privacy of my cabin, I was in a fever, struggling with my hair, powdering my nose, trying to find something to wear that was reasonably smooth and unstained. And then, when I'd tried and discarded at least half a dozen items, suddenly I was childishly apprehensive at the thought of what he might say, the questions he might ask when we were in a position, at last, to talk.

Having longed for a chance to explain myself, I found myself dreading it. But on my way up to see him all at once I was reminded of the house on Southgate, and his room at the top of the stairs.

The door to his cabin was hooked open, the curtain swaying with the ship. To reinforce that feeling of time slipping back, he was seated at his desk, writing, but there the resemblance ended. It was a man who turned to face me, bearded, freshly washed as I could tell from the wet curls at his neck, wearing a clean shirt, a flamboyant blue tie, and a crumpled linen uniform.

With a warm yet uncertain smile he offered me the other chair, which like his own was anchored to the deck by a short rope, and asked what I would have to drink. He was drinking brandy, so I said I'd have the same, and while he was pouring it I glanced around for photographs. I could see only one, and that not clearly. It was attached in some way to the

364

panelling above his desk, and seemed to be of a small family group, which I was afraid must be Jonathan, his wife, and three young children. I forced a smile and peered rather obviously, thinking we might as well clear up one point at least. When he saw me looking, he released the picture with a smile, and handed it across.

'You'll remember my brother, Dick? He has the chandlery now – that's him, with his wife and family, taken last year.'

I felt my mouth begin to twitch. 'He looks prosperous,' I said, studying his somewhat smug expression, and the plain faces of his wife and children. 'And a proud family man.'

'He is indeed,' Jonathan said drily. 'Dick weighs everything, and chooses well.'

'Not a gambler, then?'

'No, he's a good man, but he never took a risk in his life.'

We shared a conspiratorial smile across a space that was small, yet several times bigger than that in the passenger cabins below. I felt my spirits improving, even more so as the fortifying spirit took hold, and was bold enough then to ask after his parents. I discovered that his mother was dead and had been for many years, while his father had married again and was living at Bay.

'He likes it there – says it puts him in mind of Cornwall.'

'Yes, I've heard others say that.' I paused, just long enough to make the question sound casual. 'And you, Jonathan – are you married?'

He shook his head. 'Never found time, somehow. But I keep a cottage at Bay.'

Robin Hood's Bay. The name brought back so many memories, I felt choked by them and couldn't speak. Jonathan gazed into his glass for a moment, and then at me. 'You know, I've been wanting to talk things over with you ever since you arrived on board – but it took me a few days to adjust to the reality. I'm sorry if I seemed a little stand-offish, before.'

As he paused to add more brandy to his glass, I saw his hands were unsteady, and that he was far from sure of himself. At once a warm flood of sympathy – and, I must admit, a modicum of triumph that I could make him nervous – made me feel better than spirits ever could. 'It's understandable,' I said. 'It's taken me a while, too.'

Before I could become too complacent, he mentioned the storm, and began to thank me for keeping going, for looking after the other passengers when the weather was so bad. I didn't want to be thanked, and had no desire to talk about the weather, but he would not be diverted. 'No, about the other night,' he said, 'I feel I should apologise . . .'

'Apologise? What for?'

'Well, in case you thought –' He broke off, his mouth twisting with just the merest hint of irony; then, as he glanced up to meet my enquiring gaze, he said drily: 'I don't know what you thought, but please try to imagine it from my point of view. I mean, here you are, with all you possess – and all your influence in the world I inhabit – and suddenly, without any warning, you're aboard my ship. I still can't believe it. And then, without so much as a by-your-leave, this ignorant Whitby shipmaster takes advantage of your fear and a nasty bit of weather, and makes a grab at you in your own cabin. I didn't intend to,' he added, 'but it might have seemed like that. So, I'd say it wouldn't be surprising if you felt angry and insulted.'

'Oh, I see,' I responded with equal dryness. 'And there I was, thinking you were just concerned for my safety.' Before he could respond to that, I smiled and raised my glass. 'Anyway, how did you know I was frightened?'

'I knew,' he said simply, all cleverness and pretence abandoned. In that moment, I saw the innocent boy he had been, and felt a pang of longing; then he gave me a smile which was very much of himself. 'And if you weren't, you should have been. I certainly was.'

I was tempted to believe him, and the fact of danger now past struck me forcefully again, as it had that afternoon. He seemed to read my expression at once, and as I put out my hand he grasped it in his strong, capable one, entwining his fingers in mine. For a moment we simply gazed at each other; then he drew me closer until our hands clasped, until our knees were touching and we were leaning forward, face to face, breath to breath, skin prickling with awareness.

'How dare you refer to yourself as an ignorant Whitby shipmaster?' I whispered, swallowing hard.

'Because that's what I am.'

I laughed, shakily. 'In that case, I must still be an ignorant Whitby fisherlass . . .'

I felt the warmth of his sigh and his lips moved briefly against mine. But the kiss was barely there before he said, 'I liked her, you know, that girl, Damsy Sterne – I always thought she had courage. Not one to make idle promises, either. So why did she go? Why didn't she leave word for me?'

Instinctively, I moved back, but his hands tightened their grip. 'I need to know.'

'Didn't they tell you at the time, Jonathan? Surely they must have been eager to put you in the picture!'

'People told me lots of things at the time – I didn't necessarily believe them.'

'You should have done,' I said harshly: 'they were probably true.'

He shook his head, released one of my hands, but only to reach for his glass. 'That man – the one at Newholm, or wherever it was – was he the one you married?'

'Goodness, no. He was married already – that was part of the problem.'

'With that sort, it generally is,' he commented, and drank some more. 'Did you love him?'

I nodded, barely able to trust my voice. 'Yes, unfortunately, I rather think I did.'

He set down his glass then, and cupped my face in his hands. He kissed me very tenderly. 'Well, then, I'm glad you loved him. I'm just sorry he let you down.'

Twenty-eight

Looking like a wraith, Dr Graeme joined us at table that evening. He was the butt of some friendly jokes, mainly from the Chief Engineer, who was closest in age, but he responded readily enough. I was grateful, since the jesting drew attention from Jonathan's air of abstraction and my somewhat forced spirits. After dinner, I was in two minds about rejoining him, but since Alice and Miss Fenton seemed to be enjoying a cosy chat over soup and water biscuits in Alice's cabin, I felt my attention there was no longer required.

Climbing the stairs to Jonathan's cabin, I could hardly believe my change of heart in so short a time. I still wanted him, but it was hard on my conscience having all those old suspicions confirmed, discovering that he had learned of my affair with Bram all those years ago, and been hurt by it. In mitigation, he said we were barely more than children at the time; but even so, he hadn't forgotten, and nor had I.

Words had come more easily before dinner, but having broken the thread, it was difficult to recapture anything but small-talk. Above the desk were a pair of oil lamps, which moved in gimbals with the motion of the ship, casting soft light and shadows over the dark mahogany fittings. The steward brought a pot of coffee from the galley and poured two cups, together with some brandy, before disappearing back to the nether regions. If we'd both been inclined to gulp nervously before, now we sipped carefully, each watching the other while pretending not to, each waiting for an opening which seemed determined not to come.

I was aware of every movement, every blink of thick dark lashes against tanned skin. There were shadows beneath his eyes, and he seemed to be undergoing a struggle similar to my own, less to do with the morality of the situation, I was sure, than this battle between then and now, this conflict between apprehension and desire. We were like unarmed combatants, edging round a ring, looking for some kind of satisfaction, but half afraid of the pain involved. It was unbearable. I drained my coffee and set the cup and glass on the desk. 'I'll go,' I said at last, aware of the catch in my throat. 'Perhaps we can talk some other time.'

'No, please don't.' Frowning, he rose and touched my arm, lightly – then firmly, as he turned me towards him and closed the door. 'Please, I want you to stay.'

Another moment of choice presented itself, in which I knew I should do the right thing, and leave – for his sake as much as my own. But with his touch fear and conscience fled, and then the burning of his mouth against mine banished everything beyond desperate need. We clung together, intoxicated by taste and touch, swaying between the two stabilities of desk and sleeping-place. He fumbled with the tiny buttons of my blouse; I opened them at once as he pulled off his tie and began to unfasten his shirt. But we paused then, breathing hard, aware that a boundary had been crossed, some kind of commitment entered into.

'What about –?' I raised my eyes, to where an

occasional creak of timbers signalled watchkeepers moving across the deck above.

'I told the Third Mate I was going to bed,' Jonathan said with a sudden, mischievous smile. 'Don't worry – he'll call me if he needs me.'

With that he unfastened my skirt, and as it dropped, lifted me up into the bunk. It was high and box-like, with cupboards above and below and curtains to the side; and, while not nearly a double bed, spacious compared to mine. Extinguishing one of the lamps, he turned down the other, slipped off his remaining clothes and climbed in beside me. For a little while we simply lay against each other, kissing and caressing, laughing softly with relief that we'd reached this far. Then he helped me undress. Words were superfluous. He made me feel desirable and intensely alive; when he rose above me I wanted to cry out for the joy of it. He knew, and watched as he penetrated me, stifling both our cries with kisses as he withdrew to thrust again and again. At the last, when he would have pulled away, I held him to me, shuddering with pleasure as he climaxed deep inside.

Afterwards, we were both emotional, torn between laughter and tears, in a whispered conspiracy of tender words and smothered kisses. Cradled in each other's arms and rocked by the sea, with the curtains of that curious little bed half drawn against the night, it was like being nursed in the safety of a womb. Jonathan slept while I watched over him, and in the contentment of sleep he looked so very young, with glossy hair and beard, and soft dark curls across his chest. His skin was smooth, his muscles firm to the touch, and he seemed such a boy to me. I had to remind myself that he was older than I: by only a year, but older, nevertheless.

I fell asleep, and woke some time later to find him

371

leaning over me, fully dressed. 'It's all right,' he whispered, 'not yet midnight. I woke and thought I'd better go up top, check all was well. It is – and I managed to scrounge a hot drink. Cocoa, I'm afraid, not coffee. Do you want some, or will you go back to sleep?'

I was alert at once, feeling strangely relaxed and complete, as though I'd had an excellent night's sleep. It was impossible to recall the last time I'd felt like that. I sat up with the sheets around me, drinking hot, sweet cocoa while Jonathan made notes. 'Wind westerly, force 3, slight sea running,' I intoned, inventing an entry for the log book. 'Unexplained appearance of female passenger in Master's bed . . .'

'. . . with gorgeous red hair, white skin, and a pair of *very* pretty breasts,' he continued, grinning. 'Must investigate further . . .'

I chuckled at that but he shushed me, pointing upwards. 'They'll be changing the watch soon – and the Second Mate's got a bit more about him than the young lad . . .'

'Oh dear, perhaps I'd better be going?'

He stopped writing at once. 'Don't you dare! It's not every night I manage to entice a beautiful woman into my bunk – please permit me to make the most of it!'

And he did – we did – finally parting just before dawn. He dressed and came down with me, and for a few minutes we stood out on the boat deck, watching the sky grow lighter along the horizon, the black sea turning to gunmetal as we watched. And then we kissed and he climbed the steps to the bridge, while I crept indoors to bed.

We ate our meals at the same table, in our usual places, with Dr Graeme and the Chief Engineer beside us, and two younger officers, Alice and Miss Fenton opposite. Nevertheless, over the succeeding two weeks I felt we were connected by invisible cords, and that our lightheartedness made them dance. Jonathan called me Mrs Lindsey in public, but since Damsy was the name he preferred, that was what he called me in private. He said Marie was for other people, and I had to go along with that. Meanwhile he and I kept up the pretence that no one else could possibly know about the two of us, yet it must have been something of an open secret. Alfred, the steward who looked after the Master's cabin, often caught my eye and winked, while everyone else discreetly looked the other way. Aboard passenger ships, I imagine these things must have happened regularly; and possibly some kind of unwritten law existed amongst the men, to the effect that nothing was ever mentioned ashore. But there again, perhaps they were forgotten as soon as they left the ship.

Alice maintained that Miss Fenton never did catch on, simply because she was so self-centred; and Alice, bless her, made sure her attention was distracted anyway. To begin with, I worried what Alice would think – not enough to stop me, to be sure – but in the end I realised that she was far more worried about what would happen when we reached London.

I didn't want to think about that, so did my best to behave like the proverbial ostrich, while over the final few days of the voyage Jonathan became increasingly concerned. We were approaching the Isle of Ushant and the Channel when he said to me in desperation one afternoon in his cabin: 'Damsy, my love, I've measured my regard for other women against what I felt for you all those years ago. It wasn't that I imagined myself still in love, but rather

373

that I remembered how it *felt*, the bad bits as well as the good. I've known women since, none very well – there was never time to know them well – but I've never been able to recapture that feeling. I'd honestly begun to believe that it was something of a delusion, part of youth, one of those things that can never be repeated. I'd stopped looking for it. But then, suddenly, on a voyage from Bombay to the Port of London, you came back into my life again.

'And do you know what? When I saw you on deck that day – when I recognised you – it was like a blow to the chest. I couldn't believe how shocked I was – I couldn't understand how difficult it was to adjust to the idea of *then* and *now*. But when I did – when I began to accept you as you are now – I realised that all the old attraction was still there, only much deeper and stronger than before. And since then,' he added intently, 'you must know how much I love you – you must know that?'

'Yes,' I whispered, 'I think so.'

'So what do I do? Now I've found you again, what happens next? Do you expect me just to stand by when your husband arrives aboard my ship to collect you? To shake your hand and say, *Goodbye, Mrs Lindsey, it's been a great pleasure knowing you* – is that what you expect me to do?'

His intensity cut me to the quick, but there was nothing I could say to alleviate it. I kept reminding him that I was married. I kept explaining about Henry and my business as a ship-broker and part-owner of ships, but he didn't seem to understand how much I owed to Henry, and how impossible it was for me to contemplate leaving him.

'Besides, what about your profession?' I demanded later, as the sun went down over the western sea. 'Do you expect me to leave my husband – and a business which has been my life – in order to sit about somewhere for months at a time, twiddling my thumbs and just waiting for you to come home? I can't do that.' Over the past few days I'd privately considered such a life, but I knew I couldn't do it, not even for the sake of what we were sharing now.

'Why can't we compromise?' I suggested gently. 'We could meet when you're in port or on leave? Or even when you're expected on the Continent? Hamburg, or Ostend – we could have a few days together – Henry need never know –'

'Good God, Damaris – this is your *husband* we're talking about! How can you contemplate a life of lies and deception like this? What about truth and honour – don't they mean anything any more?'

I wanted to say that life was made up of warp and weft, a tapestry of compromise, but he was in no mood for such pragmatism. Time was running out, and I longed for him to agree, but he seemed quite unable to do so. Then we were entering the Channel, and he was busy with other shipping, too busy for any lengthy conversation. Not until we were anchored in the Thames estuary, waiting for the pilot, did the opportunity arise again.

It was about dusk, very mild and still, with a mist hovering mysteriously over the mudflats and the lights of other ships reflected like lanterns in the water. There was a melancholy beauty about it that reminded me of pictures by Whistler, and by reflection, later, those pictures for me *became* that evening, with all its sad nostalgia.

By next day the worst part of the crisis would be over, I knew that. Henry would be waiting for me as the ship docked, and – no matter what was decided – I would have to go home with him, and either find some way of explaining what had happened to me on the way home from Egypt, or some way of living with my memories. I'd fallen in love with Jonathan, and he with me – it was, after all, part of the price we had to pay – and the idea of never seeing him again was almost unbearable. But then I thought about giving up my work and living alone, for months on end, and I knew I could not do that either. For me, the only answer was compromise, which really meant deceiving Henry, and Jonathan was too proud for that.

He came out on deck and we walked the length of the ship in silence. On the way back, he said: 'I'm nearly thirty-seven years old, Damaris, and I've been at sea since I was fourteen. I've been thinking for a while that it's about time I packed it in, took a superintendent's job somewhere, settled down, had a family before it's too late ... We could do that, you know – it wouldn't have to be in London, there's plenty of other places ...'

He talked on, illustrating the possibilities of a shared home and family, while I struggled to contain my feelings. It was an impossible dream, part of these weeks aboard, and part of me longed to respond to it, to continue the illusion; but I was also angry and irritated that he couldn't see the realities. I dared not trust my voice to speak, and he interpreted my silence as disapproval. Before we reached the steps to the boat deck, he said with whispered frustration: 'Haven't you thought about what might happen? You and I have made love almost every night since the storm, sometimes two and three times, with absolute abandonment and no thought for the consequences. What if you discover you're expecting my child?'

He was watching me closely. I couldn't hide my reaction to his question, and he knew as I winced and turned aside that something was wrong. 'What is it?' he demanded, grasping my arm, 'what have I said?'

'I'd hoped you would realise,' I said, leaning against the rail for support. 'I didn't want to have to explain. I can't have children.'

Until that moment, the inability had never really bothered me, had been one of those things I considered more fortunate on balance, since I was able to follow different paths as a consequence. But now, strangely, it hit me hard. I don't know why. Perhaps because I thought I was in love with him, and I wanted to seem whole and perfect in his eyes, if only for a while. Admitting that lack – though not the cause – I felt crippled suddenly, unwomanly, unworthy of his regard. And it came between us in a way that nothing else could. It made the decision, solved the problem, and to my eternal shame I used it to end things.

Now that I knew what he really wanted from me, I said, I would always feel inadequate in not being able to provide it. I said there was no point in my leaving Henry, none whatever, since it would make no one happy, and him unhappiest of all. He didn't deserve that.

I hated myself. Jonathan seemed bemused as much as grief-stricken, uttering questions that were less than half complete, turning away, exclaiming, cursing the hand of fate which spirited me away when he loved me first, and then, cruelly, set me before him, only to take me away again.

'All right,' he said desperately, 'we'll meet. Tell me when and where and we'll meet. I love you too much to lose you again . . .'

But it was too late for that. We'll leave it, I said, for a while at least. Think things over. That will be best. Leave me an address, I said, and I'll get in touch. You can reach me at my office in the City . . .

And then the Thames pilot came aboard and there was no more chance to talk.

The ship berthed in the early morning, not long after first light. Although I'd hoped that Alice and I would be able to leave before Henry had the chance to come aboard, we could not disembark until officialdom had set its seal upon us, and unfortunately by that time Henry – in company with the Addisons' agent – was already climbing the gangway.

I dreaded a meeting in Jonathan's cabin. To avoid it, I created a fuss over the luggage, pretending that one of my small trunks was mislaid, which excused my nervousness to some degree, and occupied Henry as well as Alice and myself in a fruitless search. Only when I saw Jonathan out on deck with the Mate, checking one of the cargo holds, did I suddenly 'find' my box underneath the lower bunk in my cabin, and then, seized by relief, I embraced my husband, apologised for my absent-mindedness, and was suddenly all haste in the move to disembark.

Henry, dapper as ever in a pale grey frock coat, picked up his top hat and cane, viewed me quizzically for a moment, and then said he must first pay his respects to the Master. Alice caught my eye, pursed her lips and looked down as we made to follow him. She went down the gangway with Dr Graeme and Miss Fenton as we met the agent on deck, while I would have given anything to be able to follow them. Instead, I dragged myself behind the two men to where Jonathan was leaning over an open hatch and speaking to one of the men below. He knew we were there, but did not look up until the last moment, eyes dull, mouth grim, every gesture one of slow reluctance. He was wearing his navy-blue uniform but his hands were filthy, covered in oil or wax from some tarpaulin nearby; deliberate, I imagine, since when they were introduced, Jonathan was able to bow to my husband rather than shake hands.

They were much of a height and of similar build. Fleetingly, I saw a resemblance between them, and wondered for a startled moment whether it was that which had attracted me to Henry in the beginning. Having expressed his thanks, my husband listened with raised brows and a broadening smile to Jonathan's account of my help with the invalids during the storm. He responded with his usual blend of formality and charm, then turned to me and instructed me to say goodbye. That was very much out of character; but what was worse, like some doll-wife with no volition of her own, I found myself obeying, while Jonathan stood in the guise of a mourner at a funeral, with hands behind his back, gazing at the deck.

I expected no reply, but somehow he forced his mouth into a smile, and said, 'It's been a pleasure, Mrs Lindsey. I hope we'll meet again some day.'

As he escorted us to the gangway, I thought the weight of guilt and regret would drag me down. Somehow we crossed the deck and reached the quay. Henry assisted me into the waiting hackney, Alice confirmed that all the luggage was safely stowed, and we were on our way home, crunching across the cobbles and into the busy traffic of a London morning.

I felt physically wounded, as though flesh had been torn in that parting, and there were occasions in the succeeding weeks when I wept my heart out in the privacy of my room. Alice was a good friend to me then, but even so I had to strive to overcome my feelings of loneliness and remorse, and for Henry's sake had to find the spirit to converse both at home and in the office. Work was difficult, and I made the excuse that ten weeks away had undermined my ability to concentrate; but at home, when Henry embraced me, it was hard to explain my sadness.

'I thought your voyage to sunnier climes was meant to cheer you,' he chided gently one evening, 'not cast you down like this. What's wrong, hmm? Can't you tell me?' And when I apologised for it, said I didn't know what was the matter, he said rather sadly: 'Well, if you should discover the cause, my dear, remember I'm always here.'

One day, when we were dealing with insurance on a vessel lost off Heligoland, he asked me to tell him about the storm in the Mediterranean; and another time, when the *Holderness* came into conversation for some other reason, he made a point of telling me that the ship had her old Master back again, Barlow having recovered from his illness. He didn't tell me where Jonathan had gone, however, and I felt he expected me to ask; felt too that he suspected the nature of my unhappiness and was seeking either confirmation or denial. It may even have been that he was trying to be kind. But I didn't dare respond. For both our sakes, my feelings were bearable only while I kept up some sort of pretence.

I hardly expected any news from Jonathan, although I longed to hear from him. It was foolish, but part of me hoped he would give forewarning of his next visit to London, with perhaps some tentative suggestion that we meet for lunch or dinner or a companionable walk in the park. But nothing came. Even if he wanted to see me, I imagined he knew himself too well for such subterfuge, and had too clear a sense of honour to be able to make love to me under such circumstances. And if I might have been prepared to fool myself just for the sake of seeing him, I knew by then that I could not fool Henry.

For some time I kept to myself, saw no one except on business or in my husband's company, and stayed away from ships and the docks. I was glad to have work to do and the office to go to, since to be at home with the ticking clocks would have driven me mad. It took the rest of the summer, but eventually I learned to marshal my thoughts, and by Christmas I thought of Jonathan not in terms of guilt and loss but as something not meant to be. When he came into my mind I tried to be cynical, telling myself he was part of another time, a different life; we'd shared a brief but intense holiday romance, that was all, and if he couldn't see it in that light . . .

But the intensity was what I couldn't forget.

By comparison, my life with Henry was unexciting and predictable, but I knew I'd been fortunate in my husband, more fortunate than perhaps I had any right to expect. Throughout that difficult time he remained unfailingly kind and courteous, organising little treats to cheer me: trips to the country, visits to the races, walks across the Downs. As a consequence I felt bound to respond to him with courage and good humour. It didn't always work, but at least I tried.

In that last year we achieved a measure of contentment that pleased us both; and if there were occasions when I hugged Henry just because I saw a repeat of that fleeting resemblance to Jonathan, then it did neither of us any harm. The only time I felt bitter was when I had a missive from Isa Firth. Each time I kept thinking I would go to Whitby one day and settle my score with her, but I knew it needed courage and a convenient moment, and the coincidence of those seemed never to occur.

But after that brief period of contentment the

following winter was a worrying time. Throughout the autumn Henry seemed far more tired than he should have been, and a nagging cough which had persisted over Christmas developed into a bout of bronchitis in the new year. He was confined to bed for over a month, and to the house for a further six weeks. We joked that he was swinging the lead, that it was the worst time of year and he'd never liked travelling any distance in winter, not even as far as the City; but the illness weakened him, and he aged visibly in those last few months. Dismissing my anxieties, Henry's doctor said he was pleased with his progress; everyone seemed to expect him to get better, and with the spring and good weather I told myself he would soon be well. By the middle of April he'd recovered sufficiently to potter about in the garden, and was even talking about taking a trip to Cornwall in June. On the day he died, Henry had gone for a short walk on the Heath in company with an old friend, but it turned out to have been too much. He was stricken by a heart attack on the way back, and died before I could get home.

In the months that followed, all I could think of was Henry. Not just his death, but his absence, and the work which had been so important to both of us. To begin with I blamed myself for being at the office, for not being with him when he needed me; and yet where else could I have been? While he was ill, I had to carry the responsibility, just as he had carried it for me. In a way the business was like our child; it had brought us together and kept us together, and I couldn't just let it go. For his sake I had to find some means of carrying on.

And I had to find a man with the necessary background to replace the name of Henry Lindsey at the Baltic Exchange, a man who was willing not only to work with me, but to accept me as the senior partner. Temporarily one of the senior male clerks acted as proxy, but although in a mad moment I thought of Jonathan, there was something so distasteful in the idea of inviting him to take Henry's place, that I dismissed it at once. I even thought of my brother Jamie, but for the past ten years he'd been living in Fremantle, the owner of a successful boatyard. Besides, he was married, with children, and Australia was now his home.

Eventually, after long discussions, I entered into partnership with two of the younger Addisons, under an agreement which benefited both sides. In effect they became my apprentices, providing the necessary names for trading in return for my expertise and Henry's contacts. Ned and Bob were cousins, twenty-three and twenty-five years old respectively, who had been bred to the shipping business. The elder one had even spent some time at sea, and both had more than a little respect for the formidable grandparents who had started the company, and even for Henry and myself, who had been on the periphery for years. It did me good to realise that I'd become something of a legend in the Addison family and, as I started work with the boys, that I was in fact repaying their grandmother's kindness to me. She had been my friend and mentor, as well as my inspiration, and I never lost an opportunity to remind her grandsons of what an extraordinary woman she'd been.

That sense of continuity went some way towards curing my sense of failure as a wife. I hadn't borne the children Henry wanted, but I was passing on his knowledge and expertise to these young men, who would in turn carry the business into the new century.

It took time and effort but it was just what I

needed, and when Ned and Bob came to lodge with me in Hampstead at the end of the summer, they soon transformed that sad and somewhat dreary house into a place of light and music and laughter. I found myself wishing that Henry was still alive; he'd known the boys since childhood and would have enjoyed their adult company. And I liked to think he would have approved of my decisions.

The boys were good for me, so determined not to leave me brooding that they took me home with them over the festive season, for the kind of family celebration I remembered with gratitude from the old days. But the following year, as we toasted their first anniversary, I was very much aware that our initial impetus had settled into something less exciting, if more dependable. In a business sense the cousins had grown up, they knew what they were doing as brokers and were developing their own style; they even had their own apartments in St John's Wood, and no longer needed 'Auntie' to show them the ropes. In short, my presence was no longer essential, and I could afford to sit back for a while – permanently, if I so required. When that awareness dawned, I wasn't sure whether to be happy or sad, but within a day or so I'd realised something more important – that I'd discharged my obligations, and no longer had anything to prove.

For the first time in my life I was unfettered, and it was a light, heady sensation. I hardly knew where to start, much less what I really wanted to do in the long term. The boys suggested that I should take a holiday first of all, to visit my brother and his family in Australia, and with that, I agreed. In principle at least. I didn't tell them the first and most important item on my agenda, since it would have been meaningless to them, but I had decided to look for

Jonathan. Our parting had been too abrupt, some-how; our liaison had not been resolved in any way, just broken off, and, now that I was free to do so, I felt the need to settle things properly. To confess my sins and do my penance if necessary, but I had to see him. The emotional pull was too strong to ignore.

Nevertheless, I was unsure whether he would want to see me. It had been three and a half years, after all – ample time for change, as I knew well . . .

Privately, I wrote to the company offices in Hull, seeking the name and whereabouts of his current ship. The reply I received was hardly a surprise, but I was dismayed by it. Having left Addisons' the year before, Jonathan was now employed by a company trading out of Singapore. After many attempts, I wrote a brief letter which outlined my present circumstances with what I hoped was the right degree of friendliness and warmth, and posted it to the forwarding address. I wondered how long it might be before I received a reply. Three months at least, was my calculation, and it was with an anxious heart that I settled down to wait.

With the excuse that I would set sail for Australia in the spring, I kept working at the office on a part-time basis. Even so, waiting for Jonathan's reply made for a frustrating time, and as the weeks ran on and Christmas approached, I wondered whether he'd moved on again, whether my letter was on a wild-goose chase around the China seas, or stuck in some pigeonhole in a damp and airless office in Singapore. I was even wondering whether I could risk making enquiries in Whitby, through Mr Richardson, when the news reached me of Bella's death. At first I couldn't accept it, thinking it must be a mistake, or some kind of cruel hoax. But as the facts sank in they cut deep, and I was angry that no one had seen fit to let me know she was ill. And because we were the same age, I was also deeply shocked. It was a herald of mortality, when I was just beginning to realise that the years were marching on.

The next blow came very soon afterwards. Mr Richardson wrote again, this time with the news that Thaddeus Sterne had died peacefully in his sleep, only a few days short of his ninetieth birthday. Grief overwhelmed me then, mainly for Bella, for the shortness of her life and its many hardships, although I felt saddened, too, at the passing of things Old Uncle had represented. For all my contempt when young, latterly his mark had been the one I aimed for, and since my marriage a measure of respect had grown up between us. With his going, there was no one else in the Sterne family who mattered, and I knew I had no option but to go to Whitby. For the time being all other business would have to be shelved.

That decided, I telegraphed Mr Richardson to make money available for a decent funeral for Bella. Left to Cousin Martha I felt it might well be a pauper's grave and a few tots of gin afterwards, and I couldn't bear that.

In addition, I felt I could also make some discreet enquiries about Jonathan, but it didn't relieve my feelings. For years I'd been saying that when the time was right I would go to Whitby and settle my scores in person, and, like it or not, it seemed that the time had at last arrived. There would be Isa Firth to deal with, of course, which made for elements of fear and loathing, but I was beginning to suspect that with regard to those photographs, fear had always been the strongest emotion. For all my surface bravado, I'd gone on preferring to pay up rather than face what those pictures represented. Now, it seemed as though Whitby had grown tired of waiting, and had issued its own summons for my return.

Twenty-nine

The reality of that journey was even worse than might have been expected. Bad weather and slow progress, rising emotions intensifying as the train crawled further north, all conspired to increase that feeling of dread. I thought I'd shed my superstitions a lifetime ago, but with every passing mile I became more and more convinced that everything comes in threes, and those two deaths in Whitby were almost bound to herald a third. Who would be next? With fear for Jonathan lurking at the edge of my mind as I stepped off the train in York, I was totally unprepared for the shock of meeting Bram.

Age and illness might have taken their toll, yet when I heard his voice I knew him at once, just as he knew me. And when I looked into his eyes, that sense of recognition, of time moving backwards, was almost terrifying. It was like meeting my fate, my doom, my own grim reaper in the guise of an old lover. If I hadn't loved him so intensely all those years ago, it wouldn't have mattered at all, but I was afraid of what the meeting signified. What had he come to do to me? What more could he possibly want?

I don't think he realised the extent of it. He had little inkling of the damage he'd inflicted so could not know the wild swings of emotion that assailed me as we faced each other before that falling curtain of snow. For some people the past might have been laid firmly to rest, but for me it had been kept alive by books and blackmail and a barren womb.

Over dinner I kept trying to reconcile the man before me with the image in my mind. If I closed my eyes and listened to his voice I could almost feel myself being seduced again, by memory as much as the sentiments he expressed. And then I would look at him and experience the same disorientation that had attacked in the beginning. How could he be so old? In my memory he was no more than forty, the age that Jonathan would be now.

Eventually I told him about Henry, and Henry's death, but something – some remnant of superstitious dread, I think – stopped me from mentioning Jonathan. I kept his name to myself, although as the night wore on I was glad of the chance to talk about Bella and Isa and Jack Louvain. Bram seemed genuinely sorry to hear of Jack's accident and that painfully protracted death, but evidently found it difficult to understand my taut and brittle manner. Until, that is, I mentioned Isa and the photographs. But that was much later, after midnight, when the hotel had quietened down and we were almost alone in our corner of the reading room.

As coals fell in the grate, I reached out to pour myself more coffee. 'Whether Jack intended it or not,' I said, 'Isa Firth seems to have inherited much of his work, including the plates of some – well, some of his more *unusual* pictures.' I glanced up to meet his perplexed expression, and added tersely: 'Pictures of you and me – together – at Saltwick Bay.'

'Together?'

'Naked,' I whispered fiercely, watching his eyes widen in appalled understanding, 'at sunrise, making love.'

On a sharp intake of breath, he said: 'But how? How could he –?'

'Oh, Bram, please! How do you think?' Conscious of other people at the far side of the room, I made an effort to lower my voice again. 'I don't know – from the cliffs, or even from Black Nab. It was certainly light enough, and distance wouldn't be a problem. In the studio, I imagine he discarded the landscape and enlarged the figures –'

'I meant morally,' my companion interjected. 'He was a friend, for heaven's sake. How could he justify taking photographs like that?'

'Quite easily, I imagine. The same way you justified abandoning me.'

There was a momentary silence. 'Come now, my dear, you dismissed me – you said you never wanted to see me again. And I believed you,' he added heavily, 'in spite of what you're saying now.'

His words were not untrue, but went so far against the spirit of events that I felt he wronged me yet again. I was furiously angry. Longing to scream at him, instead I hissed, 'Well, be that as it may, Isa Firth's been blackmailing me for years on your account. Be thankful she never managed to put a name or an address to you!'

Even in the firelight I could see his sudden pallor, and felt a fierce stab of satisfaction that seemed to lance my fury. I hated him, but I was glad he was there. It was a relief to speak the words and share the anguish. To my astonishment he seemed to understand. Reaching for his stick, he said: 'Let's find our coats and go outside – I think we could both do with some air.'

The blizzard was over, but in the blue-white moonlight the frozen tracks looked more like eastern Europe than England. Apart from muffled railway employees going hurriedly about their business, the platforms were deserted, and, as we walked, I wondered how long either of us would withstand the cold. The main line was clear in both directions, but workmen were busy with shovels, their faces hidden by caps and scarves. They moved out of the way as a snow-plough came chugging through, followed by a sooty old tank engine, incongruously swathed and swagged like a wedding car in ribbons of white.

'Why didn't you get in touch with me?' he demanded as we paced the platform together. 'I might have been able to help.'

'Why didn't you reply to my letters?' I snapped back. 'I wrote several times from Whitby.'

'When did you write? I never received anything.'

'When I needed help, for goodness' sake. As you asked me to.'

He stopped and turned, and scanned my face. For a moment he seemed mystified. 'I had nothing from you. Of course, I knew you'd cashed the cheque,' he declared with sharp emphasis, 'because it was presented to my bank. By that I assumed you were all right. Other than that, not a word.'

I burned at that, but not even indignation could warm me against the bitter wind. 'Then what happened to those three letters? I sent them to the Lyceum, as you said. One to thank you for the cheque, one to tell you about the cottage, and the other –' I stopped as the words rose to stick in my throat, threatening to choke me. It was unbearable. As he reached out for me, I clenched my fist and beat at his chest, and at last got out harshly: 'The other was to tell you I was expecting your child!'

He gazed at me, incredulity changing to dismay, while hot tears poured down my cheeks. It felt as though furrows were being burned into my face. For a long moment we stood unmoving, and then, as I

390

scrubbed at the tears, he reached out for me in distress. 'Oh, dear God, dear God – I never knew – why didn't I know? I thought – I thought so many things – that you hated me, despised me – oh, my dear, I'm so sorry –'

I could have twisted free, but his grip tightened, and with a whispered exclamation he pulled me close. Locked together, we stood for what seemed a long time. Eventually, calmer, he said: 'What happened? Tell me – what happened to the child?'

I shook my head. I couldn't answer. As I covered my face, he held me more gently, murmuring words of comfort that seemed as necessary to him as they were to me. I welcomed his embrace, needed it, even though I still wanted to strike at him, hurt him, make him feel some of the pain which had pursued me over the years. The worst part was that I could feel it dogging my heels even now, and with a sharp gesture I broke away, retreating from his questions and his sympathy.

'If you'd been there, Bram,' I ground out accusingly, 'if you'd been willing to stand by me, even in secret, it might have been different – but you ignored my letters! You said you loved me, but in the end it was a lie – all lies – you were just *using* me! When Irving turned up, off you went, with barely a hesitation! That's what I couldn't forgive – your *eagerness* to escape!'

Ignoring his protests, I marched away, heedless of onlookers or the picture I presented. There was even something bleakly appropriate in giving way to hysterical emotion in that echoing, arctic cavern of a station. Like steam from one of those great engines passing through, the pain seemed to grow and expand to fill the space, and its growth was accompanied by a similarity of coughs and moans and cries

391

of torment. But somehow that noisy outburst propelled me forward until I came to a gasping halt at the very end of the platform, where the wind tore at my scarves and skirts and reminded me of Whitby and Bella and winter over the cliffs. I longed to be there, alone, to grieve and mend my wounds in the sharp salt air. I longed to touch the past and heal it, and I cursed the ice and snow which kept me here.

When he came up beside me, I was calmer, more stricken than angry, too spent to protest when he took my arm and led me away from that exposed spot. In the shelter of a tobacco kiosk he paused to put his arm around me. He seemed very much upset, and said gruffly: 'I think I know what happened, but I need you to tell me. You were alone, and expecting my child, so you –' He broke off, shaking his head, as reluctant as I'd been to use the word.

'Yes,' I said wearily, 'I had an abortion and nearly died. Bella saved my life.'

As memory overwhelmed me, he held me close. At last, he said with difficulty, 'I'm sorry. All I can do is beg your forgiveness. I didn't know any of this, and I'm ashamed that I didn't. I should have done, might have done, if only I'd written ... and you don't know how many times I began letters to you, only to destroy them. There was so much to explain, and so much more beyond that, in the end it seemed better to let things lie ...

'But that doesn't answer the question of your letters,' he added heavily, 'and in that regard, I'm afraid there is only one explanation.'

'Irving.'

'Yes, Irving!' he echoed with sudden bitterness. 'Ellen always said he had no scruples, and she was right. No wonder he was so keen during those first few weeks of my return – in first thing, every day. I thought he was concerned to get everything running

392

smoothly again, but all the time he was making sure I received no communications from you!'

There was such weight of truth in that statement, I felt bowed down by it. We'd both been duped by Irving's craftiness, I blaming Bram for being less than honourable in his dealings with me, Bram trusting a man who seemed to have no sense of honour at all. Whatever he wanted he took, excusing all by virtue of his great talent. Because of him, because of that monumental self-interest, one life had been denied and another almost wiped out, while Bram and I had been kept effectively apart until time took care of everything. That was bad enough, but it was when I thought of my marriage to Henry, and his longing for children, that I trembled with impotent rage. Irving was dead, yet he'd somehow managed to sour all our lives from the beginning. Even Jonathan's.

I had an obscure sense of being laughed at from beyond the grave.

Shuddering with cold, we returned to the hotel to hug the fire and warm ourselves with fresh coffee and spirits. My emotions veered between sorrow and anger; between rage and pain and fury at the unfairness of it all. I found myself going over everything. I'd ceased to be astonished by the coincidence of meeting Bram at such a juncture, and nothing he could say about Irving surprised me at all. Not even the matter of the letters. In that respect, both Bram and I had been made fools of, and if that were the sum of it, then after all these years it should no longer matter. But it wasn't all, and it did matter. Irving had managed to pervert everything, and I burned with the desire to make him suffer. Since that was impossible, I vented my bitterness on Bram.

But even in the midst of my own sufferings, I could tell that he was wounded too. We talked on, until about two o'clock, when, needing sleep and peace, I went up to my room. I would have rested in the chair, except that Alice woke and insisted on changing places. The bed's warmth was a great comfort, but it was a long while before oblivion claimed me.

Thirty

I imagined he'd be leaving by the first train, and told myself I couldn't wait to see the back of him; but as I came downstairs I saw him waiting for me, and was caught by an unexpected surge of gratitude. Although we were both tired, in the early morning light he looked grey and weary, and his voice had descended to even more gravelly depths. As we were shown to a table in the crowded breakfast room, he said tentatively, 'I've been thinking – I'd like to come to Whitby with you, if I may?'

Startled, I regarded him steadily for a moment before replying. He was halfway through a series of engagements to publicise his recent biography of Irving, and I knew the book and its success were important to him, for financial reasons more than any other. 'What about your lectures?'

'After all these years,' he said gruffly, 'Irving can wait. You and I left a lot of unfinished business in Whitby, Damaris – I hadn't realised how much. I think the time's come to deal with it, don't you?'

I was surprised that it should matter to him and said so; and was surprised afresh by the remorse I felt at his quick, wounded glance. From somewhere I found the grace to apologise, but he brushed my apology aside with a generous remark.

Fortunately, Alice had been with me long enough

to accept most situations as normal, but I did wonder what she was thinking as Bram took charge of luggage and porters and found us seats on a very crowded train. He made sure I was comfortable, and took a seat facing mine. The sun was shining, our compartment was warm, and with the steady, rocking motion of the train he was soon nodding. So was I, and what seemed only seconds later I woke to the rapid flashing of sunlight through trees. The wide, snowy moors were behind us and we were already in the narrow Esk Valley, with the river flowing strongly beside the tracks.

We stopped between deep white drifts at Sleights, then came the straight run down to Ruswarp, and suddenly I was thinking of *Carmilla* and the ghost of Old Goosey, and the presence of Old Nick up there in Cock Mill Woods. Stories and folk-tales of long ago, but the memories were extraordinarily alive. Catching a wistful glance from Bram, I straightened at once and turned to Alice, telling her briskly to be sure to watch out for the viaduct carrying the Scarborough line across the Esk; beyond it she would see Whitby.

But a better view stopped me as we were leaving the station. Framed by the great arch of the station doorway, a winter forest of masts stood between us and the town, perhaps a thinner forest than in my childhood, but a heartening sight, even so. Beyond, through the town's smoky haze, the east cliff was no more than a brooding blue-grey silhouette, while the old parish church crouched as low as ever against the skyline, with the skeletal ruins of the abbey above.

I felt Bram's hand at my elbow and a gentle squeeze, but I was anxious not to let sentiment overtake me. As we sorted the luggage I was at pains to point out that the reason I was staying at the Royal on the west cliff had more to do with personal satisfaction than any feelings of nostalgia. And it was true, since I'd booked from London, just for the private pleasure of knowing I could afford it. In any other place it would not have mattered where I stayed, but in Whitby, for me, having a suite at the Royal was akin to saying a childish 'So there!' to the ghosts of the past.

When Bram had gone along to his room and Alice had unpacked, I opened the window on to the narrow balcony and looked up and down the harbour. There was snow on the high ground, even here, but the tide was out, masts and spars were all at an angle and the river, like a glistening snake, was winding its way between banks of mud on either side. From the balcony I could smell all the old familiar smells of fish and salt and seaweed, and smoke drifting up from chimneys on the Cragg. I heard the cries of gulls and the rattle of carts on the cobbles, and briefly I was a girl again, hurrying along St Ann's Staith with a basket of fish, stopping in at the studio to see Jack . . .

But this was no time to be indulging in false nostalgia. Gritting my teeth I closed the window and tried to prepare myself for harsher realities. The service for Bella was at two o'clock, and I wanted to visit Cousin Martha beforehand. On the point of departure from London, I'd had a letter from her, thanking me for my offer to pay for the funeral but explaining that someone else had already insisted. And owing to the circumstances, she felt she must accept.

I wondered what those circumstances might be, whether in fact Bella had found a kindly protector in the last year or so, especially since giving up prostitution in favour of more respectable work. Perhaps not entirely respectable to some, but it seemed wonderfully right to me. She'd been acting as model for a group of artists, which struck me as being the kind of work ideally suited to someone like Bella. She could be beautiful, and had always known how to show herself to great advantage, yet she had no vanity at all. Remembering her as she'd been when we were girls, it wasn't difficult to imagine an artist falling in love with her, although it was rather more difficult to picture Bella appreciating such adoration. For her sake I hoped he was a good man, an understanding man, and that I might have the privilege of meeting him later.

I didn't think I would ever forget my way to the Firth house, but with Pier Lane behind me I was suddenly confused in the Cragg's maze of yards and alleys; I took a wrong turn and had to retrace my steps. In twenty years things had changed, the top storey of one house had been demolished, while another had been extended, making a different corner; but I found my way eventually. The old house looked more dilapidated than ever, as though crumbling into the dust around it, and I hesitated before knocking on the door.

A young woman answered, dark-haired and pretty, her resemblance to Bella catching me unawares; but she didn't know me, and I had a moment's difficulty explaining who I was. Cousin Martha appeared then and invited me in. She'd grown very fat in the years between, and had lost several teeth, but she'd done her hair and was wearing her best black, and she led me into the house like some noble lady receiving guests into the medieval hall. There was a fire lit, the kettle made a welcoming sound on the hob, and someone had made an attempt to tidy the kitchen and clean the hearth. As she moved a chair for me to sit, I noticed a bottle and glass on the high mantelpiece, but she

seemed sober enough, while the young woman –
whom she introduced as Meggie – was content to
look on in silence from her place by the window.

'I expect you've come to see poor Bella,' Martha
said emotionally, raising her eyes to heaven as she
lowered herself into a creaking chair. 'God rest her
soul, she suffered something terrible at the end, you
know. Thin as a lath and yellow as a Chinaman,
you'd never have recognised her in the last few
weeks.' Wiping away a tear with a corner of her
apron, Cousin Martha sniffed noisily, and cleared
her throat. 'But Nan Mills has done her best, I must
say. Prettied her up when she laid her out. She's a
good sort, Nan is.'

'Nan Mills?' I said faintly, not having expected
such an icy breath from the past. 'I remember that
name – I thought she'd have been dead and gone
long since.'

'Nay, she's not that old. Sixty, sixty-five maybe.
Still brings 'em into the world, and sees 'em out
when the time comes ... 'Spect I'll be next,' Cousin
Martha observed morosely, making an automatic
gesture towards the high mantel, then consciously
diverting her hand towards the teapot. 'Anyway,
poor Bella's in the best room, when you want to go
up. I'll make a pot of tea for when you come down.'

'Yes,' I said hesitantly, 'thank you.'

'Nay, Damaris, it's we should thank you – and we
do, Meggie, don't we? 'Twas good of you to offer the
burial money, and if it hadn't been for Bella's friends,
we'd've been right glad of it. But 'tweren't necessary,
as it turned out, they all wanted to contribute,
especially Miss Gwyneth, the lady she kept house
for. Anyway,' Martha went on, leaving me mystified,
'all's fixed for this afternoon. Service at the new
cemetery chapel, and the Star'll be serving victuals

afterwards, in the back room, for whoever wishes to partake.'

'Very kind,' I acknowledged, wondering how to ask about these other friends, especially Miss Gwyneth, who intrigued me most of all. Could she be the lover I'd been imagining? Not a man at all – no, of course not – but a woman who could love Bella and respond to her with warmth and understanding. Eventually, clearing my throat, I said: 'Bella modelled, didn't she – for a group of painters?'

'Oh, aye, she did. Like I said, she made some good friends, the last year or two. They all thought well of her. She could keep still for hours, our Bella – never a word of complaint. And they did some lovely pictures of her – enough to make you cry, some of 'em.' And as she heaved herself out of her chair, Cousin Martha raised her apron to wipe away a stream of tears. 'Here, just look at this,' she said, reaching for a small charcoal drawing, framed in passe-partout, of a woman gazing wistfully from a window. It was a study in light and shade, yet I saw at once that it was Bella, so telling and sensitive was the likeness.

'That's beautiful,' I said softly.

'Gave me that, Miss Gwyneth did – very attached to Bella, she was. Broke her heart, bless her, when she was ill ... Wanted to care for her, but Bella wouldn't have that. She knew, you see – knew she didn't have long. Wanted to come home to die ...'

I found tears blurring my own eyes, and it grieved me to realise how much of Bella's life I'd missed, although I was pleased beyond measure to think she'd enjoyed better times of late. I said: 'I thought well of her too. She was a good friend – and a good daughter.'

'Aye, she was that,' Martha said gruffly. 'Unlike some ...'

Unlike some, I echoed silently, thinking of Isa.

At Cousin Martha's prompting, I went upstairs. Foolishly, and in spite of the warning, I had been expecting to see the friend of my youth laid out like a princess in a fairy tale, a pretty, ruddy-cheeked girl, with full red lips and glossy brown hair, just awaiting a true lover's kiss to release her from enchanted sleep. And in a way, that was almost what I found. For hanging on the wall was an unframed canvas, a portrait in oils of a half-dressed woman, rich with life and colour. It was a portrait painted with love, I recognised that at once; a picture that celebrated all the warmth and generosity of which Bella was capable, a picture that would let her spirit live on.

Silently, I thanked whoever had painted it, who-ever had thought of placing it there, for the body that was left had little to remind anyone of Bella's youth and beauty. I wept over it, nevertheless, and as I gazed at the ravaged face in the coffin I could see that Bella's death from cancer must have been terrible indeed. And, by that, even more terrible for her mother, trying to ease a depth of suffering that could not have been borne for long. It seemed to me that Cousin Martha must have paid in full for whatever she'd been guilty of in the past, and for the first time I didn't begrudge her the gin, and even had the grace to wonder whether I had any right to judge her actions at all.

She had suggested I might like to travel in the carriage with the women of the family but, even though it seemed unlikely, I declined on the grounds that Isa might turn up. She didn't, that I was aware of, but when I arrived at the cemetery I noticed at once a group of people whose mourning garb stood out amongst the rusty blacks and dated millinery of

Cousin Martha's friends and neighbours. Fisherfolk and jet-workers didn't generally appear in black silk and trailing velvet. There were three men and two women, and one of the women seemed more obviously distressed than the others, which drew my attention at once. Was she Miss Gwyneth? She was perhaps my own age, or a little older, with a long, thin, sensitive face, and eyes that were swollen with weeping. It was a face of deep lines, that looked as if it had struggled with life; a face that I hoped had looked on Bella with love.

During an address which was mercifully short, the minister at the cemetery chapel managed to express the best part of Bella and leave the rest unsaid. I could feel my sense of detachment wavering, but it was not until he mentioned the family's tragic loss of their father, twenty years before, that my self-control almost crumbled. I felt myself trembling, remembering poor Bella and what she'd suffered, the revenge she'd taken, and the years of punishment she'd chosen for herself. I knew then that for all my promises and good intentions, I'd stayed away because I hadn't understood and could think of nothing to alleviate her suffering.

With an effort I pulled myself together as we left the chapel for the interment. Douglas escorted his mother and a young man who might have been Davey stood up with Lizzie and Meggie, both grown into lovely young women. Another brother, dark and heavily built, whom I took to be young Magnus, fell into shambling step beside me, which set my nerves on edge. His eyes were red as though from weeping, and he was shivering as we followed the minister outside. Together we withstood the icy blast on that windswept slope at Helredale.

Miss Gwyneth, supported by the younger woman and one of the men, stood close by, while Cousin

Martha wept against her eldest son's shoulder. We saw the coffin into the ground, and one by one cast a handful of earth as a parting gesture. I thought of Old Uncle Thaddeus and his folk legends, and prayed that at the last Bella had found some kind of peace and forgiveness. 'Rest in peace, Bella,' I whispered fervently, 'no need to come again . . .'

There were mourners enough from the Cragg and thereabouts to support Cousin Martha and the family. I stayed long enough at the Star to take a steadying glass of port wine and to introduce myself to the smaller group of Bella's friends. We talked for a while, and I sensed enough to confirm my earlier assumptions. Whether Miss Gwyneth understood my sympathy, appreciated my sincerity, or even knew who I was, was impossible to tell. She seemed sensitive and kind, and warmed at once when I mentioned her picture of Bella. I asked whether she'd given it to my cousin, and at once she shook her head. 'No, it's only on loan – I couldn't bear to part with it. I just wanted people to remember dear Bella as she was – in life, not death . . .'

I pressed Miss Gwyneth's hand and took my leave.

Making my way back to the hotel, I clenched my jaw against a strong desire to call down curses upon Isa Firth's head. For my own sake, I was glad she hadn't turned up at the funeral, but she should have been there. To have ignored her twin sister when she was dying was unforgivable. There was no question of her not knowing: each member of the family told me that she'd been informed. They told me about the shop too, maintaining that Isa had turned her back on them after the photographer died and left her most of his money.

'Ashamed of us, she was,' Lizzie had said bitterly,

'with her little shop and her stuck-up ways. Sweets and gifts for the visitors – you know, bits of carved jet, fossil paperweights, stuff like that. A few picture postcards. Seasonal trade mostly, but she seems to keep going. God knows how – there can't be much profit in it.'

But I knew about the shop, and had suspected for years that my quarterly contributions to the mythical Jack Louvain Memorial Fund were helping to keep Isa Firth in business.

Well, there would be a reckoning, and very soon. In my luggage at the hotel was a collection of Isa's notes and photographs that I had deliberately kept for some such opportune moment. With Henry's death I could have stopped the blackmail, but she didn't know about that, and, having saved this moment, I wanted her to understand that I had no compunction about taking her letters to the police. I wanted to frighten her, and frighten her badly.

'Perhaps her only intention was to hurt you,' Bram hazarded later, over tea in my sitting room. 'To enjoy hurting you – there are such people, you know. Even if she knew who I was – and she may have done – it could be that she was afraid to approach me. With my connections, I might have seemed too risky a proposition – whereas she knew you, could estimate your reactions. It was a calculated gamble, d'you see? You would pay up rather than risk exposure, but I might well have sent the police . . .'

That possibility had not occurred to me before. To me, Isa Firth was interested in money and social position, one leading to the other; and though I knew she was vindictive and had always detested me, I never imagined she would use blackmail purely for those reasons.

'To inflict pain,' Bram repeated, 'and exert power.

404

They might have been her prime intentions. You have to consider that she might not have needed the money at all.'

'But a little extra always comes in handy, doesn't it?' I remarked acidly.

'Oh, yes, indeed it does. But I was merely pointing out that if Jack Louvain left her money enough to set up in business – and if she had enough photographic plates to reproduce his pictures – then perhaps she didn't *need* what was extracted from you.'

'Perhaps not,' I said thoughtfully, chilled by the idea of such malice. 'Perhaps I was the only one, after all. Sometimes I've imagined her collecting money from men and women all over Whitby. Women particularly.' As always the idea made me feel sick. To combat it, I rose briskly from the table. 'Anyway, I intend to find out.'

'And I intend to come with you.'

I was about to refuse again when he checked his pocket-watch and turned to glance out of the window. 'Look,' he said, 'I have an idea. It will soon be dark, which could prove helpful, so why don't we revise that plan of yours?'

Thirty-one

Wraiths of mist like widow's weeds were gathering over the sea, and as Bram and I left the Royal Hotel the herring gulls were muttering and settling on their rooftop nests. Smoke spiralled upwards with scarce a disturbance in the frosty air, collecting in a lilac haze somewhere far above us, while below in the town the glow of gaslights defined the line of streets and harbour. Brighter beams from the lighthouses gilded the ends of each pier, attracting cobles from the fishing grounds as though they were moths. Across calm seas they came speeding in between the piers, each man at the oars, eager to escape the freezing clutches of the mist.

We saw it coming in as we made our way along Pier Road. There was no hurry, so we leaned over the harbour rail to watch some fine catches being brought in, and followed the cobles up the harbour to the bridge. Killing time, we even looked in the window of Jack Louvain's old studio on St Ann's Staith, but the place was a now a hardware shop and could not have been more different. I didn't know whether to be pleased or sorry at the change, and nor, it seemed, did Bram.

He turned away with a sigh, and, without thinking, I squeezed his arm. But as he patted my hand I withdrew it, faintly alarmed by the ease with which we seemed to be slipping into partnership again, into those old, seductive, easy ways. When we were together, talking, I could feel whole chunks of the past beginning to slide away from me, and when I looked back they had sunk without trace. It was alarming, I had to remind myself to hold on, not to let go; I'd clung to them for years and without them I might drown.

Fog was rolling in now, great freezing billows of it, obscuring everything as we crossed the bridge. I was glad Whitby's streets hadn't changed too much in the time I'd been away, and that I knew almost to the door where Isa's shop must be, at the town end of the long narrow street which serviced the east side's docks and boatyards. Facing Southgate, it looked like the ground-floor rooms of a house with at least one and perhaps two separate residences above. These 'flying freeholds' were common in Whitby, where habitations of several storeys climbed the banks and cliffs on both sides of town, but many were in a sad state of repair, and there was no obligation to support the ones above. Isa's building looked drab but respectable enough from what I could see, narrowly missing a clear view down Bridge Street to the harbour.

I did not envy its position, hemmed in as it was by tall buildings on almost every side, and wondered why Isa hadn't chosen a better property with more potential. Surely, I thought, she could have afforded something closer to the Church Stairs, which would have been more attractive to holiday visitors. There was, however, a front window and small doorway to the shop, and down a yard to the side I noticed another door at ground level which probably led to her private quarters. Bram agreed to wait outside until I called him. I didn't want Isa bolting when she clapped eyes on us, then escaping through the yard and up the bank.

I looked in at the shop window. Behind big glass jars of bull's-eyes and aniseed balls I could see a gas light flickering but no customers, and no sign of Isa. The sound of the door would no doubt call her to duty: I could not imagine her employing anyone else.

On a deep breath I took the handle firmly and pushed open the door. Expected though it was, the sudden jangling of the bell was startling. My eyes took in a small counter, scales, carved jet ornaments on a shelf, a display of postcards of local scenes and photographs of –

She appeared before me as though by magic, from some screened recess or doorway behind the counter. Turning, I was dumbstruck for a second, seeing the resemblance to Bella in her coffin. Not yellow, but grey, from head to foot, since hair and skin and gown were relieved only by a black shawl and a widow's pleated bonnet. She looked an old woman, yet we were the same age. There was even a moment when I wondered whether she really was Isa Firth, but then I saw the shock of recognition. Every muscle went slack, her jaw gaped and eyes widened; her fingers clutched at the counter for support. But then, like a gate closing, the muscles tightened and she was herself again, suspicion written in every narrow line.

'What do you want?'

'Well, Isa, I'm not after sweets, you can be sure of that.' Very slowly, I peeled off my gloves. 'A few postcards, souvenirs of Whitby, perhaps – or do I mean *photographs*?'

She had nerve, no question of that. Brass-faced, she nodded towards the display. 'That's all there is for sale.'

'What about the rest?' I demanded. 'The blackmail pictures?'

Her eyes narrowed. 'I don't know what you're on about.'

'Well, that's a pity,' I said softly, watching her edge towards the screened exit behind the counter, 'because I've come to make you an offer.'

She'd been about to bolt, but hesitated at that. 'What kind of an offer?'

I took my time and reached out for one of the little jet ornaments, a lighthouse so smooth and perfect it was a delight to hold. I turned it this way and that, holding it up to the flickering light behind the counter, leaning across to see it better. And then I grabbed her wrist and called out for Bram before she could wriggle free.

He came at once, squeezing behind the counter to move the screen aside. With his bulk blocking the doorway that lay behind it, Isa stopped struggling. I let go of her and locked the shop door, turning the OPEN sign to CLOSED. Then we escorted her through to the back of the shop.

There were two rooms, a living kitchen with the usual offices, and a larger room behind, which revealed itself as a combined bedroom and store. An old oak cabinet looked familiar to me from my days at the studio, together with a set of shelves that were divided up like pigeonholes. Jack Louvain's filing system, lettered like the alphabet, still contained photographs. Reaching out I grabbed a handful and began to flip through them: mostly local views which had been reprinted recently as postcards, a few local fishermen captured by Jack while mending crab-pots, some girls flither-picking on the Scaur. I recognised one of them as Lizzie, which made me pause, and then saw a fine picture of Bella with a long-line coiled and balanced on a skep on her head.

She looked magnificent, proud, with her chin held high, shoulders back and full breasts pushed out, one hand up to hold the skep, the other balanced on her hip. The Bella I remembered. My chest tightened painfully as I thrust the picture away out of sight, into the covered basket I'd brought. I had to bite hard on my fingers to regain control, to remember why I was there, and how little time there was at my disposal.

I turned to the cabinet. It was locked. 'Keys,' I snapped. 'I want this thing open.'

From her chair by the kitchen table Isa refused, said she would call the police, have us charged with robbery. None too gently I pushed past Bram and thrust my face up close to hers. 'Don't mention the police to me,' I hissed. 'Because I've got enough evidence in your handwriting to put you in gaol for the next ten years! Give me the keys!'

She looked alarmed; then, as she reached under her apron for the chain that held them, her mouth twisted into a smirk. 'And what'll your husband say when he sees that fine picture of you, eh?'

As she glanced at Bram I realised she didn't know Henry was dead, that she thought Bram was the man I'd married sixteen years before. I could have hit her. Instead I snatched at the bunch of keys. 'He'll be impressed,' I said pointedly, trying each of the likely ones. With the third I felt the lock turn and I was facing an array of shallow drawers, with a series of vertical compartments below. My heart sank when I saw the dozens of glass plates stored there, each one of which would have to be examined before we could leave this place. And the drawers were locked.

'Well,' I said heavily, 'it seems we might have a long search. You'd better keep quiet, Isa, because I mean it about the police. Believe me, I'd be pleased to see them.'

Bram might have been embarrassed by their arrival, but I refused to worry about that. He'd volunteered for this outing, and had even modified the plan, so it was important to press on. First of all I tried the drawers, patiently finding the key to each one before I examined their contents. As expected, they contained a lot of old, unmounted prints, not all of them different; in many cases there seemed to be several copies of each one. Some were even vaguely recognisable from a series Jack had completed when I was working for him, and I flinched, thinking of the temptation his fees had presented in those days.

The vast majority were studio photographs, which was something of a relief to me. Almost all of them were what might be termed compromising: young women in various stages of undress, some almost naked in the poses of famous paintings, and a whole series which included men. The men were generally fully clothed as they attempted to portray the seduction of various young women, and it was these photographs which I found the most distasteful, although not entirely unexpected. Others, involving women with canes and cringing men, seemed merely ludicrous. The truly shocking part for me lay in the faces I recognised. Quite a few, and not all from the poorer parts of town.

As I wondered at the extent of Isa's blackmailing operation, the one thing that comforted me was the posed nature of all of these pictures. One series had been taken outdoors, but even those had a self-conscious quality, the subjects obviously aware and willing to be photographed. Only those taken of Bram and myself appeared to be stolen, and I found only three, all taken in the same place and on the same occasion.

I was so familiar with each of them, they barely registered. I was looking for something different, something that might yet illustrate my worst fear: that Jack Louvain had followed us around, stealing pictures every time Bram and I were together. Finding nothing, I was so relieved I could barely stand. Trembling, I pushed all the pictures together in one drawer and took it into the kitchen. Dropping it before the hearth, I considered Isa for a moment in anger and despair, before speechlessly feeding photographs into the fire. With a gesture I indicated that she should carry on with the task, and, ignoring Bram's questioning glance, I returned to the other room, pulled out the first batch of glass negatives and deliberately dropped them on the floor.

At the crash they both leapt up, and it was hard to tell who was the more horrified.

'I know,' I snapped in answer to Bram's protest, 'but it's the only way –'

'Damaris, you'll have people at the door, wondering what's going on. Put them in the basket – I'll carry them – we'll dump them somewhere.'

'There's too many!'

'Find a box, then – but do as I say.'

He turned to Isa, who was glaring malevolently at both of us, and brushed past her to begin burning the contents of the drawer. If she'd been capable of weeping, I think Isa might have wept then at the loss of her power, but she hated me far more. As it was she stood and watched, hands and face working horribly, while I tipped out the contents of a wooden box on her bed, then started piling in the glass plates from the cupboard.

'You've no right,' she spat out at last. 'You're thieving, d'you know that? They're not all rubbish, those plates – some of those are Jack's best work, that I saved when his family came and sold up.'

'Oh, I see, I'm thieving, am I, while you were just saving things for posterity. And what about the blackmail, Isa? What about Jack's *models*? The ones who posed for him, the ones I can recognise even now? Don't tell me you didn't drop them the occasional note too, when you were short of cash?'

'I didn't do it just for the *money*,' she said on a bitter, plaintive note. 'I had to *show* folks, hadn't I? Show 'em I was somebody to be reckoned with. But you wouldn't understand that, would you? You've always had everything, everything I ever wanted. Even Jack – even Jack,' she repeated, spitting his name at me, 'even Jack didn't understand. Even he thought you were *somebody* –'

'And I thought he was something special too,' I retorted furiously, 'until I saw these – these pictures of his. Until I heard from you. Then I realised he was no better than a peeping Tom –'

'Don't you call him that! You were just a whore!' she hissed. 'Just like our bloody Bella – giving it away, going with anything, when I – *I* –' she was stuttering with rage, spitting at me in her effort to get things out – 'I always kept myself decent, I never let any man *touch* me – not even my own father, and believe me, the old bugger tried often enough. But our Bella took him on – oh, yes, she *enjoyed* it, and he – he thought she was *wonderful*, she was his favourite then, not me. She was his pretty little girl after that – he couldn't keep his filthy hands off her!'

I smacked her face, hard, in a reflex action that shocked all three of us. 'She's *dead*, for God's sake,' I hissed at her, 'we buried her today!' I stood over her like an avenging angel, dry-mouthed, full of grief and hot, outraged protest. It took Bram, looming behind her, to find the words I longed to say.

'I don't think it was like that,' he said gently. 'Whatever Bella did in those days – however wrong – it was done to protect the rest of you.'

'What do you know?' she sneered. 'Who d'you

think you are, anyway, coming in with her, thinking you've got the right to destroy my life – just because you married Damaris bloody Sterne, you think –'

'I didn't marry her,' he cut in, 'I was married already. You've got it all wrong, you see. I'm the man she lived with that summer of '86 – I saw your father's body brought ashore that morning in Robin Hood's Bay ...' He paused for a moment, and I dreaded what he was going to say. *Don't*, I thought, *please don't bring that up now!* But all he said was: 'I'm the man in the photograph', and then, at her aghast expression, added: 'Yes, I know, I've changed a bit since then – but tell me,' he went on in that relentlessly equable tone, 'why didn't you try black-mailing me? You must have known who I was – Jack must have mentioned me?'

'Oh, aye, he did. I knew who you were,' she said dismissively: 'a fine figure in London, I dare say, but you're nowt in Whitby, and even less to me.'

Bram shook his head at that and turned to me in appeal, but I could only nod in confirmation of what he'd suspected all along: that Isa Firth was interested in power, not money, in wielding Jack's photographs like instruments of torture rather than as a useful source of income. Even so ...

'Who else did you blackmail, Isa? Folks in Whitby? Ones you hated as much as me? Who? Come on,' I said irritably, 'tell me who they are before I start searching for the addresses. I'm angry enough to start breaking things – and I don't care who hears and who comes to investigate. I'll have pleasure in telling them just what an upright citizen you really are. In fact I'll go one better: if you don't tell me who these people are, I'll put an announcement in the *Gazette*, to the effect that the blackmail days are over.'

'You wouldn't dare!' But for all her bravado she

was twitching with nerves, and when Bram confirmed that I would carry out my threats, and without giving a damn for the consequences, she seemed on the verge of collapse. Pushing past me, boots crunching on broken glass, she went to the cabinet and reached into the back of one of the smaller drawers. With trembling fingers she handed over a small account book, complete with names and addresses. 'There,' she hissed, 'take it and get out.'

I glanced through the book, then pocketed it. Later I would write a reassuring but anonymous letter to each one, saying that Isa Firth was no longer in business. Part of me would have liked to drag her through the courts, but her humiliation would also be mine – and that of too many other people. I would have to be satisfied with the dark joy of destruction.

Hastily I stacked the remainder of the glass plates, while Bram collected up the photographs and pushed them into my basket. We lifted the box on to the table and he hoisted them into a reasonably manageable position. I checked the cabinet and had a last scout round the back room; I even checked the kitchen cupboards for anything suspicious, but found only the meagre stores of an ill-fed single woman. With a sense of having meted out a certain justice, I followed Bram through the shop and out of the door. I was shaking so much I thought my knees would give way before I went a dozen yards. Never in my life was I glad to see such dense and blanketing fog.

Thirty-two

The hotel was out of the question. Staggering along to the White Horse, where we'd supped that very first evening, we were both grateful for a chance to sit down and collect ourselves. Bram drank his whisky almost in one and ordered another; I took my brandy more slowly, but was no less in need. With the box and my basket on the bench between us we sat quietly for a while, gazing around rather than at each other. The place had been altered, its old scrubbed, bare style become more modern with polished wood and elaborate mirrors, yet we both regretted the change. It was easier, I think, to pass trivial comment than talk about what had just taken place.

Draining his glass, Bram took my hand under the table and squeezed it. 'What trouble I've caused you,' he whispered, indicating the box between us.

I nodded and gave a reluctant smile. 'In one short space of time you changed my life entirely.' Feeling suddenly emotional, I had to take a deep breath. 'It's been the repercussions, you see.' I patted the box. 'This was just one of them.'

His gaze was too earnest, the pressure of his hand on mine too sympathetic, for me to endure either in such a public place. 'Let's go back to the hotel,' I urged, searching for a handkerchief. 'There at least I can drink too much and give way to my feelings in private.'

With a soft, rumbling laugh, he went off to order a cab. In the swirling fog it seemed to take for ever to reach our destination, but at least we didn't have to carry the box. The problem remained of how to dispose of the contents, but inspiration came a little later as we crossed the hotel foyer, and passed the entrance to the dining room. I found myself remembering an abortive attempt to get a job in the kitchens of the Royal, and that memory produced an image of the service area at the back of the hotel, with its range of dustbins for ashes, rubbish, food waste. Broken up, the photographic plates could be tipped into a half-full bin of ashes, and no one would be any the wiser.

The idea lightened my mood at once. Setting the box before the fireplace in my room, I pulled on my gloves, took off my shoe, and started to smash the plates with the heel, two at a time, on the tiled hearth. I didn't care what pictures I was destroying, whether they were art or pornography, I felt that at long last I was wiping out years of anguish, years that had stultified my marriage and cast a blight on my life.

The laughter, of course, soon gave way to hysterical tears, but I wouldn't give up. Probably half the box was splintered in the hearth by the time Bram took hold of me and pulled me away. 'Please, Damaris, please stop this. You'll make yourself ill if you go on . . .'

I made some bitter comment at that, but in spite of my struggles he held me firmly until I was calmer. Afterwards, when he'd neatly broken every other plate into four or five pieces and overseen the entire disposal, he said with some satisfaction: 'Well, now, let's hope that's the end of that.'

As he poured us both a drink, I shook my head in bewilderment. 'Why did he do it, Bram?'

'What? Take saucy pictures? Well, they've always been a popular commodity, and you might say Jack brought his talents to a very jaded subject –'

'No,' I said impatiently, 'I meant the others. The pictures of you and me. Why did he keep them – that's the question that's tormented me all these years. Jack always seemed such a decent man, that's the strangest part. That, and whatever he saw in Isa Firth. He had some kind of partiality for her when she was young – God knows why. He couldn't stand Bella. And he can't have had a fancy for me, either, because in all the time I worked there, I never had so much as a hint of it. So why he took those pictures – and kept them – I can't think . . .'

Bram shrugged and made a face. 'Nor me.'

But on consideration I thought he must have known a different side of Jack Louvain, a side I didn't know at all. So after a while, pondering aloud and trying to draw him out, I said I'd always found Jack difficult to understand. He hadn't been in love with Isa Firth, and it seemed to me that the only thing that mattered to him was what he did, observing people, photographing them, making a record of the way they stood and looked and behaved. If he was in love at all, I said, it had to be with the pictures he took, images captured on glass and paper – people and places at a distance.

'He could go back to them, you see, whenever he wanted.' I paused, and Bram was nodding, not meeting my eyes, but agreeing. 'Like those pictures of you and me,' I went on, aware of a sudden catch in my voice. 'They were too good for him to destroy. I don't suppose he ever considered what might happen to them after he was gone . . .'

'No, I don't suppose he did.'

I waited until he turned his head to look at me. As our eyes met, I knew. It seemed so obvious, I wondered why I hadn't always known. But in that moment my lungs seemed to collapse, and I was pinned down by lack of air. 'It was you, wasn't it?' I asked, when I could breathe again. 'He kept those pictures because they were of *you* . . .'

With the briefest of nods he agreed, then abruptly moved away. He lit a cigar and stood by the window, smoking, with his back to me.

We were both embarrassed. The revelation cast such a different light I hardly knew what to think, where to begin. Eventually, it seemed I had to speak, just to break the silence. 'That last night,' I said anxiously, turning round to look at him, 'before Irving arrived – you were out for hours, alone. I thought you'd gone walking over the moors – I was worried sick about you. But when you got back you said you'd bumped into Jack Louvain, that you'd been drinking with him –'

'Yes. Yes, I had.'

I paused, aware of the tension between us. 'What happened?'

'Nothing,' he said quickly. 'At least, nothing very much.' Limping slightly, he began to pace the room, while I followed him with my eyes, willing him to tell the truth. 'We had a few drinks, and something to eat, then we ended up going back to the studio with a bottle of whisky. As I recall, we drank rather a lot. We looked at some of his latest pictures – he showed me some of the saucy ones too. But more as an introduction, I think, to what he wanted to say, which – in short – amounted to the fact that he found women rather less attractive than men.

'That was not a complete surprise,' Bram admitted, clearing his throat, 'although I was surprised – and not a little embarrassed – to discover that he was

419

attracted to me. I was drunk, of course, and so was he, which cushioned things a bit, but still . . .' He shrugged as though to rid himself of uncomfortable memories.

'Did you find *him* attractive?' I asked, and I could see the question embarrassed him further.

'Well, I liked him – I always did like Jack, you know that.' For a moment he paused, then added quickly: 'I suppose, if I'm honest, there may have been an element of attraction, but it wasn't something I'd been aware of. Although for a while that night, I must admit to a mixture of temptation and curiosity which nearly got the better of me . . . Nearly, but not quite. In the end, good sense won. Or was it cowardice?' he asked of himself, with bitter irony. 'I've often wondered. Anyway, I left.'

Drawing deeply on his cigar, he paced up and down the room. Eventually, he said: 'The encounter left me in a strange mood. I remember feeling furiously angry and frustrated because I thought I'd found the simple life here in Whitby, yet it was turning out to be incredibly complicated.' With a humourless smile he went on: 'Everything seemed against me – even my own sensibilities. All the usual curbs were failing. I'd even found myself responding to Jack, which was completely out of character, while my behaviour with you earlier that day had just – gone too far. I didn't understand it – it was very alarming. I needed to know that I wasn't losing my grip . . .

'Except I wasn't in control of anything, least of all myself, and when I got back to the cottage I – well,' he finished despairingly, 'there's no need to elaborate, you know what I did. And I know how wrong it was.'

Briefly, our eyes met, and in the midst of my own anguish I sensed his shame and distress. I could tell that, like me, he'd spent a long time, years ago, trying to account for his behaviour then, and had not entirely succeeded. 'All I can say is that I was in love with you, Damaris – madly in love – and at the same time half mad with anxiety because I knew it was doomed to end. The last thing I wanted was to hurt you – God knows, I just wanted to love you. But I – I don't know, somehow, somewhere, everything went wrong . . .'

'It felt as though you hated me,' I said with difficulty, 'as though you blamed me for something – for not giving enough, or not *being* what you wanted me to be . . .'

'Was that how it seemed?' He paused, frowning; and then as I stood up he came to me. With a sigh, he reached out tentatively, touching my hair, my cheek, my shoulder, his eyes full of concern and affection. 'It wasn't like that, Damaris, believe me . . .'

I was stiff with resistance. My throat felt dry, but I managed to say, 'I always thought, afterwards, that you'd used me as a substitute.'

'For what?' he asked in surprise.

'For Irving.'

Taken aback, he shook his head. 'No. No, Damaris, you're wrong there. I can see why you would think so, but believe me – no! Jack Louvain *could* have been – don't you see? But not you. You weren't a substitute for anyone or anything – I loved you, I wanted you, you satisfied me. You gave me the freedom I'd always longed for –' He broke off abruptly, breathing hard.

'But?' I asked sharply.

'But I was beginning to be afraid of what I might do with it,' he declared. 'The more you gave, the more I wanted. It was as though I couldn't stop. I wanted to possess you, body and soul. It frightened me.'

'Me too.' Even so many years distant, the memories were chilling. I shivered, and he turned to me at once in mute appeal. I felt he needed my warmth just as much as I needed his, and, in spite of everything, I opened my arms instinctively.

'I felt there was something wrong with me,' he said as we embraced, his voice rough with emotion, 'something sick and evil that would destroy you if I stayed. I wasn't even sure that it wouldn't destroy me too, but I knew I had to leave. It was almost a relief when you said you didn't want to see me again . . .'

Moved by his remorse, I was aware, more disturbingly, of wanting him to go on holding me. A sense of comfort and familiarity made me cling, as though he could and would defend me now, against all the maladies of the past. As though we could share the better times again.

It had been too long since anyone had touched me, much less held me with affection. With an effort I forced myself to move away from him, and dragged my mind back to the matter in hand. A pulse was beating furiously against my throat, but now we'd begun, I had to see this thing through to the end. Now he'd told me about Jack Louvain, I had to know whether sexual desire had been part of his feelings for Irving.

My voice sounded strained but he heard me out, standing perfectly still, with his eyes closed, for what seemed a very long time. I thought I'd gone too far, that he wouldn't answer, or would make some excuse and leave. Instead he picked up his glass and drank from it, and when he'd put it down again, he said quietly, 'Damaris, my dear, you must understand that Irving and I worked together, closely, for more than twenty-five years. Friendship changes. Feelings change. In all that time there was often hostility as much as affection, and if there were times when I loved him, there were times, I swear, when I loathed him, too.'

But I couldn't leave it there. A little desperately, I said: 'Yes, I believe you, but there had to be more to it than that. Tell me the truth, Bram. All those years ago – did he tempt you – sexually, I mean?'

At first he shook his head and, with something like exasperation, ran fingers through his hair. But then he said abruptly: 'Oh, for God's sake, Damaris, yes, he did, of course he did, but I was blind to it for a long time.' He broke off, and tension was dispelled on a long release of breath. A moment later, with a kind of weary resignation, he added: 'The thing is, even when I recognised it, I wasn't sure about him. I thought it was just me, a combination of fatigue and frustration, my own lurid imagination getting carried away. It took a while for me to realise that all the looks, gestures, touches, were deliberate, that he was well aware of what he was doing. He used his appeal to manipulate people – men as well as women. But he did it in such a way that it appeared innocent, unintentional, charming – you were never quite *sure*, you see . . .'

He described Irving in the early days, before success changed him: young, handsome, possessing an amazing mind as well as that prodigious talent, and the kind of charm that was later to mesmerise audiences both at home and abroad. From their first meeting, the two men had seemed to understand each other; on his part, Bram described the feeling as akin to finding a soulmate, even though he could hardly believe that such a dazzlingly talented man would choose him for a friend. In fact he'd been chosen for his own talents, for the energy and organisational ability that was to assist Irving in his great venture at the Lyceum. But in those days, Bram was far too inexperienced to see that, and was overwhelmed by the offer at a time when he felt his own life was stagnating in a backwater.

And at that time his mother had used the word infatuation to describe his behaviour; she'd sensed Irving's power without understanding it, and was afraid for her son. And even though the position was exactly what he wanted, everything he could have hoped for, Bram admitted that he'd had qualms about it. They were mostly to do with Irving. 'I was certain we could reach the heights, but at what cost, I wasn't sure. Rather like Faust, later,' he confessed with dry self-mockery, 'I think I was afraid of losing my soul.'

I remembered the impact Irving had had on me, and shivered. 'And did you?'

He shook his head. 'I hope not. I think I paid with more immediate things – my peace of mind, my marriage, whatever talents I possessed – and you.' Reaching for his glass, Bram sighed and swilled the whisky round for a moment before drinking. 'I was never able to forgive him the petty cruelties he indulged in while we were producing *Faust*. He was always affected by a part, which is why I tried to ignore it, but he came close to destroying everything – he abused his power, he did everything possible to belittle those of us who had been with him since the beginning. Ellen, who'd been in love with him for years, he treated abominably; and as for me, well, it was as though he was determined to bring everything to the surface, just to make me suffer. And he did. Love, hatred, jealousy – the full gamut of emotions. I thought I was going mad.

'He was playing Mephistopheles, of course, and I knew it was the part, but he took it too far – much too far. He'd flirt with his coterie – quite openly, often with a sly look to be sure I was aware of it. And

424

when I was angry, holding on to my temper with the greatest difficulty, he would come to me and slide an arm around my shoulders, for all the world the affectionate friend he'd always been. But then he would whisper, say something lascivious as a joke, and laugh at my reaction, which I'm afraid could never quite match his. I was too serious, you see, too intense, too obsessed by his cruelty and my own response to it.

'I felt stupid and angry – powerless to do anything. I wasn't eating or sleeping properly, Florence and I were arguing all the time ... between home and the theatre,' he admitted with bitter humour, 'it was like living in a Shakespearian tragedy! I racked my brains for alternatives – writing for a living, retiring to Scotland or the West Country, as far as I could get from Irving and the theatre. Then there was talk of arranging the next provincial tour, so I seized the opportunity with both hands ...'

I recognised the edginess of the man I'd met then. That was when he'd come to Whitby for the first time, when, as he said, he'd braved the cliffs to do battle with the elements, and gone away feeling that I'd cured him of his megrims with a blast of real life. But the cure was temporary. In London, through the winter, although the play was a success – which brought its own peculiar pressures – his relationship with Irving had worsened, bringing him back to Whitby at the first opportunity. As we talked, I saw it all quite clearly: the strain of overwork, torment from Irving, lack of sympathy from Florence, too little rest and a complex build-up of resentment and anger and fatigue. At the time I'd joked about that need to escape, but for Bram it had been more of a nightmare; and having got away, his fear of discovery was very real.

'It sounds slightly mad now, that I should have

been so fearful. But I was. I knew that once Irving discovered my whereabouts I'd have to face him again, and I couldn't bear that. It made me desperate, made me cleave to you ever more fiercely. You were my salvation, Damaris – I wanted to be part of you, have you be part of me. Only then would I be strong enough to defeat him. Because I knew, as soon as I saw him, that it would start all over again.'

'And did it?' I asked after a while.

After an even longer pause, he shook his head. 'No,' he said, sounding mildly baffled, 'not really. All those uncontrollable emotions had somehow been dispelled. I was still moved by him, still in awe of his talent – but by some miracle, when we came face to face, I could see who and what he was. I was no longer dazzled.'

I knew the symptoms. 'You were no longer in love with him.'

'No. I was in love with you, that's why.'

Thirty-three

It was getting late and we had yet to dine. Since neither of us could face formality, we studied the menu and ordered a light meal to be sent up to my rooms. Afterwards I felt calmer, more relaxed, and as waiters brought coffee and cleared away the remains, I found myself thinking how strange it was that Bram and I should be sharing such intimate secrets after all these years. In the beginning, chance had brought us together, calling up passions that might have been better left dormant, leaving us prey to consequences that had haunted the rest of our lives. Looking back on the past two days, I felt there was a kind of predestination in the way we'd been brought together again.

Painful emotions had come to a head, and had finally been lanced. And some unmistakable truths had been revealed at last. I was satisfied that Irving had not won his battle for Bram's soul, no matter how clear the victory had seemed to me then. Also, I must confess, I was vain enough to be glad that Bram had forgotten very little of that time. It had been etched as deeply into his psyche as mine.

In truth, I was even glad when he told me that he harboured regrets about his writing, too, which over the years had been accommodated between the twin pressures of Florence and Irving. Everything had always been completed in haste; he felt that if he'd been able to devote his entire attention to writing, the stories would have been fuller, the characters more rounded, his editing better executed. Nevertheless, in spite of that, the books had been successful; not enough to make his fortune perhaps, but he'd managed to prove Irving wrong, and I found that particularly satisfying.

'But tell me, what did he think about *Dracula*?' I said slyly. 'I looked it up – it doesn't just mean Son of the Dragon, does it? It also means Son of the devil. Mephistopheles, indeed! Did Irving recognise the analogy, d'you think?'

With a little grunt of surprise, Bram said, 'Well, I'm delighted you read it, although I'm not sure he ever did.'

I stared at him, unable to credit the truth of that. It didn't seem possible that his closest friend could have ignored such a powerful piece of work. But, having also produced a rough playscript to protect the copyright, Bram maintained that Irving had given it no more than a glance, before flatly refusing to have anything to do with it.

'It was a great shame,' Bram sighed: 'one of the few times he was wrong about a part. When I think of his other mysterious roles, Dracula would have been perfect ... You should have seen him as the Flying Dutchman – his eyes glowed red, just like burning coals. Amazing – I don't know how he did it.' With a wicked smile, he said: 'Just think what he could have made of the Count!'

'Mmm, yes, I can imagine,' I replied, with perhaps too much emphasis. 'The part was made for him. Why wouldn't he play it? Did he ever say?'

Bram pursed his mouth and, with a negative gesture, leaned back into the chair. 'I imagine it was too small for him, too much offstage. He never did explain, apart from making one ringing comment at the end of the read-through. *Dreadful!* he said, and that was that. I told myself afterwards that he was referring to the hasty adaptation, not the plot, but even so, it was the kind of remark I'd come to expect from him. Anything that didn't have Irving at the centre was never worthy of his praise.'

With a sharply drawn breath, I said, 'Well, then, it's a pity he didn't recognise himself! Or did he, do you think, and that was just his way of capping you?'

Bram shook his head. It was doubtful, he said, and anyway, the character was not intended to be a portrait of Irving; in the beginning his description of the Count had been based on much older men, powerful, striking figures like Tennyson, and the American poet Walt Whitman. Even my uncle had been part of those early descriptions.

'But then – because of the essential theme, which is, of course, the struggle for power – I began to realise that in character the Count bore more than a passing resemblance to Irving. And because of the Count's insatiable thirst for knowledge, his ability to concentrate and *absorb* – which Irving was incredibly good at – I became very much aware of the similarities between the two. And then I began to think of possibilities for the stage, so –' With a shrug he broke off to light a cigar. 'But because he never commented, I always believed that he hadn't read the book. Do you think he might have done, and was offended by it?'

'Not necessarily offended,' I said, 'he might just have been *disturbed*. Didn't *you* find it disturbing, when you were writing the book?'

'Not while I was writing, no.' Pondering, smoking his cigar, enveloping us both in aromatic clouds, he apologised and left my side to go to the window. An underlying tension in him brought me slowly to my feet; a moment later, watching covertly through the overmantel mirror, I was astonished to see him disappear. Alarmed, I turned at once, only to realise that he'd simply opened the window and stepped out on to the balcony. In his dark clothes, he blended with the night.

As I joined him, he was peering through the fog, towards the east cliff. 'That's where it began,' he said quietly, 'up there at sunset, when I used to wait for you by Lucy's tomb. You remember the stories we told, the plots we used to weave? It was as though they were setting the scene, providing the framework for what was to follow.

'I had this idea, you see, about an eastern European nobleman of ancient lineage, coming to England as a vampire in the present day. I wondered how he would survive in our modern world – *against* our modern world. But I kept dismissing it, because a story about a vampire didn't seem so very original – there were too many excellent precedents – and surely the modern world was too sophisticated for such a creature to survive for long. But then, with the Whitechapel murders, all that changed. Someone – some*thing* – committed the worst crimes this country has ever seen – and *got away with it*. How?

'Hall Caine and I discussed it endlessly. All kinds of people were questioned – he even knew someone who was briefly arrested – but the police had no evidence to link anyone to the murders. It was more than strange, it was uncanny. All kinds of rumours were circulating in London at the time – including the nonsense that members of the royal household were involved – but in the absence of rhyme or reason it seemed to me that one could weave all kinds of fantastical theories around those gruesome events. And suddenly, my idea of a vampire wreaking havoc in the present day, in the most advanced and populous city in the world, was no longer foolish – it became possible, credible, frightening.

'From then on, I knew the story had to be written, together with all the elements which not only belonged here in Whitby, but which had inspired it: that tremendous storm the day we first met, the wrecks, the Russian ship, the great black hound – and most especially Lucy, and the friends we'd invented for her . . .'

'While the central character,' I murmured, expanding for him, 'was based on the medieval nobleman whose name you found in that old book. Whose bloodthirstiness you changed into a literal *thirst* for blood . . .'

'Oh, yes,' he whispered, turning to me, 'that's *exactly* how it was . . .'

I shivered then and looked away. Staring blindly, I saw nothing but a dazzling haze of particles in the fog, although the cold was like a tightening physical pressure all around us. I tugged at his arm, urging him inside, but the wraiths came with him, clinging about his shoulders like a cloak. I had an image of the Count entering Lucy's bedroom to seduce her into the ecstasy of death, and it made me tremble uncontrollably. Closing the window, dropping the curtains back into place, I tried to shut it out, but I had a sense almost of something entering the room with us.

Slipping a cashmere shawl around my shoulders, Bram apologised for his thoughtlessness and led me back to the warmth of the fire. 'You asked whether I found it disturbing, but it was strange, you know, I nurtured the story for years, and while it stayed in my head, everything was fine. I'd written four books, and had three published, and that achievement alone made a tremendous difference to my life. Writing made everything else bearable – can you understand that? It seemed to bring the separate pieces of my existence together, to resolve the conflicts about who and what I was, and what I was perpetually longing to be. Writing fiction, I discovered, enabled me to be *me*, without excuse or apology or reference to anyone else. I found I was satisfied and content, probably for the first time in my life.

'But perhaps more importantly,' he went on, 'writing enabled me to deal with Irving and my paying job, which was running the Lyceum. And the Lyceum was making money, Irving was enjoying success after success, and then, as a culmination of all he desired, he was awarded his knighthood. It was as though the entire profession had been raised overnight from the status of rogues and gypsies to that of the nobility. We were all tremendously proud.

'It was a week of madness,' he added. 'You know my brother Thornley was knighted too? And of course, the entire family felt honoured by that – but, I don't know, between the excitement of the Palace and the despair of poor Oscar being sentenced, I felt exhausted, glad to get away. Florence felt it too. I wanted to come to Whitby and write, but she wouldn't hear of it, so we went to Scotland instead, and there I began to put together the notes and ideas I'd been nurturing for almost ten years. That was when I started on the writing.

'It wasn't the easiest book to write – it took much longer than the others, and I found it oddly draining. I'd written on holiday before, and always felt invigorated, but for some reason this time I was exhausted by the work, and the book seemed to take for ever to complete. In fact it took well over a year, and I was never so glad to see the end of anything.

'When the book came out I was disappointed. The cover wasn't what I'd expected, and the reviews were no more than lukewarm, in spite of all the hard work. And then things started to go wrong. Small things throughout the summer, but they rapidly got worse. That autumn Irving slipped and fell and badly injured his knee. It was immediately after the first night of *Richard III* – and, for the first time ever, he was unable to appear on stage. We were even forced to close the theatre for three weeks at the height of the season, which cost a fortune and was tremendously damaging. But the damage to his self-esteem was worse – Irving suddenly realised he was not invincible, and it was a shock. Then his little dog was killed in an accident with the stage-trap, which upset everybody. But the worst, the very worst thing that happened, was the burning of the Lyceum Storage ...'

'I read about it – it was reported in all the papers.'

Bram nodded and said tersely, 'That fire cost us something like £50,000, and we weren't fully insured. I'd been dicing with fate for years, paying premiums to cover us up to £10,000, simply because Irving wouldn't hear of any increase. But after the débâcle of *Richard III* he insisted on halving it. We'd been using the railway arches as storage for years, and he thought nothing could go wrong. And in theory it shouldn't have – except that it did, God knows why. The fire was incredible, the heat ferocious – and they never discovered the cause. It burned the arches three bricks deep, and turned the coping stones to powder ...'

'Yes, I remember,' I murmured, disturbed afresh, and shamed, suddenly, by a recollection of old suspicions. There had been a moment, at the time, when it had seemed to me that Bram might have had something to do with that fire. But being with him now, listening to him, watching his face, I knew it to have been impossible.

'It was a horrifying sight, Damaris. I can see it still. And ever since I've wondered about it . . .'

With a despairing shake of the head, he went on: 'Irving was like a man who's had his entire family wiped out before his eyes. The shock nearly killed him.'

'But the eyes were yours,' I said softly, understanding how deeply he'd been involved, that the Lyceum had meant as much to him as to Irving. 'And it was your life too.'

The hand which held mine almost crushed it then. He said: 'I'd been thinking of retiring. Can you believe that? I was so frustrated by the extravagance and endless entertaining, by the sheer impossibility of controlling it. Latterly, I felt I was killing myself, trying to curb Irving, save money, balance the books. I was exhausted. In fact that week of the fire, I had another novel coming out – an old one and not one of my best efforts, to be sure – but in order to break free, I had to have the money. However, while I was still dealing with the insurance companies and trying to fend off a court case, Irving went down with pleurisy and pneumonia and was bedridden for two months. So,' he added on a long release of breath, 'all my great plans had to be shelved.'

'So you stayed,' I murmured sympathetically, feeling something of the frustration he'd endured. 'How on earth did you manage?'

He raised his eyes to mine. 'Didn't you know? Irving sold the Lyceum – sold it without telling me.'

I gazed at him, aghast at the betrayal implicit in such a move. Although I'd never trusted Irving – and, in that, shared common feeling with both Florence and Charlotte Stoker – Bram had loved him, which made the betrayal worse. I wanted to know why, what lay behind such treachery, but the matter had become a forbidden subject, he said, and was never satisfactorily explained. The deal had been made while Irving was ill and obviously worried about finance; but the timing – which was just as Bram was due to set sail for New York – seemed to be deliberate. Irving didn't want anyone to know that he'd sold out to a syndicate, not until the deal was complete. But it was iniquitous, and took no account of the fact that the Lyceum was still a going concern. Bram could have secured far better terms, if only Irving had trusted him, given him just an inkling of what was going on.

The only possible reason for such folly, he said, was that Irving may have thought he was dying; but that to me was no excuse. I felt Bram and Ellen and the rest of them should have packed their bags and left the old tyrant to himself – they wouldn't have been short of work, and it would have served him right. But Bram shook his head, said they all knew Irving was a sick man, that it was only a matter of time before death settled everything. 'He needed his friends around him – he needed loyalty at the end of his days, not betrayal.'

'He betrayed you,' I reminded him softly.

As though in denial, he shook his head, then said with difficulty: 'I know. But I had to stay and see him through. I owed him that. It was the book, you see – somehow, with the book, I felt I'd had a hand in his fall.'

I made a vague protest at that, said he was being overly dramatic; but at heart I understood, because I'd felt it too, that connection between Irving and the destruction of the Count. As Bram began to talk about the run of events, I felt a chill along my spine. Disaster had followed disaster, until it began to seem rather more than just a series of unfortunate coincidences. He'd begun to look over his shoulder while walking home at night, and felt his heart pounding at every potential threat or accident. It was as though he and Irving had been granted their successes, but were now being forced to pay the price in full. As though unseen moneylenders were calling in the chips.

He went on to say, with evident discomfort, that he felt haunted by those events, and guilty too, because he'd resented the way success had turned Irving from friend into despot; he'd even wished him ill at times, if only that he might be taught a much-needed lesson. He'd wanted things to go wrong, just so that Irving could see who his real friends were; to prove that he, Bram, would still be by his side, even in adversity.

'But it doesn't work like that, does it?' he commented quietly, as I watched his face, his eyes, the sadness of his mouth. 'When everything fell down, I was crushed too. And I couldn't get over the feeling that I was the one who brought it about.

'It was the book,' he said, taking a deep breath. 'Somehow, evil was written into it – inadvertently, perhaps, but it rebounded on all of us. I don't know why, but what was intended to be a simple vampire tale turned into something else along the way, and, once it was complete, it seemed to take on a life of its own – as though I was merely a vehicle, a medium through which it could be told. I don't think it matters that good won out in the end,' he said; 'well, yes, it does matter, because good *has* to keep evil in check – and has to be seen to do so. But it seems my writing gave it life, allowed it to flex its muscles, gave it a chance to work its mischief. Nothing too dramatic, of course – an accident here, a fire there, deaths, doubts, arguments, betrayals . . .'

436

I shivered, but not with fear. Something primitive inside me was unpleasantly satisfied to know that Irving got his come-uppance in the end, that he was paid back for all the pain he'd cost me. And Bram. And Florence. And the boy, Noel. And I didn't care who caused it or what the vehicle was. I understood instinctively what Bram meant about evil rebounding. I thought of Irving's powerful personality, and that mesmeric quality he had, which I'd experienced myself that day at the cottage. The elements of attraction and repulsion were part of him, as direct and disturbing as the presence of the Count in Bram's novel.

'I don't think it matters,' I said brusquely, 'what caused his luck to turn. Irving had talent as well as power – and he abused both, in a direct and very personal way. He used people and cast them aside. He betrayed your friendship, your loyalty, your talent – as a matter of foolish pride, he even turned down an absolute *gift* of a part,' I added with forced laughter, resisting the urge to heap further coals upon his head. 'Who knows? Maybe the old Count couldn't bear the insult – maybe he did wreak his revenge, after all!'

We parted a little after midnight, to go to our respective beds. Bram assured me that he felt better than for many a month, and was sure to sleep, but I was not so confident. I found myself tossing and turning, thinking of the past. In that embrace before we parted, I'd been very much aware of wanting him to stay. Not to indulge in the antics of twenty years ago, not even because I was lonely – which I was – but to be assured of his warmth, his lasting affection, and even to offer him something of myself in return.

When I looked back on that summer I could see how in the passion of youth I'd rejected good sense and good upbringing, everything, in fact, that I knew to be straight and sensible and the accepted way. The accepted way was not for me, and was probably never intended to be, but in the course of finding a more amenable path I'd taken a detour that might easily have proved fatal. When it came to Bram, I couldn't blame fate or even ignorance entirely. I'd embraced that liaison with my eyes open, unblinkered by anything beyond the desire to be admired and indulged a little, to break the rules and find my own level, and in the process to cock a snook at the staid moral values my background represented. Ultimately, life, fate, doom or whatever, had decreed the price I was to pay in return. It might have seemed severe but, to counter that, Bram's generosity had provided my passport to another world – a world of ships and commerce and personal wealth. Whether the money was directly his or lent by Irving, it didn't matter. The point was, he hadn't abandoned me entirely, he'd taken care of me in the only way that was open to him at the time. He hadn't seduced me, either. Initially I'd made love to him, and the decision to seek out Nan Mills had been mine, not his. Irving had altered the balance, but there had been compensations, even for being childless. I had no right to complain that life had been unfair.

All in all, I was immensely glad that Bram and I had met again. Our conversations had balanced the scales. Especially when it came to Irving.

And I kept coming back to Irving, that shadowy figure in the wings of my life. I couldn't help going over those last years when he was so beset by illness, yet still working, still touring, eventually making a very professional exit during his farewell tour of the country. After playing *Becket* at the Theatre Royal, Bradford, the great actor had collapsed, dying shortly afterwards in the foyer of his hotel. The date was 13 October, and a Friday.

His death had seemed so elegantly stage-managed, I remember thinking at the time, just like his funeral service, held in Westminster Abbey with representatives of the royal family in attendance. But although his friends could be proud of that honour, for Bram, Irving's death had been like losing a close member of the family. After all those years, the sudden emptiness had been filled with unexpected grief for other losses. Bereaved and despairing, finding it difficult to work, Bram had barely noticed that he was physically ill. Then he'd suffered a stroke, and was unconscious for twenty-four hours.

I could tell that the sudden lightning strike had come as a great shock to him, who'd always been so fit, and it explained much about the change in his appearance. His speech and general faculties were mostly unimpaired, although for some time his mobility had been badly affected. He said he'd always been too busy to notice the passing years, but in the last twelve months had had plenty of time to muse on the past, to consider his mistakes as well as his successes.

Florence, he confided, had shown unexpected strength. His illness had brought them closer together than at any other time, and it was apparently thanks to her that he was walking again. She had nursed and bullied him back to health and strength, and, when things were at their worst, refused to let him give in to despair. I was pleased about that, if a little envious, and even found myself sympathising with her. Now Irving was out of the way, she had Bram to herself, and was evidently determined to make up for those difficult early years. But one thing Florence could not get over was the fact that when Irving's estate was settled, out of more than £20,000, there were no tokens of appreciation for his oldest friend and colleague. There was not so much as a memento to mark the years they'd shared at the Lyceum.

I too felt very angry about that.

Thirty-four

On the high ground inland the sun was shining on snow, we could see it from the road. But last night's fog was still clinging to the clifftop, veiling the abbey ruins at ground level, so that turrets and gables seemed to be floating on a milk-white cloud. The cab dropped us on Abbey Plain and at once we were in the heart of it, veiled and cold and aware of a hard frost underfoot. Pulling my mantle up to my chin, I looked up at the ruins and shivered, asking myself whether this visit was such a good idea, after all. I remembered that first night with Bram, the bold way we'd trespassed, and the brazen way I'd encouraged him, almost forcing him to take my virginity. I wondered what on earth had possessed me.

I glanced at Bram. He too was looking up at the smoky, mist-wreathed abbey; then he turned to me with a quirky, conspiratorial smile. I felt my own lips twitch, and, as the cab creaked away, we entered the churchyard together for the first time in more than twenty years. Apart from the cold it felt right, familiar, as though we'd been here only yesterday – or just a few months ago, last summer perhaps. Rimed with frost, the path looked treacherous in places, although the sexton had been out, scattering salt. We took it carefully on the slope, then it occurred to both of us, passing the church porch, that we'd been in separately, but never together.

Since our last visit a tall new cross in the old style had been erected to commemorate the Anglo-Saxon poet Caedmon. We paused before it but then with one accord carried on along the path, diverting here and there to read the old favourites, memorials to long-dead explorers and master mariners who had sailed from the harbour below, and seafarers dead in foreign places, whose wives and children had learned to endure the years alone. I thought of Jonathan then, squeezing my eyes tight shut against the sting of memory. Later, I thought; later, when Bram has gone, I will go to the chandlery, ask whether anyone knows . . .

A slight stirring of air made the fog patchy, while here and there the sun broke through with dazzling beams of light. Across the way, the roofs and chimneys of the Royal Hotel kept miraculously appearing and disappearing like some castle in a fairy tale, but the grey chill between seemed ever-renewable. From where we were, it was impossible to see the sea, or to know where the cliff ended and infinity began. Despite Bram's assurances that we were safe enough on the path, I had a fearful suspicion that he was intending to stray. Ignoring his protests, I clung to his arm.

'But I just want to see whether I can find that old table tomb,' he insisted. 'There was a seat nearby, at a bend in the path – and the path divided what must have been two parts of the graveyard. Don't you remember? Where the old cholera burial ground would have been.'

He pointed ahead to the ghostly outline of a public bench that stood beside the path. Beyond it, to the right, I could see several upright stones illumined like soldiers on parade, but to the left was a blank wall of mist. As he strode confidently towards it, I had the most powerful sense of disaster. 'No!' I exclaimed, leaping forward across the grass to grab his coat. As we stopped dead, I could see that no more than a yard or two of level ground remained. In front of us, the crisp white grass had fallen away, together with a section of the cliff.

We stood there, trembling with shock, for several seconds. Then, very carefully, holding on to each other, we edged back along the path. The bench, where Bram had so often waited for me in the past, provided a welcome resting point. 'How long,' he murmured softly, 'do you think it's been like that?'

'I don't know,' I said carefully. 'Small sections keep falling all the time.'

'I suppose Lucy's tomb could have disappeared years ago?' When I nodded, he squeezed my arm and said, 'Thanks for stopping me. I was so sure I knew where it was.'

'It was the fog,' I said bravely, but some instinct in me was aware of an uneasy presence, the ghost of Irving perhaps, or even the restless spirit which had given birth to the novel he disliked so much. *I wish I'd left it there*, he'd said to me last night of that disturbing tale, *amongst the tombs of the east cliff*. This morning, so did I.

We were both chilled through and shivering, with shock as much as anything else. It seemed a good idea to take refuge in the church, whose interior I knew less well than I might have done. Despite those ancient walls, I'd resisted the place while living here, out of a stubborn dislike for established custom as well as an insistence on pleasing myself. Yet I felt the atmosphere embrace us with welcome as soon as we entered. The interior was less like a place of worship than like an old sailing ship, crowded with box pews and ancient galleries, and a mass of eighteenth-century furnishings. There were plain leaded windows and a shallow roof with skylights, which had surely been fashioned to withstand the ferocious northeasterly storms. I had a feeling it would be here until the cliff collapsed from under it, and even then that it would sail, like a well-founded schooner, across the seas to eternity.

We found an open pew and seated ourselves gratefully, eyes taking in the extraordinary detail all around. I chanced to look down, and saw the strong, clear lines of a small brigantine carved into the woodwork.

There was such power and liveliness there, it brought a smile to my lips; Bram's too when I pointed it out. 'Who do you think carved that?' he asked. 'A small boy with a new penknife, or a budding naval architect?'

'A bored and frustrated shipbuilder,' I said, feeling my voice tremble between laughter and tears, 'in the middle of an interminable sermon!'

We laughed then, softly, while Bram squeezed my hand. He turned to gaze at me with quizzical affection, and I saw that he was moved too. He'd begun to ask me something when suddenly, behind us, a door closed. We both paused, breath halted, before turning to see who else had entered the church. But no one had.

The porch was deserted. Outside, no one was visible and the fog was rapidly disappearing, sinking like fluffy meringue to the level of the rooftops below. I told myself that we'd not closed the door properly when we came in, although it seemed a feeble excuse for such a physical occurrence, and strange not to see the visitor walking away. I was uneasy, but after glancing round, Bram said it was probably nothing. Anyway, he wanted to have another look at the edge of the cliff, to see for himself

444

that Lucy's tomb had disappeared. The sun put a different complexion on things, but I was reluctant, nevertheless, to venture forth again.

We walked with care to the far end of the graveyard, viewing the surrounding area from various angles until we were sure that the main fall had been some time ago. The old tomb was long gone, which was a great relief, but from below came the surge and pull of the sea against the rocks, sounding with all the regularity of a heartbeat.

In the cold, still air we stood in silence, a little apart, like mourners beside an open grave. Bram shifted his walking stick from one hand to the other and tugged at the brim of his black felt hat. After a pause he said slowly: 'Is possession too strong a word? Or was it just an unhealthy fascination?'

Remembering his state of mind then, and the times we'd spent here, fingers tracing the wind-scoured stones, I understood what he was asking. For a while the dead had been part of our lives, the creatures of the night had stalked us in the moonlight, and old superstitions had been reborn. Blood had taken on new meaning, and I was still the victim of paralysing fear whenever I cut myself; I didn't like graveyards, and I never walked in the moonlight.

With an effort, I said, 'It doesn't matter now. It's over. They're all dead, including Irving. You're free, and so am I. We've survived.'

'Yes. And now Lucy's gone, too.'

'Are you sorry?'

'No, not a bit,' he said decisively. 'Relieved, I think. Unburdened – yes, that's how I feel, as though a great weight has gone from me with the falling of the cliff. I'd like to think of the sea carrying it all away – complete with my sense of guilt!'

That sudden lightheartedness pleased me, but still I stood there, watching the mist as it dispersed in the sunlight, listening to the sea. 'By the way,' I said, 'that name you gave her, in the book . . . ?'

'Lucy Westenra?' He gave me a broad smile and squeezed my hand. 'Didn't you guess? You spotted so many things, I thought you'd have worked that one out. Lucy Westenra – light of the westering sun . . .'

'Oh.' I smiled at that, picturing the sunsets here, understanding at last the surname which had always mystified me. 'Oh, yes, I see . . .'

As I glanced up, still smiling, in the distance I noticed a man in black watching us from the north transept. He was too far away for me to distinguish his face, but there was something disturbingly familiar about him. Something that made my heart race in apprehension. Was he real, or a ghost?

'What's wrong?' Bram asked as my smile faded.

'Nothing,' I said abruptly. 'Shall we go?' But when we turned the man had gone, which disturbed me even more. All at once I was keen to be back at the hotel, where blazing fires and hot coffee might dispel these lingering fears.

When the time came for Bram to collect his luggage and say goodbye, it seemed too soon. We'd had two days of each other's company, two days of intensity in which sorrow and anger had been turned to greater account; two days of atonement for all the wrongs of twenty years before. I felt soft, weak, wrung-out, but at the very last, I didn't want him to leave me, didn't want to be alone. He knew me so well, and with him there was no need to pretend. I even wished – but no, it wouldn't do, even to wish. Better to leave things as they were. I think we both knew, without it needing to be said, that he and I were part of some other existence, never destined to be together in this.

Aware of the bond between us, we came together naturally, with understanding this time, and affection. Reminded of our first embrace, I clung to him, and his arms tightened around me. I felt the softness of his beard as he rubbed his cheek against mine, and the warmth of his breath as he kissed me; he felt safe and familiar, a proverbial rock in my ocean of uncertainty, and I didn't want to let him go.

'I know, I know,' he whispered, 'but you don't want me, my dear – not now.' He kissed me again with tender affection, and then, like a father to a daughter, put me from him firmly and said: 'You're young yet, and beautiful – and you still have so much living to do. For goodness' sake don't waste yourself on widowhood. Go to Australia – see your brother and his family – enjoy your life!'

'I will – I promise!' And I felt guilty then at not mentioning Jonathan. Next time, I promised Bram silently; when I've found him, then I'll tell you ... I managed to smile, even to laugh a little at my own sentimentality as I wiped away a tear. 'But we'll meet again,' I said, 'in London. I'll let you know my plans.'

'Be sure you do,' he said with mock severity. 'Remember, I have your address.'

And with that we parted. I watched from the balcony as he left the hotel. He looked up and raised his hat to me, waved from the cab, and then he was gone. Not for ever, not this time, but when next we met it would be as friends, not lovers and no longer enemies. It was right, and it pleased me.

Once Bram had gone, Alice was inclined to fuss, but there was barely time to rest and no time to eat. With Old Uncle's funeral to attend shortly in Robin Hood's Bay, I knew I had to keep moving. It was either that or sleep, I told her, and sleep would have to come later. I set off to walk along the harbour, enjoying the sun, feeling the pull of old memories, and wishing I had the rest of the day to myself.

Passing the fish stalls on New Quay, I paused briefly to gaze at the rows of cod and turbot, inhaling the wonderfully fresh salty smell and wondering why I'd hated it so much, once upon a time. But then I looked at the raw red hands of the girls and women minding the stalls and felt the agony of their chilblains through my fine leather gloves; saw the perpetual anxiety behind their smiles, and knew how fortunate my life had been by comparison. The cold blurred my eyes as I stood there by the harbour rail, listening to the voices, to the cry of the seabirds mingling with the sound of sawing and hammering from across the water. I breathed the scent of steam and wood shavings and wet canvas from ships being overhauled and refitted up and down the Esk, and thought anxiously of Jonathan. It was hard to turn my steps towards West Cliff station and the waiting train, when all I wanted to do was cross the bridge, go into Markways' and have my questions answered.

The station was busy, and I found myself examining the faces of several black-clad men and statuesque women, looking for my Sterne relations. I spotted three or four, who might or might not have recognised me, but we bowed to each other as a matter of course and later walked in a loose kind of group from Bay station to the house at Bank Top, which was full to overflowing.

The gathering for Thaddeus Sterne's funeral could not have been more different from Bella Firth's. Honour had been done to his memory by following all the old traditions. Every blood relative was invited, together with friends and colleagues, and representatives from all the families in Bay. Food and refreshment were available throughout the day for the funeral guests, who dropped in to talk, commiserate, and eat and drink until the time came to leave for the service. About two o'clock the procession started to form, and the coffin was lifted to the sturdy young shoulders of six of Old Uncle's closest male relatives. The long procession followed on behind, winding its way up the steep incline from the house to the little old church a mile away.

There must have been at least three hundred people. It was like a medieval pilgrimage. I had forgotten that feeling of pain and humility, that sense of doing honour to the dead, which for me was not just honour to Thaddeus Sterne, but to the whole of my family: mother, father, grandfather and grandmother. Before, there had been no chance, I was too young, too ignorant, I had not understood. I did now. And Thaddeus Sterne in his ninetieth year was the last of his generation. We climbed the hill at sunset, we crowded into and around the little church, and we heard him lauded and applauded as a grand old man who had not only served his time before the mast but lived through five reigns, from George III to Edward VII. He had been a shipmaster, shipowner, author and local historian. We all knew that he would be greatly missed, not just in Bay, but in the much wider community beyond.

I bowed my head in acknowledgement. In the shipping world I had discovered Old Uncle's reputation for astuteness, and while I'd never done business with him personally – he was retired by the time I came to work with Henry – it had pleased me to be able to claim a connection. After my marriage we hadn't met again, but we'd corresponded occasionally. Mr Richardson said he'd always asked after me, and had seemed proud of my achievements as well as vastly amused by them.

But he'd been a hard old rogue, amusement or not, no matter what plaudits they heaped upon him. An old Viking at heart, I thought as everyone flooded out into the midwinter dusk. As we prepared to follow the minister to the appointed place in the graveyard, there came a sudden flare of light. Torches were lit, at least a score of them, blazing against the coming night, lending an unexpected air of pagan joy to the final proceedings.

Cheered by the warmth, by the flickering lights, it seemed there were fewer tears than smiles of triumph as we saw Thaddeus Sterne into the ground. Even the earth which followed was scattered with a hearty sound. Remembering the hand he'd had in my early life, I bade him a silent if rueful goodbye.

As I turned from the grave, the man behind said softly in my ear, 'If you ask me, they should have taken him to the Wayfoot at high tide – laid him in his boat with the sail set, and thrown the torches in after him . . .'

The comment followed so closely on what I'd been thinking, I shivered with the aptness of it. Half amused, half afraid, I turned, prepared to meet a typical Sterne countenance, and was overwhelmed to see a thin face and lively dark eyes, together with a clean jaw and sweeping black moustache that almost disguised the man's identity. Almost, but not quite.

Rooted to the spot, I felt myself begin to smile; I could hardly believe that he was real. He took my arm then, with a firmness that proved his existence beyond doubt, and led me apart to where purple shadows disguised even the stunted trees. For an eternity we gazed at each other, and then he cupped my face in his hands and kissed me. Fiercely, deeply, even angrily, until he remembered where we were and broke away. As for me, I was beyond speech, in a world of stunned, delighted acceptance, where all remaining volition was channelled purely into movement.

The train was crowded, too crowded for conversation. He looked at me from time to time but mainly kept his eyes on the window for the fifteen-minute journey to West Cliff, which was probably fortunate. My smile, I'm sure, was far too revealing. Then it was into a cab for the short distance down to the Royal Hotel. What the reception staff thought as I asked for my key I hardly dared to imagine, since I'd walked out the door with one man that morning and was now arriving after dark with another. But I was past concerning myself with such trivialities.

He remembered Alice, and when we reached my suite had the wit to lock the bedroom door before casting aside my raven's-wing hat, loosening my hair and divesting me of my clothes. I didn't protest – the entire situation was too erotic for that – and he barely spoke, but even in my bemused and delighted state I was aware of his tension as he stripped me down to my chemise, a self-control that contrasted alarmingly with the dark glint in his eyes. He didn't hurt me, at least not intentionally, but his grasp was firm and his intentions clear. After all the restraints of the past couple of days, I found his forcefulness intoxicating. Within moments we were naked on the bed, and, with few preliminaries, making love with single-minded intensity.

For both of us the crisis came quickly, in great, heaving gasps of release. He held me fast, face hidden in my hair, body locked to mine, his reaction deep but wordless, while I seemed to be spinning endlessly in a darkened, star-studded world. Gradually, by the rhythm of his breathing, I knew he was calmer, and just as gradually I was restored to earth. In a daze of dreams, I hardly knew what was real and what imagined. He was alive and well, I could

451

feel him, taste his salt on my lips, recognise the scent of his body, but I could scarce believe he was by my side. Eventually, I opened my eyes to find him gazing at me, and, with a smile, I raised my hand to smooth the frown away.

'Jonathan Markway,' I said, on a deep, indrawn breath of satisfaction, 'you came back . . .'

He traced the line of my cheek and brow, pushing back wild tendrils of hair. 'Damsy Sterne,' he whispered, 'when I had your letter, I couldn't stay away . . .'

But still, the frown stayed, the darkness in his eyes did not disappear. After a little while, he put some space between us and said carefully, 'This morning, Damsy, on the east cliff, you were with a man. Who was he?'

I knew then that Jonathan was the man I'd noticed, watching from the north transept, but as I began to protest he reached out to place a finger over my mouth. 'I wasn't spying, I promise you – at least, not intentionally.

'You see, I went to your house in London, only to find you'd gone to Whitby. I came on by train, but it was late when I arrived, so I went straight to my brother's. This morning, early, I called at the Royal, on the off-chance you might be staying there, but you'd already gone out and no one knew where. I couldn't believe the ill-luck – I was so angry I just walked, back through town and up to the east cliff. But as I came through the churchyard, there you were, arm in arm with a man –'

'You followed us into the church.'

'Yes,' he admitted gruffly, 'I did. I thought perhaps he might be ill, some stranger you were assisting. But it wasn't like that, was it?'

'No,' I said calmly, wondering what interpretation

452

he'd placed upon those tender gestures, those affectionate smiles.

'Who was he, Damsy? Will you tell me?'

I hesitated, closing my eyes against an image of Isa Firth and the photographs which had so recently been destroyed, and my ears against the suggestion of jealousy in his tone. I'd spent my life hiding that affair of twenty years ago, but if Jonathan and I were to be together for any length of time – and I hoped we might be – then it could only be with honesty between us. I would tell him everything – eventually. But not now. For the time being he would have to trust me.

'I think I mentioned him to you before,' I said gently. 'I was in love with him once. He was the man who wrote *Dracula*.'

Author's Note

Most of the characters in this book – the Sternes, the Firths, the Markways and the photographer, Jack Louvain – are fictitious and not intended to resemble real people, either past or present. By contrast, Bram Stoker, his family and friends, were very much alive in the early years of the twentieth century, and Whitby is known to have played a notable part in their lives.

Bram Stoker was a complex and secretive man, one who left few direct accounts of his life and experience. This is frustrating for the biographer, but leaves considerable scope for the imaginative writer. My interest in him sharpened considerably in recent years, and I gradually came to the belief that all the major components of his most famous novel were to be found, in his lifetime, in the little seaport of Whitby. The result is my own attempt to explain the man and that extraordinary novel, *Dracula*.

This book has been a long time in the preparation, and many people in Whitby who talked to me, lent me books and gave their help must have wondered whether it would ever appear. Well, here it is: a view of Whitby as Mr Stoker might have known it.

My thanks to all those who gave assistance, from staff at Whitby Literary and Philosophical Society, to individuals like Des Sythes and Pat Beal who were so generous with their time and information. Special thanks to Valerie and Joe Blakemore for continuing support through the difficult bits!

It remains only to say that I could not have begun to understand Mr Stoker without the work of his excellent biographers: Harry Ludlam, Daniel Farson, and Barbara Belford. Ms Belford's recent work, *Bram Stoker: A Biography of the Author of Dracula*, was particularly informative, as was Clive Leatherdale's *Dracula: the Novel and the Legend*. Amongst many other books consulted were: *Whitby Lore and Legend* by Shaw Jeffrey; *Forty Years in a Moorland Parish* by Rev. J.C. Atkinson; *The Streonshalh Files* by John Tindale; *Whitby* by Rosalin Barker; *A History of Whitby* by Andrew White; and *Frank Meadow Sutcliffe: Photographs*, published by the Sutcliffe Gallery, Whitby.

Ann Victoria Roberts
Whitby 1999